CHAPTER 1

When she opened her eyes under the blanket it was midnight and, as she had for the past four years, she momentarily forgot where she was. As always, the first thing she thought of was Khanoum. Then, as though someone had switched the light on, she asked herself, 'What's Nanaz doing now?' When Nanaz had last come to see her she had wondered why she was so happy.

'Nanaz, are you looking after Mother?' she had asked.

Nanaz had burst out laughing.

'On the contrary, Khanoum's looking after me!'

She wanted to open her eyes and talk to Narguess, as they always did whenever one of them was feeling low. The thought of tomorrow, however, had made her restless. This had nothing to do with Narguess so she'd better let her sleep.

'Close your eyes,' she told herself. She could think better with her eyes shut and she always felt better when lost in thought. It was Mrs Sediqi, actually, who had taught her that one felt liberated when one had one's eyes closed; she could then take a trip with whomever she liked and to wherever she fancied.

Narguess said, 'You have an educated and well-mannered soul but mine is unruly. I can't keep hold of its hand!'

Narguess is truly a slave to her unruly spirit which never ceases to get her into trouble.

'Are you awake, Narguess?'

She felt Narguess was awake and so wanted to spend this one last night chatting to her.

1

'How can you say that? How could I possibly forget you? You, too, will be released one of these days. I hope you haven't forgotten what Akram said? Well, if you can't rely on what she says, then I am not to walk free tomorrow either! But, for now, come and rest your head next to mine so that we don't wake Mrs Izadi up. Let me tame your soul and you can tell me why you have difficulty sleeping. But let's not talk about those nights, let's talk about the future. Do you recall the book that said, "Tomorrow's beautiful because it's neither like the past nor like anything else that is old"?

'What? I didn't hear what you said; I just felt your breath on my ear. Are you crying? Come on, this is my last night and tomorrow I'll be free to leave and go to Khanoum, and to Nanaz, who can't wait to see me. Have you already forgotten what you said to me; that you'd even be happy to stay here in my place so that I could go back to Khanoum? So why did you knit that scarf for her? You've never seen her before! Didn't you promise you'd come and stay with us when you walk free? With us, Khanoum, Nanaz and me? Perhaps Akram wasn't right after all and I shan't be released tomorrow. Are you listening to me or are you asleep?

'Listen to me, you ninny! You can give me your restless mind to take with me. I'll set your diary free as well, but I shan't take my books and notes. Take them with you when you leave this place. So now, please sing for me ...

O little sparrow,
You'll be a ball when it snows;
You'll be wet when it rains ...

'When you come we'll shut ourselves in your room and then we'll sing freely and out loud, like the other night when you were ranting for no reason. I want Khanoum and Nanaz to hear your voice. Will you promise to read something by Forough[1] to them?

... I'll plant my hands and they'll grow ...

To Aty, my wife and my best friend

THE KNOT IN THE RUG

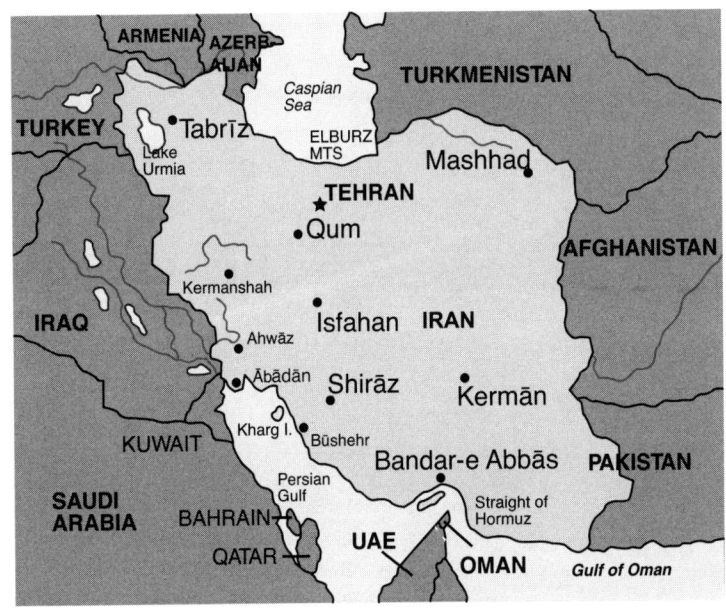

'Narguess, are you sleeping? Lucky you ...'

When she got up the next day, she was busy folding the blanket when she saw Narguess's face, but it was difficult to tell whether she had heard her the previous night. Everyone began to wake up to Aqdas Khanoum's loud voice. Akram was also there and, as usual, she was calling them to go to the washrooms. They both looked to see whether they could read anything in her expression that hinted at the release of prisoner number 820. Her eyes met Maryam's and she beamed. As soon as Maryam had finished washing her face she said, 'I hope you're not suddenly going to pounce on Khanoum!' – something she had repeated over and over again.

She kept to herself for the next half-hour while the other twelve inhabitants of prison cell number 99 were chatting away. Akram nodded, and when Maryam had finished kissing everyone goodbye she took her bag and quickened her pace as she followed Akram to the guard's room. Akram answered a couple of questions for her. She then signed a bundle of papers and heard a young man's voice asking her not to 'remember him for the bad times behind bars'. She then heard Akram's last words reminding her to help Narguess out of prison as soon as she could.

'Will you go to Faramarz?'

No, she hadn't forgotten; Maryam was aware that Faramarz was Akram's only son who was buried in the martyrs' corner in the public cemetery.

When they passed through the last exit Akram patted her on the back. They were both tearful. They had not been referring to one another as prisoner and guard for some time now. She managed the remaining formalities without Akram's help and an hour later the large gates finally opened and Maryam swung one leg over the iron bar surreptitiously separating her from the outside. As she lifted her other foot she was seized with fear; there was daylight and noise on the other side. She was relieved that no one had come to pick her up. She felt so lonely, loneliness far more profound than anything she had ever experienced.

For a moment, she felt that everyone around her was also a fellow prisoner. The cars driving past and the woman carrying a plastic bag took no notice of her as she stepped into their world. Maryam began to walk uphill when she caught sight of the familiar figure of the young man in the tower. Her shoes felt loose but they made her feel good. A man brought his *Paykaan* to a halt; the most popular car assembled in Iran, the old Hillman Hunter; and she heard the military anthem blaring from its radio, which was duly interrupted by the narrator, who gave a passionate monologue about the 'Godless' army under siege by brave Islamic forces. The driver said something Maryam couldn't hear. She caught sight of a telephone booth and went to the corner shop across the road. After obtaining a coin from the shopkeeper, she started to dial …

She closed her eyes and let 'Allo, Allo' travel through her ears. She could vaguely hear a young man talking to the shopkeeper about a couple of air strikes somewhere in mid-town. She was about to pass on the news when her eyes suddenly encountered those of a man who was smiling broadly at her. She put the receiver down and began to walk briskly uphill until she reached the market. There was a memorial ornamental kiosk right outside the mosque, still in Evin, near the notorious prison. The loudspeakers began transmitting the chanting of the verses of the Holy Qur'an when she sensed the smiling man was still following her, but by now she had reached the mosque. She sat on the carpeted floor watching a group of women busy wrapping packs of dates intended for the war front. She was soon so absorbed in helping the women that she didn't even notice noon arrive. After a while the women stood up to get ready for prayers, but she didn't move. When lunch was laid out on a cloth over the carpets, someone offered her a bowl of broth. An hour later she was resting her head against a pillar, and soon she was unrecognisable, completely covered in her *chador*. In the quiet of her cover, she was once again on her own, and her memory could lead her back to New Jersey. There she was, in her graduation gown sitting in the front row, on the lawn. Her mother, Khanoum, looking elegant and distinguished, was chatting to an American gentleman, one of the many parents. She was delighted her mother had managed to come all the way from Iran to attend her graduation despite the complications. Clad in a blue silk dress and a hat, she was a princess who had captivated Nader, her beau, and everyone else. She found herself encountering her mother's adoring gaze. With a rolled diploma in her hand she was now standing between Khanoum and Nader.

As she leaned against the pillar in the mosque, Maryam suddenly remembered the mosque in New Jersey: she was marrying Nader, and her mother was giving him a pocketwatch, an antique on a gold chain. Then came the necklace; she knew this was her mother's own wedding memento that she had been keeping safe for such a day. She had seen the same necklace in a picture of a young woman dressed in early nineteenth-century fashion, wearing a hat and holding an umbrella. Soon she remembered Nanaz's first screams in a New Jersey hospital, the sound of life, and … she fell asleep. They were standing inside the airport, Nanaz and her. She found herself explaining to the little girl.

'Nana, we're going to Iran; to Khanoum my love, and to Tehran, city of Revolution, city of "Down with the Shah" and "God is Great, *Allah Akbar*" shouted from the rooftops.'

There she was, Khanoum, sitting on the veranda listening to her radio, beaming with happiness; those were the days of flowers and tears.

And now she was pleading with her husband.

'Please come with us Nader! We'll never see such days again. I know what you're thinking but it's not as though I'm mad or vengeful even. We're not going over just to see the fall; this is not just a fall, Nader, this is history in the making, please come! We shan't be alone in the house; there'll be Manssoureh and her family, Ali Akbar and his children, a full and lively house.'

The curfew, the Shah's escape and the joyful tears of Khanoum, her darling mother; the social nights when Khanoum listened to the radio; the days of demonstrations and the fear of a *coup d'état*; the siege of the garrisons; Hussein and Hassan, Ali Akbar's sons, and the weapons; the young people meeting in the basement and planning the next day's moves; the day happiness burst out; spring in the middle of winter … The victory of the Revolution!

'I'm sorry Nader, Mother doesn't wish to come over any more, and we'll stay here as well. Why not come and join us? Mother's been waiting for this day for fifty years!'

Maryam suddenly felt short of breath under her *chador* and she began to sense a sharp pain starting in the back of her head and moving down her spine. She lifted her head so that her eyes were no longer covered with the *chador* and she could see the ceiling of the mosque and the light pouring through the window onto the pile of donations. She knew she would soon have difficulty breathing.

'Oh Narguess,' she sighed, and then her voice petered out; she was unconscious.

An anxious-looking woman went to her, and began to wipe her moist brow with the corner of her scarf and brought a glass up to her mouth.

Maryam managed to hold the glass, and returned the woman's kindness with a faint smile and then propped herself up.

'Where am I?' she asked but it didn't take her long to remember.

Someone in the crowd said, 'Give her some *halva*, she looks so pale!'

The morsel of the sweet paste taken with some flat bread tasted familiar; the flat golden long triangle of bread that Muhammad Ali used to buy every morning.

Picking up the telephone receiver, she said, 'Nanaz, is that you? I'll be home soon … don't say anything to Khanoum.'

'Where are you?'

'Not far at all!'

The radio in the car that she managed to hail, as one did when there were no taxis, was playing military anthems. She sat neatly in the backseat, just as she had done four years ago, but going then in the opposite direction; to prison, to Evin.

'My goodness, you've grown so much, Nanaz!'

She then turned to Mr Ali Akbar and said, 'I owe you a great deal; I'm not sure what would've happened without you. Where are the boys, Hussein and Hassan?' But the man was quiet; she had to find the answers for herself.

She was talking to them, Nanaz and Ali Akbar, in the alleyway. The road was named 'Hussein' after the shy one who dropped his gaze when she left, biting his lower lip and kicking the edge of the flowerbed with his boot.

'I don't really need a bath, Nanaz.'

But the smell of lavender, her favourite aroma, had filled the air in the bathroom and she could hear Shirley Bassey's voice seeping through the steam. She spotted a few grey strands when she looked in the mirror, where Nanaz had traced out 'I NEED U' in the steam. She suddenly noticed her mother; Khanoum was standing in the doorframe, leaning on the same old walking-stick. She had a brown and beige scarf on her head, just as she did when she was watching her leave through the window.

'Naughty Khanoum!'

Maryam had never heard anyone refer to her mother in that manner, which made her glare at Nanaz. But then she heard her mother say in return: 'Go away, you little rascal!'

She went forward into her mother's outstretched arms and, as she did, the 1623 days' captivity, Akram and Narguess, were all forgotten. Nanaz was supporting Khanoum's body from behind, by placing her forehead against her spine; her walking-stick was shaking. Once again they were together, inseparable – and she had yet to find out what had passed between Nanaz and Khanoum in the past four years.

Early on she noticed that her daughter was guarding her mother like some Old Master painting, and she sensed something in their eyes that was sweet, familiar yet strange. She'd never come to feel as close to her mother, but in the days that followed she discovered that in Khanoum's care Nanaz had grown into a strong young woman. She was no longer an insecure little waif of a girl, but a rock on which one could lean, or a large tree laden with fruit, spreading its wonderful shade in the heat.

Barely three days out but she was already thinking of all the things she had to do. She went to Shiraz to visit her cellmate's sister and brother, Narguess's siblings. She also accompanied Akram to the martyrs' corner in the public cemetery to visit the spot where Faramarz, Akram's beloved son, was lying. She had also not forgotten to visit another cellmate's sick, blind mother as well, and …

One evening they were sitting in the basement, a safe haven where her mother had everything she needed. Next to her antique bed was a desk with an old typewriter. There was also a tape recorder that had been brought down from the floor above, as well as a box of tapes. There was another bed nearby where Nanaz slept so that she could attend to her grandmother should she feel unwell during the night. There was also a framed photograph of Nader and herself.

'You don't seem to have had such a bad time!' Maryam had hardly noticed the Shirazi accent she'd picked up.

'I guess Narguess must be speaking English with a downtown New Jersey accent!' Nanaz teased. Their laughter filled the room.

'By the way,' Maryam said, 'she's going to walk free one of these days and you'll see for yourself!'

And that wasn't news. Maryam's daily visits to the public prosecutor and the preparations in the room upstairs were all testament to the imminent arrival of their guest, someone who was going to stay some time.

And so she did. In just under a month, after Khanoum had gone into intensive care, Narguess joined them, and they tried their best not to worry her with their concerns for Khanoum. Once the visit to Shiraz was out of the way, Narguess went to the hospital with them every morning. Khanoum was sleeping peacefully surrounded by tubes and wires. Narguess and Maryam had repeatedly had to pull Nanaz away from the incubator; she would rest her forehead against the walls of the corridors at the hospital and mutter something, as though she was reading a prayer or calling 'Khanoum' over and over again.

'Don't go, my dear Khanoum!'

Her voice was far more upsetting than hearing someone sob. And she went on, until someone disconnected all the tubes and wires, and covered her grandmother with a white sheet. It was as though she had lingered on just long enough to hand Nanaz over to her own mother.

Nanaz had promised to be quiet and not to disturb the other patients, so she was allowed to follow the head nurse towards the body of her grandmother, lift the sheet, and stare at her peaceful face. She pecked on her forehead and said: 'I promise you!'

She didn't weep any more.

* * *

Our story is about Khanoum, the story of a life she had told to no one; a story that she had narrated and Nanaz had recorded during the dark nights when Iraq sent its missiles to Tehran. It was a story that inspired the little girl to believe in the power of the human spirit. She had come to learn that, although encased in a fragile body, humanity could endure pain with the strength of a rock.

Khanoum had told her story in such a way that the little girl had fully understood its magnitude. You, too, are about to hear it in the memory of a woman who was truly a *khanoum* – a lady. She was never called by any other name, nor was there one that better suited her character.

She is buried under a black slab in the middle of the Emamzadeh Abdullah cemetery in Tehran. Written on the slab is, 'Khanoum, born 5th April 1900, died 5th December 1986', and here is the tale just as she narrated it.

CHAPTER 2

I was born in the spring, in a room in the corner of a large mansion in the middle of our estate, in a district named after my father and grandfather.

Yahya, our muezzin, was standing on the roof, chanting the verses of the Qur'an, announcing the time for prayer, when my mother fainted; whether it was from pain or happiness, we'll never know. The Armenian midwife, who looked after the women in the Qajar court, was busy dealing with the umbilical cord. The physician to the imperial court was having coffee in the adjacent mansion where male guests were received, ready to intervene should there be any complications. But there were none: the delivery was a smooth operation. An hour later, the news of my birth was telegraphed to our embassy in Paris. My father was in Paris at the time, but the telegraph was addressed to the Shah, Shah Baba, my grandfather.

Muzafareddin Shah, my maternal grandfather, was receiving medical treatment at the time while on a state visit to Europe. Later, I learned that on seeing the contents of the telegram he had summoned my father, giving him five imperial coins as tradition dictated, as a token of the happy news, and everyone else was offered pastries. My grandfather was due to receive Gustave Eiffel, when he telegraphed a message to the Imperial Palace in Tehran:

I have just received news of my dear daughter, Princess Monii, giving birth to a little girl – she will be a khanoum – congratulations – I am delighted – we have given Khan five imperials. Seyyed

Ahmad, the cleric, recommends a reading of the six verses from Nessah Surah to be whispered in the baby's ears at dusk, at the time of night prayers, this will be a good omen.
Paris, 1900.

There and then, everyone began to call me Khanoum, and this remained my name. Later, Khanoum was also endorsed on my birth certificate and my travel document. Shah Baba was going to give me a title, but sadly it wasn't to be.

Before me, my mother had given birth to a boy who only lived for two months. She had no other children after me and so I remained an only child. But I was hardly alone; from very early on I was surrounded by bustle and noise. My nanny had two daughters around the same age as me. She had come to our house as part of Mother's dowry. Her daughters were a little older than I. Then there were a number of sons and daughters of relations and servants who all lived in the same household. But my principal playmates were princesses, Shah Baba's other daughters and grandchildren, who were my cousins.

I remember us receiving tuition in one of the rooms in the outer part of the mansion. Our tutor wore a green shawl around his waist and always carried a pointing stick. He sat on a wooden bedframe covered in animal skin. The girls sat on one side of the room and the boys on the other. The girls would then go to a different room to do homework, and also for lunch and prayers. We would then return to the classroom an hour later.

I so wanted to ride but could not understand why boys of my age were allowed to ride horses but I wasn't. I had to learn how to embroider, cook, and run a household instead. Activities such as riding were considered inappropriate for a girl; this made no sense to me and I was tormented by the desire to do everything considered unsuitable for girls. After school the day was filled with girlish pastimes. Nanny had made various outfits for our homemade dolls. Going to the *hammam* was one of the highlights of the week. Morvarid, my mother's black maid, would sing and mimic the others. Sometimes, we took two other maids as well, one of whom, as well as attending to the beauty needs of the female courtiers, would pick up a pan in the *hammam* to play tunes and mimic the men and the elders. Anvar, one of the maids, was one of the late Nasser al-Din Shah's, the 'martyred' Shah's *siqehs*, married under a temporary contract. She mesmerised everyone with her magical voice. Her anecdotes from my grandfather's harem were quite something.

My first memories go back to the receptions held in the drawing room. When the sun shone through the stained glass of the French windows, it was as though the voices became colourful, and we played with our toys bathed in the glow of the colourful light passing through the stained glass. Somehow I was always the empress in our games, while Nanny's daughters were my ladies in waiting. Their mother, Nanny, was actually my mother's companion and, after my mother, the most important person in the house.

Hard as I try, I have very little memory of a 'father'; Khan everyone called him. He was seldom there yet one always sensed his presence. Morvarid, Mother's maid, would prepare his bed, and then leave a bowl of water covered with muslin on the shelf. When the temperature soared in summer, this would have a piece of ice jutting out of the muslin. My father had a chamber in the courtyard, which was always filled with intoxicating aromas emanating from the line of ceramic wine jars on one side and jars of pickles and syrup on the other.

We spent hours in the courtyard watching the herbs being spread out to dry in the sun. The servants cracked the shells of fresh walnuts that were delivered from our country estate in Shemeeran and their hands would be stained black for the rest of the year. They would then spread the walnuts on a white sheet and, once dried, they ended up being stored in new sacks or in the stone mill in the courtyard, ready to be ground and used in *fessenjan*, my father's favourite winter dish, a stew made with pomegranate purée, ground walnuts and poultry.

Soltan not only minded the larder and the pantry, she also supervised the making of provisions for autumn and winter. When she made tomato purée with stewed tomatoes boiled in large pots over firewood, the acrid smell filled the house. When sour cherries were ripe some were dried and some pitted for use in jam, always with a separate jar kept for Khan. Others were stewed and poured onto large trays to make *lavashak*, sheets of fruit paste, as a snack for me.

'Soltan likes spreading it all under the sun,' Mother always remarked, thinking maybe of winter, when they would be laid on the *korsi*, the low table which housed a brazier underneath and colourful layers of blankets on top to keep our feet warm. There were plates of *halva* and *sholeh zard*, the saffron-infused rice pudding. Pastries were baked the day before Mother's guests arrived, when the sweet smell of cardamom and saffron filled the air. No one was allowed to climb down the cool, dark staircase leading to the larder without Soltan's permission; this was where one could find anything from melons and apples to sweets and pastries, all kept in sealed pots.

I remember the winter I was taken ill. I was feverish and couldn't leave my bed. Shah Baba's foreign physician came and sat on a chair next to the fireplace in the drawing room and talked to my mother. He spoke Persian with a heavy accent, which would normally make me laugh, but now I hadn't the strength, though I did remember Anvar the maid's imitation of his accent when we were in the *hammam*. He prescribed some bitter powder to be taken on an hourly basis. I also had to take almond oil and other liquids, all of which tasted and smelled foul. There was a pitcher and a pan on the windowsill and, worst of all, there was a colon hydromat behind the curtain.

One night, when I was delirious with fever, my youngest aunt, Nezhat, was at my bedside and told me later that I kept asking a white horse to leap out. I suppose I must have had the image of Nasser al-Din Shah, my great grandfather, on his white horse, emerging from the large picture hanging in the drawing room. The thought of flying made me happy but Mother was in tears and kept fiddling with her rosary while she prayed. Nanny was doing the same. Even Khan walked in with his imposing figure encased in a fur coat and shining boots.

'You'll begin to perspire tomorrow my love, and feel better,' he said and then began to dish out orders to the servants.

I can't recall whether he actually touched my forehead or whether he demanded that the senior court physician be called in the next day if I didn't begin to perspire. All I could see through my eyelids was that it was snowing outside and the sky looked red, and the anxious shadows kept passing through via the veranda.

In the morning I woke to the sound of the snow being shovelled away to clear a path through the garden. The bitter powder prescribed by the doctor was clearly taking effect, or perhaps it was thanks to Soltan's syrup or even my mother's prayers. Every time I opened my eyes I saw her wipe her tears. By noon, the sun had spread across the snow. The frostbitten sparrows were picking the seeds Nanny had sprinkled in the garden and I could hear the pigeons on the mansard roof. I was beginning to feel better but I still had to wait a few more days before I could go onto the terrace and sit in the sun, well wrapped up in a blanket, hat and woollen scarf. They eventually took away the bedding and left the windows and doors open to get rid of the smell of fever and illness. My cousins were playing on the frozen surface of the pool, and seeing my smile my mother turned to heaven as a sign of gratitude. Nanny was burning *espand*, the seeds of wild rue that was supposed to turn away the evil eye, and fanning the fumes into my face. Soltan had brought eggs in for the same purpose; she mentioned the names of relatives and acquaintances and drew a cross on the egg each time until finally the egg cracked on one of the 'evil' crosses. I wasn't told to whom the evil eyes belonged until later that evening, when I finally discovered that they belonged to one of my aunts! I was sure that it could not have been Nezhat: she was my dearest and youngest aunt and I loved her. My older aunts, however, though good to my mother and me, could not stand each other, mainly because of their husbands. One of them was married to Farmanfarma, the most prominent, prosperous nobleman of our times. The other was married to Eynud-Dowleh, Shah Baba's dearest son-in-law. At the time of my illness, when I was six years old, Eyn was the Vizier. Nanny believed he was the right-hand minister and Farmanfarma the left-hand one, but Soltan referred to them as the sun minister and moon minister! My mother, though, regarded them with respect and due courtesy, and always referred to them as Mr So-and-so. Did she, perhaps, lament that her own husband was not of the same standing?

The day after I finally left my sickbed, my eldest aunt came to pay me a visit and the household was, as usual, at her service. At lunchtime my uncle made quite an entrance in our drawing room before proceeding towards the men's quarter. As he stood in the doorway holding his walking-stick he resembled a statue. He took one look at me and said something in Turkish to Nanny, which I reckoned was about the sickly-looking girl who was now thinner than usual. He quite fancied having me as his future daughter-in-law.

My other aunt, Farmanfarma's wife, had four sons. She always looked melancholy and I once overheard her consoling my mother with the thought that perhaps it was fortuitous that Khan was not involved in the running of the country as politics was a dodgy affair.

'One group has the upper hand today, and another the next.'

Why my eldest aunt always looked depressed only the adults knew and the truth was never disclosed to the younger members of the family. I had another aunt, Fakhr, who was more or less the same age as my mother. In contrast to Mother's quiet and dependable nature, she was a resourceful woman with good social skills and, in contrast to my father's pretentious attitude, her husband Mr Amin was meek and under her thumb.

I must have been six when Nanny's daughter's engagement to one of my father's foremen was arranged. This was celebrated in our home and Mother presented the future bride and groom with gifts. From then on the bride changed and did not participate in our games as often. She would write to her fiancé and he would reply. She was only one year older than I, which meant I, too, had to become attached to someone pretty soon, which made me anxious: I knew there was still much I needed to learn. One name making the rounds of the ladies' social events was that of my cousin Firouz, Farmanfarma's son. But all that came to an abrupt end when the Shah sent Farmanfarma into exile and my aunt and their children accompanied him to Karbala in Iraq. The Shah was said to be annoyed with Farmanfarma but Mother sympathised with his wife. I understood for the first time that she was the granddaughter of Taqi, the Vizier everyone remembered with great respect. It was said that at one time he had been the most important man in the country. He was determined to move Iran forward and turn it into a more European administration, but Nasser al-Din Shah ordered his murder; at least that was what our teacher believed. The princesses, however, did not have a good word to say about the Vizier and, when my aunt was not around, they said Taqi was an assistant cook turned premier who betrayed his benefactor and jolly well deserved his sentence.

Nezhat seemed more attuned to what went on behind the scenes and thus advised me not to listen to their nonsense: Taqi, she believed, was a victim of the collaboration between the British and the Shah's mother. Taqi's daughter never had a good word to say about her uncle and for this reason everyone gave him the cold shoulder. This was the root of Nanny's melancholy, Taqi's great granddaughter.

'What a destiny! Ever since they murdered the Vizier we haven't had a moment's peace; the British at work again – my grandmother didn't live in peace, nor did my mother,' she complained to my mother when she discovered that her husband, Farmanfarma, was being sent to Iraq. Firouz's name never came up again.

Every now and then another name would come up, but I began to discover that Mother was not entirely happy to part with me. My father never seemed to interfere. Consequently, when Nezhat mockingly revealed that Mother and Malakeh Jahan, the wife of the heir to the throne, had finalised the arrangements for my forthcoming engagement to her eldest son, Etezad, I did not believe her. Years afterwards though I understood that Mother didn't want the match. I was not aware of her reasons but later I learned that Etezad was a child from a *siqeh* marriage rather than an official wife, and that she preferred Ahmad, the eldest son, who would be heir to the throne and eventually the Shah.

Ahmad was a couple of years older than me and I had often seen him in our games, particularly when Mother and I went to Tabriz, where we would spend two months at their home. Ahmad was overweight and lazy but kind and the girls often outsmarted him. The doctors had cautioned him about food and advised physical activities yet everyone took pleasure and pride in feeding him. I felt my mother, too, treated him differently because Ahmad was particularly well mannered. My mother was his aunt on his father's side, and as a child I never knew how much my mother's sisters resented Muhammad Ali Mirza, the crown prince. Malakeh Jahan, his wife, felt closer and warmer towards my mother than all the other princesses. The two cousins were related through their fathers and were inseparable. Little did I know that my destiny would come to depend on the two women's profound affection for one another.

CHAPTER 3

H e was always unwell and out of kilter, and preferred to spend most of his time with the children. Despite his thick moustache and formal attire, he enjoyed spending hours playing with us and didn't take much notice of the adults. This didn't please the grown-ups at all but he took delight in seeing them line up with their arms folded spending hours standing to attention in the ground outside or inside the palace watching us playing.

My grandfather forgot his troubles when he played with us but the doctors had to interrupt our games from time to time. We were proud to see the grown-ups bow to Shah Baba, pay their respects and take his orders. One day, my dress was spoilt during one of our games; the very dress he had brought me from one of his trips abroad. Upset by my tears, he ordered one of the chests to be brought to him. The large wooden chest was filled with children's clothes and foreign dolls. He sat next to us, pulled out whatever was inside and distributed the contents among the children. He gave me a lovely dress which was embroidered in red on the chest, much prettier than my own dress. Then he ordered a folding screen to be brought as well so that he could help me change.

I liked him, not so much as my grandfather but as one of my playmates. There were seven or eight princesses but he seemed to pay more attention to Nezhat and me. Nezhat was the result of one of my grandfather's unions and we were both the apples of his eye. Years later I discovered that there was a lot happening in the country while we were at play. A constitutional revolution was upon us and when I understood how significant this was I resented his carelessness. As a child, however, the happiest times were when we played at various palaces and returned home at sunset filled with joy and with lots of presents. I would be quietly given a pair of earrings here, a necklace or ring there. These I would pass to my mother so that she could keep them in a safe place.

'May God give him prolonged health,' she would exclaim and then ask me whether I had kissed his hands in gratitude. I would then rush to show my dolls and new dress to everyone else, all of whom, except my father, shared my happiness.

My father belonged to an old aristocratic family and his father and fathers before him had all been given titles of some sort as a reward for their services. He commanded a great deal of power and respect. The Shah's other sons-in-law such as Eyne and Farmanfarma were ministers, governors or prime ministers, but my father seemed to spend his days hunting and gambling. He never hesitated to use abusive language directed at the Shah, which upset Mother but she couldn't do much as she was effectively a respectable prisoner in her own home. My father didn't dare acquire a second wife or take mistresses – or so it seemed – and the atmosphere in our home was melancholy and quiet. When he travelled, my mother would open the doors to lavish ladies' lunches and dinners to mark different occasions, be it religious festivals or anniversaries, and our home was filled with joy.

As far as I can remember I resented my father because I could see that he made Mother suffer; her jewellery and possessions were periodically sold to pay his heavy gambling debts. She always gave in to him to avoid public embarrassment. Rumour had it that my paternal grandfather had been even wealthier than the Shah but that my father and his brothers had managed to squander his wealth. He died before I was born and my father was abroad at the time and took months to return to Tehran. He even threw a lovely fluffy cat Shah Baba had given me into the pool once, while cursing his name as usual. I felt I was dying of anguish. I cursed him, and Mother consoled me.

My memories of childhood are filled with Mother anxiously watching over the gardens from behind the French windows. Whenever Father was in she was uneasy, and everyone was aware of it. Dressed in black and looking smart, he would usually step out of his quarters into the gardens around noon. His moustache was thin and twirled, and he always managed to find an excuse to look cross. He never missed an opportunity to use his beautifully made walking-stick to hit Heidar Beig, who was in charge of the coachhouse, on the head, or point in the direction of the rest of the household and look for faults and errors everywhere. As soon as he climbed up the stairs to come to the sitting room, where Mother would be sat leaning against a huge carpet-covered cushion, the servants would immediately disappear, and I would be kept busy in another room unless he called for me.

I can remember in detail the sitting room where my mother ruled. In the evening Morvarid, with her black face framed in the white scarf pinned under her chin, would prepare Mother's bedding in the middle of the room. The bedding consisted of a large mattress and a thick blanket decorated with pink satin. My father led his own life in his quarters: he would arrive late or bring friends with him, in which case one heard the sound of music and raucous laughter well into the night. Mother would read a book at such times, or keep herself busy with embroidery. Nanny occasionally stayed up late and kept her company. I would sit on the edge of her bed some nights and watch her. She held a hand mirror with the picture of a winged angel on the back while Morvarid undid her plaits, combed her hair and let it rest on her shoulders while she admired the beauty of the princess. I think no one had ever seen my mother with her glossy black hair loose except Morvarid, me and, at times, Nanny. She always wore a white headscarf tied under her chin and fastened with a pearl-studded pin. When she went outside she wore a *chaqchour*, a *chador* tied at the waist, and a veil so that her face was not exposed. When she was at the palace, she kept only her veil, but in the privacy of her quarters she donned a white *chador* printed with tiny flowers. The white of her *chador* was striking and smelt of jasmine, but her prayer *chador* was plain white.

Her nightgown was trimmed with lace and fine pink and mauve embroidered butterflies were sewn to the shoulders and chest. When her hair was combed, she resembled the angel on her hand mirror, but to me she *was* the beautiful angel. Morvarid would dip the corner of a muslin cloth in a bowl filled with milk to remove her makeup.

I was content as I lay on my tummy by my mother's bed with my hands under my chin and watched both women's movements. Once the makeup was removed Mother's fair complexion was exposed. The small muslin handkerchiefs soiled by makeup each night were lined up on the laundry line the next morning. By the time Morvarid had finished her task, a few dark spots floated on the surface of the milk, like a constellation of eyes. And when Mother called Nanny to take me to my bed in the east wing of the building, I pretended I was asleep so that I could stay with her, and I did occasionally get lucky when Father travelled. But as a rule I would share a room with Nanny, who would wake up at my every move. The best nights were those when Nezhat came to our home and we would both sleep in the same bed, chatting until sleep caught up with one of us. Four years older than me, with fair hair and hazel eyes, my youngest aunt was my childhood friend.

On one rare occasion that I slept in Mother's room, I suddenly woke in the middle of the night in such pain that I screamed: what had happened was that my father had fallen asleep in the middle of the bed and his huge, heavy body was resting entirely on my leg. I was about to cry when Mother pressed me against her chest and kept rubbing my leg. Once she thought I was asleep again, she tried to undo the buttons of his uniform and remove his boots, with great difficulty. He snored away, and with one of the lights left on I could see Mother folding my father's clothes and putting them on the chest. The pungent smell in the room was only too familiar; although very young, I knew the smell came from the ceramic jars placed side by side in the courtyard and I had seen the servants fill the glass jugs with their scarlet liquid and take them to his guests. I smelt the same thing coming from the funny-looking fat bottles sitting in the cupboard in the sitting room.

Whatever went on during the night, nothing could be read from Mother's face; she would peacefully draw her prayers to a close and then sit down to breakfast while overseeing the tray containing his breakfast, which was taken to him, often towards noon. While I ate, Mother would talk to the servants about their duties for the day, which also helped me find out about our own plans: whether we were supposed to have guests or go to the palace; whether I was to play with my friends or be taught by my tutor.

Despite the passage of seventy or eighty years, pain and sickness creep over me when I remember the night Father collapsed on my leg. Mother rubbed the bruise and put her lips on it. She was miserable: the sad princess whom everyone envied. She, however, never uttered a word and never shed a tear until the day we went to see Shah Baba one last time.

CHAPTER 4

I had not appreciated how unwell my grandfather was until I saw him lying under the *korsi*, keeping warm. The foreign court physician, with his upturned moustache and a *kolah*,[2] held his hand while kneeling by his side. Mother was the first to go to his room but she emerged tearfully.

'Shah Baba's unwell; go in and kiss his hands.'

I knew how to behave towards a sick old man and so did Nezhat, but he never actually allowed our lips to touch his hands; instead, he raised my little hands and kissed the palms.

'Nezhat-ol-Saltaneh?' he asked, using her full title, and Nezhat went forward. He then murmured, 'Have you, my beloved Khanoum, come to say goodbye as well?' and he burst into tears.

I put my arms around him. I could not believe how old my playmate suddenly looked. I could smell some bitter solution about him and can still hear his gentle Turkish voice in my ears.

'Pray for Shah Baba, I am dying.'

I didn't know what dying was but clearly it was a bad thing. The air in the room felt heavy. When the physician separated Nezhat and me from him, I began to realise how feverish his body felt. Mother was standing in the corner of the room wiping her tears with her handkerchief. As Nezhat and I went to cling to her we heard the king's faint voice while pointing towards a dwarf servant who was wearing a red *kolah*. A box was brought out and Shah Baba turned its tiny key with his eyes closed and the box opened. He was feeling his way and searched for something until he finally found what he wanted and, with the object still buried in his fist, he pointed to my mother. Looking like a crow in her black *chaqchour*, Mother reached for her father. I then saw his shaking hand press something into hers. Her silent weeping affected both Nezhat and me. The physician nodded towards the two maids, who separated Mother from the *korsi* with difficulty and helped her to the door.

The drawn curtains in the carriage driving us away from the palace created a dark and gloomy atmosphere. This carriage belonged to the king's mother with whom Nezhat was living at the time. On the way back, Nezhat and I clung to Mother, who wept quietly while stroking our heads. I felt fortunate that my little aunt was joining us in that cold house where Mother's distress filled the air; we could seek refuge in each other's company.

From then on, Mother did not take me with her to see Shah Baba and every time she returned she seemed more anxious. I saw her pray for long periods of time and make vows. After prayers, she sometimes covered her face with her *chador* and we could see her shoulders shake. But I didn't weep any more; I was somehow certain Mother's prayers were going to make a difference and that my grandfather would soon recover. This situation lasted about a month.

I went to see my grandfather once again the following week when the whole city was illuminated with fairy lights. He was still in the same state. Later that evening, when we went to see Nezhat at her home, I saw a banner erected in the little *bazaar* near the water fountain but there was no sign of jubilation in our homes: the adults feared something that we could not comprehend. Nezhat explained to me that Prince Eyne, who had been a guest in their house the other day, had hit someone's head with his walking-stick when the servants were offering him pastries. The servants were saying that His Majesty had signed a decree to set up a court of justice, an idea the courtiers did not like. My father, too, had forbidden the mention of 'constitution' and 'justice' in our household. Then I further heard that the Vizier had lost his position when the clergy and the people demanded his resignation. Rumour had it that the prince was involved in a number of murders, and the clergy cursed him when they preached.

Nezhat, the girls of our age and I never paid any attention to what was happening around us. Nezhat took piano and French lessons from Madame Hakim. I also had to do homework or embroidery. There was a heavy snowfall that winter and, despite the gloomy atmosphere and the fear outside our home, we were happy with our lives. But it wasn't long before the day Mother and the princesses had so feared finally arrived.

Father rushed home one afternoon and disappeared into his quarters. A few minutes later he sent for Mother. As this was rather odd all the servants began to eavesdrop, our lesson stopped and Nassir, one of the servants, kept hovering around nearby with his watering can, which he kept refilling from the pool. I was anxious as we'd kept hearing that the Shah was so unwell that the foreign and local physicians were covering their nostrils with their handkerchiefs because of the awful smell in the Diamond Hall and the Holy Qur'an was recited at his bedside. News had been flowing in the whole week and everyone was praying. Yet Father's hurried return, followed by Mother's summons, made everyone curious; everyone knew that Father had brought ominous news of the king.

When Mother finally emerged she seemed to have aged in that short period. My aunt rushed to hold her arm and Father climbed down the steps. Clad in military uniform, his sash and sword made him look taller than ever. In contrast to Mother, who seemed to be withering away, he went towards the pool with an air of jubilation; his riding boots seemed to gleam brighter than ever. He summoned Nassir, who promptly dropped the watering can and hurried to the poolside. Servants suddenly emerged from every corner and went towards him by the pool bowing.

I saw some of them burst into tears on my father's first words but they were quickly silenced by his rage. He then began to give his orders. In the end, everyone bowed and some stepped back, still bowing, until eventually everyone scattered. He paced up and down for a while and then rushed to the coachhouse.

Having seen my father from a distance, I rushed to Mother's quarters, together with my cousins. Mother was sitting in the middle, beating her head. Her headscarf had slipped down and she was pulling at her hair, whereupon all of a sudden everyone started wailing. My aunt started to sing a mournful serenade in Turkish and women started to beat their faces and hands, as one does at times of mourning.

So Shah Baba was dead. Black garments were taken out of the wardrobes and the mourning period had officially begun. Mother went to sit at the top end of the room and the other female members of the family and the neighbouring princesses came pouring in. Every new arrival made Mother burst into tears, sobbing; she had become an orphan. I was dressed in black, too, and Mother would turn in my direction from time to time: 'Finally lost your Shah Baba, haven't you my love?'

An hour later, the Shah's mother sent for us to go to her palace. I could see the Cossacks dotting the roads through the drawn curtains of the carriage. The shopkeepers had hung something black outside their shops as a sign of mourning. Some shops had even closed for the day. I was sitting next to Nezhat. She had already lost her mother and was now fatherless as well.

The king's mother, seated at the far end of the room, could barely move when we approached to kiss her hand. I thought to myself, if this woman passes away as well, Nezhat is going to be left with no one in the world, but she seemed to have read my mind. According to the Shah's will, she was to be brought up under my mother's guardianship. The air was awash with the sound of the Qur'an and wailing. The two of us were pondering a destiny, the painful depth of which was yet to unravel. Nezhat's

Georgian nanny offered everyone sherbet and peppermint drinks. The sweet aroma of *halva* wafted through the palace.

The next day we were taken to *Tekyeh Dowlat*.[3] Shah Baba's body had been placed in an ebony coffin which rested on a marble mantel. Save for a few clerics, and those reciting the Quran, as well as some boys dressed in black who were beating their chests, the only other people permitted in the *Tekyeh* were the female courtiers. A large picture of the Shah had been placed above the coffin. I felt my crowned playmate was asking me to go and play with him; he was looking into my eyes and his moustache seemed thicker than ever.

Everyone was sobbing, but Nezhat said they were really weeping for themselves. Later that evening I asked her whether we were crying for ourselves as well, which made her smile and say, 'No, we must ...' but she did not complete her sentence. I was young for my age, too young for what I'd been about to hear, but she was older than her years, as I came to discover later on.

CHAPTER 5

Z aynab, one of the maids, had told us a great deal about Father's quarters on the outer periphery of our home where he received guests and held social gatherings. She had to clean and dust the quarters under his housekeeper's watchful eyes. She would then come back to us with her stories and the tales kept us entertained in the winter evenings. Like everyone else, I couldn't wait to step inside what stood there like a locked fortress where only my father's male servants were granted entry. According to Nezhat, Eyne and Farmanfarma were received in the drawing room and even they were never ushered into the forbidden side of the building.

There was, however, a sudden change, and Zaynab was given other duties since Mother did not care for gossip. She gave the task of cleaning the mysterious rooms to Soltan, her own maid, who was dumb and who would certainly be good at keeping secrets! Our curiosity, though, had already been aroused and we couldn't wait to see what went on inside. Nezhat was the only person who showed no interest in gossip and generally did not talk much; she objected to idle chatter. Her gracious and haughty manner brought respect to that thirteen-year-old, golden-haired and hazel-eyed aunt of mine. Not only the servants, but even the tutors and the princesses, who were a little older, felt obliged to watch what they said in her presence. Nezhat's demeanour endeared her to Mother and she wanted her to be my role model. But I already felt great affection for Nezhat and wished, one day, to be able to speak to Madame, our tutor, in French, read books in French and play the piano. When Shah Baba and his mother were alive this was possible, but Shah Baba's death changed everything.

When Shah Baba's body was about to be taken to Karbala in Iraq, Mother, Nezhat and I, dressed in black and looking tearful, were taken to see everything from a distance. Having lost their father, Mother and Nezhat sobbed, but *I* had lost a very kind playmate whose presence I felt everywhere in my carefree childhood; the old man was the epitome of affection and kindness. Father escorted the hearse to Karbala, and in his absence Mother felt free to honour the mourning ritual with the rest of the imperial family.

The arrival of the heir to the throne, now Shah, and his family and entourage, meant that certain positions changed hands. This became the subject of endless gossip. Not all Shah Baba's daughters were as fortunate as Mother in having their own homes, and not all the youngsters led Nezhat's life in private estates with servants. Their carefree days were over and they were anxious about their future. The welfare of these women became Mother's main preoccupation for some time to come. Every time she went to see the new Shah and his wife, Malakeh Jahan, the future of some of the wives and daughters was sorted out. Nezhat and I were completely removed from the troubles, but a few weeks after Shah Baba's death we came to sense a new turn in our lives.

Shah Baba's mother died and was buried in Karbala, as per her will. From then on, Nezhat came to live with us, following which the new king ordered the palace to be closed down. Nezhat's nanny, who also moved in with us, complained that Nezhat's belongings had to remain behind. My nanny was shocked to hear that the princess's entire household, consisting of a number of servants, had been dismissed. Nezhat listened and simply smiled; perhaps she knew her belongings were soon to be packed and brought over.

Nezhat's possessions were indeed brought over and stored in a room at the end of our garden. Her piano, however, had to remain behind. We had to wait for Father's return so that we could learn of the Shah's decision as far as a home for his youngest sister was concerned. Upon Father's arrival, the doors to his quarters opened to us as well; now Nezhat would sit behind the grand piano in the salon while I got on with my homework. Mother kept Nezhat's box of trinkets safe in her own wardrobe.

The two months that took Father to and from Karbala heralded a new beginning for us, as Nezhat's presence changed the atmosphere in our home. Having taken Nezhat under her wing, Mother was no longer as melancholy as she had been. Everyone seemed to have forgotten that on Father's eventual return all the freedom and excitement that Nezhat had brought to us, along with her enchanting voice, was to come to an end. Nezhat's presence meant that no one was idle: not only did I give my dolls away to my cousins, but the exciting ladies' suppers, when everyone was entertained by the singing and dancing of the imperial harem's dancers, lost their appeal. Instead, Nezhat read aloud from foreign literary works such as *Hamlet* or *Othello*, while Mother would lean back against the cushion and puff at the hookah. Nanny would sit next to her doing her embroidery. We were all ears.

While Nezhat was slowly opening our eyes, our ears were filled with the news of the events taking place all over the country. The new Shah was not getting on with the parliament and the courtiers had no time for the constitutionalists. We didn't really understand what constitution meant; the only thing we knew was that, before his death, Shah Baba's decree had been designed to bring Iran in line with those countries which enjoyed a constitution. Nezhat, however, read in a book that the French Revolution had brought about the liberation of the people; prisoners were released and Louis XVI and Marie Antoinette were guillotined. Mother would look in the direction of Nanny and Morvarid and exclaim, 'Dear, oh dear!' – she was concerned about the impact such literature might have on them.

One day, my Persian tutor didn't show up as she wasn't feeling well so I ended up revising with Mother. I asked her about

Nezhat's mother since I had heard a great deal about her. Mother, who had so far avoided the subject, quietly explained that Nazgol was a Georgian girl whose father was a member of Nasser al-Din Shah's army in Tabriz. Ever since she had joined the harem by becoming Shah Baba's *siqeh* – Shah Baba was the heir apparent at the time – the rest of the women hadn't been able to contain their jealousy. She had many talents not to mention beauty – so that was where Nezhat's golden locks and fair complexion came from. It was said that Nazgol had an enchanting voice; she sang, played music and danced admirably. Mother recalled that she was an outcast in the harem, a harem which was filled with malice, and women never ceased casting spells on her in the hope that she might come to lose the heir's affection. Nevertheless, her integrity and good nature came to her rescue every time. The scheming was at its worst when everyone discovered that Nazgol was with child. As a result, the heir decided to leave his new wife in his mother's care, where he would visit her every so often. The young Georgian girl, who was only fourteen, eventually developed some curious disease and, when Nezhat was six days old, passed away. Mother said that Shah Baba spent an entire week mourning his favourite wife. Afterwards, he ensured that all that belonged to Nazgol was passed on to her little girl and asked the Shah to choose a suitable title for Nezhat: Nezhat-ol-Saltaneh, the reigning Nezhat. Hence the framed, gilded order that Nezhat brought along with her and which now hung in my room.

Nezhat was only one year old when the Nasser al-Din Shah was assassinated. Shah Baba became Shah, which meant that he had to leave Tabriz for Tehran. Mother said that he missed Nezhat and longed for her, but Nezhat and his mother did not arrive in Tehran for another year. Upon their arrival, he put them in an impressive estate with an army of servants, which only fanned further envy in the harem.

Nezhat learned how to play the piano and speak French from an early age, and she loved to read. While still in her early teens she already had many suitors, but they were all turned down. When Kamran, the regent, sought her hand in marriage, Nezhat's manner of speaking and the questions she put to the young man in the presence of the princesses caused his mother and sister to regret the proposal. Mother explained that Nezhat's knowledge and quick wit took everyone by surprise and made her suitors look rather stupid and ignorant; she proved too strong for their palate. Before he passed away, Shah Baba was heard to say to his mother that during one of his visits abroad he had met the Austrian Emperor's sons and, taken by their manners, had thought either of them would be a worthy match for Nezhat. Breaking all the rules and customs of the imperial household by galloping on her horse, Nezhat resembled one of the European princesses in the stories she read to us. The women of the harem would bite their lips saying: 'Such a demeanour's not becoming for a girl, particularly the Shah's daughter.'

Nanny always informed Nezhat of whatever was being said behind her back but she simply smiled, revealing the dimples in her cheeks. She would then give Nanny a peck on the cheek and change the subject.

Nezhat taught me that time was precious and one should not waste it. I feared the day she might finally get married and leave us. Mother could clearly sense our attachment and as well as not objecting to it, wanted me to follow Nezhat's example. But how?

Nezhat would sit behind the piano, under the crystal chandelier in Father's quarters, and when the sunlight struck the crystals beads, they spread their colours on the large Tabriz rug in the middle of the salon. The scene resembled the picture on one of the postcards we received from Europe. The Russian bookcases covering the walls had precious objects on display behind their glass doors: crystal glasses, clocks, lead soldiers clad in helmets and shields, and other memorabilia purchased during Father's visits to Russia and Europe, or presents from the Shah. At the top end of the salon there were also guns with mother-of-pearl butts, fine pistols and bejewelled swords with hammered gilt scabbards; you could spend hours just looking. There was also a large picture of my grandfather painted by my father. In the middle there was a large dining table and many chairs. He had bought the table in Spain and, on arrival in Tehran, I had been told it took many porters to carry it to the house. The carpenters had, however, spent a week putting it back together as it would otherwise have been impossible to get such a table through the French windows. The tall gilt mirror placed on the mantelpiece had created the same problems; it was so large it reflected the entire salon.

Nezhat was oblivious to her surroundings. She would sit next to Madame Hakim behind the piano and, when she played, she would ask me to pay attention when my tutor spoke. She always seemed in a hurry and somehow passed her sense of urgency on to me. Unlike the other women and girls in the family, Nezhat was always busy, unprepared to engage in idle talk. I was slowly drifting away from the environment I grew up in; I was stepping into the world in which Nezhat strolled with confidence, a most enticing world indeed. I was not alone; I sensed Mother, too, was slowly being drawn to Nezhat. Despite the immense respect that Nezhat had for her elder sister and guardian, Mother would listen to *her* and nod in approval every now and then.

Nezhat had not only brought *joie de vivre* and excitement to our home, she had also made us reflect on our lives and the future. She made us want to relinquish all the rigid customs and habits that were *de rigueur* in the imperial households, the necessity of which no one ever dared question. I recall the evenings when Nezhat read to us aloud about the lives of important women in the world. In response to Nanny, who said that those women were fortunate and, unlike us, were not born miserable, she retorted: 'It's up to us whether we allow it or not. God didn't intentionally create us as unfortunate, meek and submissive, did he?'

Was this the first important lesson of my life?

CHAPTER 6

I was so enthralled at the thought of stepping into a new world that I almost failed to notice Father's return from Karbala. With his return, it soon dawned on us why Mother was so upset about losing her father, and why she always complained about having become an orphan with no one in the world. Shah Baba's death meant that cracks began to appear in the mutual respect and civility between my parents. Not long after Father's return, news of a 'second wife' struck like lightning. His new wife was related to the Court Minister and she was only three years Nezhat's senior, five or six years my mother's junior, though Mother's unpleasant life made her look older than her twenty-four years. Behjat, the rival wife, had spent a pampered childhood in Istanbul and resembled a doll newly unwrapped from the shop. When I heard the news I felt like strangling my father because I knew how belittled this would make my mother feel. She could no longer conceal her profound unhappiness, and it became impossible to put a lid on everyone's endless speculation.

Nezhat could not contain her fury; for the first time ever she looked tense, and she pushed me away from the door. She then raised her voice saying that I could shout as much as I liked but had no right to weep – she considered weeping pathetic. She went on to explain that our lives did not have to follow those of our mothers who had succumbed to their fate.

'But how?' I managed to ask amid my tears.

'We have the right to choose and shape our destiny; we shan't become submissive. We're certainly not an item of furniture that can be moved around, sold or swapped.'

She terrified me. Mother, too, was terrified of what went on in Nezhat's mind as she paced the room in fury. She had assumed Nezhat and I were going to lay our heads on her knees and sob, but now she turned to her hot-headed sister.

'How my dear, how? Daughter of the Shah or not, women are born unfortunate. Forget about my disposition but how are *you* going to prevent your own misfortune?'

Her tone was melancholy. Nezhat embraced her.

'We shan't allow it! If necessary, Khanoum and I will leave this country and take you with us as well.'

It was the first time I had ever heard such a thing; though I had seen it in my dreams I never imagined it possible: an unmarried woman travel abroad? As though reading my mind she said, 'Yes, it *is* possible! Who said only men could travel? In other parts of the world women become empresses, patrons and ministers, yet in this part of the world we think we are duty bound to give in to what's decided for us.'

Mother had stopped shedding tears and was now looking at Nezhat. Our lives seemed to have changed dramatically: a day that had begun with tears had changed by lunchtime. I was bewildered. Nezhat, however, seemed to have braced herself in preparation. She took the tray of bugloss tea and asked Nanny not to let anyone in the room. She then locked the door, crouched on the floor and looked at Mother as she fiddled with the key. She asked Mother why she was so upset. Mother explained that she had never wanted to marry Father. When she had heard the Shah's decision and was faced with the *fait accompli* she had initially decided to commit suicide, but then gave in to her mother's pleas and Shah Baba's orders. Since then, she had never let anyone find out what went on in our home.

It was heartbreaking to hear that she had spent the best years of her life imprisoned in a golden cage with no one to talk to. My resentment was at its height but there was no trace of chagrin or tears on Nezhat's face. She waited for Mother to calm down and then explained that we had to be tactful. But before going any further, she asked Mother whether she genuinely disliked Khan and whether she was at all envious of his new wife. No, she did not feel any affection towards him; she was actually pleased that he was going to be occupied with his new life so that we could now live in peace. Nezhat leapt with joy and went towards the door to ensure no one was eavesdropping. She then began to explain. The plan was simple: we were to facilitate Khan's means of pleasure and by doing so we would be able to work out a plan of attack. I didn't know exactly what battle she was thinking of, but I found Mother completely taken by her little sister; she seemed only too happy to leave the decision making to Nezhat.

Father and his new wife set up life in the extensive Ferdowse Park, with a new, Western-style building constructed at its centre. Nezhat had inherited the property from her grandmother but, rather than lease it to foreign diplomats, as was originally planned, she was now asking Mother to let Khan use it. Father was, of course, delighted and, when he left, our large home was completely at our disposal. We even got hold of his quarters except for the salon and one minor room; the door to the bedchamber and its library was locked. A carpenter was brought in, and a door was made and locked with a huge padlock. I could no longer peer through the windows either, since these were now blocked by shutters. The whole thing resembled a fortress that only opened up when Father returned every couple of weeks to take chests full of stuff away with him.

CHAPTER 7

We welcomed spring, a cheerful beginning to a new life. Nezhat and I were growing up with Mother nominally in charge of the running of the estate, but everyone knew that it was Nezhat who had masterminded our new situation, and it was thanks to her that our way of life and relationship with people had changed.

Madame Hakim visited Nezhat regularly, and I would study scripture till lunchtime, when the blind Abbas enchanted us with his wonderful voice. He knew Ferdowsi's *Book of Kings*, the *Shahnameh*, by heart and also recited poems by Hafez and Sa'di. Sometimes he was asked to stay on so that Tiny Hassan, his assistant, could sing with him, making the ladies' *soirées* even more pleasurable. Mother enjoyed such gatherings.

Our bliss was disturbed whenever we received disappointing news. Muhammad Ali, my uncle and now Shah, did not get on with the constitutionalists – a monarchy with limitations did not agree with him. He had sworn to observe the constitution that his father had decreed a month before his death, but it was a mere sham. Though the majority of notables and even aristocrats had joined forces with the clergy and were supporters of the constitution, any inclination to go along with the changes on his part would be questioned by the courtiers. The Shah wanted to maintain autocracy, just as his ancestors had done before him. As far as he was concerned, the parliament and the people had no right to interfere with affairs of state.

The Shah had hardly sat on the throne when we were invited to go to the palace. Before the visit, the Shah had sent his father's wives and daughters dress fabric and new clothes to mark the end of the mourning period. Nezhat, however, preferred not to go to court or to wear colourful clothes so soon. Mother felt the same and a message was thus sent over to Malakeh Jahan. A message was received in return: the ladies were free to come in the clothes of their choice!

It was hard for me to encounter my grandfather's absence in his home. When we entered the Diamond Hall, we saw the dulcimer player, with his face covered to avoid looking at the women; he had been court musician since the time of Nasser al-Din Shah. The music created such a gloomy atmosphere that we all burst into tears.

Malakeh Jahan, the king's only wife, was seated at the top end of the room beside Shah Baba's daughters and grandchildren, followed by his wives and, further on, the daughters of Nasser al-Din Shah, my mother's late grandfather, and some of his youngest wives. The princesses were chatting away and sherbets and pastries were being offered. The loud voice of the chamberlain announced the arrival of the Shah. Everyone rose and the sound of *espand* seeds sizzling could be heard in the ensuing silence. Upon seeing the Shah in the doorway, the women went over to offer their usual pleasantries. I was standing next to Nezhat and my eyes caught sight of the Shah's sons: Ahmad, the crown prince, was his usual short, chubby self, and as soon as he saw me he smiled and I felt embarrassed. Muhammad Hassan, tall and slender, was in military uniform. Unlike his brother he looked distant and arrogant. The arrival of the young men started the women whispering and winking messages to each other. Nezhat found the whole affair silly. I was now used to her delicious anecdotes, especially when she highlighted the false manner of the others. Considering the country was in turmoil, I, too, found their demeanour out of place; these women seemed to be trapped in their own world and had no fear or even knowledge of what was happening outside.

It was snowing and the heat from the burning logs formed condensation on the windowpanes. The Shah sat on a gilt armchair with his sons behind him. The room was filled with women and a few eunuchs dotted around here and there. The Shah raised one eyebrow and his low-pitched, angry voice emerged from his double chin.

'Ladies! I have summoned you here so that I could have a word or two with my own family in the privacy of my home.'

He then motioned the maids and the eunuchs out of the room. I felt I was about to hear some dreadful news and my heart was pounding. Nezhat had narrowed her eyes as she always did when she wanted to focus intently on something.

The Shah started off by cursing his father and 'a few godforsaken traitors who surrounded our late father and manipulated him and the monarchy', at which point a few women burst into tears. He then sprang to his feet, put his hands on his waist and retorted:

'I have not called you here to weep and I don't believe I am chanting a mourning serenade; do save your tears for Muharram, the martyrdom of our saints, which is upon us!'

Everyone fell silent.

'A bunch of traitors has filled everyone's head with talk of a "constitution and a court of justice" and such nonsense. They are trying to provoke the common people. They took advantage of the late Shah's disposition to have some decree signed and by doing so they are determined to put an end to monarchy.'

Most of the women had no idea what he was talking about and so followed his line and began to curse the traitors.

'I am not a coward and am not going to leave the throne to these lackeys. I'll have them shot if necessary!'

He then asked us to be vigilant and report whoever spoke of 'parliament' and 'constitution', be it their husbands or even their sons. They had to take particular care with the servants; if they suspected they were involved with the rebels and were seen to handle any pamphlets, they would be better off sending them away on leave until the conspiracy was over. There was absolute silence until the Shah finally sat down and I sighed with relief. So that was why we had been summoned. But it was not quite over.

'Pamphlets are being distributed in people's homes to awaken the peasants. Be vigilant so that these scrap pieces of paper do not taint your homes, as they will bring about your ruin …'

As soon as the Shah had fallen silent, Malakeh Jahan picked up a plateful of pastries, and offered him some. She was about to summon the servants when Nezhat stood up. Mother watched her anxiously. Nezhat's height, fair complexion and hazel eyes always contrasted sharply with the dark-haired, olive-skinned women of the court, and now, dressed in black with a black scarf fastened under her chin with a pearl-studded pin, she looked quite striking standing in the middle of the room with a few golden strands escaping her veil. Her docile voice penetrated through the noise and she called upon her crowned brother to forgive her for her impertinence and to take a moment to listen to what she had to say.

No one had anticipated a speech; women had no right to stand up to men, particularly when the man happened to be the king and the leader of a nation. Everyone was silent and the crown prince's mouth opened in a faint, neutral smile. Nezhat began by paying homage to Shah Baba. She then reminded the king that he had sworn to abide by the constitution and, as far as people were concerned, he was bound by its terms. She then landed her first strike.

'I have read about some of these pamphlets and have been through some foreign newspapers as well. There's nothing in them but the mention of people's rights and the denunciation of oppression. Every educated and godly person likewise believes that a country must not remain in poverty and chaos, and the reason behind all this is the cruelty that the oppressed suffer without a system of justice in place. And now that the people have come to rely on the parliament, it is unfair to let them down. It makes people happy that their country has finally come to have a constitution.'

The Shah was agog, the princesses were transfixed, and there was a sense of fear. I felt proud, but I was perspiring despite the cold weather. And when Nezhat spoke of the French Revolution, the Shah became impatient, rose from his seat and responded:

'Enough! What nonsense I'm hearing! The bastards have gone as far as penetrating the privacy of our homes ... What nonsense ... brat ... call the executioner ... I'll have the lot of them shot ...'

He was heading out yet we could still hear his angry words. Malakeh Jahan and the ladies, who had been sitting at the top end of the room, were getting up and following the Shah. The assembly broke up in disarray with everyone muttering:

'Unbelievable! How dare she give the Shah a sermon? Luckily, he's a compassionate Shah, otherwise ...'

Nezhat stood there for some time without saying much. Then a furious woman approached her. Nezhat finally lost it.

'You miserable soul! What do you know about what's going on out there? Life's not just about making oneself up. You seem to be content sitting here waiting for people to climb up the walls of your homes and hold you prisoner. The only thing you're capable of is to dress up and weep. How long, just how long ...'

Mother was now desperately trying to stand between them.

'Come, come!'

I had never seen such a show of resilience and strength from Mother. Upon hearing her retort, the other princesses, quiet up to then, having noted her mourning attire, began to feel embarrassed and decided to pull back so that we could leave. We followed Mother and Morvarid followed us, carrying Mother's veil. As the three of us climbed down the stairs, I felt I was being watched by myriads of eyes behind the steamed-up windowpanes. The servants had cleared a path in the snow. We passed by the glasshouse and towards our carriage. Resting behind the steamy glass, the plants were silently looking forward to the spring, and I suddenly felt like someone who had just been liberated. The coachman rushed to open the door for us. The horses' breath condensed in the air but my cheeks were burning despite the cold.

By the time we sat inside the carriage I was no longer an eleven-year-old: Nezhat had pushed the years forward. No one thought of her as a mere fifteen-year-old. Even Mother seemed to have grown older. I had never been overwhelmed by feelings of independence and power before that day. My heart was glowing and suddenly we didn't feel bereft any more. An hour later, Mother's strength was put to the test.

We were standing in the middle of the sitting room, and had hardly removed our veils, when we received a message that Mother had been summoned back to the palace. The message was from Malakeh Jahan and we knew this had something to do with what had taken place earlier. The Shah was in command and Nezhat was at the receiving end. The time dragged as we waited to find out what punishment the Shah had in mind for his little sister. Meanwhile, Nezhat was reading a book. I, too, wanted to appear as though I was reading but my mind was occupied with the events. I was terrified at the thought of Nezhat leaving us; she knew a great deal that I did not know. My only hope was the relationship between Mother and Malakeh Jahan: they were cousins, and so close it was as though there was but one mind in two bodies.

When I saw my mother's drawn face on her return I realised I was right to be anxious. She had hardly arrived when she used an excuse to yell at one of the servants, and as she approached the room it seemed as if she were carrying a heavy load. She sat down next to the fireplace, leaning back against the cushion. Nezhat and I remained in our room until Nanny came for us.

I had guessed right: the Shah was infuriated with Nezhat's bold demeanour earlier. He now wanted Nezhat to get married within a week and she was given two choices of husband. All Mother and Malakeh Jahan had managed to do was to remind him that the war minister, Bahador, was a common and ignorant man, and that his son was unlikely to be any different: it was not sensible to offer him the icing on the cake. No one, however, could fault Nezam, who had a successful record of holding ministerial posts.

So, the Shah had decided to marry Nezhat off. 'Why in heaven's name had Nezhat remained unmarried at fifteen?' he'd raged. Mother broke the news as carefully as possible. We expected Nezhat to explode, but we were taken aback when she asked how long she had, looking quite composed.

'In a few days Muharram is upon us followed by *Safar*, which are both inappropriate months for such events. We've plenty of time as a result and when the apple's thrown in the air, who knows where it'll land.' And then she changed the subject.

The next day, however, something else happened. Father returned home. Wearing his fur coat and riding boots he went straight to Mother. Nezhat was called in an hour later; she donned her informal *chador* and went along. I wanted to be there as well, but an hour passed and no one came for me. It was almost lunchtime and I had not heard a word of what my tutor had tried to teach me, so anxious was I concerning my courageous aunt. Though she gave the impression she was merely waiting for her mistress's orders, Morvarid was eavesdropping behind the doors on the veranda, despite the cold.

Nanny finally came to call me. Father was now standing by one of the French windows as Morvarid helped him with his boots. I said hello and reluctantly allowed him to give me a peck on my forehead, upon which the scent of his cologne filled my nostrils. Ever since he had acquired another wife he paid more attention to his appearance. He then picked a mouthful of food from the tray held in front of him. In addition to the pistol he always carried, a gunman always escorted him. He had a collection of some fifteen expensive rifles.

'The country's in such turmoil that in some regions governors and landowners have even been murdered. I shan't be surprised if the capital also comes to experience the same situation,' he remarked as he walked towards the gates. He then turned to Mother. 'Hasn't Khanoum grown?' he said, as though referring to something that had come up in their earlier conversation.

The Shah had asked Father to keep a watchful eye on Nezhat and the sooner she was settled with a husband the better. Clearly, Mother was not at all happy with Father's getting involved. Nezhat, however, saw it all from a different angle; she was fearless and confident.

'I'll never marry someone with my eyes shut; I must get to know the person who's going to share my life and I have to like him first. I've no objection to meeting Bahador but they must bring their son over as well.'

Bahador's ignorance and stupidity was legendary. When he was attending a meeting with the head of the parliament, at the first mention of the constitution he had taken out his pistol.

'I'd never allow a bunch of commoners to interfere with the rights of the monarch', he'd said; 'if necessary, I shall personally shoot them all.'

But Nezhat was in no way put out.

'All the better, since it'll be much easier to get rid of him and his family rather than Nezam, who sounds quite sensible and high up.'

The conflict between the Shah and the parliament was, by then, at its height. Without Father's knowledge, pamphlets reporting the terrible state of affairs kept coming. It was not difficult to see that the monarchy was being sucked into a whirlpool. This was worrying because *we* were members of the imperial family.

With the arrival of Atabak in Tehran everyone held their breath; his diplomacy, wealth and open-handedness were legendary. We had heard that he was neither as tactless as the Shah and his entourage, nor as inexperienced as the nationalists. He had spent years serving Nasser al-Din Shah and Shah Baba as head of government. His wealth was greater than the entire treasury and he was a well-established figure internationally. After years of travelling as the guest of emperors and presidents, he was now happy to accept the Shah's request and come over to Tehran. Those who had been to Atabak's extensive park described the large containers that he had brought over from his trips to Japan and America. It was said that his premiership meant that the conflict was going to settle down and that the country would once again be peaceful. My uncle Amin, who could not stand Atabak, nevertheless agreed that only Atabak could rescue a country in turmoil. The other news reaching our home was that Nezhat's hand had been asked for in marriage to one of Atabak's sons. Nezhat winked again.

It was spring, and we began to study outdoors. Sometimes we were invited to the homes of our relations; at other times the imperial family and princesses came to visit us. It rained a great deal, which made the arrival of spring more pronounced. In the evenings we would sit on the veranda close to the sweet-smelling stocks and talk about the day's events. Changing Bahador's mind was far easier than Mother and I had imagined. Nezhat's arrogance, as well as a demonstration of her knowledge in the presence of some ill-educated women, soon made them flee!

Summer had hardly ended and the city was already in turmoil. Atabak was shot in front of the parliament while conversing with the leader of the constitutionalists, and died on the spot. This was hard to believe; the government had depended on his diplomacy, and the parliamentarians had slowly been getting over their anger.

'By doing this they've effectively terminated your brother's rule; Atabak was his only hope,' Nezhat reminded Mother, who replied very quietly so that the servants could not hear: 'He did it, the Shah arranged for his assassination!'

'But my dear sister, he was guardian of the crown and the country. If what you say is correct, that's too bad for your brother.'

'Your brother' was what the Shah had become ever since he had shouted at Nezhat.

We saw a lot of Nezam's family, and Father made himself available during their visits as a matter of courtesy. The men would gather in his quarters as usual and talk politics while puffing away at the hookah. As well as the family of the suitor, a few members of the imperial family, Mother's sisters and nieces and nephews, would also be invited on such occasions. Nezhat and I would remain in our room and keep ourselves busy with our books while we tried to guess what was being said, until someone eventually came for Nezhat when Mother wanted her in the sitting room. Nezhat then reluctantly checked herself in the looking-glass before stepping out. We curtsied to the older ladies but before the mother and sister of the prospective groom could embrace Nezhat, she went to sit next to Mother. The sister of the groom-to-be was complimentary on Nezhat's attributes, but Nezhat tried to brush it off.

'Thank you. Everyone likes pleasantries and flattery and I am no exception. May I take the liberty, however, and say a few words before this place comes to resemble the slave market in Baghdad, or the horse markets in Europe …'

She then began by describing some of the girls in the family who had only recently got married in sumptuous circumstances and with superb dowries. She did not mention any names but everyone knew what she said was absolutely true. She related how these young women became captives in the end: from the moment they woke up they made themselves up and waited for their husband's return from partying with friends, gambling, hunting and male social events.

The women were mesmerised by Nezhat; at times they shook their heads with regret, at other times they whispered to each other. They were eager to hear the outcome of what Nezhat was describing. She then launched onto the liberation of women: in Europe and other parts of the world women even managed to reach the throne. She used Catherine the Great as an example and then mentioned the long reign of Queen Victoria and her supremacy.

She told everyone that she had looked into the religious doctrines and had found no impediment to women reaching power. The sturdy women in the room were exchanging meaningful looks when Nezhat landed the final blow:

'Have you heard of the uprising in Shiraz?'

She then spoke of Azerbaijan, followed by the sale of Turkman girls, the account of which deeply moved a couple of ladies in the audience. Nezhat was urging them to show an interest in the pamphlets that appeared in their homes daily, and to prepare themselves for an imminent event, a 'revolution', the uprising of a nation that had come to learn what went on in the world. They should no longer be prepared to live like tamed animals at the service of their rulers.

What Nezhat was saying was not only hard for those women to digest – after all, they were either princesses or wives and daughters of prominent individuals – it was not suited to the nature of that gathering either. She even turned to the suitor's mother and said: 'I'd like to see Mr Nezam and ask him not to accept any ministerial posts proposed by the Shah because he'd have to face the same fate as Atabak!'

'What nonsense!' came one reply from the top end of the room.

'Mr Nezam and all the other old and experienced politicians hardly need *our* preaching,' was heard from a different corner.

'Well actually they do, since they have no more experience and wisdom than Atabak, who for thirty years was the second most important person in the country and had seen the world. A great deal of fuss was made of his return and see what happened to him!'

Thus she left everyone astounded.

An hour after we had left the room the commotion of servants carrying lanterns suggested that the guests were on their way out. We were busy reading when Mother entered the room. By then she had got used to Nezhat's outbursts and, although at times anxious, she was rather amused. Later that evening we were having a good time mimicking the eligible bachelors and their families. We were hysterical when we heard His Eminence's arrival. Mother got up, undid her *chador* from around her waist and pulled it over her head. She then, reluctantly, went to greet him. Father wasn't staying overnight these days, except that evening. The two of us were summoned to his quarters shortly afterwards. Nezhat did not want to go but then it dawned on her that Mother might need her assistance in dealing with him. So she got up and tidied her hair under her head scarf. We donned our *chadors* and went over.

The sound of the frogs hovering by the pool resonated in the garden and the aroma rising from the large pots of jasmine placed in front of the mansion was intoxicating, not to mention the stocks which were releasing their scent in the evening air. I had braced myself for Father's unbearable temper, but we were surprised to find him sitting on the armchair under the chandelier with a crystal jug and glass on the small table next to him. He even rose slightly as soon as Nezhat arrived. Mother seemed relaxed sitting on the sofa near him and her *chador* had slipped down and rested on her shoulders, revealing her hair in the light of the chandelier, which enhanced her beauty, especially when she smiled. I had never seen them both together, seated in the same room at the same time. No wonder I was surprised and rather delighted. Father hugged me and gave me a peck on the forehead, but, despite Mother's gestures, I could not bring myself to respond in kind; I did not know how, nor did I love him. Father then invited us to sit on the sofa next to Mother.

'Whatever did you do, Nezhat-ol-Saltaneh, to make them flee?!' he began, sounding as though he was being supportive.

'I sang some blasphemy in their ears that they'd not heard before!'

Father burst out laughing and fiddled with his moustache. He then started talking ill of Nezam.

'And the rest of them are a bunch of cows, with no idea how to run a country.'

He followed this with a description of Nezam's 'spoilt and stupid' son. Talking about the current affairs in the country, he demonstrated his usual resentment at the thought of allowing commoners to have a say. Turning to Mother and Nezhat he said: 'Your brother's not decisive enough and too hesitant for his own good. I'm concerned that it'll eventually be too late.'

In his opinion, the Shah had to take action to save the monarchy; he should bombard the parliament with shrapnel and execute all the constitutionalists. I found the expression on Nezhat's face changing, as though hearing his bloodthirsty words had made her nauseous. I was sure she was going to voice her own, contrary opinion but I was mistaken; she didn't say a word! Just as Father was becoming enthralled, she suddenly got up and apologised for not feeling well. I used the opportunity and got up as well. It was midnight, but he wanted to hear Nezhat play a tune on the piano and was rather hoping she was going to change her mind. However, over the years Nezhat had made everyone understand that once she had made a decision no one could alter it.

We were lying under the muslin sheet inside the mosquito net and chatting. The light in Father's sitting room was still on and the bedding in Mother's room had not been touched. Nassir and another servant were beating the water in the pool to keep the frogs quiet. This was routine whenever my father was at home, but we loved the sound of the frogs. It was rather unjust, according to Nezhat, to keep the household servants awake well into the night just so that we could sleep soundly.

It was a peaceful night and the sound of water and the breeze played in gentle harmony. We had no idea what had gone on in that room by the time Mother returned to the cool of her bed.

CHAPTER 8

There was something in Mother's manner the next day which was unusual, but it took us some time to find out why. She had become aloof and preferred to sit in the sitting room puffing away at the hookah, watching us doing our homework. She seemed to be worried about something but didn't wish to involve us. She was being particularly meticulous about Nezhat's financial affairs: she spent hours going through the books with the bookkeeper. Nezhat, of course, would know about the decisions made on her behalf.

The other visible change was Mother's absence from our gatherings in the evenings. She no longer read the books Nezhat had given her, nor did she join us. She was certainly not in the mood and we could occasionally hear her having a go at Morvarid or the other servants. Father came home regularly now. When he didn't have parties of people gambling in his quarters, he would talk to Mother, and her subsequent drawn face and puffy eyes were indicative of the nature of these conversations.

Though the atmosphere was no longer a happy one, other aristocratic households were no better off. They, however, didn't have Nezhat to distract them from the turmoil. Her maturity and experience outdid that of several people put together, and whenever we faced dilemmas she came to our rescue with a suitable solution. One such occasion was when Mother, after months of secrecy, could no longer contain her pain, and finally opened up to Nezhat.

Every day we received news of unrest in different parts of the country and every day a new dispute brewed between the Shah and the populists, yet Mother seemed to be suffering from something quite different, the cause of which was her husband Khan. And so it was that the next day, after a night of heated argument between my parents, we found her still in bed by noon and quite upset: Father intended to divorce Behjat and was using this as a pretext to sell Ferdowse Park. Father was well aware that once he had managed to convince Mother, Nezhat was not going to pose any problem over relinquishing her assets; she didn't feel attached to material things. Moreover, she was wealthy enough to afford another property. Needless to say, Mother was not prepared to succumb to Father's impulse and let go of what belonged to her sister. She was also aware that he had recently lost heavily at his gambling; divorcing Behjat was merely an excuse to ask for more funds to be made available to him.

I managed to overhear only a fraction of their conversation that day. It appalled Nezhat to see her beloved sister's bruised face; Mother was the only close older relative she felt she had. She began to pace the room like an angry wildcat and kept retorting: 'What do you care, dearest sister, let him sell it! So what, we'll buy a better one. I never liked the damned estate anyway.'

But Mother was stern and reminded her that, so far, to avoid spilling the beans, she had been obliged to sell a great chunk of the assets and jewellery that Shah Baba had bequeathed to her, and she was not prepared to throw away someone else's as well. Then, to confirm her intentions, she added that she had just written to the Shah begging him to protect her sister's estate against her cruel husband. Nezhat was emphatic in her response.

'But you're so naïve. To save his pride, your brother would sell us all, if necessary. He's effectively mortgaged the country to the Russians so that he can fund his military. I wouldn't be surprised if he's already made provisions in some foreign bank for his imminent departure. What makes you think he'd concern himself with this injustice against us? Are you not aware that ...'

I couldn't hear the rest of the conversation, though I do remember that Mother finally calmed down.

CHAPTER 9

S pring was upon us once more, and green was appearing through the trees. We saw the passing of the season and winter's last breath when we sat under the large *korsi* in the evenings, laid out in Mother's room. Nezhat would enlighten us by reading the foreign papers out loud and, when no one was around, we also read the pamphlets. These pamphlets unravelled the true face of our family and acquaintances. We weren't surprised to discover that the men married to our aunts and many of our relatives were with the people, and the people demanded justice. The elite, however, wanted to maintain their privileges.

It took me days to discover how expediently the Shah had commissioned Father as commander-in-chief, hence his departure for Khorasan in the north-east to suppress the insurgencies; a plan contrived by Nezhat and Mother, and effected thanks to Malakeh Jahan.

'Had it not been for you, dearest Nezhat, our lives would have become unbearable with the demise of Shah Baba. What are we going to do when one day you leave us to marry a very lucky man, who's bound to show up any day? I suppose I could put up with your absence, but what about my poor mother who'll be crushed in the grip of a man who's already destroyed her life?' I wondered.

When we lay down, I undid her golden locks and spread them round her shoulders like a waterfall. She always listened to me and my worries, and always chose something appropriate from one of her books, or a quote by a foreign philosopher, to console me.

'Life flows like the river, and only fools think it is still and sorrows are eternal.'

Her reassuring voice helped me fall into a peaceful sleep and the sound of the pitter-patter on the rooftop played background music to my dreams.

Noruz, the New Year, arrived. Everyone was busy: Mother was getting the preparations underway and the servants were carrying out the spring-cleaning of the house. We visited Malakeh Jahan, who presented me with two gold imperials on the first day of the New Year. She was particularly affectionate towards me and gave me a peck on the cheek, but since our thoughts were elsewhere we were oblivious to the significance of her show of affection.

Father's second wife, Behjat, came to see us in the afternoon along with a couple of her companions and maids. Mother was kind to them and stretched her hospitality well into the late afternoon, the two of them speaking privately behind closed doors. Something seemed to be emerging from the visit. Nanny couldn't help but curse Behjat in my presence and we were astounded to see Mother's kindness towards her. The accountant, who also dealt with Nezhat's affairs, arrived with his books. Though we later discovered that Mother had parted with her few remaining assets and an item of Nezhat's jewellery, the two women seemed delighted and Behjat embraced Nezhat and bent to kiss my mother's hand before she left. She was pleased to be saved from Khan! Later on, when Mother was explaining everything to Nanny and me, she was, as usual, full of admiration for Nezhat's wisdom and graciousness. Nezhat then frowned and responded: 'One's possessions must serve one's happiness, otherwise they're worthless.'

We received a letter from Father, who was in Mashad in the north-east at the time, as well as items for the household, including a couple of rugs for Nezhat and me as New Year presents; it seemed he was being handsomely rewarded for his work. Mother, however, thought otherwise.

'I suppose he's had a major win on the gambling.'
Over the years she had got the measure of my father.

On the third day of the New Year festivities Malakeh Jahan and a few princesses came to return our earlier visit. They then proposed a match between Nezhat and Moshir's eldest son. When we were in our room later Nezhat said that Malakeh Jahan had also asked for my hand in marriage for her son Ahmad. Although I knew this was coming, I suddenly experienced a sinking feeling. I found it hard to think of that kind, overweight boy as my husband-to-be. Though I was still a child, girls of my age were little by little becoming engaged, or were already married, and their lives were changing. But I felt I had much yet to learn about life.

'How could you sound so pleased? Didn't you tell me that living in palaces doesn't bring anything but misery and unhappiness? So how come when it comes to me, you change your mind? You keep mentioning the crown prince, the future Shah? I'm not going to part with you and Mother. But you need to get ready; Moshir's son's a politician and sounds very knowledgeable and widely travelled. I assume he'll take you along, as well, to wherever it is you want to go. What shall we do with Mother then? Have you thought about that?'

Nezhat laughed and said that my survival might well depend on the rotund, rather spoilt one. And then she paused, as though she was tasting the secret in her mouth before letting it be known.

'With the way everything is progressing, I wouldn't count on a monarchy that's going to be permanent; I don't think it's going to last much longer and then you can fly this cage. While they're having cakes celebrating, all will come to light. Your mother's pleased as well.'

Yet what Nezhat disclosed to me did not cure my anxiety: I knew Mother was pleased but she was thinking purely of me and not of herself.

'What would Mother do when we're not here?'

Mother and Nanny arrived at this moment, looking tired after a busy day. The air was alive with the sound of canaries and swallows, and the scent of blossoms on almond and black cherry trees.

CHAPTER 10

I t was Muharram. We were in the regent's mansion, dressed in black. In the mosque where the martyrdom of Imam Hussein was commemorated, a barrier made of cloth had been erected to separate the men from the women. The story of Imam Hussein was being retold and the usual mourning ritual for the martyrs of Islam was in progress. I felt everyone was watching me, particularly the members of the imperial family.

The crown prince's grandmother asked me to sit next to her and asked me a few questions that, luckily, I managed to answer. Then, with a voice loud enough so that everyone could hear, she complimented me on my education. I felt hugely embarrassed to receive the compliment with so many people present. I felt the blood rush to my cheeks and wanted to leave as soon as possible.

The massive pots were full to the brim, ready to feed thousands of people. Some food was brought to us. We were busy eating when the crown prince suddenly made an appearance; I could not swallow the food in my mouth. He was so overweight that he had difficulty sitting down. As usual, the women showered him with endearing remarks. He sat on a chair and started chatting to Nezhat in French. He said a few words in my direction, but I seemed to have suddenly forgotten everything I knew! Despite his youth he behaved with decorum. I had heard that he spent a good part of the day with his tutors. I was busy watching his every move from under my *chador* and imagined myself one day, like Malakeh Jahan, sitting at the very top end of the room and everyone curtseying and bowing, though I wondered whether this was really going to happen. Later that evening, Nezhat confirmed that it was, indeed, quite possible. She had also been able to have a quiet word with Ahmad about me.

We were to go to Sohanak Park after Muharram. I had already met my husband-to-be but this was going to be different. Mother was even more apprehensive than I was and she never let me out of her sight. The only downside, as far as the Shah was concerned, Nezhat remarked, was that I was living under the same roof as my rebellious aunt! He was concerned that I might become like her. I wished I could: I wished I had her wisdom and knowledge. One could not ignore the envious looks in the social gatherings. Nezhat never intended to make anyone jealous but some lady courtiers were so uneducated and ignorant that they just could not tolerate her presence.

The younger women, on the contrary, were mesmerised by her and wanted to be everything that she was. A number of girls and young women had begun to frequent our home but I was considered too young to be permitted in their gatherings.

'Nezhat's leading everyone astray!' Mother commented with light-hearted affection.

I knew she admired her youngest sister and thought of her in the same way as me. At times she said she had two daughters but, in reality, it was she who was led by Nezhat; Nezhat had helped her be herself. This became evident in the course of my father's visits before autumn. She no longer behaved as though completely submissive to Khan and she was never in tears.

The night before he was leaving on duty, I heard Mother's confident voice, 'The war will soon be over and you must then think of your future. As for me, I know what I'll be doing with mine.' As though Khan had noticed the change in Mother lately he simply said, 'God willing!' No more threats and no more embarrassment, as had been the case every time they had conversed since Shah Baba's demise.

CHAPTER 11

It was winter and snow was fast covering everything. The servants chopped the logs and piled them up at the back of the building. Soltan's courtyard was filled with charcoal drying in the sun for use in the *korsi*. Nezhat's women frequented our home, and now there was talk of what was going on in Toupkhaneh Square: under the Shah's command and with his regent's financial backing, a group of people had gathered to demonstrate against the parliamentarians and the constitutionalists. The populists were eventually caught and hanged. We once heard Nouri's followers chanting in the small *bazaar*:

> We don't want a constitution;
> We want Muhammad's institution.

Nezhat was muttering something in anger but didn't say anything until we were in the carriage on our way home. Nezhat advised Mother to start storing food for the dark days that were looming. When we arrived we noticed a couple of donkeys being unloaded in the coachhouse. The men were being paid while Soltan's son was busy with his scales. Bags of wheat and flour had piled up in a corner; our household of forty had to be fed.

A few days later, when we were sitting under the *korsi* reciting Sa'di's lyrics with our tutor, what Nezhat had predicted materialised. A terrible sound startled everyone. This was a time when the contents of the pamphlets had become truly offensive and we could not really read them out loud: criticism of the king and the courtiers was relentless.

63

Upon hearing the terrifying sound, the guests emerged from the sitting room looking concerned, until Heidar finally arrived. Breathless, and without the usual formalities, he asked for Mother. She quickly donned a *chador* and climbed down the steps.

While trying to catch his breath, Heidar managed to say, 'They threw a bomb at the Shah.'

The news took Mother by surprise and she had to sit down on the steps. The maids burst into tears but everyone was in reality frightened for their own future rather than for the Shah. Having put her *chador* on, Nezhat rushed towards Heidar and questioned him in an attempt to establish the source of the news.

The guests rushed to their homes and, shortly afterwards, the three of us sat in the carriage with Heidar, with two gunmen up top, and headed towards the palace where the Shah was.

The place where we had spent our childhood playing happily with Shah Baba was now filled with hundreds of women and men. The soldiers had blocked the roads to prevent people coming in. The water in the pool had frozen and the snow had piled up. Many people were wandering around and they looked anxious. From beneath our veils we saw the Cossacks and rushed in to reach the inner rooms. A tall eunuch was standing at the threshold asking everyone's names. A great number of people were left outside the door and the eunuch was firmly asking them to leave.

'His Imperial Highness is in good health.'

Inside the palace, the female courtiers had surrounded Malakeh Jahan, who did her best to compose herself and, maintaining her smile, tried to answer everyone's questions. As soon as she saw us she hugged Mother and kissed Nezhat and me. She then whispered in Mother's ear to go to the salon, as she did not want to be overheard. Once there, we saw the Shah, the crown prince and Muhammad Hassan. They were standing while *espand* was being burned around them to ward off the evil eye.

Two clergymen were reading prayers, but the Shah, sporting his fur overcoat, looked apprehensive.

He kept saying, 'Bastards! I'll show them!'

Malakeh Jahan raised her voice and asked everyone to sit down. The terrifying sound that everyone had heard was the explosion of a bomb thrown at the car in which the Shah usually travelled, but he hadn't been in it that day. One woman then remembered the day when the martyred Shah, her husband and the current Shah's grandfather, had been shot at, and I looked at the large painting hanging in that room. He looked magnificent. Neither Shah Baba nor this Shah looked anything like him.

We were sitting in our carriage heading home when Nezhat told Mother that she did not think her brother was going to be able to save the monarchy.

'Unfortunately, there doesn't seem to be a courtier around who can "think" properly. As you saw, your brother was merely waiting for the Russian ambassador to turn up as if, heaven forbid, he was praying towards St Petersburg!'

'Nezhat, you may not get on with our brother, but however he may behave, he's the Shah and our lives depend on him.'

Mother sounded anxious and impatient. I knew that when the time was right Nezhat would ask Mother not to pin her hopes on the Shah.

'What would've happened if the Sha had been in the vehicle?' was my thoughtless question.

Nezhat's response was void of any emotion.

'Absolutely nothing; the situation couldn't get any worse.'

And once again Mother bit her lip.

CHAPTER 12

It was summer and we were getting ready to go to the country. Nezhat found it difficult to part with her piano. The night before, she had played till dawn while I was sitting on the sofa reading the biography of Mirabeau, the French statesman whose debates had helped to advance the course of events leading to the French Revolution. I had ended up falling asleep there. It was a balmy night. Nezhat woke me up and we went towards the gardens without our *chadors*. A mosquito net had been erected on a frame and, as soon as I reached it, I threw myself in the cool of the bedding. I didn't realise that Mother was still awake.

We had a tough day ahead of us. We left a large chest filled with books for Heidar to bring over, as well as an easel and paint brushes, together with a case of clothes. There were disturbances in town and a couple of gunmen escorted our carriage. Listening to Nezhat and Mother's conversation, I understood the situation had worsened. Armed national committees were forming while the grandees were trying to mediate. The courtiers encouraged the Shah to make promises only to break them later on. They were also spreading rumours against the constitution. Mother was hoping that there was not going to be a civil war. We never concerned ourselves with Father, who was at the time in Khorasan and whose telegrams we received every week.

Mother always said, 'He prefers to leave the fighting to others and use whatever funds are available to pay for his pleasures.'

It took us a couple of days to settle in the country, in Qolhak, north-east of Tehran. There was a medium-sized house with a crimson mansard roof and a stream passing through its gardens. Several cottages had been constructed at the end of the park where the servants and watchmen could sleep. We settled in and began to receive visitors practically every day, but life was generally quieter here. There was a large tub full of water on the veranda with fresh walnuts floating on its surface. Nanny occasionally peeled the walnuts and then placed them on a plate adorned with jasmine; there would also be a platter of berries covered with muslin. Our hands were forever red and black because of all the berry picking.

Even in the country Nezhat and I had to do homework. A rug lay by the stream of clear water coming from the local *qanaat*, the subterranean canal which, after feeding the pond, became a stream again and flowed out of the park. The gardener always carried a spade and regularly opened up the route of the stream. Soltan was busy as usual: peeling apples, removing the pits of the cherries and black cherries, and then throwing the fruit in large pans to prepare jams and syrups.

One day, an area was curtained off where Mother could sit on a wooden frame in the arbour. She puffed away at the hookah, making the jasmines in its glass container dart around. Nezhat and I were bathing in the cool water coming from the mountains. Nanny and Morvarid were sitting by the stream on the other side of the barrier so that they could keep an eye on things. When Nezhat dipped in the water and then emerged, it was as though she had a straw hat on, which covered her head and face. We seemed momentarily to forget all the troubles and worries hovering over us. An hour earlier, a servant had brought the pamphlets over from town and they now lay under a stone near the easel.

Nanny was waiting with our clothes and some towels.

'You need to hurry!' she said.

Nezhat winked, 'His Imperial Highness the crown prince is about to arrive!'

A few minutes later Nezhat was quickly plaiting my hair and tidying my eyebrows. I was anxious; in the past two months no one had talked about the crown prince and me. He had just written me a few lines in French, which had been delivered to Nezhat by a member of the regent's household. It was written on paper bearing the gold imprint of the lion and the sun, the imperial coat of arms, with 'Golestan Palace' beneath it in blue. It was a pleasant note signed 'Affectionately', the only amorous part of a letter that would have passed secretly through many watchful eyes before it reached me.

Now he had arrived in the park, in a white carriage drawn by three brown horses. The servants and coachmen remained at the entrance to the park, while he sat on the wooden frame next to Mother, who wore a white *chador* sprigged with flowers. Just as I was ready, Nanny took out a pair of turquoise earrings, which I recognised, from the box Mother always kept by her side. I was wearing white stockings and pointed shoes with open toes, the straps of which were hurting me. When we greeted him he stopped talking with Mother and, looking at the plate piled with sliced watermelon, asked Nezhat: 'How is Her Ladyship, Nezhat-ol-Saltaneh? I hope I'm not intruding.'

Mother responded in endearing terms, and asked his permission for lunch to be served.

But he apologised and said, 'Mother's instructions were that I should only come to pay my respects.'

He seemed tense and even more embarrassed than I was. A few minutes later Mother asked him on our behalf if we might be excused. But it wasn't long before Mother called for Nezhat. I couldn't understand why she insisted on discussing important issues with her alone. I realised that my high hopes were unfounded; the crown prince had come to discuss a far more important matter: Malakeh Jahan had explained in a letter to my mother that the Shah had become aware of the gatherings in our home and he was wondering why Nezhat was not settling down.

I sensed that these were really the empress's words expressing concern about my future. However, more important than that were the Shah's words to my mother about Khan's imminent return, at which point he was to take charge of managing Nezhat's estate.

'Why on earth is the Shah meddling in people's affairs? I am merely another one of his subjects but worse off than the servants since they seem to marry whenever and whomever they fancy!'

Mother reasoned that the Shah had the last word.

This merely made Nezhat blush in fury, and the only thing she said was, 'I wish I were a man so that I could do whatever Malek Motekalemin did!'

We had read in one of the pamphlets that Motekalemin had given a speech right outside the mansion of the head of the Qajars in which he had revealed that Ala, a ruthless and dictatorial man, had hit his head against a column in frustration.

'I don't wish to ruin your future but someone's clearly reported the gatherings and I assume they've now summoned Khan to distance me from you.'

I had been expecting this for some time and now I was in tears. For the past two years Nezhat had brought me excitement and I had put childhood behind me. I did not know how to cope without her. Soon afterwards, she splashed some water on her face and turned to me.

'We shall manage somehow. But the problem is that fighting is brewing,' she said, adding that Malakeh Jahan had disclosed to my mother in her letter that the Shah was determined to quash the parliamentarians with the Russians' help and have the constitutionalists hanged.

It did not, therefore, come as any surprise when, that Thursday, we received news of a group of soldiers emerging from Arg Square carrying rifles and demolishing whatever got in their way. It was almost lunchtime when we heard the shooting. We were not surprised, either, to hear that the king had, meanwhile, decided to leave Golestan Palace for the Imperial Gardens in his carriage.

Even in Qolhak the weather was getting warmer. We spent the balmy nights sleeping inside the mosquito net outdoors, and in the daytime kept ourselves busy in the basement. Nanny turned up every now and then, bringing sherbet or other cool refreshments made of grated cucumbers mixed into a sweet drink.

Amid all the uncertainty in the city we decided to spend a day at Zahir's park. It was hardly the first time yet it felt different this time round. A number of tents had been erected for the Sufis[4] by the large pool in the middle of the park. Ice and a few glasses were floating in a small marble tank for those who needed to help themselves to cold water. Through the stained glass in the salon, I saw a gathering of women under a large portrait of Safi Ali Shah, a Sufi Master, and they were about to begin *Sama*, the Sufi dance. We had previously been invited to the park and I knew that Malakeh Iran, an aunt for whom my mother felt profound respect, and her daughter Foruq, who was the same age as Nezhat, were hosting the event.

Zahir was governor of Guilan, a province in the north, and rumour had it that he supported the constitutionalists, an offence against the king. Since the king and Malakeh Jahan were respected figures, no one in the gathering mentioned them; Malakeh Iran forbade mention of politics. In the days following the king's departure for the Imperial Gardens, along with the Cossacks and the army, fear and anxiety were palpable throughout the city. Given the circumstance, it was impossible to tame people's tongues.

'*Ya Ali*, help your followers!' Malakeh Iran began.

Everyone else murmured, '*Ali madad!*' which reverberated through the park when the Sufis also joined in.

Nezhat and I were sitting by the window looking round the room, which boasted superb plasterwork. A giant chandelier bearing numerous lights was hanging in the middle of the room.

One occasionally heard the sound of the drum, and at other times, away from the men, the Zahir diehards were engaged in the whirl saying, '*Ya Ho Madad*'.

This continued well into the night and when they lit up the candelabra the room adopted a different aura.

Foruq then came forward and ushered us into a smaller room where some other women were waiting. I knew them all: they attended Nezhat's gatherings and I knew they had contacts with the populists but I was never allowed in their gatherings since I was too young. This time however, to my delight, Nezhat let me join them. A lot was discussed that evening. For instance, I heard that the Shah and the Cossacks were planning to besiege the parliament and the populists. The latter intended to bring the situation to a head and put an end to the monarchists' subterfuge.

'It's about time we put our lives on the line to save the country. We've had enough of misery and backwardness.'

Pamphlets and notes were being handed around the room.

A woman in a white gown and with her hair loose came and sat next to Nezhat, saying, 'One of these days the Mojaheddin are going to sort it all out, which means that Om Khaqan will have to mourn her son and Ahmad will take his kingship to an early grave.'

I was well acquainted with this woman: she was a member of Zell's family, the king's oldest uncle, and some said even older than Shah Baba. Zell had claimed the throne once but because his mother was not a Qajar his hopes had been dashed. When they spoke of Ahmad my heart sank; the thought of a revolution taking place with the Shah and his family being beheaded like Louis XVI and Marie Antoinette, and Ahmad being harmed as a result, made me tremble, but I never dared express my fears. I knew full well that everyone was resentful of the Shah, but Ahmad had nothing to do with all this.

Before everyone went home, they took their bangles and earrings and threw them in the drum the woman in the white gown was taking around. Nezhat looked at me and I took off one of my bangles and threw it in as well. So the whole thing had been a pretense, and the fact that we were involved with the populists and the parliament made me feel good. I trusted Nezhat's wisdom. On the other hand, I was mindful of my mother's relationship with Malakeh Jahan and Ahmad.

When, later that evening under the mosquito net, I revealed my fears to Nezhat, she stroked my hair and, as usual, as though she had a great deal of experience, said, 'Time will untie all the knots. It's not too late to resolve everything, but the careless Shah has become the Russians' puppet, effectively selling himself. The populists have paid the price of their freedom with their blood and now they're ready to fight the despots for stopping progress in the country.'

The pamphlets had said the same thing.

'Muhammad Ali Shah, in his foolishness, wants to keep the clock moving backwards, and nobody can do anything about it.'

I knew when they talked about foolish courtiers they were also referring to my father, who never lost an opportunity to revile the parliament and the people. He also condemned Shah Baba for having signed the decree in the first place.

Every day the servants delivered news in the shape of parcels, which were passed on to Mother or Nezhat. Once in her room, Nezhat would open up the bundle and would occasionally share the contents with me. Sometimes she wrote a note and then took it to the end of the park. I was aware that Ebrahim acted as an intermediary between Nezhat and the others. When we were in town I hid the papers under my *chador* just to be on the safe side, and as soon as we arrived we would retire to Soltan's room. Everyone knew that I had loved this room ever since I was a child so my frequenting it raised no suspicions and no one took any notice.

At the end of a day when all hell broke loose, with the Shah parting for the Imperial Gardens, Nezhat took me along to Soltan's. She had made *halva* and the air was filled with the aroma of saffron, butter and roasted flour. Mother had gone to see one of her acquaintances and we were left in charge of the household, but we were mindful of the servants, my father's in particular. In the evening, Ebrahim arrived and, moments later, Nezhat went to the corner of the gardens and I saw Zahir, a prince dressed like no other prince. He always wore a turban and had a good voice; he was renowned for his eloquent speeches. He was one of the followers of Malek and was a very able speaker. He spent about an hour chatting to Nezhat. Meanwhile, Ebrahim kept an eye out in case someone turned up. Soltan, her *chador* round her waist, looked around and then came back to her son to let him know that all was well, but as soon as we heard the sound of horses' hooves in the coachhouse everyone stopped talking. Zahir left by the back door and we took a plate of *halva* and went home. Mother had already arrived and was by the pool, splashing water onto her face while Morvarid held a pitcher. At night, not only did we have to put up with the heat, we also had to suffer the sound of sporadic shooting.

We were back in town earlier than usual. That year no one seemed to want to stay in the country but no one complained either. I watched Nezhat reading the notes Zahir had brought over and began to fall asleep. She had also kept a paper hidden in an envelope for me to read as well. The excitement of reading made the heat of summer more bearable, but when I remembered Ahmad I became distracted; I was anxious to know whether he was going to be harmed if, in the course of the revolution, the king was dethroned. I never dared put the question to anyone, not even Nezhat, just in case my secret was revealed, nor did I wish to come across as thoughtless at a time we were experiencing a national crisis.

Later on we received news of the supporters of the parliamentarians holding the fort around Baharestan, the district where the parliament was situated, and the Sepahsalar Mosque. We also heard that an army of gunmen was in position guarding the parliament. The Shah, on the other hand, was busy holding talks with his supporters in the Imperial Gardens. He subsequently asked the parliament to dismiss Malek and his leading supporters, and asked them to leave the city. We had already become familiar with their names by reading the papers and pamphlets that Ebrahim delivered. Malek was such an accomplished speaker that had the king ever listened to one of his speeches he would doubtless have become a constitutionalist himself, despite his obdurate despotism.

Nassir watered the flowerbed frequently, but despite the stream of underground water running through the park the heat had become unbearable. About twice a day large blocks of ice were collected from the cool house and left in the pantry in large pans covered with muslin, but they did not take long to thaw. Nezhat and I spent the entire day in the basement since it was the coolest place to be, and so we were completely unaware of the events that were fast brewing. I felt anxious, but when I saw Nezhat's excitement reading the pamphlets, I began to feel calmer again, a calm that was short lived!

At night, when the social business died down, she read Victor Hugo's *Les Misérables*. In those days we didn't call it '*misérables*'; Nezhat referred to it as 'the paupers', but Madame Hakim, who sometimes helped Nezhat out in translation, called it 'the helpless'. From time to time we imagined ourselves in the same situation, and immersed ourselves in Jean Valjean's worries.

That night we were busy doing the same thing when we heard a noise. It was alarming to begin with but later we understood that my father had returned from his posting. The sound of hooves, wheels and men helping with Khan's luggage continued well into the night. My father's valet rushed in to put all the trunks and boxes in place. The sacks and boxes of food were left with Soltan, who had been woken up despite the hour and was busy putting them away in her pantry. Then we heard the horses whinny from the other side of the park, but it turned out that my father wasn't with them. Just before reaching Tehran he had received orders that he, together with some other governors, should report to Imperial

Gardens immediately. When he eventually returned it was past midnight. Although Mother tried her best to keep her anxiety at bay, it was clear that she was unsettled. She called the servants and gave instructions, but her tone was abrupt and impatient.

The soldiers finally left and the tumult that the arrival of Khan's carriage had caused outside gradually died down. Nezhat and I were resting in our beds under the mosquito net when we heard him arrive. We were about to fall asleep when we heard the sound of something heavy fall in the water. A little later we discovered that Khan had thrown himself in the pool after a long and dusty journey and, as was his style, completely oblivious to the fact that a number of people were fast asleep, was dishing out orders at the top of his voice. We pictured him lying on the bamboo chair by the pool, wrapped in his robe, drinking. We could hear him talk to Mother through the sycamores and spruces and I was filled with fear; something was not right. Despite his cruelty towards my mother, he always tried to put a good face on things and started every sentence with Princess, though after Shah Baba's death and having taken a second wife, he was not as courteous; at times we even heard him raise his voice when they disagreed. That night, however, was different. Something had changed in him, and I could sense this even at such a late hour. I knew Nezhat was awake listening and thinking the same. I wished she'd get up and talk to me. Among the words that penetrated the mosquito net I heard him twice refer to Muhammad Ali Shah as 'His Highness' or 'The Centre of the Universe', the manner in which the king was referred to in those days. He had never paid so much respect to Shah Baba, whom he had habitually cursed. I couldn't work out why he was so different now. I had heard him refer to my mother using the familiar '*taw*' rather than '*shawma*' for 'you.'

'I hear it's you who's the source of all evil', he said.

My mother tried to hush him as usual and she murmured a response I did not hear. We decided that all would become clear by the morning.

Chapter 13

M orvarid woke us up just before dawn as usual so that we could say our prayers. In the course of our prayers we heard the sound of conversation from afar. We didn't take much notice and after the morning prayer we went back to sleep in the basement, as we always did. There was complete silence; everyone was asleep. Although we were in the privacy of the inner sanctum of the house, traditionally women would retire to the basement when the sun was up.

The sound of an explosion woke us up, but this was now routine, given the state of the country. We asked for breakfast to be brought to us earlier than usual. Meanwhile Nanny and Morvarid arrived looking as though they had overheard the conversation by the pool the night before. The atmosphere became even heavier when Mother arrived. On Mondays we usually went to the *hammam*, but before she sat down we realised that plans had changed: she mentioned to Morvarid that we were not going to the *hammam*!

When everyone finally left the basement, we understood that what Mother had feared most had finally materialised: the Shah had commissioned my father to become Nezhat's official guardian and take charge of her estate. Nezhat was to marry a person of my father's choice and leave our home. In the meantime, she was not permitted to leave the estate or hold meetings with anyone.

'Why doesn't he order lock and chain to be brought over as well! It would've been better to send me away altogether,' Nezhat said casually.

Mother didn't say anything; it seemed she, too, was convinced Nezhat had become an issue for the family. She looked down so that she was not influenced by her sister's expression.

'You can't fight with them ...'

'Please don't bother yourself, sister, you've done your best for me, far more than necessary and I thank you for it. So if you'll allow me ...'

I don't know what she was about to say because my father's *'Ya Allah'* meant that he had arrived. He climbed down the stairs dressed in a strange outfit which made him look as though he was going hunting. Nezhat donned her *chador* and I rose. As usual, a chair, which Nanny had carried down the stairs, was brought to him. He didn't bother greeting me and sat down with a frown. He seemed to have slimmed down in the past month, which made him appear taller. I was desperate to know what Nezhat wanted to say but I was not supposed to be present during adult conversation.

While holding his cup of tea, my father issued his orders as though he was a military commander.

'I've asked Baba Hassan to close the doors and no one has permission to come in or to go out.'

We were looking down when Nezhat complained: 'I see; we've become prisoners ...'

He looked tired and began to shout. 'That's right, you don't deserve respect. I hardly needed a Russian colonel, who barely knows how to wash himself, to look me in the face and report to me that a bunch of unsuitable individuals frequent my home!'

He then referred to my mother with sarcasm. 'I trusted everything to her and went to fight for my country, but little did I know that I was rearing vipers in my bosom. I really feel like kicking ...'

Nezhat got up, wrapped her *chador* around her and interrupted. 'Forgive me, Khan, it seems to me you're going too far; you are, of course, in charge of your household, but I ...'

'You, too, I'm now in charge of you, and I shan't allow you to leave this basement and ...'

Nezhat by now had lost her calm; her *chador* had slipped to her shoulders and part of her golden locks could be seen projecting from her scarf. She made a move, even before she had placed her fine feet in her slippers protesting, 'I shan't have anyone speak to me in this manner. We're not butchers or greengrocers!'

I was agog when I saw my father take a leap towards Nezhat. I had seen his aggression so I leapt to stand between them. Then I suddenly felt my head spin; my father had slapped me so hard that I was thrown onto the rug in the middle of the floor.

'You shameless man! Why on earth are you harming the child?'

My mother jumped up like a wounded leopard and held me close to her chest. Though I felt I had been deafened by the impact of his hand on my ear, I knew the entire household was listening. Mother and I were in tears. We couldn't tell how Nezhat felt, since she was facing the wall with her back to us. Father had opened his leather belt and rested his hand on his pistol. I so hoped he would shoot and relieve us. We could hear the sound of shooting and shouting from outside, which only began to reach us once momentary silence had been established in the basement. Nezhat then broke the silence, removed her slippers and came to join us on the rug. She wiped her tears so that no one could see her distress.

'This isn't the way! Forgive me if I've been impudent. Please allow Khanoum to leave ...'

But I had found some courage and, while swallowing my tears, I screamed, 'I'm not going anywhere; I'm staying here.'

Father didn't utter a word, since he believed he had won the war.

Nezhat continued, 'Please give me your orders calmly. I *am* a guest in your house and shall obey what you say. You're older ...'

'His Majesty has commissioned me to express his utmost dissatisfaction with this household and particularly with Nezhat-ol-Saltaneh. He's asked me to see to it that your life is set in order in the next two days. Therefore, you're not permitted to step out of the basement and, to make certain of that, I've positioned someone right outside to guard this place.'

'But I must say that, as of today, I am by law under the guardianship of someone else!'

We all looked at her incredulously as we heard this. I can't remember which one of us asked her, 'Someone else?'

'That's right; today I've become betrothed to someone who asked for my hand in marriage. Perhaps you'd like to know who he is. I don't feel it's necessary to disclose it but it doesn't matter: I am talking about Ebrahim.'

My father looked as though lightning had struck him and he sprang out of his seat. While holding my head, Mother kept slapping her own chin with her fingers. The silence in the room did not last long because Morvarid screamed and suddenly appeared in the basement.

'Sir, they're throwing bombs!'

Indeed, we could hear the explosions and the shouting of men in the park. Someone was calling for Father. I knew it was the gatekeeper. My father was hesitant; he went towards the stairs and took out his pistol. He paused near the stairs.

'Stay here,' he said; 'no one's to leave until my return,' and then he disappeared.

Despite Morvarid's presence, the three of us were in tears. Nezhat sat down and embraced Mother and me; she could no longer hold back her tears. She gave me a peck on the cheek and my mother one on the forehead. Mother then placed our hands on her chest, where we could feel her heart pounding.

According to Morvarid, the Cossacks had intervened and thousands of people were being shot at. They had demolished the parliament building and Sepahsalar Mosque, and had either killed or chained up the populists. Down in the basement we kept receiving up-to-date news of the state of the city thanks to the servants. Father had been summoned and, before his departure, had stationed soldiers to guard our home; no one had permission to pass through the gates.

I had by now forgotten the burning pain on my face and was lying in the dishevelled bedding still on the floor from earlier that morning. Every now and then my thoughts took me to the Imperial Gardens, but the sound of explosions diverted my attention in the direction of the parliament and I could not stop picturing the injured bodies of the populists. In between, the image of Ebrahim seeped through my thoughts. Was it true? I had known Soltan's son since I was very young; he was always reading. Lately, though, he tended to go to the Sepahsalar Mosque together with Zahir to study. I knew they were both staunch and enthusiastic followers of Motekalemin.

The king had clearly received reports of secret meetings between Nezhat and Zahir, but what about the shocking news: did Nezhat really wish to marry Ebrahim, Soltan's son? She had rejected a number of eligible suitors, and had more recently also turned down the son of Moshir, the premier, who, despite his youth, was quite educated and had travelled widely. He was also the ambassador to the court of St Petersburg.

I knew Mother was equally desperate to know the answer to these questions. She was somehow hoping that Nezhat would turn round and tell her that it wasn't true and that it was a strategy aimed at surviving the orders of the king and now my father as well.

'I beg of you, Nezhat, tell us it isn't true and you're not going to leave us. Did you not tell me that it was becoming to accept Ahmad's proposal? Didn't you say I'd then be free to go abroad? It's because of you that I've begun to contemplate the thought of becoming the future Shah's wife and empress; how could it then make sense that you should marry Ebrahim? How?'

The questions were racing through my mind, though I did not speak them out loud, and I felt my eyelids getting heavy. A bowl and pitcher were brought to Mother to refresh her face and hands. I had closed my eyes and was still going over the sudden storm in the basement earlier; the thought of my father unfastening his belt made me tremble. I knew Father had gone to the Imperial Gardens. What if the place was under siege? Just like the tale of the Bastille, which Nezhat had read to us over and over again. If the Shah and the empress were beheaded then what would become of Ahmad? Would they murder my father as well? He had only recently joined the courtiers in the conflict against the populists. I wasn't actually concerned about my father, nor was I bothered about the brutal slap which had left a mark on my face. The only thing that remains engraved in my memory today is the way he spoke to Nezhat that day, and his discussions with Mother the previous night. He had no place in my heart, but what about my poor mother ...

Just before noon, Khaleh arrived with fresh news: the Cossacks had been bombing various sites since that morning and there was nothing left of Baharestan or the minarets of the Sepahsalar Mosque. The parliamentarians were still shooting, but every time the Cossacks shot hundreds were knocked down. Nanny was saying that she had witnessed Malek and others being shot, and then, with their hands tied and their faces and hands covered in blood, their bodies being dragged on the streets towards the Imperial Gardens.

At this point, Nanny suddenly arrived looking distressed, pulling her hair out and cursing the villains, Yazid and Shemr, the murderers of Hassan and Hussein. She said that the servants had seen the clergy, having lost their turbans and robes, being taken away by the godless Russians. They had been beaten on the head and their beards been pulled. No one seemed to have any fear of cursing my mother's brother in her presence and everyone prayed that the Shah's house of oppression might fall on him and his family. As though my mother and Nezhat had forgotten that their brother was at the root of it all, they prayed for the victory of the populists and the ruin of the Shah!

The corpses of the constitutionalists were now covered in shrouds, lying in Baharestan Square; the surrounding houses, such as those of Zell, Mother's aunt and uncle, were all under siege or ruined. In the city and the area surrounding the parliament, the angry cries of the gunmen were mixed with the groans of the people who had been shot and the whinnies of frightened horses.

When lunch trays were brought in, no one felt like eating. The unbearable heat, coupled with the horrific news coming from town, was stifling. Mother had undone the top buttons of her dress and every now and then moistened her fair skin with a wet cloth. She was breathing heavily. Nezhat had put her *chador* aside and was silently pacing the basement. She looked like an injured leopard. The servant who had gone to the Imperial Gardens to bring news turned up. He had clearly been beaten up and reported that the Cossacks were beating and shooting everyone. He had been lucky that one of my father's old servants had recognised him and managed to rescue him.

It was an hour past lunchtime and we could still hear the sound of the bullets and cannons on the rooftops. We were informed that Soltan had suddenly disappeared. Mother sent for her but she didn't show up. When she finally appeared the maids had to help her as she had difficulty climbing down the steps to the basement. Nezhat jumped towards her to help her sit on the carpet before she passed out. A mixture of clay and thatch was held under her nose so that the pungent smell could revive her. Nanny also offered her and everyone else cups of herbal tea. This consisted of bugloss and other herbs, which were known to alleviate anxiety.

The old woman finally began to talk. Everyone knew that she had gone to search for Ebrahim, her only son. His name, of course, had recently come to have a certain connotation for us, a matter we were still trying to comprehend. She was pulling at her grey hair and saying that she had been looking for Ebrahim amidst all the bloody corpses of so many young men. She had been able to reach Baharestan, which was in ruins, the mob busy looting its fine rugs and pictures. The furnishings, which had once been carried on hundreds of large trays, were part of Taj, Nasser al-Din Shah's daughter's, dowry; she had recently been married to Aziz Soltan.[5] The festivities, to which the residents of Tehran had all been invited, had lasted seven days and nights. After the Shah's death, Taj divorced Malijak, and Baharestan Park, which had earlier hosted foreign monarchs and guests, became Crown Court. Muhammad Ali Shah, however, was now demanding that it should be brought down over the heads of the populists and the constitutionalists.

Soltan talked and wept, reducing her audience to tears as well. When she said that she had seen Zahir, who had been tied and dragged behind a horse on the streets to the Imperial Gardens, I shook with fear. Motekalemin had confronted the Cossacks with his bare chest but a soldier had thrust himself between Motekalemin and a Russian officer's pistol. A group of people were standing behind him when he had raised his face to the sky and said: 'O Lord, you have been witness to our sacrifice for the liberation of the people from despotism, yet our reward now is the cannon and the bullet. But we shall fight for the people of Muhammad, the Prophet, as long as we live.'

Nezhat seemed beside herself, as though there was a volcano inside her, and was pacing the basement. For a moment she lost control and shouted at Soltan.

'Where are Zahir and Ebrahim now?'

'If they are still alive, they'll be in the Imperial Gardens waiting to be hanged. O Lord ...' and she fainted.

Nezhat then yelled at Nanny to bring her *chaqchour*.

Mother panicked and asked, 'Where?'

'The Imperial Gardens.'

My mother started to sob.

'Dear God, why don't you take my life so that I might not suffer any longer?'

By then everyone in the room was wailing. Nanny and Morvarid were holding Mother's hands and when she tried to release herself her movements shook like those of an epileptic.

Nothing could calm the gathering of these terrified women until they heard the noises from the estate: Malakeh Iran, Zahir's wife and some other people had stormed the coachhouse. The gatekeeper, despite Father's orders, opened the gates upon seeing the princess and allowed the women inside. This powerful woman was the oldest of the Qajar women and she was now seeking refuge wearing her worn-out *chador*. Her daughter, Forough, was even worse off: she had been in the *hammam* when the Cossacks started to shoot. The walls of the *hammam* had collapsed and she had been forced to extricate herself from the wreckage naked. The maids had covered her in a *chador* and climbed the ladder to get out; with great difficulty they had managed to reach our home. The thought of Zahir's park and the Sufis' gathering place in ruins, and the looting of a place a hundred times grander than the imperial palace, made everyone forget their pain. Mother stood up and held Malakeh Iran in her arms; she then helped Forough, who was still shaking, lie down on the bed. When Nezhat went forward to kiss Malakeh Iran's hands, she burst out with anger. 'They are destroying the home of Molana's servants. This is merely a worldly home and a mortal one; I hope God may destroy their home in the after-life!'

The maids followed with 'Amen!'

Mother ordered some lunch to be prepared for Malakeh and then she wrote a note I knew was addressed to Father, asking him to take the soldiers to the Imperial Gardens.

There seemed to be no end to a day that had started with such disturbing events. However, when a response to Mother's letter was received the mood changed a little, and we were finally able to leave the basement. The guests were accommodated in different corners of the estate: Malakeh Iran and Forough were placed in the reception room and so we were free to go back to our quarters. Nezhat went straight to her notes and books; she had prepared a bundle ready for Nanny to take and I didn't enquire where.

The household had gathered around Malakeh Iran, who was describing the events of the morning in some detail.

'A week ago I received a letter from Rasht in the north, which contained a premonition that before long the agony would be over. I am not sure if His Holiness would be happy for me to quote him. I can't reveal all as some affairs are secret; otherwise I'd tell you tales to raise your estimation of Mr Zahir's position.'

The excitement and curiosity of the gathering, which by this time had forgotten the tumult of the day, was such that Malakeh Iran finally relented.

'About a month ago, His Holiness wrote to me that the chandeliers would fall one by one, shattering into pieces. If, in the course of this, we were to be injured and start to bleed, we would not be innocent. If, however, no harm was done and we were not to be injured, then, beyond doubt, we would clearly be the disciples of righteousness and would have another chandelier light up above our heads in this world. When the cannons fired this morning, the chandelier in the large room exploded with the most fearsome sound and shattered into tiny pieces. Extraordinarily, although I was at the time sitting underneath it, I wasn't affected at all. I prayed deep down and thought, bravo, Mr Zahir, Sir, how fortunate you are to be held in such esteem, and to reach such a high rank despite poverty. The next shot brought the two other chandeliers down as well.'

Malakeh Iran gave an overblown account of the events with unbelievable fervour and pride, which continued well into the night. She didn't seem to have any intention of retiring and so the household was fully entertained. Zahir's years as the court's Master of Ceremonies had increased the size and splendour of the park. The fact that the whole place had been plundered and now resembled a heap of rubble was not as shocking as Malakeh's calm, which stemmed from her belief that 'Worldly possessions are like dirt that can be washed off one's hands.'

Midnight was approaching and everyone was still listening to Malakeh when letters arrived for Mother and Malakeh. A lantern was brought in and we realised that one was from the Shah, written on his crested paper. He had apologised to his beloved aunt for the events which, he said, were due to an unfortunate error; he thought the soldiers had gone mad. Not only had the king extended an invitation to Malakeh Iran to go to the Imperial Gardens, he had also confirmed that she and her husband would receive compensation for the extensive damage to their estate. When Malakeh read the letter out loud, she grinned, 'We have the Lord. *Ya Ali!*' and everyone else followed suit. The other letter was from Father asking us to prepare ourselves to pay a visit to His Majesty the next day. At the same time, he'd made it clear that no one could leave the house. We worked out that he would be on guard in the Imperial Gardens for a while to come. Amidst all this, Nezhat came in from time to time, sat and listened to Malakeh and then disappeared through the door again. She seemed restless. I wasn't aware at the time that something had perturbed her and that she was busy planning.

We were getting ready to go to bed. It was a balmy night and the bedding and mosquito nets lay on the veranda. Soltan arrived. She had wept and beaten herself so much in the course of the day that now she seemed quite worn and dishevelled, hardly resembling the woman she'd been earlier that day. Malakeh Iran tried to console her; when Soltan was desperately seeking her son, Malakeh had recited Saadi's poetry:

If Sa'di's to lose it all
What better cause than for thou.

She then reassured her that she was going to mention Ebrahim when she sought Zahir's release during her meeting with the king. She spoke with confidence but Soltan wouldn't calm down.

'What am I to do if they execute him tonight?' she said, at which a shock ran through Nezhat's body.

I suddenly wanted us both to go to the mosquito net so that I could find out the truth. Nezhat didn't sleep a wink all night and it wasn't long before we discovered that what Nezhat had so casually announced that morning would result in someone losing their life, and that at that very moment, among all the prisoners in the Imperial Gardens, a colonel would single Ebrahim out, only to throw his corpse next to Motekalemin's and the rest of them.

The next day, in order not to wake our special guests after their morning prayer, my mother asked everyone to be very quiet. When I was getting up, I reminded myself that had it not been for Malakeh Iran and Zahir's family taking refuge in our home, we would still have been imprisoned in the basement; their presence had altered Khan's terms. Everyone was awaiting the return of Malakeh and my mother with up-to-date news. Before leaving for the Imperial Gardens, however, Mother went to Nezhat's room and talked to her for about an hour behind closed doors. It transpired that Zahir had, a couple of days earlier, recited verses of the Quran, making it possible for Nezhat and Ebrahim to become intimate enough to discuss political issues. Nezhat then mentioned to Mother that she had planned to go somewhere else and set up life with Ebrahim, the location of which she had yet to decide on. It hardly mattered to her that he was Soltan's son. And when Mother had asked her if she should break the news to the Shah, Nezhat had responded, 'If this could buy Ebrahim's freedom, by all means!' But she had also warned that if she felt this could further endanger his life then perhaps the matter should be discussed at a later date.

The news of Ebrahim's execution was kept quiet from everyone and all we learned upon Mother's return from the

Imperial Gardens was that Malakeh felt much better and was evermore confident in the Lord's mercy and Zahir's righteousness. But Mother seemed dazed. In order to reach the inner sanctum in the Shah's residence, they had had to pass through crowds and chaos. Malakeh Iran had finally managed to have a word with the Shah while Mother exchanged a few words with Father. Khan was apparently in charge of everything in the Imperial Gardens and the Shah would do nothing without consulting him. No one was immune from disrespect, even the head of the Qajar clan, who was older than everyone else and had shut himself in his home; others had sought refuge at the embassies. If anyone wanted to survive execution they would have to go through the Regent and my father. Rumour had it that Zahir was to be released but there was no mention of Ebrahim since he was hardly worthy of mention; after all, he was one of the many hundreds of people who had been shot that day, either on the streets or in the Imperial Gardens.

It was almost lunchtime when Mother and Malakeh Iran returned. In the next hour a few carriages arrived to take our guests to Azod's country seat in Shemiran, to the north of Tehran, and so we were left to deal with our chaotic situation. The liveliness of the past two years in our home had given way to morbid silence. Nezhat was quiet, and as soon as Mother had seen Malakeh Iran off, she disappeared into Nezhat's room and later kept to herself. I desperately wanted to know what was happening. I felt we were going through a metamorphosis: it felt as though we had jumped off the roof of the Shams-ol-Emareh palace and our bones were about to shatter on impact with the cobbled street below.

When Soltan left our house the silence was finally broken. The heartbroken woman had not even been able to establish where her son had been buried so she was suffering in silence, which was painful for others to see. Nezhat had bought her a house yet she was not able to console herself; no matter how hard my mother tried, she could not prevent Nezhat frequenting Soltan's empty room. At first I seriously began to believe that she'd been in love with Ebrahim and that her passion for her lost love had caused her misery. I was actually hurt: she used to tell me everything and I couldn't understand why she had not discussed her love. Perhaps I had unjustifiably considered myself grown-up and mature; otherwise Nezhat would have disclosed everything to me considering that she knew me inside out. She had not even bothered to tell me why she had rejected so many respectable bachelors.

Later on, however, I discovered that my concern was unfounded; there had been no passion. Mother and Nezhat had used the matter of dowry for Soltan's daughter to give her many things but the woman was not moved. Her departure brought a chapter to a close; the chapter of a book that I had not yet read. Until the day I went to call Nezhat for lunch and overheard a conversation which stunned me.

'Why are you doing this to yourself? This wasn't your fault. Whether we had said anything or not he would have been executed, like the rest of them who were hanged, which had nothing to do with what we said.'

'My dear sister, why are you fooling yourself? If I had not mentioned Ebrahim the other night he would be alive now. I have killed someone who was worth hundreds of aristocrats and courtiers.'

'This is what I am trying to say; you mustn't blame yourself; someone else pulled him out and hanged him, not you.'

Was it true? The person who had pulled Ebrahim out and had him hanged could not have been anyone but my father, presumably because Nezhat had expressed her decision to become his wife? Did this mean that my father was enraged at the thought of a brother-in-law such as Ebrahim? No, this was not possible! I went away from the sitting room and returned to my room. I did not love my father yet I could not bring myself to think that he was capable of such a deed. I remained in my room and tried to come to terms with this until Nezhat came for me, when I let it all pour out. I said that I was not a child any more. I told her that she had taught me to learn not to live like a donkey, but she had now taken sides with the world to fool me.

This led to the discovery of the secret that had been behind the state of unease in our household ever since the shelling of the parliament. Nezhat explained that Khan wanted her for himself and had so far sent her several notes. He had asked the Shah to be put in charge of her estate, and since the Shah needed the support of people like him he had agreed to the match between my father and Nezhat. Thus I began to understand why my father had yielded his support when it came to rejecting everyone who had asked for her hand in marriage. I could now comprehend the reason behind the release of Zahir mediated by Malakeh Iran, but Ebrahim, who was guilty of backing Zahir, did not survive. I began to understand the agony Nezhat's conscience was experiencing. She believed if she had not mentioned Ebrahim's name that day for her own protection against the Shah's command and that of my father, who was now his agent, the young man would still be alive.

It took me a while to compose myself and ask Nezhat what we were to do. I knew she would not give in to such humiliation. She was not prepared to succumb to such a fate; how could she? When Nezhat said that there was a religious impediment to the marriage, she thought it would calm me down. Although I was not aware that according to our religion a man could not acquire wives who were sisters, it made me look at the situation from a different perspective: my father wouldn't have cared about letting go of my mother. My mother was not happy either, and I knew that she had put up with the hell she was in for my sake, and also to avoid public embarrassment; something which did not easily fit in with a young girl's logic.

My father needed my mother's wealth; without it he would have had to give up many things. Perhaps he wanted Nezhat's money. He effectively wanted to have it all and didn't care how he went about achieving his goals. He would have happily divorced my mother, leaving her to look after me and allowing him to wed Nezhat.

'The martyred Shah, Nasser al-Din Shah, had several sisters in his harem and every six months he'd wed one and divorce the other. The clergy managed to find a lawful way out,' she said, adding that my father wanted to use the same trick.

That evening, I learned everything there was to know. For instance, when Nezhat had bluntly told him that she'd never marry him and nothing could force her to give in, I could vividly picture my father fiddling with his moustache as he said: 'You are mistaken; you have yet to learn the meaning of good fortune.'

'I looked on you as my father, and I am not going to stay here any longer!'

'You stay, I'll go, and time will prove that you will never come across a better opportunity in your life.'

So our two weeks away in the country were intended to remedy the situation, but I couldn't understand why Nezhat decided to go back to a house where a demon was awaiting her. How could my mother have been happy for her to return?

Nezhat was perturbed and reluctantly disclosed everything. She also agreed to deal with my other question: when my father was posted to Azerbaijan, he had told Mother that he was no longer keen to wed Nezhat and that he had changed his mind. Upon his departure, therefore, Mother had returned and brought us back to our park. However, what Khan had claimed did not turn out to be the case, as was apparent from his letters. I read those that he had written, in a vulnerable state, to Nezhat: he was mad about her and could not sleep; every day he died and wished that, were he alive for only a single day, he could spend that day with her.

I was disgusted to read such amorous words, which no doubt he'd stolen from some book or had asked one of his more educated servants to write on his behalf. It was obvious to everyone that nothing more than gambling, hunting and having a good time pleased my father. He didn't have much education and Mother had heard him say: 'God has a duty to provide for my leisure and entertainment.'

He was confident he could have whatever he fancied and, so far, had never encountered any obstacles. In one of his letters to Nezhat he had written that he had never heard 'No' for an answer, and since he was not used to it, if she continued to refuse him, he would end his life and she would have his blood on her hands.

We spent the winter nights under the large *korsi*, sleeping next to my mother. Some unwritten pact had made us stay together and stand by each other. The city was in uproar and we received unpleasant news on a daily basis. The three of us had no fear of the revolution or the collapse of the pillars of the country. Although we never spoke of it, we were frightened of only one person, and this fear drew us closer to each other. At times I heard about the terrible confrontations in Tabriz and Maraqeh, Turkish-speaking cities in the north-west of the country, and I wished that one day they'd bring me news of Khan's death, which was, of course, never to happen.

CHAPTER 14

Nezhat's presence meant we still managed to receive news despite my father's orders. In this way we learned about Sattar Khan and Baqer Khan, the courageous men who had stood up to the Shah. State forces had closed all the routes leading to Tabriz and, as a result, there was a shortage of food. These men had nothing to eat but were not prepared to give in. My father was, of course, caught up in all this and, no matter how many letters he wrote to the Shah seeking his permission to return to the capital for a few days, his plea was dismissed. We knew he was desperate. He had written a letter to my mother in which he had enclosed his will. He had also written a letter to Nezhat saying that he missed her.

The situation worsened. One day we would hear that the Shah's Cossacks were paving the way for Russian troops to take Tabriz; on another, the constitutionalists were receiving funds and weapons from abroad. Amidst all this Ahmad came to see us a couple of times. He seemed unsettled, and we concluded that the monarchy was in grave danger.

It was spring, and the advent of the New Year slightly improved our uncertain, stagnant lives. The *korsi* was put away and the house was spring-cleaned. We spent a couple of days in Amin's park where my Aunt Fakhr lived. Unlike the other women in the family, she was savvy and able. In their extensive estate, which was situated north of Baharestan, she led a happy life with her children of various ages. She was a sociable woman but no one really cared for her husband: based on information from the servants, when the

95

parliament was besieged and its members sought refuge in their park, he had, without his wife's knowledge, quietly reported them to the Imperial Gardens. The Cossacks had poured in, beaten the men up and taken them away. Some were killed on the spot. These accounts had diminished Mr Amin's popularity. On the other hand, everyone loved my aunt, who was completely in control of everything. She always had something interesting to say and urged caution on Nezhat, advising her to be mindful of what she said in the presence of servants and acquaintances. I wished my father, too, was incompetent and under his wife's thumb like Mr Amin.

Our garden was in full bloom when Father returned, and his arrival brought only racket and commotion. The first couple of days he spent at the Imperial Gardens, and the evenings in his quarters. He received few visitors, and didn't seem to be bothered by us. The tranquillity, the sound of the trees swaying in the wind, the swallows, the cool breeze creeping in the room through the door; all were reminders of the spring, even when we were under our blankets.

One evening I saw Morvarid's shadow moving behind the door: Khan was in the sitting room. This was ominous, as was the gradual crescendo of voices. Nezhat and I were awake and silent, until we heard a shocking sound: the large porcelain vase in the sitting room had been thrown onto the veranda. I had a sip of cold water as my throat felt dry; I was sure everyone else must be awake listening to what was going on. It wasn't long before Mother's scream penetrated through the curtains, 'No, no …' Then followed the sound of lashing. It was as though I was the one being beaten; I shivered. As the sound continued I took refuge in Nezhat's bed and let my tears roll onto her face while she held me close to her. We then heard the sound of a heavy slap, at which point Morvarid opened the door, threw herself into the middle of the room and started pulling at her hair.

'He's killed the princess,' she said, as she kept on pulling.

Nanny was whispering, 'Khan never dared touch the lady when Shah Baba was alive.'

This time my mother's shrieks filled the whole building. It sounded as if she had been thrown on the floor: 'Over my dead body!'

I wished Nezhat could tell us what to do; it was usually she who had a solution. I saw her suddenly take a leap like a leopard, grab Nanny's *chador* and rush out of the room barefoot. By then we were sitting up and Nanny had come to hold me and was murmuring some prayer, but the dreadful night seemed to go on forever. The moon was above the dome of the *hammam* and had spread its light on the veranda. There was movement in the branches of the hedges, which meant that the rest of the household was up and in fearful anticipation. By now the sound of beating was louder and my mother's screams had even silenced the frogs. The frame of the French window suddenly shattered and fell with a terrifying sound onto the veranda. It was as though the willow tree was lashing itself with its branches.

Morvarid couldn't contain herself.

'Ya, Eighth Imam, come to our rescue!'[6]

I suddenly heard my father's heavy steps coming towards us. He was losing his balance and managed to collide with one of the flowerpots, which he kicked out of his way. Mother's groans were not far away. Khan kicked the door open and his height filled the doorway. His eyes began to search the room. Nanny, who didn't seem too fussed without her *chador*, got up. Morvarid was trying to avoid his eyes by hiding behind the curtain when his roar reverberated through the room.

'Where is she?'

There was no response so he lifted Nezhat's blanket furiously, threw it across the room and shouted. 'Where is she?'

Morvarid was petrified and started to cry.

'I asked you where she is, you bitch!'

Morvarid was stunned and lost for words but Nanny came to her rescue.

'To whom are you referring, Sir?'

At which he clenched his teeth and at the height of his anger yelled, 'Nezhat-ol-Saltaneh!'

'She left last night. I am not sure where she went but I think she might have gone to Amin's park …'

Had she been rehearsing this?

By then we could see Mother's figure in the doorway. Her scarf had slipped under her throat and her hair was all over her face and covered in blood. I wanted to run and embrace her but I was numb with fear and my feet were motionless.

'Out!'

Father pointed to Nanny and Morvarid, who were both trembling. As they were passing by Mother, she yelled, 'Go on, go and call everyone! Ask them to come to see this …' but she was duly silenced by the impact of his walking-stick on her head.

I saw blood running down her forehead yet she ignored it and launched herself at his silk dressing gown, which she tore. She pulled at his collar and continued tearing at his clothes, but the monster hit her with the back of his hand and she fell down.

Nezhat's grey cat had come to the veranda as though wanting to find out what was going on. I saw Father pull his pocketknife out of his pocket; it was reflected in the moonlight as he pointed it at Mother. I was so scared I couldn't help but turn my face. I heard his loud, rough voice.

'I could kill you this very minute, you miserable cow, but I shan't. However, I shall make your life hell: one eye shall shed tears and the other blood!'

Mother collapsed on the floor with blood pouring over her ashen face. Khan put his knife back in its scabbard and then took my hand and pulled. I struggled. He then pulled me in the direction of the door. He was so strong that I felt my arm was about to dislocate. I had to let go of the edge of the bed I had been holding on to and he lifted me off the ground with one arm. He was about to leave through the door when I caught at his legs, making him stagger and almost fall. I was screaming but he was taking no notice. While circling my waist with his arm he passed through the veranda. I saw the reflection of the distraught willow tree in the pool but I couldn't see where the moon was hiding.

He was staggering towards his quarters while I was desperately clutching the air and screaming, at which he raised his stick and shouted, 'Shut up!'

The gravel made a crunching sound under the soles of his shoes. Nezhat's cat was following us; my quiet sobs seemed to have terrified her. We reached Father's quarters. Afterwards he threw me inside and started putting the bolt on the large doors. He had hardly finished when I saw my mother's bloodstained face behind the window. She was beating against the door with her fist. Her voice sounded hoarse and desperate and seemed to come from afar.

'She is your daughter, you animal!'

I was shouting again; I was calling my mother who was calling everyone as though she was deranged. I went to hide behind the sofa but he came and caught me by the hair and twisted it around his hand. He then lifted me and held me under his right arm. He seemed completely drunk. The chandelier reflected the moonlight and we were moving further from the door, upon which my mother was still beating. We passed through a hall adorned with heads of reindeers and wild goats. I told myself if we passed through the next door then no one could reach us, so I began to struggle with all my might. I was hitting his arms where his dressing gown had been torn but it was useless; I could not match his strength. He finally threw me on the ground just behind the metal door leading to his private apartment, the area forbidden to us for the past two years. He then started pulling the bolts one by one, all the time pulling on my hand. The light was on and there was a large wooden bed in the middle, a tiger skin on the floor and two wooden statues of fairies on either side of the bed. I felt numb. He approached the jug, took it to his mouth, drank the yellow liquid to the end and then slammed the jug down on the tray. In an instant I was thrown on the bed. I could still hear Mother's voice and her hammering.

'You animal!'

I felt quite helpless so I implored, 'Khan, in the name of Aqa joun's grave!'

I am not sure where this came from. I had never sworn on anything, but I was begging now as he was removing his torn dressing gown. I was on the bed right between the two fairies when I saw the curtains by the wardrobe move. The barrel of a rifle began to emerge and then Nezhat's hands made an appearance. For a moment time seemed to have stopped. The moon had suddenly sunk in the pool and Mother's hammering had come to a halt.

'Go! Go!' I heard Nezhat's command but the gun was pointing at Khan. 'There are two bullets in here; if you move I'll shoot your heart out!'

I didn't have the strength to move but she ordered me again.

'Leave this room!'

I wanted to ask her how she had managed to reach that place but when I remembered Mother I began to run. I came to a wall and then reached the door with the bolt. It was too high up and I couldn't reach it no matter how high I jumped. In the dark I saw the antique Russian chair by Father's small antique desk; I pulled it and began to climb. When I finally managed to unbolt the door, it felt as though I'd been born again. Mother was very close, and the windowpane had been broken. It was as if my soul was leaping out of the window when the terrifying sound of shooting filled the room. The sound was so fierce it made the windowpane reverberate. I could now see many terrified eyes. My feet were bare and I was stepping on the pieces of broken glass but I didn't care. When I heard the sound of the second shot it took my breath away. Momentarily, I saw Nezhat fly past but I didn't feel anything else. Mother had passed out with the first shot.

CHAPTER 15

I was dead, but there were all these confused voices in my ears. I was dead and someone was carrying my body on their shoulder and running. I tried to call someone – Mother, Nezhat, Nanny – but nothing came out; it was hopeless. I was dead but once again the kind hands were approaching; the hands which gave me confidence and warmth, the hands which were searching my body. It was my mother, but I was dead: I couldn't hear anything nor did I have a voice. I felt cold, but the dead couldn't feel the cold. So was I in a coffin? No, I had pins and needles in my feet, as though someone was digging into them with a blade. So, I was alive but no one knew; or perhaps I was in a coffin. But wait! The kind hands were far away from me and my head was on her chest. The first voice I heard was my own.

'Mother!'

Her body was suddenly shaking and her hands became limp and let go of me.

'Oh, the princess passed out!'

This was Nanny's voice. Passed out? How? I felt drops of water fall on my face; someone was sprinkling water on Mother's face. I wanted to get up and help so that we could wake Mother, whose face was bruised and covered with dried blood. Her hair looked as though Morvarid had not combed it for years. The collar of her dress was torn and I could see many dark marks on her fair skin.

It took me a while to come to myself again and recall events: the door, the bolt, the rifle and the sound of shooting. I shivered.

'Nezhat?'

A cold bloodless hand as though of a corpse rested on my forehead and I opened my eyes. It was Nezhat with a couple of dark rings under her eyes. I must have been dead for some time as Nezhat looked rather old. I took her hand and held it in my weak hands. Then I rested them on my eyes, forehead and lips. I began to say a prayer; thank God we were alive and sitting together in complete darkness. Someone called me. It was Mother's hoarse voice as though calling me from afar.

'*Khanoumi*!'

None of us had any strength, and we were slowly coming back to life yet I didn't know where I was. I only knew that I was sleeping between the two of them: between Mother and Nezhat. Both of them moved from time to time; they jerked occasionally and then were motionless again.

'Get up, Khanoum, get up.'

It was Mother's voice, which was inviting me back to life. Her voice was dry and hollow.

'Get up and listen my love; we haven't got much time, as I have to go.'

I sat up. We were in an unknown room; this wasn't our home. There was an unlit lamp and a servant was entering the room through the curtains. The door was ajar.

'Listen Khanoum, we haven't got much time, listen; it's over! There's no danger; everything is over. I must leave for an hour but you must look after your aunt. Don't let her leave. Drink this tea now,' at which point a small glass tumbler approached my mouth.

I felt nauseous. The tea was lukewarm but sweet and when it travelled down my throat it was as though it was flowing down a parched gully, but I couldn't easily swallow any bread or cheese. I drank the tea. The door opened and Nezhat stooped forward as she stepped inside. Without looking at Mother or me, she threw her *chador* to one side, went to her unfamiliar bedding and snuggled under the blanket. Mother approached me.

'I'll go and come back. Asdollah is here sitting in the garden. Take care of Nezhat and I'll come back soon!'

I wanted to say to her, 'Don't leave, I am scared,' but she beckoned me to be quiet and then took her *chador* and slipped through the door.

I heard her speak to Asdollah briefly, after which I heard an outside door open and shut and someone bolting it.

There was silence. If I had not been aware of Nezhat's presence under the blanket I'd have been scared of loneliness. Her presence though, and the various scenes which were now parading in my mind, didn't leave any room for fear. I so wanted Nezhat to get up and talk to me and tell me what had happened and what had become of that beast. I had many questions but I felt feverish and my body didn't feel anything. Where are we? Why are you not getting up, Nezhat? I was absorbed in my thoughts when I heard her quiet voice. It was as though she was speaking from the bottom of a well.

'Can you hear me, Khanoum?' She was talking to me from under the blanket.

'Yes!'

'Please listen, we don't have much time. You must make a promise that you'll leave this place. You must go … you mustn't stay here. You must go as far as possible and you must live for me as well. Please promise me, don't let life dominate you; rather it is *you* who must rule your life.'

I couldn't understand what she was saying. What did this all mean? Was she planning to go somewhere? I wanted to speak to her but she got up. She must have been feeling nauseous because she was holding her hand in front of her mouth. Now a faint light was penetrating the room, allowing me to see her face clearly. She was bruised around her eyes and her golden hair was wet. She pulled her *chador* on her head, opened the door and left. I got up and watched her. When she appeared in the doorway, Asdollah, who was sitting on the steps resting his forehead on his thick walking-stick, got up but did not say anything. My eyes followed Nezhat as she picked up the ewer and climbed down the steps leading to the toilet on the other side of the garden. So we were in the house of Asdollah, husband of Nanny, who lived behind the butcher's shop where Mother used to settle her account. Mother had given Nanny this small property with its courtyard. There was a well in the middle and rooms around the courtyard. I felt better for knowing where we were. I could now recall events and recognised the room. There was a tray of bread and a chunk of cheese left on the floor and there was dishevelled bedding all over the place. I put a piece of bread in my mouth when I had a sudden realisation: I rushed to Nezhat's bedding and pulled the cover off. There was no light. I touched the mattress and it was wet. I looked at it. I was shocked. My wet hands terrified me as though I had committed a crime. I could smell blood. I buried my head in Mother's pillow and began to scream.

Chapter 16

I t wasn't four days but rather four months, or perhaps forty years, or even centuries; the three of us were still in that room. Asdollah resembled a statue sitting on the steps with his walking-stick under his chin. We didn't say much. From the two corners of the room Mother connected us like the beads in a rosary. We sat there without a sound, deep in thought for hours. Mother kept us under control with few words, and the words were repeated many times over.

When Asdollah brought in the tray of food, she effectively spoon-fed Nezhat. 'Eat!' And every time one of us got up to leave the room, she asked, 'Yes?' or she would ask me, 'Khanoum, why don't you go to the garden and take some fresh air and I'll call you in when it's time.'

I had to give them some privacy so that she could attend to her young and withering sister. We were prisoners, and only Mother could go to town from time to time. The sound of shooting never ceased and sometimes one could hear the galloping of horses. I was concerned about my mother, who would don Nanny's *chaqchour* and leave the house a couple of times a day. Nezhat and I were then left to ourselves, but very little was exchanged between us.

She often remained under the blanket and I wondered how she could go on and not suffocate in the heat. When she sniffed from time to time I knew she was weeping. I too was weeping quietly, and I believed that Asdollah, too, was quietly weeping while resting his forehead on his thick walking-stick. We didn't know where Mother went, or why, and we didn't enquire. Nezhat had a temperature, and whenever I held her head it felt like she was on fire.

One night we took her to the well and helped her sit on the ground. Mother then pulled up some water and poured it over her head. The faint moonlight made her golden hair sparkle. She was sitting motionless while the water fell on her head, and Mother used her hand to wash her face, just as Nanny had washed mine when I was younger. Then we washed her feet. Her fair skin was as dry as an old woman's, as though she had suddenly grown forty years older. I saw her shiver and huddle up to herself, resembling a chick or her own cat, which was nowhere to be seen now.

Mother informed us that the next day, when night fell, we were to leave but she did not disclose our destination. Inside the room she took out some clothes from a wrapped bundle. We dressed Nezhat and removed her wet clothes. She didn't utter a word; only when my mother stepped outside the room did I hear her voice.

'Khanoum, don't forget your promise: you promised to live for me as well.'

But I wanted to say something this time.

I wanted to say, 'Wherever we go we'll go together, we'll be together and we'll live together.'

But she suddenly burst into tears and pulled the blanket over her again. Mother returned and for the remaining three nights we slept fitfully. I dreamed that Nezhat and I had fallen into a large well and a black snake was chasing us. Although Mother was there and was hitting the snake with something sharp, the snake seemed to remain alive and to continue chasing us. We were about to drown. I had no strength to move and my hands and feet seemed tied with something. I was drowning while struggling until I woke up. My throat felt dry so I drank water from the large ceramic jug in the corner of the room. Mother had pulled her muslin sheet over her and Nezhat was breathing, but not so steadily. I returned to my bed and fell asleep again.

I couldn't believe it, and I still find it hard to believe: the next day when we were preparing to take our leave, Mother and I were the only ones to go. While we were asleep, Nezhat had drowned in the water I had been dreaming of. I was wrapped in *chaqchour* and veil the next day so that I couldn't see Nezhat's corpse when they pulled her out of the well. Though she had gone she returned to my dreams many nights over with the same golden locks and hazel eyes; just as she had been the night before when she was asking me not to forget ...

The first few nights I kept waking up in terror, but in time I became able to actually reply to her whenever she stepped into my dreams.

'Very well, Nezhat-ol-Saltaneh!'

CHAPTER 17

T he city was in turmoil, quite unlike the silence and state of
fear in Asdollah's house. The state forces had turned on the
Shah and they were returning to Tehran from Esfahan and the
northern parts of the country. What if they murdered Ahmad
along with the rest of the imperial family?

The beast was searching for us, and Mother returned looking
exhausted from her daily quest for security: she was the cat
carrying her kitten, holding onto her by her teeth. My last refuge
was Soltan's place; the very house that Nezhat had bought her.
She would remember Ebrahim and it pained me every time
she mentioned an aspect of her son. I just pictured Nezhat and
Ebrahim living in that cute little garden: my princess was playing
the piano and Ebrahim arrived with a handful of pamphlets and
papers. He courteously stood there, as he had the other night,
bringing Nezhat a report on the state of affairs.

Mother left me for two days, during which time I would sit
by the little tank that was served by a narrow stream of water that
flowed in from one side and left it from the other to flow into the
flowerbed. While she spoke of her loss I stared at the watermelons
and apples that Soltan had left in the tank to keep cool. At night,
under the mosquito net, I would always keep a space for my little
aunt, but ended up sleeping alone. I remembered her whispering
in my ear that there was no reason why we should feel our hands
were tied when it came to our destiny, yet I felt tied to the chagrin
of losing her. My void was so palpable that I had forgotten

about myself and didn't notice that I, too, fell in the same water that Nezhat had, though I wasn't sure whether it was the marshland I was slowly being drawn to or the sea which was about to receive me.

From the corner of my quiet prison I heard that the Shah and his family had left for the fort in Saltanat Abad, north of Tehran. The courtiers and officials were fleeing, either to the embassies or to their estates outside Tehran, and since there was no one left in the city, the Bakhtiari forces, drawn from the tribes in the south-west, and the Cossacks helped themselves to their properties. I was told that Russia and Britain were dividing the country between themselves and that, before long, the name of Iran would vanish from the map.

CHAPTER 18

I found myself sitting between two women who, in their *chaqchours*, resembled anyone but Soltan's nieces. Every time the carriage jerked, I felt I was getting a little further from everything, further from the memories of my eleven years, which made me feel like a grown woman. I didn't know where my mother was and didn't dare ask. Although impatient, I knew that, as soon as I mentioned it, Soltan would once again whisper that she was waiting for us. She had made bite-sized sandwiches of beaten meat mixed with mashed chickpeas in a stale piece of bread. My stomach was therefore kept busy, which also helped soften the bitter taste in my mouth. The radishes in the sandwiches were pungent and burned my tongue. I couldn't hold my tears back: they rolled down my cheeks and made my neck wet under the veil. I wished I could go to sleep and dream of what I had seen the night before under the mosquito net: Nezhat had taken a rifle and, with each shot, someone fell; tens or hundreds of them, who were all one person. My father seemed to have fragmented into a hundred other men and Nezhat was shooting them all. She was now riding a horse and the sun made her hair look even fairer. Mother and I were following her in a carriage laughing and screaming. We were in a green field with orange trees, like the ones in Shah Baba's gardens.

The journey to the unknown place seemed never-ending and we stopped from time to time. Soltan would regularly murmur some prayer and then blow at me. Every time we came to a halt we heard Bakhtiari gunmen talking with Heidar. They would ask questions, he would respond, after which we would carry on. The horses slowly trotted uphill, their panting becoming more noticeable. The clamour outside meant that we had finally arrived. A large iron gate opened up, we entered and then it closed behind us again. Hearing the sound of the horses' hooves on the gravel path gave me the impression that we were riding through rather a large park or some palace.

'Here we are,' someone said, and then they began tidying their *chaqchours*.

I noticed Soltan was holding a wrapped bundle.

'Where is Khanoum?'

My mother's voice was the best sound I had heard in two days. My whole being wanted to scream, 'Mother!' Instead I silently watched her through the curtains of the carriage. She had grown older. I wanted to shout out how much I had missed her, but I remembered the last night and how she had lectured me on how resilient and contained a girl must be. I had no strength left to talk to her or anyone else about the reality that had filled our minds ever since the final night in our own home, but we never spoke of it. Not even when Nezhat threw herself in the well. When Mother was hitting her head against the windowpane and the door yelling, 'You beast!' it was as though all our questions had been answered.

I didn't know at the time that we had arrived in the summer residence of the Russian Embassy. When I saw my mother from afar, covered in her *chador* and veil, I began to understand her efforts: disappearing in the uncertainty of the deranged city covered in Soltan's *chador* she was securing a safe haven for us. When I ran towards her she lifted her veil and embraced me. I was wrapped in her arms as though dissolving in her.

I thought, despite looking much thinner, she had been transformed once more into the princess I used to see in the imperial palace; the same woman who used to sit at the top end of the sitting room leaning on a large stiff cushion, and when the net curtain fell she would take a puff at the hookah while listening to the secretary going through the accounts.

When she stretched her arm to receive the small wrapped bundle from Soltan I noticed that her left hand was wrapped in a piece of white cloth. I sneaked a look at her face: her eyes were bruised and bloodshot. 'What an animal!'

There was a heavy guard of Cossacks at the Russian Embassy and, for the first time, I noticed women wearing white aprons and no scarf. They had all come to see us; or rather, the imperial family, whom fear of the people had driven to that place. It took many years for me to find out that while my mother and I were sitting on the bench, away from the pool, a few constitutionalists who had taken over the capital were busy negotiating with the Russian ambassador in a room a few yards away. In another room, the forlorn Shah was holding talks with other Russians, who were explaining their terms. That afternoon he signed his resignation and it was decided that his son, Ahmad, should remain in the country as Shah while the imperial family were to take their leave.

None of this, however, was of any consequence to me. What mattered to me at that time was the news Mother broke to me; that I was to leave along with a terrified family who had gathered in the embassy. When Mother mentioned this to me I felt shock waves spread in my chest and then through my veins. All that remained was fear. I couldn't work out whether it was the fear of leaving or the thought of leaving her behind all alone that was making me tremble. Mother placed her arm on my back and we walked away from the pool on the wide, clean, gravelled path with fir trees on either side. Amid the large trees, I spotted a tree covered in black cherries, a bride among hundreds of bridesmaids. In such fanciful surroundings my mother explained to me that I was no longer safe in that city and that she had asked her brother to take me with him.

'After your departure I'll tie up some loose ends and come as well.'

'Where?'

'Wherever they go.'

I asked her what she was going to do. She tried not to show any signs of frailty and weakness; she even managed to conceal the pain of losing Nezhat and parting with her only child.

'At this moment in time the most important issue is your life. Once you are gone he will treat me with more kindness. You never know, perhaps I shall come as well, but you must go now.'

What a pleasant lie! What Mother said to me shaped my future dreams: wherever we went, whenever I closed my eyes, I saw her arriving on a fast-moving horse-drawn carriage, or on a horse with a long mane, and she would embrace me. She carried on talking but I can't remember anything else; the words had no effect and she was hopelessly trying to make it all seem like a minor incident, just like any other but of even less importance. I was anxious.

'How long? I mean, how many months will I not see you?'

She replied, perhaps to herself, 'I wish we were talking about months.'

While we were seated on the bench with a continuous flow of carriages arriving or leaving, the future of the country was being decided and I felt I was being gradually released into a very large world. I recall her face with her veil up. She was holding my hands and trying to make our last encounter easy. I was confident she had arranged the safest place in the world for me but the safest place for me was in her arms.

'Mother, how could you expect me to do such a thing? What will happen to you? What will you do in this merciless hell; a place where nowhere is safe for us?'

Some seventy years have passed, and whenever I recall that day many questions come to my mind and I imagine I put all of them to her in the space of a few minutes. When I turned twenty, or even thirty, and throughout the years to old age, these questions never changed, though everything I wanted to say to her on that day had dried up in my mouth. When I became an old woman I answered them for her in my dreams or even when deep in thought.

'You must go; you must leave this hell. Go and never be feeble and a captive like me. Go and fight for life. Go and claim justice for me and for Nezhat ...'

She never said anything in reality, however, and save for that one sentence, she didn't say anything else. I had to discover it for myself. At the end of our encounter she held me and pressed me against her. She whispered some prayer in my ear and then blew it over me. She got up and guided me to the salon of the building where the family of the forlorn king had gathered. Malakeh Jahan's face, although kind, looked shattered and terrified; it was she who was supposed to become my mother from then on. She rose as she saw my mother. I had always seen her in sophisticated gowns but, at the time, she had wrapped a *chador* around her waist and was helping the convoy that was about to leave Iran. They both took me to a room with boys and girls of my own age.

I then remember myself standing behind a window at the Russian Embassy looking at Mother, who was embracing the empress, both looking tearful. I looked through my tears at the hazy image of my mother climbing down the stairs. The park was busy with people who were still arriving or leaving. Mother ignored it all and passed through the carriages. It took me years to find out what was inside the wrapped bundle Soltan gave to my mother, and which she left with the empress. At that moment, however, it was of no consequence to me. I only thought of one thing: the one whom I was worried about, and the one who worried about me.

Mother left me to the convoy and departed. I was far too weak to contest it, to follow her, hang onto her carriage, fall at her feet and beg her to find a different solution. I was too fragile to scream amid the tumult and tell everyone that a stem was being cut off from its root. She got in the carriage and left. Before leaving she left me with a woman who always smiled. The rest I heard from the empress over the years. Standing behind the window along with the other children, my last memory of our parting is the few minutes that I saw her walking with a slight limp, putting her foot on the step to get into the carriage, not looking back for an instant. She left, and for the past seventy years I have been waiting for her to come back.

When I did manage to communicate with her it was from a distance. The first time was when we settled in the carriages with drawn curtains following the black car driving the Shah. The Cossacks were riding on either side of the carriages as we left the embassy. As the moment of departure approached, everyone had someone to say goodbye to. The embassy's gardens were filled with wailing and the desperate tears of parting. The Russian ambassador with his heavy moustache was standing on the steps waving to the deposed Shah, and I was hopelessly searching for Mother's eyes. When we left the embassy's cobbled street we came to a halt at the British Embassy so that the British soldiers could escort our convoy to the borders. There I saw our carriage with Heidar, our coachman, sitting on top; I was certain she was sitting inside next to Soltan saying a tearful prayer for me, the tears she had denied me in our last encounter. For a moment I was filled with a desire to throw myself out of the carriage and I knew that if I did, she would leap out and catch me in her arms. She would then place my head on her chest and I was going to tell her not to let go of me. During our journey I sometimes closed my eyes and rested my head against the velvet upholstered side of the carriage and spoke to her. The further we got from Tehran, its green gardens and poplars, the more I had to say to her.

CHAPTER 19

M y first night away from my mother was quite an experience, as though I was born to be part of her. My chest was tight and I felt I was suffocating. Everyone thought this was because of the *chador* and the veil. When I removed these and my head and neck were bare, I was in a room with three or four other carefree but kind girls. I wanted none of them to be there, no one in the world, not even me, only her.

When we got out of the carriage we were in an extensive park with a building similar to my father's quarters planted in the middle. The resemblance was so uncanny that I was filled with a sense of horror and thanked God I had not been taken *there*! The Shah, his entourage and his sons, however, went in and we, the women, were taken to another building across the park; sadly, I took the image of Nezhat and the piano with me to the other building. The empress ordered some infusion to be prepared so that everyone could have a sound sleep, as we had to get up early the next day to continue with the journey. Taking the colourful image to bed with me meant that it took me a while before I gave in to sleep. Everyone's gentle breathing meant that I could sit and let my imagination take off.

Where was my mother at that moment? Was she still in the same house as that beast? The thought of her at his feet receiving her beating gave me a sharp pain in my stomach. I was alone on a cold, unfamiliar bed, bothered by a myriad questions and places. I began to go through the events in Father's quarters:

at Nezhat's command, I had got out of the beast's bedroom and started running in the dark hallway. I had heard the sound of shooting – twice. Had Nezhat killed the beast? I knew this was only wishful thinking; so what had happened? The girl who had used the wardrobe to ambush my father with her rifle in that dark room had no resemblance to my Nezhat. No more than Mother when she had kept striking at the snake in my previous dream.

I had closed my eyes. A bullet killed the beast, but that couldn't have been the case. Why had Nezhat become so unwell? Why did we have to hide? If it weren't for him, I would not have been here and Mother wouldn't have been so terrified, and Nezhat … My Nezhat wouldn't have been at the bottom of the well.

Just how long it took me to let fatigue and sleep come over me I can't remember. I just took another peep inside Father's quarters: a heavy chandelier hung in the middle of the ceiling and upholstered chairs could be seen around the room. Nezhat was sitting behind the piano, but instead of Mother, the monster with his narrow moustache and tall body was now seated, and his riding boots sparkled. I was hiding in a corner behind the black cast-iron stove whose pipe resembled a baby elephant's majestic trunk inserted in the wall. I was sweating as the stove generated its powerful heat. Nezhat's suffocated scream shook me and, as a result, my face stuck to the side of the stove. I saw her struggle in his hands like a fish out of water, like me the other night, and I heard the laughter of the man with the thin moustache who had taken the rifle away from Nezhat, and … The room with a large wooden bed in the middle, like Shah Baba's bed but larger; two naked fairies on either corners of the bed … Nezhat had been thrown on the bed; her golden waves had covered the leopard skin on the bed; the heat and my fever. My cheek was burning, and I couldn't bear to witness the scene before me. Around me, hanging on the walls, were dried heads of mountain goats and a row of rifles. When I turned my face, near the top of the bed I saw a tall candelabra and a pistol with a mother-of-pearl butt. I then seemed to be flying from the corner of the room to the candelabra, the only source of light in the room. The heavy curtains blocked the sunlight. I went to take the pistol out of its case. I had seen the monster targeting a stone while out in the countryside; now I was targeting him. I couldn't see Nezhat; it was as though the leopard had become alive and had swallowed her. A few drops of blood and I woke up. My breathing had slowed down and I was sweating.

The girls were fast asleep as if they hadn't a care in the world. A candle was flickering, making it possible for me to find a bowl of water. I took a sip and then poured some water on the palms of my hand, splashing my face with it. A drop of water ran down the back of my neck. I tried to wash away my tears. My nightmare had stemmed from my questions. There was no one to interpret my dreams any more; my mother wanted me to be alone. When I was going back to sleep I cursed her, I talked to her.

'Come, come to me in the morning. Sit on the bench by the pool, and let me sit next to you as well. Hold my hands so that I can tell you what you tried to keep from me. I dreamed of this bitter and naked truth. I now know from what nightmare you pulled me, but you had no right to let go of me and just drop me somewhere.'

The next morning, the weight of having cursed my mother in the night had numbed my body. When someone pulled the curtain and called us, I felt more tired than when I had gone to bed. Our area was screened so that the women could get ready to perform their prayers and leave. On the other side of the barrier there was commotion and the sound of arriving and departing. This became the order of the day everywhere we stopped. We would go to sleep having drunk some herbal tea and would wake up to the sound of shouting, perform our prayers and then depart. There were about ten carriages altogether with the Russian and British soldiers galloping on either side. We went from one house to another, by the poplars, *toots*[7] and walnut trees; we were getting away from them all. The young leaves and buds, at times washed with rain, kept us company along the journey. We were leaving spring behind and I was distancing myself from someone who was *my* spring: my mother.

CHAPTER 20

We passed through the snow-covered mountains. Every time we arrived at a convenient location we camped in old mansions in large grounds. Our feet became numb from long sedentary periods in the carriage. The children, who were excited at the thought of being able to run around and play, were always first to leave the carriages. The girls seemed happy but occasionally imitated the grown-ups by pretending to be anguished. I discovered early on that they actually had no idea why they were leaving their palaces. I, too, would perhaps have been like them without any care in my head had it not been for Nezhat. But that wasn't the case, and I knew I was becoming increasingly lonely and soon enough would have no one in the entire world. I was well aware of why I was leaving and who had brought this about. Those girls had no reason to feel resentful, but I did. During our journey, I got a diary and began to write; I wrote letters addressed to my mother and thus I spoke to her on a daily basis, which was soothing. Every day and night I would plant her on a large stiff cushion where she would lean back against another large stiff cushion in the reception room in our house. I would then hand her a hookah and place Morvarid next to her. I would do the same with Nanny and then I would begin to chat to her.

The drizzle as we were passing through one of the cities, once forced us to camp in a house where the moss on the steps made them slippery. An umbrella was held up high to cover the forlorn Shah and his wife. They went inside and the children followed suit. I had already become a member of their family but we would always stay in a room away from the grown-ups. While the fire was drying our *chadors* Abdollah, one of the eunuchs, entered.

'The empress has called for Khanoum,' his delicate, feminine voice announced.

I donned my wet *chador* and went to the other room. The empress was seated and had a haughty air about her. I kissed her hand. She was holding a parcel and from inside she took out an envelope and passed it to me. I knew full well who it was from: apart from my mother, my only relation in the world, no one else could have written to me and no one else could have been thinking of me. On the envelope my father's name and address printed in gold had been crossed out and I could see Mother's clear but childlike handwriting on the envelope. 'With Her Majesty, the empress's permission, to the light of my eyes, Khanoum.'

I took the letter to the other room. Reluctantly, I opened it, but when the letter left the envelope it was as though something was released and its aroma filled my entire being. Since no one was looking I kissed the letter and placed it on my eyes. I left it unread on my chest, close to my heart, and pressed it against my chest with such force that the skin underneath became tender, as though part of Mother was in it. I had never read a letter from Mother before.

Khanoumi, my dearest dear,

Without your tender presence our life is hell on earth, but I am delighted that you are leaving. Do not look back; there is nothing here but pain and suffering. Your future, however, is bright and beautiful. Do not miss any opportunity to live your life. Think of Her Majesty as your mother: she will look after you and you must obey her. At the same time, you must understand that Her Majesty has suffered a great deal and you must not expect her full attention. Your true guardian is God and I know that he has watched over you, and will carry on doing so. Whenever Her Majesty sees fit, she will explain everything to you, but you must not ask any questions and you must not do anything to trouble her. Write to me every now and then so that I know you are well. You are leaving this insecure abyss at a time when people's lives are worthless. No one is safe here, you and I in particular; ordinary people are subject to pain and suffering.

Khanoum, my beloved daughter, try to forget us, and every time you pray, ask the Almighty not to forget you. Please forward my kindest regards to my most honourable cousin the Empress, and kiss her hands, and I kiss your beautiful face.

Your loving Mother

I could not hide the turmoil my mother's first letter had stirred in me. I buried my head in the pillow and cried. I carried on in this manner until someone touched my back. It was the Empress; I understood that Khadijeh, her daughter, had gone and called her. I was embarrassed that I had already forgotten Mother's request and had selfishly distracted the Empress from her problems, thus drawing her to my room. I stood up and wiped my tears with the corner of my scarf, said hello and forced a smile. I then passed on my mother's greetings.

The Empress smiled and sat me next to her and, while holding my hands, said, 'Once we have safely crossed the borders, my love, God willing, I have so much to tell you girls. We have a lot to do ...'

She said a little more and then got up. She stared into our eyes and said, 'I want to ask you to do something for me; are you ready?'

Khadijeh and I nodded while we stood and looked at each other. Little did we know that this was a trick that the Empress would often use in the years to come and we repeatedly fell for it. She never wasted time and she knew many ways to calm a troubled mind. She mentioned to us that Mahmoud Khan, who kept the accounts of the harem, had that day informed her that he was not going to be able to go with us, so the Empress was asking us to take over his duties – managing the accounts for a convoy which had initially started off with more than two hundred individuals but, upon arrival in Baku, was reduced to twenty-five. Fear of such responsibility made me momentarily forget everything. Khadijeh said that we had no idea about accounting but the Empress was encouraging.

'You are educated and you have two days to learn everything.'

So that afternoon Khadijeh and I were busy enough to have no time to think. The Empress left and an hour later we were facing the accountant, who opened the books and began.

'*Bismillah*, in the name of God ...'

Later that evening, after we had dinner, we sat and listened to Khadijeh's nanny's tales and anecdotes. Every night she would narrate the tales of *One Thousand and One Nights* while I withdrew to a corner to write. I wrote that I would endeavour, with all my might, to respect Mother's wishes and become the Khanoum she had desired. I wrote about the Empress's kindness and Khadijeh's empathy, though I did not write that no one was able to fill the space that belonged to her. This wasn't my first letter, but I was confident that this was the first one to reach her. I felt I had no right to bother her by describing my pain; on the contrary, I saw it as my duty to make her happy and reduce her anxiety,

Mother,

Her Majesty's presence and Khadijeh Khanoum's company brings me much comfort, and I am confident that with the Almighty's support, the future path will be smooth.

I wish I could express a tiny part of my gratitude to my dearest Mother, by kissing her hands ...

Could Mother, through these banal words, discover how I felt, and just how much I would have preferred to hide in the room behind the tank, yet close enough so that I didn't have to dream about her? Could she come to sense how much I needed her?

CHAPTER 21

According to Mahmoud, we had to board a ship and leave on a Sunday. The drizzle was relentless. Our identity papers had been stamped and were ready. The Russian and British guards had been dismissed, as well as a group of people, one of whom was Mahmoud the bookkeeper, who were returning to Tehran. Our convoy, now at the mercy of the people's resentment, had to leave the next day to part forever from our homeland.

The night before our departure we were alarmed by the sound of shooting. We knew that, while we'd been travelling, the constitutionalists had repeatedly attempted to kill the deposed Shah, who was also travelling with us. They wanted him to pay with his life for the many people he had hanged in the Imperial Gardens, or killed during the fighting against the state forces, or who had lost their homes. The Shah, who only a few months before was so arrogant and powerful that even behind closed doors one dared not be disrespectful, was now a feeble and frightened soul terrified of the slightest sound. Had it not been for the Empress, who insisted, he wouldn't have eaten but would simply have brooded.

One night in Qazvin, in the north-west, we woke up to the sound of shooting near to where we had camped. The Empress, taking the lead as usual, sent someone to find out what had caused the shooting. But before we knew what was going on, we saw the Shah in a cloak and *kolah* arrive in the women's quarters, trying to hide among the women and children. Early next day, when we set off hastily, we learned from the pamphlets flying across the barriers that the Mojaheddin had intended to finish the Shah off the previous evening.

On another occasion, while we were crossing the snow-covered mountains, we decided to take a rest in a mansion by a fierce-flowing river. There was an ancient tree nearby and when the wind blew wildly through its branches it made for a spectacular scene. I had seen the famous poplar in Emamzadeh Saleh, a holy shrine north of Tehran, where Mother and I had lit candles on Thursday nights and tied knots. Now, near this tree, we could run around and release the tension of sitting in the carriages for so many hours. The boys were climbing the tree, and some of the women had sat down by a man who was reciting prayers and whose voice the wind twisted in the densely leaved branches of the poplar. I wanted to go and sit next to the women. The feeling was indescribable. The storm was intensifying, and lightning began to strike. The terrified grown-ups sought refuge indoors but we, being completely soaked already, were taken to the tree. At times the storm untied the knots and released them into the air. Khadijeh's nanny brought a piece of cloth and asked us to make a wish. We had to close our eyes and try to tie a knot with the corner of the cloth. We did as she instructed and, after each knot, recited a prayer. Khadijeh's nanny then tore strips from the rest of the cloth and handed everyone a piece. We waited for the storm to calm down so that we could tie a knot to the tree, but it was relentless. We then sat for lunch. The grown-ups were not about. By then we had an addition to our convoy: Etezad, the Shah's eldest son from a different wife. Dressed in a military uniform, he practically never left his father's side throughout the journey and came across as aloof. He left the Shah's room only when there were secret political talks in progress, or letters from the British Ambassador, or the Prime Minister or the Regent were received. He came to join us that evening. When he realised that we could not tie our knots as we were frightened of the storm, he decided to show off his bravado: moments later, he was walking ahead, followed by the four of us, who were younger than him. It started raining heavily. In order to approach the poplar we had first to pass along a path and then down a slope by the canal lined with mint.

We all took the first shot to be lightning, but when we saw Etezad take out his pistol and lie down on the muddy ground, we realised something was afoot, though we didn't know what to do. We huddled together behind a clay wall and no one dared make a move, as though we were paralysed by the sight of them. Four men carrying pistols, with their legs heavily wrapped and black shoes, made a terrifying sight. Their black hats added to their fearsome appearance and they were towering over Etezad with their pistols pointed at him. We huddled even closer together and were agog. It was as though the clocks had stopped. We were clutching our wet knots, murmuring prayers. The voice of Khadijeh's nanny broke the silence and, facing the gunmen, she begged them to be merciful. One of the gunmen stepped forward and took a good look at us huddling. Up close, he no longer seemed so scary. He didn't seem to want to shoot. And so the four men fired into the air, and then rapidly disappeared behind the trees and low clay walls. We had hardly begun helping Etezad up when an English colonel arrived followed by an older man a few minutes later. This man was referred to as 'Yeneral' or General. The general was a Russian and was in charge of the embassy guards. They insisted that we should return indoors but Khadijeh's nanny was adamant that the knots should not lie around, since this would be a bad omen.

CHAPTER 22

We were making slow but steady progress; every time we stopped to spend the night we would sense people's resentment. At times they turned their backs on us, or they would throw stones at us from the middle of the woods, after which the guards would shout and warn them. The sounds of shooting persisted, but having come from Tehran, this was only too familiar. The further we progressed the more attached we became to one another. The British and Russian guards were a constant presence and to cheer us up they would say: 'We'll soon arrive at the border and once we board the ship all will be over and we shall arrive in the land of happiness.'

This land of happiness gradually became more visual and more beautiful every time we talked about it. Everyone yearned for their final destination except me: I wanted our arrival at the sea to be delayed for as long as possible since I believed once we arrived my return would be improbable.

My prayers bore no fruit and we arrived at the harbour earlier than anticipated. It was cloudy and dark, and we spent a few hours at an old mansion waiting till we could board the ship. Though no one could fill Nezhat's place, Khadijeh had become a good companion during the course of our journey; she had olive skin and abundant black hair. Her French wasn't up to Nezhat's standard either. She claimed that she could play the piano but I was confident that she would have been no match for Nezhat's music. However, she was *equally* kind. We both felt seasick on the ship and had to rest in bed looking pale; Khadijeh's nanny would come to our bedside trying to alleviate her worries by murmuring prayers. My mother had clearly asked her to look after me as well. Whenever I was anxious, homesick or sad she would come and sit by me and hold my hand. She would then tease me so much that in the end I would manage a smile.

The first night on the boat I had insomnia. I got up and turned up the lantern, picked up my diary and started to write to her, to Mother, although I had no idea where she was, or what she was doing.

What is this, this folded paper that bears diagonal and straight lines? Mother, what is this that you've put in a velvet pouch, which you always wore round your neck? Which prayer can protect me, floating like a piece of straw on the angry waves? Since you have wished it and asked me always to carry it with me, I shall, and as long as I live I shall not part with it. Whenever I am lonely, I open the pouch. I kiss your ring and place it on my eye. I then close my eyes, hoping the genie may emerge and appear before me with folded arms, awaiting my command and desires. Then I could ask for you.

How many letters shall I write to you? In the past week since our departure, I have written every day. These letters were then handed to the courier who is supposed to bring them to you. What have I written? Nothing except that I kiss my gracious Mother's hand, and that I, your humble servant, have no worries except not being able to see you. But this is not what I really wanted to tell you. I would be lying if I said I had no worries: I do! Every time this restless and anxious convoy stops, everyone wants to reach the boat as quickly as possible to be able to escape all the problems. Though with every step I take away from you, I feel I am taking a step to non-existence. When I received your letter in Qazvin, I felt a sharp pain in my chest. I then had a devious thought: I wanted to escape. So I went to the vineyard and sat in a corner. I wanted to leave the convoy and reach you; I wanted to go to Nezhat's grave. Could you not let me hide somewhere near you, in the dark passageway

> behind the room that led to the moat? I would have preferred the darkness where I felt close to you. Could you not let me remain in Khaleh's room? I would have been content if you came to spend even one night a week with me so that I could see you. And when I thought of escaping, I slowly went towards the wall. I sat in a corner and took out your letter, 'Khanoumi, my dear daughter' ... and I could hear your voice in my ears, and then as though you had read my mind, 'Soon you shall go abroad and I shall join you.'
>
> I know I shall never see you again; I know I shall have to make do with the thought of you. If your comfort and peace of mind is dependent on my being away from you then I give in.

I repeated this to myself and then returned to the task. I went to the tank, put some water on my face and then lost myself amid the children's chatter and Nanny's concern.

> I decided whenever being away became unbearable, I'd talk to you; I'd write about whatever I fancied. This morning I wrote you yet another letter with the same pretence. And now we've come to this large ship. 'The sea is magnificent' I had read in books. Now I am like Sinbad, and the worldly Venetian Marco Polo whose story Nezhat read to us. I am sitting in the cabin of a ship, which will sail off when the Shah arrives tomorrow. When I swung one leg onto the boat and lifted the other from land it was as though something tore apart in me. When I was on land, our homeland, I seemed still to be connected to you, but when we left the Anzali shores,[8] all connections were lost. It was a good thing that the rain was falling and washed away my tears so that no one could discover my secret.

A week had now passed from the day I saw my father's carriage with Heidar on top watching me depart. What a week for a little girl, an indescribable turmoil! My cries were lost amid the tearful parting of the convoy of hundreds. Everyone had a reason to be in a state of terror: the princes who had lost their palaces and servants anxious for what the future held for them, as well as embarking on a perilous journey to an unfamiliar destination.

The Iranian people had risen and as far as they were concerned this was the convoy of a bloodthirsty and despotic Shah who had committed a great many murders for the sake of maintaining his grip on the throne, and was now being driven out of his country in disgrace and misery.

Travelling in the same convoy were men and women whose destinies had obliged them to leave their homes; each of them had different problems from the others. In every stopover we had so far been sheltered from the comings and goings and the watchful eyes. The Indian guards sent from the embassy to guard His Highness always searched the house. The rest of the convoy would then scatter in the surrounding houses on the estate. At times, they would also camp somewhere in the grounds. As soon as we arrived, chaos would break out. Certain individuals would arrive: they either wanted to speak to someone from our convoy, or they were merely friends delivering messages. Some were merchants who had come to trade. Anxious creditors rushed to our compound and demanded what they were due or demanded signatures on the documents relating to the debt.

Every morning there was a never-ending commotion. In every house some departed and others joined. No one understood me or had any idea what I was going through. The princesses who were in the same age group as me couldn't wait to go abroad, but when the uproar increased they became terrified. Very early on I discovered that when Mother let go of me I became a loner and my only companions were the pages that were darkened daily with my writing. The evenings were best because I could drown in the darkness and the silence it offered. At times I put Mother's ring on, or squeezed the velvet pouch and dreamed of the genie that would appear, take my hand and take me home. Occasionally, I was so absorbed in my dreams that I actually saw myself on the roof of Father's quarters looking at my father, who was resting on his wooden bed. Every night I dreamed of Mother, and sometimes of Nezhat, who had rested her head on Mother's knees with her golden hair spread at her feet. Some mornings I wished I would never wake up again, but then I told myself, 'Khanoum, remember your mother went through a great deal of trouble for you to distance yourself from Tehran.' What I really wanted, though, was to find out why Mother had been in such a hurry to take me to the embassy and leave me with the Empress, and why I had to be taken on such a long journey. The questions were never-ending.

CHAPTER 23

We had been waiting on the boat for some time. Everyone seemed anxious but the children were oblivious. Having to deal with seasickness made everyone impatient and there was no news. The boys were more at ease and managed to entertain themselves without difficulty. One day I saw them taking a stroll on the deck and I even saw one of them attempt to shoot a goose, but *we* were told not to leave our cabins. The weather was unsuitable and the ship could not sail. Night fell. Khadijeh and I huddled together on the same bed and tried to use our imagination to amuse ourselves. When she fell asleep I reflected that she was the daughter of the Shah and had to accompany her parents on this trip, but why me? Why did I have to come along with a convoy with no clear future ahead of it? Was Mother right to think that this was the only solution for me?

We tried to relieve the suffocating humidity by fanning ourselves and telling each other stories. Khadijeh's nanny, a kind old woman who did everything for us, always smiled and always seemed to have an anecdote up her sleeve. I called her Nanny Khanoum but the others called her Nanny Khàj, a name made up by Etezad, the Shah's eldest son. He had given a name to everyone and each had a meaning with specific connotations. She reminded me of my own Nanny, whose whereabouts at that moment I was not sure of. All I knew was that she was sitting somewhere and weeping; I could actually hear her somewhere in my mind.

I had asked my mother to look after her and Mother had said, 'Yes, yes.' What did she mean by this 'Yes, yes'?

Nanny whispered in my ear that I might be leaving the convoy. Not only was I unconcerned, having no questions for her; deep down I was rather happy. It was the Empress, however, who clarified the situation.

I entered the largest cabin on the ship, which I took for some floating palace. There were several portholes overlooking the sea and when one stood by them one could hear the sound of the waves. The Empress was resting on a magnificent bed and, as usual, refused to let me kiss her hand. She didn't look well; she looked pale and seasick, and invited me to sit on the edge of the bed. I was anxious. The maid who always accompanied her was asked to leave the room and I consequently felt the air became heavy. I felt that she had a great deal to talk about but neither her state of health nor her anxiety made it possible for her to do so, nor was I worthy of hearing it all. She was hesitant but said that the reason behind our one-day delay was that my father had discovered I was with them. He had gone to His Majesty and asked that I be returned to him. As the Empress broke the news to me, I was overcome with resentment; the possibility of him taking me away made me shudder.

I became daring and asked, 'Has my mother arrived as well?'

The Empress shook her head in disappointment.

'I wish she could come.'

After moments of silence she sat up declaring she was not going to let go of me. As she had promised my mother, she was going to take me with her and look after me.

'Your poor mother ...'

On the other hand, with unusual resentment, she referred to my father as 'That man'.

What could I say? I simply lowered my head and listened. The Empress informed me that my father had even gone as far as seeing the Russian Ambassador, but his request had been rejected.

'You shall become my own daughter and there is no need for anyone to recognise you as anything other,' and, indeed, so it was stated in my travel document.

'Whatever His Majesty feels appropriate,' I uttered quietly.

I didn't ask what my mother's wishes were as I already knew. The Empress talked of my 'poor' mother and how much she wished me to leave Iran. Then, seeming faint and too weak to continue, she closed her eyes. I went forward and pecked at her soft white hands and said: 'I shall be indebted to Her Majesty all my life,' at which she smiled and caressed my hair.

When the ship finally sailed and the sound of the cannon was heard, I had become the daughter of an Empress and a deposed Shah, who from then on were fugitives. Once the imperial Russian ship's horn was heard as the vessel left the shore, the passengers, having been able to leave the country in one piece, screamed with joy. After two days at sea we were slowly getting used to our seasickness and colour was returning to my face.

In the first letter I wrote to my mother aboard the ship, I explained everything, including all that I had heard from Nanny. Nanny's husband had disclosed to her that my father had fallen at His Majesty's feet and complained that he had lost his daughter, claiming that he had heard from someone that I was hiding in His Majesty's convoy.

The Shah had pulled a face and said, 'I don't suppose you would wish to search our harem, would you?!'

Father's entreaties to the other princes and courtiers had not proved fruitful either. For a convoy terrified and desperate to leave a country in chaos, this incident had been worrisome. It was said that the court minister had warned the Shah that if my father resorted to going to the Russian Ambassador, this could have grave implications for His Majesty. When I was writing this to Mother, I asked myself why Father had come to get me? Why would the beast want me? Was he not the one who had ruined our lives because of his whim for my little Nezhat? I put my pen down and thought of Mother, who had crouched down under his beating and curses. She was, nonetheless, not prepared to leave Nezhat in his clutches. Was the Empress aware of this when she referred to 'That man'? Was the Empress privy to the incidents in our home? Had Mother disclosed to the Empress how Nezhat had committed suicide to heighten the sense of urgency so that she let me go with them? Had she told her what terrible things had happened to Nezhat? But now that Nezhat was lying under a slab, everyone was told that she had gone mad and shot herself. But why was Mother so frightened? Why did she hide me and why did she let go of me so that I could pursue a different destiny under a different name? I desperately wanted the answers. Would I be able to conceal Nezhat's saga from everyone all my life?

I was staring through the porthole, looking at the water flowing on either side of the ship and foaming on the surface. I was thinking about my future when I saw Nezhat's face in the waves. It seemed as though she had found a way out of the bottom of the well and into the sea, and before parting had come to see me. I was doing exactly as she had asked me: I was going far away.

'You must leave and become a liberated soul, not an animal in a cage. You must live for me as well.'

The ship was sailing away with me further and further from my homeland, my mother and the beast. It seemed to me that the watchful eyes of Nezhat and Mother were accompanying me. So I had to be strong.

'I promise Nezhat, I promise …'

The image of the Shah I had carried in my head thus far was as sinister as my father's, though more so and more cruel. From what Nezhat had told me and the pamphlets I had read, I recalled that all the killings and ruins were a result of the unjustifiable demands of this man who did not want to recognise the people's rights. He could not comprehend that people wanted democracy and a court of justice. They wanted their country to become like one in the Western world, and didn't wish to be in chains and kept in cages like animals. I had noticed the way my father and my uncles had treated the servants and maids. They didn't consider ordinary people normal human beings and took it for granted that those like Nassir had a duty to stir the water in the pool right up till dawn so that the sound of frogs did not disturb them, or had to spend hours standing in heaps of snow with folded arms so that they were at Khan's service while he and his friends played cards or drank, with the roars of their laughter reverberating through the entire estate.

When I thought that I was part of a convoy that was regarded with resentment, I profoundly cursed my father. I had seen too many unhappy and dissatisfied people in the months leading up to the revolution. Remembering Soltan's face in mourning for her son Ebrahim, beating her chest to relieve her pain, made me resent the Shah. After all, was he not the root of all the problems? He was the one who, upon becoming Shah, had shouted at his own sister, my darling aunt, in the imperial palace. Was he not the one who took the pistol off his Cossacks so that he could personally fire at people when someone had thrown a bomb at his carriage? These were innocent people who had merely come to see the pageant. He was the one who had gone to the Imperial Gardens and had the cannon target the parliament and had so many people hanged as well. Despite hearing how miserable my mother and Nezhat had been, he had effectively sold Nezhat to my father because my father sympathised with his views. The Shah, therefore, up to the day at the embassy, to my mind was a complete monster. That day, however, I saw his true self, the one that was no longer in a palace surrounded by servants and Cossacks. He was sitting on a bench by the pool with Malakeh Iran, on the ground, holding his hands. I saw the Shah weep and beg his aunt's forgiveness for destroying her palace and life.

'Oh darling aunt, please forgive me; they fooled me, and this is what they have done to me; I wish to die, Auntie ...'

That day I was so absorbed in saying goodbye to my mother, and so concerned about my future, that it never occurred to me what an extraordinary scene I was witnessing while standing by the door in a room at the Russian Embassy. It didn't seem of any significance then but it came to make sense later on. In the days that followed, at the embassy or en route, I occasionally recalled that scene, wondering how much people could change according to their circumstances.

Up to then I had divided people into two categories: monsters and angels; they either oppressed or were oppressed; they either raped like my father or were raped like Nezhat. I must have been quite a phenomenon: the result of the union of the devil and an angel such as Mother. I reached this conclusion through the books that I had read and the foreign stories that Nezhat had read to us.

At the Russian Embassy, however, seeing the deposed Shah seeking refuge under the Russian flag, shaking like the branches of a willow tree, weeping and asking forgiveness from his aunt, I began to realise that both evil and angelic characteristics coexisted within human beings, though both were not expressed at the same time. Malakeh Iran, having spent the day in our house talking of her beliefs and seeking help from her Lord, had had her life ruined on the day the parliament was bombed. She had, later on, gathered everyone around her and spoken of life's uncertainties. She was the same woman at the Russian Embassy, as though nothing had happened. I could see from her expression that she had forgiven the Shah and was being compassionate towards him. She was fiddling with her rosary and giving reassurance to the demon that had now metamorphosed into an innocent lamb. She was urging him to believe in God and ask Him for salvation and guidance.

One day, when we were still at the embassy, the other children and I had gathered in a room when we were alarmed by the sound of sobbing in the park. We went to see what was going on. On the veranda we saw the deposed Shah embracing Ahmad, the heir to the throne, and crying inconsolably. He was in a much worse state than the Empress. They wanted to take Ahmad along. His overweight body had made him short of breath and he was in tears while clinging to his mother's skirt. He was begging to be allowed to go with them but an Arab, whose master was a Russian, was standing there ignoring the outpouring of emotion. I had heard from the nanny and servants that the nationalists now recognised Ahmad as Shah and that he had to remain in Tehran, but Muhammad Ali Shah and the Empress were unhappy and did not want to part with him. *We* were upset as well. I didn't see why I could not stay behind; now that Ahmad was Shah I could stay in Tehran.

I remembered Nezhat telling me, 'Once you become Ahmad's wife, he'll be Shah one day and you the Empress, and then you'll be free.'

Nezhat, who resented power and considered it the root of all evil, wished me a happy future living next to my overweight and harmless cousin. By doing so I could make a difference to the lives of others. If that was the case, then how come the Empress did not stop his entreaties? I couldn't answer these questions nor was Nezhat there to deal with them as she had done for so many years. I had no choice but to go about discovering life and people on my own, and I had to learn how they became transformed in different situations.

In the course of our journey, I could sense the resentment towards the dethroned and fugitive Shah from the way people looked and behaved. But when the ship began to sail it was as though he was liberated from his fears and I saw him on deck on the second day staring into the faraway waters while speaking to Khan Baba Khan, a loyal supporter of the imperial family. The others, even the British captain and the Russian general, stood courteously with folded arms, but the Shah had become thin and weak; he seemed to have shrunk, too, despite his top hat. Once in

Baku, we watched him, accompanied by the Russian army officers, board a boat heading for the shore. Despite the officers standing to attention to salute him, he was no longer the man who had shouted at Nezhat in the imperial palace. The more I saw of him in Baku the more it sank in that when men shed their borrowed 'lion' attire and become their true selves, they are completely different people. He no longer seemed the devil he had been.

CHAPTER 24

B y the time we arrived in Baku and boarded the train we were already feeling different. Up until then, none of us had travelled on a train. The *Machine Doudy*, the first train-like vehicle used in Iran, which we used to take to go to the shrine on the outskirts of Tehran, bore no resemblance to the one that was now taking us through the woods; it was more like a wind-up toy car. Whenever we took the Thursday-night *Machine Doudy* to go to Rey, my mother made sure that the whole vehicle was at our disposal: the guards would keep the ordinary people at bay until we managed to reach our compartment, the interior of which had been upholstered in red and the seats covered in leather. We would pass through vegetable plots, harvest stacks, fields of melon and modest houses made of mud brick covered with thatch. And that was all we would see until we arrived.

The train we boarded in Baku, however, was a long train, billowing out steam whenever the whistle was blown. Before the first hour was up we arrived in a tunnel; the darkness terrified us until we got used to it. The Shah, the Empress and the courtiers who had fled the terrors of Tehran, were beginning to feel at ease once again and the sense of relief made them happy. As a constant reminder of how fortunate we were to have survived our journey, the Empress kept praising the Lord, as though she could not believe they had survived the turmoil, their enemies and the shooting. The Shah was quiet and occasionally helped himself to some food. His attire was similar to everyone else's, without

medals or any kind of decoration. We kept our *chadors* on until
the evening, when the curtains fell. At night, exhausted from
several sleepless nights on the sea and the humid, greasy air of
Baku, I managed to fall asleep with the sound of the wheels on the
rails, a little like the tick-tock of a clock. Once again I dreamed of
my mother, just as I had done every night since I parted from her.
I saw her in front of the embassy pulling me out of the carriage.
Then we passed through the Indian and Russian guards; later
she placed me in a cradle and started to rock it. The sound of
the swinging became repetitive and her voice slowly began to fill
my ears. She wasn't screaming or sobbing any more, nor was she
pulling her hair out. She was calm, and in her voice I could sense
the peace reminiscent of my childhood. I was about to ask her not
to leave me or to go to the sitting room. I wanted her to stay in
the *goushvareh*. I wanted to open my eyes and see the moon
ambushed among the poplars and the sycamores in front of
Father's quarters but, hard as I tried, I couldn't open my eyelids.

When Khadijeh's nanny called me, I found myself imaging
the warmth of a bowlful of hot milk, just as my own nanny used to
bring me. Alas, she was Khadijeh's nanny and we had to get up; it
was daytime. The monotonous sound on the rails was a reminder
that I was one more night further from our home. I had no idea
where my mother was or in which bed she slept. Had Morvarid
let Mother's hair loose? Was she wearing her pink nightwear
or had she huddled under her blanket still dressed, as on those
nightmarish nights in Nanny's house where she jumped at the
slightest sound?

A special compartment had been allocated for our use and
another for our luggage, which was tightly packed into the space,
with Khan Baba keeping an account of the number of boxes and
then checking it against his book. The guards were seated in the
adjoining compartment to the front. On arrival in every station
they emerged and checked our compartment, making sure all
was well. We were still wary since we had heard that the Shah's

enemies, the constitutionalists, had supporters everywhere. Khadijeh was concerned about her parents and would pose questions as to when we were going to be free to live like other people, free of fear. I, on the contrary, would occasionally close my eyes so that I could speak to Mother. Khadijeh and Nanny did tell me that I had a habit of speaking in my sleep; apparently I jumped and at times sweated heavily. They had no idea what images passed in front of my eyes and what bliss it was that no one else could be present in another's sleep.

The further the train went the cooler and more humid the air became. We would open the windows and watch the woods, which paraded by at great speed. At times we would even see fair women with their heads uncovered, and strong red-faced men who waved at us. Despite the speed at which the train was moving, we did not have permission to wave back. Khadijeh, who occasionally forgot the orders, would remove her scarf and wave it at the children or the grown-ups on the farms. She would then be reminded by the Empress or her Nanny that a princess had to behave with decorum, even when there was no one present, and must be forever composed, serious and gracious.

'You are no longer children,' we were reminded wherever we went; we had always to remember that we were members of an imperial family.

Every time the train came to a halt at a station the curtains were immediately drawn across the windows. Our stop would occasionally drag on and, from the sounds coming from outside, we guessed that some formalities were taking place. A couple of times the Shah, dressed in formal attire, got off the train and, adopting a stately gait, exchanged a few words with those who had come to pay their respects; a few times his hosts went to his private compartment. The Empress on these occasions joined us to sneak a view through the slit in between the curtains. The two Russian and British officers and a few Indians always stood at attention by his side. Initially, I thought the poor Shah enjoyed this pomp and ceremony but when the train started to move again I would hear him say to the Empress: 'I am tired of all this and feel unwell. Damn the wretched monarchy! I wish we were ordinary members of the public. The bastards look at me as though condemning me for losing my seat and crown.'

Having completely forgotten our presence, the Empress tried to console him.

'That's enough! You are moaning like some old woman. What's wrong with being paid respect; don't complain, it'll all be over in a few days.' At which Khadijeh and I would exchange a look that asked whether it really would be over in a few days.

Once the train had stopped in Odessa we observed yet another welcoming ceremony, but it was to be the last. The neat rows of Russian officers were playing some military tune and then their commander, who was carrying a sword gleaming in the sunlight, shouted out something in Russian and they all disappeared. The commander and the Shah got into a white carriage and then we were allowed to go and sit in another carriage, which looked more like a large black coffin. When its doors closed and the black curtains were drawn, it was pitch black inside, and when the carriage began to move I felt sick. I kept pressing Mother's wrapped bundle to myself in an effort not to vomit. I really wanted the curtains drawn back but this was not possible.

When we finally arrived at our destination I ran to a corner and vomited and then, feeling rather embarrassed, tried to pull myself together. Khadijeh and Nanny rushed to see how I was. I looked pale and my head was swimming. Abdollah, the eunuch, lifted me in his arms and carried me up the stairs. I was shaken by the image before me: we had arrived in a mansion where we were to spend many years to come. What an inauspicious start! But when the sun rose and the next day began, I felt this was going to become the best chapter of my life; I had to grow up in this place, break away from the past and await the future; the shrouds of secrecy were going to be lifted to reveal what was from then on going to be translated into the grown-ups' language. Once inside, I anxiously opened my eyes to a place that was to become the bridge connecting my childhood to my adult life.

The mansion was situated on a hilltop that faced a mountain covered in trees on one side and, on the other, overlooked the sea, the Black Sea, the black colour of which was only one of the many shades it adopted in the course of day and night. The mansion was not only large enough to accommodate our group of about thirty but could hold twice the number in the day.

The day after our arrival, by which time I had emerged from my sickbed, we had unpacked and the women were to have a wash as though the beginning of our new life had to be celebrated in the *hammam*. A screen divided the terracotta-painted mansion to create a receiving area and an inner sanctum. On the very first day, two female servants entered our service. Nadi was a Christian Russian and resembled the women I had seen in the summer residence of the Russian Embassy back in Tehran. She was a large woman with a fair complexion and wore a white apron and a scarf. Jamileh, on the contrary, was olive-skinned and a Muslim from Georgia; she was reserved and had a melancholy look. In the bathroom they both kept their clothes on while we got changed.

The bathroom resembled a house in itself. I remembered Tehran with all the bitter details and kept comparing everything with our new home; the bathroom seemed a little larger than Soltan's garden, also with a well, and when I looked inside it I saw Nezhat with her golden locks floating on the water.

I could have felt happy that day if only I had not harboured the old thoughts: if only Mother and Nezhat had been there.

'Why, oh why? Did you not promise we'd go and see the world together? And now ... I wish you could twist and turn, and laugh in this round bathroom with its high ceiling and white marble interior. They are beginning to play a rhythm and sing so that they can wash off some three years' worth of desolation, war, fear and anxiety. Khadijeh's nanny has removed her usual black dress and her wrinkled flesh is on display; she looks as though she has come out of her shell and is playing the *zarb*, our main percussion instrument. I wish you were here to listen to Khan Baba Khan's wife reciting poetry. The Empress's hair is being dyed with henna and there is a platter of grapes and pomegranates in front of her. Mother, you couldn't stop Morvarid's singing in this place!'

'Light is pouring in through the domed ceiling; Nanny, you are not here to mind the prying eyes, possibly peeping from the top. There is a small silver pan on the steps that descend into the pool of cold water, and I am carrying my wrapped bundle which Mother left me. Alas, Nanny isn't here to sprinkle jasmine in it, nor can I spot Zivar and her scissors to sort my hair out.'

They sang and danced all day long. Nadi and Jamileh watched in amazement and came and went with a smile. By the time we emerged from the bathroom the red sun seemed to have fallen on the sea. Khadijeh and I went upstairs to our room from where we could see the sea through the windows. I placed Mother's photograph – which had been taken standing by Shah Baba, who had a 'smaller me' wearing my scarf sitting on his knee – on the chimneypiece. I kissed the photograph and went towards the window to look at the sea, which resembled a heated platter of copper, as feverish-looking as my heart. At that moment I could never have imagined spending a thousand days looking at the same scene. Perhaps if I had known I might not have been so eager to look at it! Khadijeh had rosy cheeks and came to my side to look at the view. She immediately understood that I was about to burst into tears so she offered her shoulder.

Mother I miss you so; my happiness cannot be complete without you; I cannot take in any beauty without your presence. It seems to me I am on that sailing boat on the sea, completely alone on its copper-glazed surface. I can't see the mermaid in Nezhat's poems, and I can't feel the sea breeze that caressed the mermaid's hair. I wish my mermaid would find a way out of the well in Khaleh's house and come to this sea.

No Nanny, I am not hungry. Please could you seek permission for me to stay here? No, I haven't forgotten my prayers. I have done *vozou* (the cleansing ritual before prayer) and I have a few things to say when I am praying. I have a wish. The white prayer *chador* which Mother has left in the wrapped bundle is there on the shelf. I want to place her ring on my finger when I am reciting my prayers. I know that on the other side of the mountains someone is standing to pray in the sitting room. She's pulled her *chador* on her face and has remained that way for some time. Perhaps she'll come tonight to sleep next to me in this bed, stroking my hair while talking to me.

'Khanoum Khanoumha, my yum-yum.'

The sailing boat is not there and the sea is black and I can only hear the sound of its waves. I must close the window so that I do not catch a chill. I am getting goose bumps. I can smell the scent of the jasmine in the air, the scent of the orange grove. I can't hear the frogs; Nassir is beating the water in the pool. The monster made a lot of noise diving in the water. I can hear shouting in Father's quarters. It is night again ...

We were quite busy in the week that followed our arrival. The Empress asked Khadijeh and me to be present everywhere. Trunks were opened, large Tabriz and Esfahan rugs covered the floors of every room, and the palace was slowly beginning to look like our home or that of one of my aunt's.

One day I asked the Empress, 'Where will Mother stay when she arrives?'

She turned to me and stroked my head, leaving it to me to find the answer.

Then, trying hard to keep her composure, she said, 'We have ample space, my dear, ample!'

She was right: there was a lot of space. We had turned two rooms into storage where the finely woven *termeh* cloths and other precious ornaments were kept. Planks of wood had been nailed to the window frames inside to block the view, also for security. A month later I, too, came into possession of a trunk and the Empress ordered my name to be inscribed on it. My mother had sent this trunk and it contained a few shawls, a prayer *chador* and a few dresses that had clearly been sewn by my mother's seamstress. I imagined Mirza Yaqoub, who would occasionally come to our house along with his assistant carrying rolls of foreign and colourful fabrics, all of which usually remained in our house and were stored behind the sitting room. Every so often Mother would take one of them out and have Badri sew it.

When the trunk arrived there was also a letter from Mother, who, as usual, cherished her daughter and made false promises; the beloved child wished she could believe in these promises. I opened the trunk and pulled out everything, while Khadijeh and her nanny looked on. I wanted to see the photograph, which had been taken by the court photographer in Shah Baba's presence, in which Nezhat and I were seated on a large cushion. I wanted many things, though I could only find a few books among the shawls, *termeh* and a prayer mat. There was also another wooden box that I had been asked to pass on to the Empress, which I did. The Empress opened the box there and then; out came a string of pearls and a gold bracelet that I was familiar with. This was the bracelet that Nezhat had given me and that I had left behind in Tehran. Of all the things that could be a reminder of Nezhat, Mother had somehow chosen this.

The following week a seamstress was sitting in the hallway on the second floor making dresses for everyone. Every Saturday Khan Baba Khan would go shopping in the city centre, and bring us anything we asked for. Little by little our rooms were filling up. When it wasn't raining or too warm we would sit on the balcony. Late afternoons, most days, the Shah would come to our quarters.

I had by then come to conclude that he was no more than a wary and feeble soul. When the weather became milder, he and the Empress would sit on the large stiff cushions in the salon puffing away at their hookahs with the children sitting around. Others sometimes joined us for supper, after which Khan Baba Khan's wife would tell our fortune.

We had a lot of spare time and the days passed slowly. The best times were when we had new arrivals from Tehran and when we received news. This was much better than the stories Etezad and the other two boys would bring from their daily trips to school. We considered them most fortunate to be able to socialise with the people outside our compound; indeed, we were envious of their tales of the outside world. We were given the same books to study at home, as a result of which our knowledge of French, History and Geography didn't fall short of the boys'. We, however, felt like prisoners; we didn't even know what went on in the receiving area or who the guests were. The only thing we managed to work out, by looking at the copious lunches and dinners that were prepared, was their large numbers. These visitors came from Iran; they would spend the night in hotels but in the daytime they'd be with the Shah.

We had not completely forgotten the nightmare of our last days in Tehran and occasionally talked about it. Tehran had, in those last days, brought me into contact with the harshest realities of life. Now, however, I missed it. On the face of it, I may have become a member of the Shah's family, but I always dreamed of my home, that damned establishment with the ominous Father's quarters. When I slept, in my dream, I would ask the others where Mother was. Sometimes, at dawn, with her bruised and beaten face, and her torn *chador*, she would come and pull the blanket over me. Alas, she never stayed.

Winter caught us by surprise. The bitter cold blowing from the sea kept us indoors and under the *korsi* most days. The Shah would join his wife and speak of the letters he'd received from

Iran. One evening he read a letter written by Ahmad, who was 'paying his respects' and 'kissing his parents' hands'. At the end of his letter he had also included me: 'Her ladyship is always on my mind', at which I lowered my head.

'His Majesty thinks of everyone,' and, with that said, the Empress was, as ever, swallowing her tears.

'Why don't you write a letter to His Majesty?' Khadijeh whispered later that evening. I hadn't even thought about it. I was actually mindful of what the Empress thought. I occasionally had the picture of Ahmad's face in my head, but it seemed as though I was even banned from thinking about him. Moreover, I was no longer the princess back in Tehran; like everyone else in that mansion I was floating on the sea, and such a letter only occasionally passed through my head. If, indeed, writing a letter were permissible, no doubt the Empress would have reminded me by now.

CHAPTER 25

I can't remember whether it was that winter or the following one. The arrival of a letter from Tehran dealing with financial and property matters seemed to have angered the Shah and he kept cursing someone I didn't know. He then turned to the Empress and said: 'Wait till I get to Tehran, I shall teach the bastard a lesson he will never forget.'

I had just got used to not expecting every courier to bring me a letter from Mother. We would occasionally go for a boat ride and see the sights. Nadi had told us exciting stories about St Petersburg, the capital, and we could not wait to see it. It was as though we no longer thought of our return to Tehran. The Shah, however, conducted meetings on a daily basis with a number of Iranians and Russians; only a month later we bade him farewell when he embarked on a journey to Europe. At the time all we could think of were the presents he would bring us from foreign lands.

The only men left behind were Khan Baba and a sturdy Russian who took the Empress's orders and effectively looked after us. The Empress spent a great deal of time receiving people in the reception area; I hadn't the faintest idea who they were and couldn't have cared less what was going on. From time to time news of the Shah's travels reached us. We heard he had gone to Vienna; we even received a chest full of presents. As soon as General Khabayev's wife saw us in European dresses she was thrilled and started to clap her hands; she was so delighted to see us 'dressed like dolls' that she immediately sat behind the piano and played some Russian tunes. She then noticed that everyone was clapping hands rather than dancing, at which point she leapt up from the piano to take our hands and make us dance in the middle of the room. I was twelve by then and had grown taller than the other girls of my age. Our teacher at school had promised to teach us dancing, but though I kept looking at the Empress to see whether she minded our dancing I couldn't read any expression in her face. Wearing a white scarf, she was seated on the sofa and was clapping her hands like everyone else, but we knew her mind was elsewhere.

In the two months that followed we stuck to the routine: our days began with the tutors followed by embroidery and cookery. We would then do music in female company. One evening, Khadijeh and I noticed a bundle of newspapers in the reception room. We took them to our room so that we could read them in secret. There had been a reshuffle in the cabinet and there were reports of uprisings in different regions, conflict in the parliament, terror and general unrest. The reports were of no use to us, however, because we didn't understand the implications. One newspaper had a special report on His Majesty's birthday, for which Tehran had been illuminated and receptions held in the imperial palace. I searched for his picture but couldn't find one; at that time, Iranian tabloids, unlike their Ottoman counterparts, did not have any pictures.

'Did you know when His Majesty's birthday was?'

No, I didn't know, but the question made me ponder: I had not had any news of him for some time now. Every time the Empress received letters she would become emotional reading her eldest son's.

'His Majesty has asked after you,' she would tell the rest of us.

That was all, but why didn't I pick up a pen and write? Whatever had happened to our engagement? For some time now no one had spoken of it, except Khadijeh, and that was purely out of girlish curiosity.

One day the Empress received an envelope full of photographs, which she pored over one by one. Later that evening Khadijeh picked up the photographs and we went to our room. His Majesty was quite rotund now; he was holding a walking-stick, just as the grown-ups did, and the crown prince stood behind him, tall and upright with a cocked hat. They were both surrounded by a group of elderly men, arms folded, who looked like court tutors. I wondered what it would have been like if I had remained in Tehran. Had it not been for the demon destroying our lives I'd now be in the imperial palace. Then I pictured my mother fiddling with my hair and preparing me for the crown prince's visit as she had done when he came to see us in Tehran. Oh Nezhat, I wish you were here! You so wanted me to taste life; you read to me and spoke of the world's great empires.

The pictures from Tehran took me, once again, back to the city I still dreamed of. A year had passed and yet I could not rid my mind of Nezhat, Mother, the beast, our home, the stuffed heads of goats hanging on the walls of the salon, the grand piano, Nanny, Madame and the precarious last few days.

The Shah was no longer in Europe, we heard from the Empress, but had gone to Iran to fight for the crown. He had gone to open the way for our return, Nanny said, so we could once again live in the imperial palace and be the imperial family. By now the Empress's anxiety was palpable and she kept pacing the room. One of the maids would offer her herbal tea to calm her down. It was not difficult to work out what went through her mind when she held the rosary and sat down to pray. Naturally, we soon lost interest in our studies and Javad Khan, our new tutor, clearly sympathised and was quite lenient with us. No one really felt at home in that mansion. I was, perhaps, the only one who welcomed the idea of returning to Tehran despite all the bitter memories. Khadijeh wanted to see other countries and Etezad claimed that even if everyone else returned to Tehran, he would go to Europe to continue with his education.

The whisperings behind closed doors eventually came to an end as the situation in Tehran unfolded and our destiny with it. The Empress and the general's wife cursed the British on the grounds that the constitutionalists were receiving their orders from Britain. According to the Empress, her husband's enemies had conflicting interests and were now paying for their deeds. When we had been in Rasht, we had heard that Nouri had been hanged. The news had distressed everyone and they unanimously blamed Abdollah. The Empress believed that Abdollah had had Taqi Zadeh murdered and that the holy men of Najaf had cursed him. Even though he was a member of the parliament he had fled to Europe. When we were in Tehran we knew that, among the parliamentarians, Taqi Zadeh was the Shah's staunch enemy; during the shelling of the parliament the Shah had sent the Cossacks to find him. Had he not sought refuge in an embassy they would have assassinated him.

I would read the news and then explain everything to Khadijeh. She didn't know anyone and didn't have a clue. I reminded her that she should not curse just any old constitutionalist or parliamentarian.

The news continued to be disturbing: having assassinated Atabak earlier at his home, the state forces, plus the Bakhtiari troops, had now launched an attack on Atabak Park, where Sattar Khan, Bagher Khan and the rest of the Turks were based. The next day, in the reception room, we mentioned the news to the Empress. I had heard a great many extraordinary tales about Sattar. I knew that my father and uncle, along with a large army of soldiers, had not been able to take Tabriz despite a long battle. My uncle had had to part with the throne as a result and had ended up in the Russian Embassy. Sattar had become a hero, just like the heroes of the French Revolution, whose bravery Nezhat used to recount to me. I didn't know just how long it had been after we had left before Sattar and Bagher had arrived in Tehran, but I could imagine the lengths people had gone to in erecting victory arches and sacrificing numerous cows to celebrate their arrival. Hearing the news of their assassination now hardly made sense. The Empress considered it the well-deserved fate of all those who had opposed His Majesty and made us homeless. I had no choice but to conceal my feelings, but I tried to draw my own conclusions: after expelling our convoy, the constitutionalists must have developed conflicting interests and begun to fight amongst themselves.

The next day the papers had a large picture of Azod the Regent above reports of his death; the white-bearded man was the head of the Qajar clan and the young Shah's guardian. I continually searched for news of Ahmad, but there was little or nothing more than that he had attended the opening of a new establishment or the parading of the troops. One evening Khadijeh was looking at the sea through the window in our room and I was drawing.

'I imagine the whole nation must be welcoming my father but I find it difficult to imagine that those who so wanted us to leave have now suddenly changed their tune.'

I stopped painting and dried my brush on a piece of cloth. I knew she was upset and couldn't talk to anyone but me, just as when I felt depressed and we would carry on talking until I forgot my pain.

Despite my mixed feelings about my uncle, the thought of him having gone to a place where everyone resented him worried me. Though I had become a member of his family I couldn't disagree with *all* his enemies.

We realised that the Shah had gone to fight the state forces and, to do so, had bought artillery from other countries. Khadijeh and I were anxious: she had pictured people erecting victory arches and sacrificing sheep to mark the Shah's renewed reign; his enemies had either fled or were killed and everyone was going to be jubilant on our return. But what we were to learn shocked us. We took some of the papers the next day and slipped them under our mattresses. It was Ramadan and we were all fasting. After the sumptuous *eftar*, the first meal after sunset, with a spread dotted with butter, jam and small bowls of honey, Khadijeh and I rushed to our room only to learn that the truth was even worse than we had assumed. No wonder the Empress and the general's wife were so anxious. We learned that the Shah had adopted the name of Haj Baghdadi and, travelling aboard a Russian ship, had made a secret arrival in the north of Iran. Salar, who was reputed to be insane, had also arrived via Kerman Shah. The country was in turmoil and there were insurgencies everywhere. Mansour, Khadijeh's uncle, and one of my uncles were accompanying the Shah. Their arrival had created some excitement but their supporters were limited to a group of Azeri and Turkman clans and, other than that, everyone in Tehran opposed them.

We kept passing the newspapers back and forth. Some of the articles were so aggressive and worrisome that I preferred to keep them from her: the parliament had put a price on the heads of the Shah, Mansour and Salar, and the state forces under the command of Yeprem Khan had left Tehran to assassinate the Shah. Khadijeh was apprehensive and at times in tears; she loved her father and, although I resented mine, I sympathised with her plight.

'It is not as simple as we think. You must trust these Russian generals who support His Majesty; they are quite powerful in St Petersburg. His Majesty would not do anything without having thought it through. We are too young to understand but the grown-ups know what they are doing.'

But Khadijeh was quite right when she screamed through her tears, 'They have far less wisdom than us; damn the throne, why does he want it anyway? What's wrong with my brother being the Shah?'

When, early the next day, the Empress met us for the meal just before the day's fasting began, she noticed Khadijeh's puffy eyes and, surprisingly, shared the same opinion.

We had performed our prayers and returned to our room. The Empress, still in her nightwear since it was quite early, wrapped her white prayer *chador* around her waist and came in.

'Men never grow up; they behave like children. When you grow into adults you will see for yourselves!'

What a strange night! Having read so many histories of the French Revolution, the storming of the Bastille and the beheading of Louis and Marie Antoinette, I was now mesmerised by the Empress; she mentioned to us that the power acquired by sitting on the throne ensured that danger was never far away. She began by talking about Napoleon, whom she considered to have been an outstanding ruler.

'He defeated the whole of Europe as well as Egypt, Africa and Asia, and became more powerful even than Genghis Khan and Alexander, but that didn't seem to satisfy him so he decided to launch an attack on Russia as well.'

Later she told us that the British had brought misery to him and, in the end, taken him prisoner.

'The British are to blame for everything.'

'Mother, are the British also opposing His Majesty?'

'Yes, but their influence does not extend to the whole world: the Russians are powerful. The Ottomans, too, have been fighting with the British; they don't much care for the Russians either but at least they stand on their own feet.'

Dawn was upon us, and we didn't seem to be able to go back to sleep, so we remained with the Empress and listened to what she had to say.

We regularly received Russian and Ottoman newspapers and sometimes also managed to get papers from Tehran and Tabriz, which we would smuggle to our room! I sometimes read well into the night; the news worried me so much at times that I could not sleep. Reading the papers slowly helped me to become aware of the realities that were usually the concern of the grown-ups alone, but we were aware of the state of the inner sanctum months before the Shah's departure. The Russian Ambassador and generals were coming and going, plus there were endless meetings and talks, and when, in the evening, the Shah had a quiet moment with the Empress he would discuss everything with her, until the day he passed under the Qur'an for luck before departing for Vienna. Once in Vienna, he sent us a postcard followed by the chests of clothes, as well as furniture, all of which was shipped from France. The papers reported that he had purchased armaments, and that he had gone from Baku straight to Astarabad. We were well aware of the day it all happened; the Empress hurriedly said goodbye and left us in Madame General's care, headed for Baku to greet the Shah. She returned some time later full of news.

The newspapers reported that, upon arrival in Astarabad, the Turkmen had gone to greet the Shah and declared their allegiance. The Prime Minister and some members of his cabinet had secretly sent a message through the Russian Ambassador that they, too, would lend a hand upon his arrival in Tehran. They had said that two years of unrest and harassment had made people impatient for the Shah's return. The nationalists and members of the parliament, however, had combined forces with those who were not prepared to accept the return of the former Shah, 'the Russians' puppet'. The parliament had placed a huge reward of 100,000 tomans on his head, and half that amount for Salar and Shoa.

The newspapers also described the details of the fighting, in which hundreds had perished on both sides when the Shah's forces, headed by Arshad, were approaching Tehran. Yeprem Khan had defeated Arshad and taken him prisoner. I had so much to tell Khadijeh about the two of them. Yeprem was the same man who had conquered Tehran when we had taken refuge at the Russian Embassy. He was considered a hero at the time and everyone talked of his bravery. Nezhat had also mentioned his name. Arshad, with his towering figure and moustache, was the subject of our conversations and gossip at bedtime back in Tehran. When I eavesdropped behind the sitting room doors or pretended to be asleep, I also overheard Mother and Nanny speak of Arshad. I knew that when Nasser al-Din Shah was alive, Arshad had directed Malijak's musical ensemble. The Shah had forced his daughter Akhtar to marry the ugly commoner Malijak, despite her mother's pleas, and she had reluctantly departed to Baharestan Palace where she led a 'happy' and affluent existence. She had earlier fallen for Arshad and despised Malijak. And when Kermani assassinated the all-powerful Shah, Akhtar, cursing her father for having imposed such a husband on her, left Baharestan for her lover's home. I was aware that my mother and her sisters were displeased with Akhtar and thought she had brought disgrace on the imperial family. Arshad was my father's hunting, gambling and late-night companion, and whenever he went to our house my mother turned her face aside. In contrast, everyone liked Malijak; 'the Honourable Commander' was a harmless, simple and kind-hearted man, who bore no resemblance to the Shah's darling boy, who was taken along on his foreign tours and always given the best place at table. We were invited to his marriage to one of Malakeh Jahan's sisters, and his daughter later became one of my playmates.

When Arshad was taken prisoner, he confessed everything to Yeprem Khan in the presence of British and Russian reporters. He even declared that the Russians had been behind it all. The next day, before he was executed, he took off his necklace and sent it to Akhtar with a smile. His execution appeared to have put an end to plans to recover the country and the Shah had escaped.[9]

When Khadijeh mentioned to the Empress that Arshad had been executed, the Empress seemed to known about it already.

She shrugged and said, 'Frivolous man! He was a nobody. In any case, this has nothing to do with your father as Tehran would have been bombed if anyone had dared touch him.'

I was old enough to know that the Empress didn't believe what she said, otherwise she would not secretly have cursed the Russians when Madame General was not about. I can't remember whether it was Khadijeh or I who asked her mother what would become of it all.

'We thought the Russians were going to help us return to Tehran and that the wretched people, having had their ears filled by the British with "national assembly" and "palace of justice" would grow dissatisfied with all the turmoil and wish to return to their homes,' the Empress responded. 'You know, these Russians, and the Ottomans even, are themselves troubled by their people making the same demands for national assemblies and justice. The Ottoman Sultan has been held prisoner in his own palace, and every day the situation is worsening here in Russia as well. It seems that life is not as it used to be; people have become rebellious.'

Khadijeh, at this point, sprang up and asked whether that meant that her father, too, would be imprisoned or killed.

'No, your father will soon return. His Majesty your brother has the reins in his hands in Tehran; pray for his well-being. Now we must get on with our lives. God willing, you'll soon go to your own home, but just put yourselves in my shoes: I'll have to put up with a dispirited man for the rest of my life. But don't you worry; if necessary I shall single-handedly manage our lives. Now you must get up; dawn is upon us, and we need to do our prayers and pray for Ahmad Shah to reign honourably. Don't be downcast; I have reports of people's love for His Majesty.'

And from then on, she would use 'His Majesty' only when she was speaking of Ahmad. So we went peacefully back to sleep thinking of my uncle's return after months of absence, even though his high hopes had all been dashed. Indeed, 'Haji Baghdadi' returned two weeks later. He had lost weight and constantly cursed everyone. In the evenings he would pace the corridors and the gardens.

The Shah's journey to and from Iran, according to the Tehran newspapers, represented a *fait accompli*. As far as our convoy was concerned, any hope of returning to Iran was dashed, and I never received any more letters from there.

CHAPTER 26

I recall an evening back in Tehran when Zahir and his family were invited to our home. The prince in his robes and copious dervish-like moustache was sitting at the top end of the reception room reciting poetry and admiring Molana, the thirteenth-century Sufi mentor. Everyone was enthralled.

'What is the meaning of this line "Whatever comes the disciple's way is meant for his prosperity"?'

Nezhat and I had written it in our diaries, something she had taught me to do.

'Sometimes the Good Lord grants good fortune by placing one's reward at the bottom of a well; one must first fall in the well, and just when one's desperation has reached an all-time low, driving one to part with life, one suddenly stumbles upon one's reward predetermined by the Lord.'

Two or three months had passed since the traumatic days of the former Shah's expedition to Iran. It was as though our convoy had finally reached its 'good fortune'; everyone except me had given up on the homeland, and the gardens of Odessa were bursting into colour. The two neighbouring gardens were purchased and the connecting walls knocked down. As well as a fathers' quarters and the beautiful old building in the middle of the park, already facing in the preferred direction of Mecca, a new building was commissioned. The walls surrounding the park were raised so that we could stroll unobserved in the park.

A grand piano arrived from Vienna with one of its legs broken en route to Odessa. This was repaired and, by the time I sat behind it, practising the forgotten tunes, it had become the means of putting my unhappiness behind me. It was then decided that Khadijeh and I should take private piano lessons with a French woman who coached the privileged young ladies at her school behind the cathedral in Odessa.

The Empress had instigated all the changes, and everyone now understood that *she* was the commander of the convoy; since his return, the morose Shah seemed to have washed his hands of his duties. He spent the days in the receiving area playing back-gammon with his usual guests and smoking the hookah. At times he also had his lunch brought to him there. In the late afternoon, when the gates of the park closed and the carriages were taken to the coachhouse, he would go back indoors. Since the addition of the new buildings, the original one had become the Empress's residence where her husband would spend the night. The Empress not only dedicated herself to dealing with household affairs assis-ted by her ladies-in-waiting and her two maids; she also supervised the affairs related to her properties in Iran. She would also spend time on business in Europe and Istanbul, and was always busy. Khan Baba Khan would arrive every morning and take note of her instructions as well as presenting the balance sheet.

Most evenings, Doctor Jarozelski, the Shah's physician, who also looked after us, was at the dinner table together with his wife and Khanbayev, the Russian general. They spoke Persian and were practically members of the family. The general was, as ever, reserved, polite and courteous to the Shah, who was by then well distanced from his throne. He treated him as though he were still Shah and the present Shah merely his adjutant.

Khadijeh and I had our own bedrooms on the second floor of one of the new buildings. There were also four other bedrooms to accommodate guests who turned up from Iran and Europe, and who would spend a couple of months in Odessa. I was growing out of my clothes and could see the changes in my body. I read, painted, played the piano, learned about housekeeping and sewing, and, from time to time, missed Iran. This usually happened once a month when there was news and talk of Iran. I had begun to experience menstrual pains ever since I had reached puberty back in Tehran; these confined me to bed and left me not fit for much. At such times I felt my mother's absence. I pictured her in the gardens of the Russian Embassy, by the pool, and remembered her injured hand and bruised face. Then the events of that God-forsaken week would begin to race through my mind: Nanny's house, Mother's screams, the monster's father's quarters, Nezhat's golden locks, her blood-stained bedding ... Everything rushed back and I woke up in a sweat. At times, while awake and in pain, I was transfixed, staring into space and reviewing the nightmare in agony. I was terrified that after experiencing the recurring nightmare night after night I might eventually become insane.

During those days of the month, the Empress always came to my bedside. We were all now in possession of shining chrome-plated Russian beds with springs. Known as *varsho* beds, they also had headboards with two flowers engraved at the top. As time passed, the Empress's manner of speaking to me at such times became more grown-up. When I was in pain, she was adept at somehow distracting me. She was effectively my only pillar of support and I knew that Khadijeh kept her informed of my state. Nevertheless, I sensed a certain barrier between us that was never lifted.

I had not received a single word from my mother for four years, nor did I even know how she was, yet the Empress never prompted a situation in which I could ask about these things. Even so, I knew the day would finally arrive – and indeed it did. The Empress seemed to have waited for years to break two things to me, one of which was to ease the pain of the other.

I was neither in discomfort nor in bed when all was finally revealed, nor was I at the dinner table. It happened one afternoon when we returned from school. Nadi called me and I went to the reception room. I became anxious; the Empress was sitting on the sofa and the Shah on an armchair by the window reading the newspaper. The air felt heavy and the absence of Khadijeh or any other person put me on my guard. There was a bundle of letters on a side table next to her. I curtseyed as usual and went forward to kiss her hand but she wouldn't let me. The Empress had asked Nadi to bring in some tea; she then took Mahmoud, who was by then five and the youngest member of the family, out of the room.

For the first time the Shah referred to me as 'my dear niece'; although he was my mother's brother he never referred to it. As soon as I had sat down he said: 'Do you know that I, too, have lost my mother?' and then tried hard to swallow his tears.

I not only heard 'too', I understood the full extent of what he had said, so I tried to mop up my tears with the corner of my scarf when they were not looking.

Having broken the news in the gentlest possible way, I could not understand why it came as such a surprise. If she had been alive she would have written. The Empress, who was by then wiping her tears with her pink muslin handkerchief, tried to make it short. She began to talk about the news of the death of her mother-in-law, Om Khaqan, that had been received in the past hour. She continued until the Shah rose and went towards the window and looked through the window pensively. Though it wasn't yet really dark, we could hear the sound of the gas lanterns. Ever since these lanterns had been brought to the estate, they were turned on at dusk, and only turned off when Hassan Beig signalled. At that hour the sea looked spectacular, with the tiny lights flickering at a distance, together with the boats' lanterns.

They didn't seem to want to discuss my mother any further, but now that the curtains had been lifted, I didn't want to let them get away with not revealing more. No matter how hard I found it, I still asked. 'Where did Mother go? How?'

168

At this the Empress gestured towards her husband, who was still standing by the window looking out, and uttered a brief sentence, which made me understand that we had to talk privately.

'Your poor mother ...' was all she said.

I kept quiet and the forlorn and orphaned Shah, having lost his own mother and looking more destitute than ever, turned and sat down. He held his hookah to his lips but did not puff. Then he let go of it and said, 'You've grown, my dear.'

This opened up an issue that was no longer spoken of: my engagement to Ahmad. He kept talking, and every time the Empress heard her son's name mentioned she sighed, as usual, and then her eyes welled up with tears. The only time the Empress relaxed her imperious manner was when Ahmad Shah's name was mentioned. With such a prelude they effectively informed me that I had to prepare myself for an important event: I had to return to Tehran, to the imperial palace, and become the Empress of Iran. To do so I had to acquire the skills expected in such a role. My uncle was talking and the Empress expanded on what he said.

'The world has changed and women have stepped into the arena and are no longer to be kept behind the veil. Everywhere in the world women go to college or write in the newspapers. In the Ottoman Empire they are present in court and practise law. Although, unlike Russia or Britain, it is too early for a woman to be on the throne in Iran, they still have their duties and have to manage the court.'

According to them, I had every tool at my disposal to prepare myself for the day I had to part with them and lead my own life.

At the end of our meeting the Empress picked up a letter and a necklace with a row of emeralds that had been sent from Golestan Palace and handed them to me. The letter was addressed to me, 'Her Ladyship, Khanoum, my dearest cousin'. The Empress picked up a photograph of His Majesty that was on the small table by her side and passed it on to me. The photograph was put in a frame and, without the slightest regard for what others might say, was placed on the shelf in my room. This formalised our engagement, the purpose of my invitation to the reception room. Enayat Saltaneh, the sister of His Majesty's wet nurse, was arriving the following week. I had previously met her in Tehran and now she was to become my lady-in-waiting and prepare me. Nezhat and life after Nezhat had already distanced me from my childhood. For some time now I had run out of conversation with Khadijeh, let alone the older girls on the estate in Odessa. The Shah and the Empress had also come to sense this. The Empress often discussed the running of the household and even the finances with me, and I knew she valued what I said.

That evening I left the reception room holding my praying *chador* under my arm. While I was passing through the hall I began to feel as I had on the day I had been stuck in Father's quarters and was struggling to reach the latch. I needed Mother with the same desperation and couldn't reach my room fast enough. I climbed down the stairs and passed a couple of people on the ground floor without seeing them. I carried on. I opened the door and ran alongside the hedge until I reached the building where my room was. The white rabbit, for which I always left some food, was under the lamp-post waiting for me. She, too, I passed unnoticed. I ran up the stairs. My face was wet and I wanted to scream. Once the door to my room was shut, it was as though I was liberated. I held my *chador* in front of my face and kept on screaming.

I had, over the years, thought about Mother and wept. I knew she wasn't there, otherwise she wouldn't be able to bear not to receive news of me. But, somehow, we always have this need to fool ourselves; to colour a dark little corner of our minds; to paint the sky very blue; to plan a forever-green garden then leave the garden and look for flowers to plant in the garden. I had created such a garden in my mind and over the years I had watered it in anticipation. I had then placed Mother in a corner, just as she had sat in the sitting room leaning against the large stiff cushion, laughing at Morvarid's jokes, revealing her dimples. Just as, when in the *hammam*, she dried her hair and her pink skin glowed. She always sat in my imaginary garden and yet I was never able to draw her on paper. I had drawn portraits of everyone in our compound, and General Khanbayev had said that I could sell my drawings in Europe, yet I was never able to draw my mother. Now it felt as though floods had destroyed my garden.

I had once again become as obstinate as a child and I wanted to know: I wanted someone to describe every moment of what had happened to Mother, not like the Empress who refrained from discussing it. I could not wait. I wanted to go back to the park and run, go up the stairs in the reception room, put pomp and ceremony aside, and without prior announcement enter the room where the Empress had broken the news to me. I wanted to scream that I did not want to become Empress, neither the Empress of all Iran nor the Empress of the entire world. I didn't want to exist at all, I just needed someone to tell me the whole story: how and where my mother passed away. I suddenly had a question bubbling up in my mind, which prompted me to dry my tears. I uncovered my face since my *chador* was now wet. I cleared my voice and, as though someone was standing in front of me, I raised my voice.

'Where is she buried?'

That evening, since no one came for me, not even Khadijeh, I can only assume the Empress had asked everyone to leave me be; no one brought me supper either. I was so glad I could go to my chest. I placed around me everything Mother had sent or I had with me: the letters, the photographs, her ring, the prayer set, the rosary and the Russian hand mirror. I never noticed the lamps being turned off. I never looked at the sea and didn't see the lanterns either. I had lit a candle and was reading Mother's letters and the diary in which I had made notes, sometimes just a few sentences. I placed her first letter on my chest. I closed my eyes and it was then I heard her voice: it was she who was gesturing that I should get up from under the *korsi*. Nezhat was there and she got up too. She closed her book, removed her canary from its cage and held it in her hand. We were both wearing galoshes as it was snowing. Mother put her *chador* on. Flakes of snow were landing on her black *chador*. We passed by the dust-mat placed at the entrance to the sitting room. She was moving ahead and was carrying a lantern, the light of which made the snowflakes sparkle and lit up the marks her footsteps left in the snow. She walked towards Father's quarters, but went round the pool and passed by the short tree that usually bore berries but now looked bare.

The snow made a crunching sound under her steps. She then turned towards the gardener's cottage. Behind it there was a store of buckets, watering cans, a spade and a pickaxe. She rested the lantern by a broken wooden chest buried in front of a wardrobe. She opened the wardrobe, and when the rusty mirror swung to face us, Nezhat and I were stunned and silent; we couldn't see anything. She stepped inside the wardrobe. Then we heard the sound of a lock and a key turning with no trouble. Another door opened and we, too, stepped inside the wardrobe. She then closed the door behind us and kept moving forward holding her lantern. Snowflakes slipped down her *chador*. She climbed down the steps ahead of her and continued along a corridor with large openings to one side. We then arrived in a small area with a round tank in the middle. She held the lantern high enough for us to see where we were going. She proceeded to the right past further turns. She came to a door and opened it. This time we had to climb the steps. Nezhat and I quietly followed her up without asking any questions, Nezhat still holding her canary that occasionally fluttered up to perch on her shoulder. The corridor suddenly turned into some long, narrow garden. There was a cool breeze, but winter seemed suddenly to end at this point and spring to be in full bloom. The ancient trees were full of leaves but even their trunks looked green and were covered in flowers. Mother kept going and so did we. She stopped, and a rabbit hurried past her feet. Right there, in front of our terrified eyes, my father appeared carrying his rifle. He shot the rabbit and blood spurted out everywhere: first onto my mother's face, next on her body and then all over us. The canary was covered in blood.

Mother approached and guarded us, holding her arms in front of us. Nezhat and I hid behind her. The monster's eyes looked red and puffy just as they did when he was drunk. He was facing us with his rifle ready to shoot. Mother immediately threw me into a chamber and, before the bullet could hit me, shut the door. But the bullet pierced it and I looked through the hole in the door. My mother was about to throw Nezhat into another chamber but Father's powerful hands clutched Nezhat's waist and, laughing raucously, he lifted her off the ground. Nezhat's canary was flapping its wings and kept flying above them until Father, with incredible dexterity, shot the canary. It burst into space and sprinkled us with scarlet powder. Nezhat was weeping and tearing at her face as though the unbearable pain had penetrated right through her bones. The monster, however, seemed suddenly to be filled with joy and, once again, burst into raucous laughter as, while holding Nezhat, he jumped into the middle of the tank, which looked like the pool in our house. Through the hole I saw Mother also jump in the water with her bloodstained *chador*. The surface of the water was covered with large water lilies. The monster's hands suddenly looked very large, covering her head and pushing her down amid the water lilies. Mother went in and then came up. Her plait was floating on the surface of the water. The monster's hands once again pushed her down amid the lilies. I was sweating and shouting from inside the chamber but somehow the ability to move had been taken from me. I felt crippled and could do nothing but watch.

For a last time Mother went under and never came up again. I only heard her faint voice from inside the water begging me to leave. Her voice seemed to return my strength. My hands and feet began to move and I ran. The corridor, narrower than before, seemed to twist and turn. At the far end, on a sumptuous throne,

Ahmad Shah was sitting looking rotund and compassionate, and I was running towards him. Before reaching him, I had to run on the frozen surface of a tank. The ice broke and I fell in. Inside the tank a different world appeared. It was full of big cities with European people with their umbrellas and top hats bearing feathers, warm cities, naked people in the water, churches, cemeteries as well as tall, magnificent buildings. I kept drowning in the water but the others carried on living, laughing, dancing and happy. But at times they also appeared to be in the middle of a battle,occasionally carrying rifles. I was still suspended in the water when someone called me; I didn't listen but the voice called me again.

When I woke up, I saw Khadijeh's anxious expression looking at my tear-stained face. It took me a while to find my bearings. I had huddled in bed and the contents of my chest were all over the place. Dawn was upon us and I seemed to be alive. My nightmare had taken hours. I was in pain. Khadijeh helped me remove my clothes and then dropped them in a pan under my bed. She, too, had one of these under her bed for when we wanted to wash certain clothing items ourselves so that we did not expose the signs of growing up to anyone. I was silent, thinking of that dream, the nightmare in which people and places all seemed familiar: the cool house under Father's quarters with its twists and turns, and even Nezhat's canary, which she always kept in a European cage in her room, and the rifle. However, I did not know how to interpret it. Before reaching the throne and the person seated on it, the ice broke and I fell in. I told myself that I should never discuss the dream with anyone. I no longer had anyone to discuss my dreams and life with. My mother had disappeared amid the water lilies. I seemed to have found an answer to my question and no longer needed the Shah, the Empress or anyone else to tell me how she had passed away.

The next day I woke up just before lunchtime, and I felt sick.

CHAPTER 27

I had seen Nanny Aqa: she came from Khoy, in the north-west, and it was said she had looked after Ahmad ever since he was born. Her accent made her sound sweet. She was kind, selfless and her happiness depended on the well-being of that overweight child. Back in Tabriz she was never anywhere far from his cradle, later his bed. Shah Baba's demise had shifted the family to Tehran since my uncle became Shah and Ahmad the crown prince. Nanny Aqa was always there, even on formal occasions. He had dozens of tutors and yet Nanny Aqa was at hand, as though born to fulfil her duty.

She didn't really have anyone else, but her sister Enayat, having been rewarded with the title of Enayat-ol-Saltaneh, was a different kettle of fish. She was younger than her sister, married to Moeen ut-Tojjaar from Tabriz, and the mother of a four-year-old girl who had accompanied her to Odessa. In the course of our first meeting I found something in her eyes that put me off. Khadijeh and I saw her arrive through the windows overlooking the park. She seemed to be getting off the carriage with difficulty, and had a number of leather-bound chests with her, which we assumed were filled with presents for the Empress or us. When we finally got to see her fair, round face, she had dolled herself up and seemed to be communicating certain instructions to the coachman. She then picked an expensive-looking case and followed Nadi. She was holding Behjat's hand, approaching our building. We went to my room and, shortly afterwards, Nanny

Khaj came to announce the new arrival: 'Nanny Khanoum has arrived!' Then she left.

The Empress had earlier that morning summoned me to have a few words about the new arrival. She seemed to be concerned about something, and though she wasn't showing her displeasure, she said that the Regent and her own mother had insisted that the woman should become my nanny, something that was disclosed much later. The Empress tried to make me understand that I had to be careful when talking to this nanny. I even remember her using herself as an example: as a child she had a nanny whom she resented. Her nanny's attitude had affected her and made her suspicious and mean as a child, until one day her tears had persuaded her mother to get someone else instead.

'Your situation is different; you are mature and so cannot be affected by the unbecoming influence of someone else, let alone some illiterate woman, but I thought I'd better open your eyes to the background.'

I then learned that the new nanny had for some time been my uncle Shoa's *siqeh*. According to the Empress, Mansour had the contract annulled because of some terrible event, and she was thrown out of the harem. Later she had become Tojjaar's wife, but that had not lasted long either and ... At this point the Empress hesitated, seemingly unsure whether to continue or not. She finally went on.

'She is somewhat too aware of whatever goes on around her and keeps us entertained, though we have not lost our vigilance. It is said that when we left Tehran she became acquainted with the Russian captain Smirnoff and used to sing for him, but perhaps this is only some cheap gossip of the kind circulated about everyone in Tehran.'

In the end, the Empress re-adopted her usual reserve.

'What shall certainly *not* happen in *this* place, unlike Tehran, is the temptation to gossip and engage in sorcery. You, too, need to be vigilant my dear!'

What she said concerned me, but Khadijeh and I kept our heads buried in our studies, and then I sat behind my easel and painted. An hour passed; the woman didn't turn up and we had no intention of going to her either. Then Nadi arrived and asked us to go to the reception room to have tea with the Empress. Nadi broke the bad news: Khadijeh had to go to the empty room on the other side of the corridor where the guests occasionally stayed. Khadijeh argued and left the room in a huff with the intention of getting her mother to change her mind. She couldn't, and was the first person to take a dislike to Enayat, but soon enough the others followed suit.

In the reception room, the Empress was sitting in her usual place. At first glance I saw a woman in a short *shaliteh*[10] revealing her sturdy, fair thighs, something so far unseen in this place. She had a gold necklace and several bangles on her wrists, which clinked noisily with every move she made. Though furious, Khadijeh had a silent smirk on her face.

I curtseyed to the Empress as usual and then went towards the woman. She had already opened her arms.

'My, my, look how much Khanoum has grown. How silly of me to think I was expecting to see a child!'

I couldn't work out the sarcasm in her reference to my age since I was Ahmad Shah's junior by only two years. She proved more forward than I had anticipated: with one hand she lifted the *chador* off my head and with the other she clasped my wrist and twirled me in the middle of the room. She looked me up and down, and tilted her head so that she could study me in detail. She must have seen my anger when I pulled myself together and locked eyes with the Empress, who was frowning by this time. I released my hand and went to sit next to Khadijeh on the sofa. In order to improve the atmosphere, the Empress asked Nadi to bring some tea and then, with a certain haughtiness, said to Nadi: 'Ask Nanny Khanoum if her daughter, too, would like some tea or ...'

'If Her Majesty permits, I can be called by my own name, just as His Majesty always does.' As she spoke she raised an eyebrow and, without waiting for the Empress's response, then turned to Nadi and effectively to everyone else. 'Enayat-ol-Saltaneh. My daughter has also been named by His Majesty Behjat-ol-Saltaneh.'

The Empress puffed so vehemently at her hookah that the flowers floating inside the container began to dart around. Khadijeh became impatient and asked her mother if she might take her leave. From then on, my nanny, who incidentally began referring to herself as my companion, began to speak of Tehran, the Regent, the Empress's mother and all the events that had been taking place: deaths and marriages and so on. I began to wonder how on earth we were going to put up with such a woman in the days that lay ahead. My only hope was the Empress; her strength had even tamed and calmed the men of our compound, yet I doubted her ability to deal with this one. As though the Empress had read my mind, whenever she looked in my direction her smile quickly vanished.

An hour later I was relieved when the Empress allowed me to leave the room.

She turned to Enayat and said, 'Nadi shall spend the next hour showing you around, explaining the ways and customs we have had to adapt ourselves to in our foreign place of residence and the way things are done …' And before she continued she motioned me to leave.

Making my curtsey more pronounced, I pulled my *chador* on my head and left.

In the hallway, Nanny Khaj was playing with the woman's child, at which point I growled, 'Behjat-ol-Saltaneh …'

And so began an ordeal I had to go through for the next seven months. I had no idea how unpleasant and hard I could become. I didn't know that some people were adept at bringing out the worst in others. Just as I didn't know that some people enjoyed igniting resentment in others. It was as though this woman had arrived in Odessa just to demonstrate to us that human beings were not as pleasant as they seemed. Before her arrival the Empress's wisdom had created an atmosphere where we came to realise that even a person like my uncle, who was the subject of a nation's resentment, was only a human being. As a result, there was no sign of malice in our gatherings. If, occasionally, something disappeared, or someone treated another badly, no one got to know about it; we would just learn that someone had been sent away to Tehran or Tabriz.

Prince Zell, who was reputed to have been my uncle's blood enemy and was considered the source of all troubles – rumour had it that he had funded the opposition – arrived in Odessa and stayed for a month. His family also arrived, either from Tehran or Esfahan, and their presence meant bustle on the estate. They all spoke with a heavy but sweet Esfahani accent and their presence made our evenings enjoyable. However, prior to the arrival of Zell and his family, the Empress had summoned the children and younger people, as well as the servants. She told us that not everyone was alike and, without the slightest note of disrespect, further explained that during the coming month it was best to keep oneself away from any mischief. She further advised us to have no more contact with the younger members of the group than the rules of hospitality demanded. After they took their leave, an entire week was spent clearing up, as was the case every time someone came to stay. One of the servants, meanwhile, busy talking behind their backs, failed to notice the Empress.

'Just as you are washing everything, also wash away and discard the past and whatever was said.' She repeated the same remark each year when we were spring-cleaning the house in preparation for the arrival of *Noruz*. Order and peace meant a great deal to her.

A few days had passed since Enayat's arrival. One night in the sitting room, when she was not present, the Empress turned the conversation to Tehran and, as though she were merely chatting, revealed to us that when we were in hiding in the gardens of the Russian Embassy, the revolutionaries were holding meetings discussing their terms and the Russian and British ambassadors were acting as messengers and mediators. This was the day Mother had left me with them and, though others had gradually forgotten, I could recall every moment as clearly as if it were yesterday. The Empress carried on.

'We felt quite dreadful; everyone had become rebellious; the roads had been blocked except those to Qolhak and the Russian Embassy. Once the imperial family were in hiding and Tehran was conquered by the constitutionalists, there was talk of the crown prince becoming Shah.' Everyone had indeed witnessed how my uncle and the Empress felt, and the sound of wailing reverberating throughout Qolhak. Ahmad, too, had been inconsolable and unwilling to let go of his parents. There and then, the Empress had proposed that Ahmad should accompany them and Azod the Regent manage the country on his behalf while he was brought up under the Empress's supervision until he reached his majority. But the British Ambassador disagreed and said that in that case the Qajar dynasty should cease to be. They tried every possible solution yet, in the end, the separation was inevitable.

'It was unthinkable to be away from the crown prince; I would have preferred to have been sliced in two rather than part with him, but the Regent and my parents arrived and tried to persuade me. They promised to take good care of him. They promised that Ahmad would be raised in their guardianship, something which seemed acceptable to the ambassadors and the constitutionalists. I had no choice and, although I was only too familiar with the set-up in my father's home, I didn't give it much thought at the time. I knew that his loose rein on his household meant that the servants had become powerful. I also knew that the Regent was busy with his responsibilities, and my mother had done nothing but pray, fast and attend every religious and social gathering since she was a child. I was confident that Mr Azod, who was the head of the family and also Regent, would see to my child. However, he was an old grandee and couldn't keep an eye on every detail, and I was powerless being so far away. I now keep hearing news that is a source of anxiety to me. Thank God, His Majesty will be eighteen in two years and will take charge personally. If I had not been preoccupied with this house and establishment, I'd forget about my husband and go and become a mother to him, but you can see that this is not possible.'

She was right: if she had left, our vast establishment in Odessa would have disintegrated. I always tried to copy her way of managing everything, even her dispirited and feeble husband. Everyone got the impression that he was such an able and dignified person, but he depended on the Empress even more than anyone else and was incapable of doing the simplest of tasks.

The Empress used the events in Tehran and the circumstances that Ahmad Shah had been brought up in to help me look at Enayat from a different perspective. Perhaps she also wanted to help me develop an understanding of the nature of my future husband, to understand that, like his father, someone had to manage him. Her words, as usual, gave me strength, and I began to wonder which one of us, Enayat or me, was actually going to be influencing the other. Enayat, this chubby woman, barely had an education, while I, on the other hand, had not only benefited from a mentor such as Nezhat since I was a child, but the Empress had also coached me over the years. Everyone in our household, and anyone who was invited to Odessa, admired my manners, knowledge and talents. I knew my limits and yet I also had to live for Nezhat, for whom I was in eternal mourning. I hadn't taken this woman as seriously as I should have. Having barely arrived, she began slowly to make an impact on the peaceful atmosphere in Odessa and her main target was me. But to do so she had to use others in the process.

Only a day after her arrival, when we returned from our lessons with Madame Francis, I found that everything in my room had been moved: the bookcase had been pushed to the window which overlooked the sea and as a result blocked the view. I could no longer see the framed, signed photograph of my future husband: it had been placed somewhere in the corner. I then went to my dressing room to find my clothes had halved in number. And when I realised that my mother's chest was not in place I'd had enough and ran to call Tal'at, who was in charge of the housekeeping. When I called her she turned up with Enayat. Enayat placed her hands on her hips, looking rather defensive.

'Whatever is it?'

'Who has …' I began while facing Tal'at, but I couldn't finish what I wanted to say.

'Me!' she declared with confidence.

I don't know why but I began to stammer and, later on, was cross with myself for losing confidence during our very first encounter. But what could I have done?

I began to head toward my room but changed my mind and with an air of indifference asked, 'Where have you put my chest?'

'It's with me, in my room!' I just about managed not to lose control entirely. I was about to leave when she answered my next question.

'I threw out the clothes which were no longer suitable and we shall have some new ones made instead.'

And so began the game. I had no peace from then on. She had a split personality and was just like an actor: in the evenings, when everyone else was there, she was a completely different person, yet in the daytime, when she was alone with me, I would see her other side. Later that evening, as well as us, the general, and the Russian physician and his wife and children, were also present in the reception room. The gathering had actually been organised in Enayat's honour. However, everyone, even the Russians, who had difficulty with the pronunciation, called her 'Enayat-ol-Saltaneh'. After a short while her see-through *chador* slipped down and fell onto her shoulders, and she was quickly transformed to resemble the Russian women who only wore a loose scarf. Until then, no woman in our compound had ever appeared without a *chador* outside the privacy of the inner sanctum, particularly when the Shah and his guests were present. Nadi and all the other servants, Iranian, Russian or Turk, wore the loose dresses with white aprons at the front that had been made for them. They also donned a white bonnet, like the women I had encountered in the Russian Embassy.

That evening, Enayat sent one of the maids to fetch the *tonbak* she had evidently brought with her all the way from Tehran. Without the Shah's permission and with a slight nod from the Empress, she began to play and sing. She was very good. She delighted everyone except Khadijeh and me. She behaved with familiarity towards the Russian general as she made his daughter get up and dance. She sang lyrics which were a reminder of the days in the *hammam* when Nezhat and I were quickly washed and sent out while my mother spent an entire day with her acquaintances in the *hammam*, where Morvarid would perform and Soltan played a tune with her fingertips on the back of a pan:

> *A seedling here, a seedling there, we're in Bagh e Shah;*
> *Don't step here, don't step there, you may be in the waters of the Shah;*
> *You shameless hussy,*
> *Plucked your brows, you fussy;*
> *You brought ruin to my home*
> *May God ruin your home …*

By then the salon was ablaze with excitement. Enayat got up and removed Jarozelski's hat; he was corpulent and always had a monocle hanging from his neck. While she played she faced the general and then sang something in Russian, enchanting both him and the physician:

> *Destroy your St Petersburg God may,*
> *Mar your sea view I pray;*

Didn't even have a single imperial to give me,
How dare you tease me so;
Gold money hardly any,
Kept your nose in the air with so many.

Everyone was so absorbed that no one noticed Khadijeh and me leave. The two guards on the estate were having their supper. I followed Khadijeh to her room so that I could calm her down. She was even more furious than I was but we decided not to mention anything to the Empress and mar their happiness. After years of silent anxiety, joy and laughter were now penetrating the house in Odessa and we had no right to allow our own unhappiness to ruin it.

It became increasingly difficult for Khadijeh and me to chat, and we occasionally resorted to having a conversation at school. Khadijeh was upset; every time she had complained to the Empress, the response was that we had to get along with everyone. This woman, though, was not like everyone else: she kept an eye on us at all times and no one could work out what she was up to. For instance, she went to the Russians or spent time alone with the general's wife. Enayat had barely been with us a week when we again quarrelled over my chest. I had no doubt that she had been through the entire contents and had learned every detail. I was determined to stand up to her and get the upper hand.

After our earlier argument, I summoned Nadi. I then asked her to call someone else to empty my books and put the bookcase back to where it had previously been.

And in order to further assert my authority, I faced Nadi and said, 'I thought I was better off with the bookcase in front of the window but I have now changed my mind.'

I wanted everyone to know that it was I who had made the decision to move it in the first place. Enayat didn't say anything, and I thought I was victorious, not only in having my chest returned to my room but in once again being able to open the window to the sea. I had hardly had time to relish my satisfaction, however, when she made another strike.

Enayat came in and, as usual, stood in the middle of the room long enough for Khadijeh to leave. She then lowered her voice and in a seemingly kind and friendly way said, 'I only want what is right for you, because no one is more familiar with His Majesty's temperament than I. For instance, I threw a bunch of your clothes away because I know that he doesn't care for the style. Eshrat's daughter became his *siqeh* for a couple of months. Although he liked her and she pleased him, her way of dressing made him send her back to her father's home and that was that. The poor girl was grief stricken and I know that she is still melancholy; she also had a miscarriage.'

My blood was boiling and I felt my cheeks burning. I clenched my teeth and decided to keep staring at a book, a French book about the life of Madame Marchelain.

In the course of the next few days I could read from her expression that she was wondering whether I still dared challenge her. I did. I actually had no desire to complain to the Empress. I spent time scheming and looking for the right moment, knowing full well that she, too, was waiting for the same opportunity.

The climax of this antagonism came to a head when Khadijeh and I went to her room while she was with the general's wife. We opened her chest: there was a heap of colourful outfits, a bunch of papers, different moustaches and pieces of fabric she used when she performed. There was also a fine-looking pistol, the sight of which terrified us, and so we decided to put it back in its place. We were frightened; it was the first time we had resorted to such an act and I was beginning to be appalled by myself. I felt ashamed that we felt the need to act like this and I shut the chest impatiently. Khadijeh kept an eye on the stairs so that she could warn us of Enayat's imminent return. She looked surprised and asked whether I no longer wanted to check the wardrobe. I cringed and said that I didn't. But Khadijeh wasn't satisfied. She found the key and went ahead. The first item she pulled out was a thick leather-bound book, out of which she pulled a photograph and asked me indifferently whether I knew who it was. I wish we had never opened the wardrobe and I wish I had never caught sight of him: that monster was my father. I trembled, rushed out of the room and threw myself on my bed.

For years I hadn't seen that face and I had tried hard not to let him into my dreams either. When Khadijeh held the photograph in front of me, he had the same expression as when Nezhat had emerged from behind the curtains. His hair was sleek and the eyes looked into my eyes; for days he kept looking at me in the same way and at night the fear of him kept me awake. I consequently spent a couple of feverish days in bed. The Russian physician came, took my pulse and prescribed some medicine. The Empress sent some herbal mixture over and came to force me to drink it. I could see that woman, Enayat, standing there expressing her opinion. She came across as sympathetic but everything she said had other connotations as far as I was concerned. When she said, 'A draught is coming through the window,' it was as though she was telling me off for what I had done with the bookcase; when she came to help me put on a dress, it was as though she was saying that I had no right to wear anything other than the ones she suggested; and when, after a week, I finally got up and announced that I was going to Madame Francis the next day, she thought it better if a Russian tutor came over and taught me at home.

'Why Russian?'

'Russian is necessary and not French.'

I looked in the Empress's direction as though to ask why we were allowing her to determine what I had to study.

'I know French quite well and I am studying French history and literature,' I said, adding sarcastically, 'Am I to start learning Russian now?'

She was stern, 'Yes.'

I was later punished for my disobedience. When we returned from school I went to my room to put my books away, and I noticed that Enayat had placed the monster's photograph on the mantelpiece.

Later, she took the frame that held Ahmad Shah's photograph, pointing out, 'I don't think it is becoming to display that picture on the mantelpiece while still waiting.'

I wanted to scream but didn't seem to have any strength, as though I was scared of her. I left the photograph of my father face down so that he didn't look into my eyes and then left the room to think. I had some dreadful plans forming in my mind. Goodness knows how unpleasant I could become! Was a human being's capacity for deviousness such that it could actually prompt one to think of a pistol? I should have listened to Khadijeh, who had very early on asked me to join her in praying profusely – for Enayat's child to become unwell, for example, or another problem to force her to leave Odessa. I had said to Khadijeh that such an evil thought must never cross one's mind, something that Mother had always said; but Mother, why did you not teach me to be disagreeable? I would surely have suffered less if I knew how to be nasty. Didn't this woman look pleased when she tortured me?

Turning my back to the photograph, I threw it in the drawer of a small table in my room, only for it to reappear the next day on the mantelpiece. I tore it into pieces and scattered the bits among the dried leaves in the park. However, whenever I was not there Enayat would place the empty frame on the mantelpiece in such a way that I could see it as soon as I entered the room, as though the image of that photograph had been engraved in that empty frame.

By the winter I felt I had failed: she had succeeded in bringing me to my knees. All she had to do in a gathering, in the presence of the Empress, the Shah and others, was somehow, adept as she was, to direct the conversation to my father, and then burst into laughter.

'Khan is a true man, a true prince. How lucky Khanoum is to have such a father!'

She hardly cared when the Empress frowned and demonstrated her displeasure. The Shah behaved otherwise: he was so simple and thoughtless that he could never remember anything. Wasn't it he who had kept me in hiding on the boat so that I did not fall into the clutches of the monster? Wasn't the Empress's hatred contagious enough to have affected him? Had the Empress not mentioned 'your poor mother' in his presence? Did Mother, his own sister, need to have suffered so much? Had power and the throne overtaken this man to the extent that he never, for a moment, remembered his sister, who that day in the gardens of the Russian Embassy had a broken hand and bruised eyes? So how could this woman succeed in fooling him by singing the praises of a man like Khan? None of this really mattered. What mattered to me was what made this woman treat me the way she did. Perhaps I was guilty of being condescending towards her.

The New Year passed. Enayat celebrated every minute of *Noruz*. We had guests who were entertained by her performance. I had been suffering her for seven months and had no strength left. Late at night, just before the beginning of the New Year, she mentioned something that indicated that she was well aware of everything, perhaps even more than I had imagined. For the first time ever, I heard the word 'sullied', and though I didn't know what the word meant, I had a fair idea.

The end of this painful episode of my life was marked by the day after *Sizdeh Bedar*, the thirteenth and last day of *Noruz*. Enayat came to my room and closed the door behind her. She looked at me.

'I thought having read so many books and having received an education you would have acquired wisdom!'

I just looked at her. She ignored me and continued.

'I am leaving but you are destroying your future. The Russians will not let you return to Tehran even if the Heavens wish it. I was the only one who could make it happen, only me. And I had merely come to warn you but you are obstinate. The reason I did this was for your father's sake and not for you or that mother of yours …'

I could no longer bear it; I turned into a wild beast: I first threw the book I had in my hand and then everything on the table. My strength was a culmination of piled-up hatred.

I screamed, 'Shut up, you whore!'

Such a word had never left my mouth, nor had it ever crossed my mind. Having heard the sound of my voice, her terrified daughter opened the door and came in, by which time I had thrown a pillow towards her. She held her daughter and rushed out. However, she paused by the door.

'You miserable soul,' she said, 'why don't you stay and become a maid? Who knows, perhaps one of the servants may take you for a wife.' And as she was closing the door, she hammered home her final words: 'Someone whose father has …' at which point I felt something well up inside my body, as though my gut was about to burst. I collapsed and could no longer hear a thing.

CHAPTER 28

E nayat, who was meant to spend a month in Tehran, left and never returned. The ordeal of the many months, and the poisonous atmosphere that she had created, lingered on for some time. Khadijeh was adamant that Enayat had had dealings with the Russians and was some sort of operative. Etezad, just before leaving us for university in Vienna, quietly mentioned that Enayat secretly visited Captain Smirnoff, the Shah's adjutant. More importantly, rumour had it that General Khanbayev and his wife supported Enayat and relied on her as some sort of agent. But what kind of agent? I could not comprehend just what kind of political service that woman could offer to Imperial Russia. I was well aware that the Russians were behind the Shah. They had persuaded him to purchase weapons and embark on a military expedition to Iran; they provided him with funds and facilities; and we were aware of the many visits that high-ranking Russians paid to my uncle while in Odessa. However, these were entirely political matters, and I could not see how they could possibly concern me.

Once, when the Shah was travelling, the Empress threw a soirée to which the grand families of Odessa were invited. As the evening drew to a close, we were sitting in the largest arbour in the park. According to the Empress, Imperial Russia was confident about the monarchy in Iran, and no law could force the Qajars to let go of their throne. Years earlier I had heard Zahir mention this; Nezhat, too, had spoken of it, but I had been too young to understand it all. I could not really understand why the courtiers had assumed that the British supported the constitutionalists and were determined to uproot the monarchy and force the Russians out of Iran so that they could colonise Iran as they had India. By doing so they would effectively have made Iranians subservient. Nezhat found the whole thing comical.

'I can't believe how foolish the British can be; the nation is really after a system of justice because the people are tired of tyranny.'

The Empress, however, reminded us that we had taken refuge in the Russian Embassy once the constitutionalists marched on the streets of Tehran. They wanted a republic with a Bakhtiari as their president; just like France. The Russians did not allow it to happen and the Tsar issued an ultimatum.

'We have secured the monarchy in Abbas Mirza's bloodline. These are the only people we recognise and no one else. Now that Muhammad Ali Shah is reluctant to reign, you must recognise his son as Shah.' The Empress then mentioned to us that at that very moment in Tehran, the Russians were guarding the young Shah and were vigilant about foreign interference.

That night I spent hours trying to reconcile what I had heard with what I had read in the newspapers. I suddenly realised that the Russians objected to our marriage, and when I thought about this I began to remember every single move that Enayat had made. For instance, when she insisted that I should learn Russian. I also remembered how chummy she was with the general and his family. The same applied to the physician and his daughters. I recalled how she had searched my chest upon her arrival and taken all my letters and photographs to her room. Amid all this, I suddenly remembered my father, the demon, who frequented the Russian Embassy and its staff. He admired the Russians but resented the British. He thought the constitutionalists and supporters of a system of justice were all subservient to the British. And the night he quarrelled with Nezhat ... Various parts of my memory were parading in front of me, and I suddenly saw everything in a different light. I then wondered what the Empress's role in all this was.

These things kept me occupied for months, and even when I read the papers, I kept searching for some clue pointing to the Russians or the British. The world of politics was unfamiliar territory and I had no one to guide me. I occasionally put some questions to Madame Francis. One day, she explained the fate of Napoleon and, at the end, mentioned Napoleon's battle with the British, concluding: 'And finally they sent him into exile and ended by terminating his life.'

The thought of the Russians or the British meddling in our affairs, even our marriages and private lives, terrified me. Bearing this in mind, I listened to what the grown-ups said and then tried to interpret it. I was convinced, as Enhayat had said, that I should forget about becoming the wife of the young Shah. I was not actually in love with that plump man, but I didn't dislike him either. After all, I had grown accustomed to what my role was to be later on, and now it was not so easy to give up the idea. Meanwhile, I was anxious: if one day they decided to ask me to leave their compound for Tehran, just as my father wanted, what could I do since I was not prepared to go back to the monster?

Amidst my anxiety there was only one ray of hope, which had a calming effect, and that was the Empress's promise to my mother, which she repeatedly spoke of. After Enayat left I spent ten days in bed, delirious with fever. The Empress was always there at my bedside and she tried to comfort me by saying that she had two daughters, Khadijeh and me. To give her her due, over the years she had behaved in such a way that I could not distinguish any difference between her treatment of her own daughter and myself; in fact, she occasionally told Khadijeh off but never admonished me. During all the years in Odessa, among some sixty people in the compound, I was the only person who was never subjected to her anger.

Nadi was aware of this and always told me, 'You are very fortunate; I'm sure that unless the Empress is completely reassured, she'll never let go of you to an unreliable person.'

Therefore, one evening, when the entire day had been spent in preparations for the annual gala in celebration of Ahmad Shah's birthday, I decided to lift my frail body from the bed to discuss everything with the Empress in the arbour: all the nightmares and delirium of the past few months, the thought of the Russians and my future life. She told me she would respond the following day. That evening the noble families and the grandees of Odessa had been invited to our home. She fulfilled her promise and late in the afternoon the following day, she took me for a walk. We sat down on a bench in the same arbour and she asked me to repeat what I wanted to ask, and so I did.

She gave me a smile and explained that she still wished me to become her daughter-in-law, although there were some obstacles. One was the fact that she had not seen her son for some years and, despite receiving his letters fortnightly, it was difficult to work out what he was up to. Although His Majesty always asked after me, what she heard from the people who passed by Odessa concerned her. Therefore, after Enayat's departure, she had decided not to discuss the matter until His Majesty's coronation, which was to take place in a few months. The Empress was delighted to mention this and seemed so happy, as though she would give anything for the encounter to take place as soon as possible. I then understood that, in one month, the coronation that would make Ahmad officially the Shah of Iran was to take place. Up to then, the Regent had been in charge of matters relating to the throne. After Azod, Nasser ul-Molk had become Regent, but the Shah, the Empress and everyone in Odessa believed him to be a British agent. I had heard Etezad say that Nasser was, at the time of the siege of the parliament, the head of government, and that Muhammad Ali Shah had wanted to hang him in the Imperial Gardens. However, the British Ambassador had intervened and Nasser had escaped, disguised in a *chador*.

Ahmad Shah's forthcoming visit to Odessa was the most important news that the Empress broke to me – the person I still took for my future husband and who had a special place in my heart. However, when we were returning to the reception room to join the others, the Empress murmured other things and asked God to keep the devil at bay.

I assumed something must have crossed her mind, but once again she cursed my father, the monster, and muttered, 'Your poor mother …' She didn't finish what she was about to say.

Finally, the auspicious event to mark Ahmad Shah's coronation dawned. Attendees at the celebrations in the gardens of Odessa were my uncle and some of his brothers, as well as a number of people who had arrived from Europe, including a few pashas from the court of Constantinople. The gala was to be the grandest ever: the entire estate was illuminated as well as the road leading to it. Khadijeh and I saw through our binoculars that a large area by the sea, where the fireworks were due to take place, had been laid out ready to receive the male guests. We had about a dozen Russian female guests in the gardens as well as an all-female musical band, who sang and danced. The Iranian imperial family and the members of the Russian imperial family were the only people to be seated in the pavilion.

Khadijeh and I were introduced as princesses, and we both wore our new dresses. The night before, the Empress had let us both borrow certain items of jewellery from her collection to match our long green and scarlet gowns. My mother's necklace gave me confidence, and I found it prettier than all the gold, jewellery and pearls that the Russian princesses wore. However, I didn't wear my ring; the Empress didn't think a diamond ring was appropriate for a young woman who was not yet married. By contrast, the Russian princesses, each accompanied by a lady-in-waiting and a maid, as well as a young officer behind each of them, wore opulent jewellery. Their gowns, decorated with pearls and diamonds, reflected the light.

Aqdas, who usually dressed the Empress's hair, was asked to do our hair in the current Russian fashion. The Empress asked us not to cover our hair, but she had her golden tiara placed over her scarf. The rest of us were in line with the princesses from St Petersburg. From time to time, Nadia and the Empress, who could speak some Turkish, made an effort to converse with the guests, with the wife and daughter of Jarozelski acting as interpreters. I was introduced as the granddaughter of the former Shah, Shah Baba, as well as the Shah's niece.

Khadijeh and I slipped away a couple of times to sneak a peek at the men's quarter through our windows. Khadijeh had overheard one of the princesses talking about her and one of the princes. We understood that the princesses and their companions had nothing worthwhile to talk about except idle chatter, discussing the young women's prospects and any potential match among the eligible young men. When we looked through our binoculars, we had difficulty seeing clearly but we could enjoy the colourful sight that the lights and fireworks had created. Khadijeh and I were conscious of everyone looking at us. Khadijeh regretted Etezad's absence as she was confident, otherwise, that one of those beautiful Russian princesses with all the diamonds and gold could be his.

I knew that a large photograph of Ahmad Shah in formal costume had been placed on a table in the men's area. At midnight, surrounded by the aroma coming from the braziers, the guests kissed the Empress goodbye while Khadijeh and I were standing by her curtseying to the grown-ups. The eunuchs bowed profusely to the Empress. We had practised our curtseys in advance and Madame Francis, who had also been invited, kept smiling while checking on her pupils in their colourful gowns, gold and jewellery, no longer resembling their everyday selves. After saying their farewells, the ladies covered themselves from head to toe in their cloaks, concealing all the colour and glitter. They then disappeared into their carriages, drawing an evening that had celebrated the beginning of Ahmad Shah's reign, on an estate north of Odessa, to a close.

Once the guests had all departed, the servants got busy clearing the chairs, tables and crockery, and the musicians put their instruments away. When all was done, the Empress let her heavy body collapse onto one of the sofas and Nadi began to massage her feet. The evening had proved a success and everyone was content. Khadijeh and I were busy removing the jewellery, which had to be returned to the Empress's coffer, but little did we know that as the Empress had always said, our destinies were shaped while we were asleep. I wasn't asleep, but even so I was unaware that the words that Sultanah Ameeneh, the daughter of Sultan Abdul Hamid, had whispered into her sister's ear were to have an impact on my life when I turned sixteen. She was a fairy-tale figure in the Ottoman Court and was in Odessa at the time because of her husband, the Ottoman Consul.

CHAPTER 29

I had come to learn that life was a river, and one couldn't tell whether the river came into being because of the stream, or was created by the mountain from which the rainwater flowed to start the stream. The river flows over stones which direct its course but which are, at other times, themselves shifted by its force. It is difficult to determine exactly where things originate. It may even be the gardener, who diverts a stream to feed the garden, helping the trees to grow and eventually spread their shade. There is always one element, however, which ends up making its mark more decisively than the others. And when the river finally buries its head in the soft soil, it begins to remember the long distance it has travelled: from the clouds to the mountains, to the rocks, to the trees, ending up with the gardener; only the river knows which one has had the most influence on its existence. It is only when Man reaches the end of his life that he can recognise, looking back, the days and events that have come to shape his life, and can then determine which was the most influential.

I was sixteen or seventeen when I thought of this. We were in Odessa and I was living with a family where my role was not clearly defined. The image of the little girl whose mother pulled her out of an inferno and placed her in a convoy going far away, a convoy sped on its way by the hatred of the people, gradually disappeared with the passage of time. Mother was lost in dust and I had very early on managed to bury my father with hatred. Nezhat's brief passage through life had played a major role in shaping me, or perhaps such was my assumption. Her golden locks always floated on the surface of the water in the well in my dream. This became a permanent image shaping my dreams, but the image of her face was lost in the course of those days and nights. After seven or eight years I was left alone to discover and understand the world. The image of a future that Nezhat had helped me to picture was not always stable: the arrival of new people, letters and newspapers, or the news of events back home, moved me like a straw floating on the surface of the water. The role I was to play, however, was to become meaningful only many years after my arrival in a foreign city; the role of the future Empress and the wife of a king, whom I always remembered for his tears back in Tehran and whose photograph was even now sitting on the mantelpiece in my room, but who had by then become king. Even this role didn't turn out to be permanent; nobody talked about it any more.

After Enayat's departure, I felt my presence in the gardens of Odessa was merely acknowledged as the niece of the former Shah or the granddaughter of Shah Baba. For a young woman without a defined place, life could become a tragedy. One was forced to ignore undue attention and meaningful smiles in the galas and gatherings because tradition dictated it.

At eighteen years of age I felt I had no future; I felt I had been left in a Moses basket and released into a calm sea, a calm that was becoming irritating. In a place where, should I have stepped outside the park, no one knew me or spoke my language, I felt insecure. This was agonising. Inside the park, however, there were many guards and watchful eyes. The worst time was when my imagination was let loose by reading a newspaper or article, and then it would wander to the future; a hazy future like an Odessa autumn by the sea, buried in the mist, making it impossible even to recognise the lighthouse; it was only the sound that one could hear, the sound of the seagulls and the waves.

But a lantern was suddenly to light up for me and, until it was extinguished, I had not realised how much it had illuminated my inner ambiguities. Some unlikely person had always held the lantern and towered over a lonely little girl in her most difficult inner turbulences. This person was neither the king nor a prince, nor any of those polite and smiling Russian princesses, and certainly not any of the men who visited Odessa with lots to talk about. Nor was this person like any of my classmates, nor even Madame Francis our teacher, nor Marina, the nun who did everything else in the classroom and taught the girls about religion and the love of Christ. He was not like the clergy who, every year, spent the months of Muharram and Ramadan in Odessa. These clerics brought excitement in the nights of mourning for the Shiites of the household as they retold the epic of Ashoura and the bravery of Hussein, the master of the martyrs. They told us stories in an effort to keep the memory of Imam Ali alive in the illuminated evenings of Ramadan.

Every one of these individuals could have been the bearer of the lantern in my life and in some ways they were, in particular and not surprisingly my uncle with his broken heart, and Malakeh Jahan with her strength and stability. Yet the person who became, more than anyone else, the light, mentor and guide to me in all those years, the person who helped open my eyes to life and whom I could understand, was a tall, thin man with a face full of wrinkles, completely bald, and with the fine, melodious voice of a eunuch, which, indeed, he was. When our convoy left Tehran he wasn't with us but he joined halfway through. I saw him for the first time on the boat, standing by the Empress's bedside with a bowl that was filled and emptied as the Empress vomited into it, looking concerned.

I always saw him with the same expression. He didn't laugh, even when the musicians were being comical, or when some joke made everyone burst into laughter as if they hadn't a care in the world. Nor, like the rest of us when we were depressed or frightened, did he weep at times of sadness. He told me about his life and how he had agreed to being castrated because his father

wanted him to be in the court and an insider in the harem. He
was a treasure trove of stories and anecdotes; everyone knew that
nobody was as aware of what went on in the court and among
Iranian courtiers as he. No one but he could maintain calm in
our dishevelled and anxious convoy as he did with his engaging
tales in the evenings. It was he who told me the true story of the
monarchy and power, not those tales the Empress tried to engage
us with during the long winter nights under the *korsi* as everyone
eventually fell asleep. It was not the sweet and amusing anecdotes
that the Empress asked him to tell to entertain guests – everyone
found his mimicry hilarious – that enlightened me, but what he
revealed of the underlying story.

For years, I never realised that, as well as the Empress, my
mother had also spoken to Abdollah Khan about me, and that he
had sworn to look after me until the day he died. I didn't know this
and Abdollah Khan didn't reveal anything until his very last night.

He didn't know his mother's whereabouts and he couldn't
remember anything before the day he was castrated. The earliest
memory he had was of becoming Taj's eunuch the moment his
wounds had healed. Taj was a Turkman, and as soon as she joined
the harem, towards the end of Muhammad Shah's life, she became
his favourite. As a child, her eyes opened up to the sorceries and
conspiracies in the harem and, despite all the vigilance, she was
finally affected; she caught some disease while she was still young
and died. After this incident, Abdollah noticed the Shah's growing
resentment towards his principal wife, the crown prince's mother,
a cruel woman who was determined to terminate Taj's son's life.

One night, during Muhammad Shah's final hours, Prince
Motamed helped Abdollah to take the child to an embassy to
ensure his safety. From then on, Abdollah remained in the harem,
until he went with Malek as a significant part of her dowry when
she married Taqi, the man who would later become Amir Kabir;
the man whose name, after sixty years, still brought tears to
Abdollah's eyes.

Many a night Abdollah would secretly come to my room carrying a cup of tea and a plateful of fruit on a tray. At such times the residents of the park were often travelling. And so he would talk to me, sitting cross-legged, about 'Mr Vizier', whom he considered unique: he had helped Iranians to prosper and Iran to flourish. There was logic behind everything Mirza Taqi Khan did, and every time he told me a tale he cursed Mahd Olya, Nasser al-Din Shah's mother, the one who made Taj's life hell and who, in the end, was instrumental in her son-in-law's death as well; the very same 'Mr Vizier'.

Abdollah didn't have a clue about politics, as he put it, yet he couldn't forget the Vizier's imposing figure and power, just as he couldn't forget Malek's sobbing when the Shah's sentence was spelled out to them. It was in Fin in Kashan, a city south of Tehran and famed for its rose gardens, that the Vizier was to receive his sentence. Abdollah had seen with his own eyes blood spurting out of the Vizier's veins, flowing into the aqueduct in the *hammam* in Fin. He had then spent many a day and night with Malek and her two little orphaned daughters. She would stretch her hands to heaven, wail and protest against the brutality of destiny. From then on, Abdollah went to live with the Vizier's two children until they were adults. He then followed the eldest daughter as part of *her* dowry when she married the future heir to the throne, my Shah Baba.

Abdollah had a great many tales from his years in Tabriz, where the Vizier's darling daughter lived. I, too, could remember Om Khaqan as I had seen her when I was little; mother to that same Shah, now a wandering soul in Odessa, who spent his days strolling in the park.

The Empress would always ask Abdollah to tell her guests or the rest of the courtiers a story. He would then describe the days when he had accompanied 'the martyred Shah' on his trips to Europe – no one else among us had seen so much of the world. He knew a great deal about the rulers and notables of the world, but when he was with me and not bound by caution or obligation, he would talk about the memories he had locked away. He wanted me to understand that power was a dirty thing, something that tainted one's mind. He talked about the many innocent men and women who had been sacrificed for the sake of the dark desires of power; people like the Vizier were permanent fixtures in Abdollah's stories.

Whenever he left my room, I would spend hours thinking of him. I had never heard him complain about his own misfortune, nor did he ever complain about the father who had brought this upon him so that he and his other three children could lead comfortable lives. Abdollah's father had died, and every one of his sons had managed to reach a position of status in the establishment. They had managed to have families of their own, as well as handsome estates, thanks to Abdollah. I always wondered why he never complained about his destiny. He was an honest and humble servant of God and could not help being grateful.

Before he came to my bedside to tell me stories, I had no idea how much he knew, and neither did anyone else. He was a philosopher who had the appearance of an obedient soul who had succumbed to his destiny. However, I slowly began to see behind the façade and began to read between the lines. I couldn't understand why he felt as he did only when he was with me. Everyone looked at him as the Empress's eunuch and nothing more; when a Russian officer came to conduct the census, the Empress commissioned Abdollah to be the spokesperson and present the travel documents. I don't imagine his name was even mentioned on the list! He never mentioned anything and no one bothered to ask: they didn't see him. He had accepted his non-existence and was never heard to complain.

Our home in Odessa was a small kingdom in its own right: it had a king, a queen, a minister, the military, a chamberlain and a warden. In this state, after some years, everyone had their role: Khadijeh, the Shah's sons and I had our studies to attend to, as well as drawing and bettering our skills at playing the piano. Abdollah, however, was more occupied than everyone else; he was always at work and no one ever saw him idle. Frequenting the women's quarters was easier for him than for the female servants. Everyone needed him, and he always carried out his duties with a smile and little jokes, which were his hallmark. He used to say,

> *It will be done early, it will be done later;*
> *But for sure it'll make no one suffer.*

I do recall the evenings I was feeling low – many evenings, in fact. At such times I would sit by the window overlooking the sea and focus on the horizon where there was nothing but darkness. He would come in with a fistful of nuts and raisins and ask permission to sit down. He would then kneel down, the way he was accustomed to, and he would always call me 'Khanoumam, my Khanoum'. When I was still quite young, he told me the story of an old man who was scared of death and talked to God.

'I don't wish to die in spring because the tulips grow; I don't wish to pass away in summer, either, because it is time to work. I need to collect in autumn for winter; so pointless dying in winter too!'

When Abdollah recited poetry, his voice adopted a certain tone, and he lifted his eyebrows. When I was older, he spoke of history and told me improving tales rather than childish stories. For instance, the story I can remember to this day was the tale of a traveller who rescued a monkey, a snake and a tiger trapped at the bottom of a well along with a goldsmith. The monkey asked the traveller not to rescue the man as he was of low birth. The traveller paid no attention to the request and rescued everyone. In the days that followed, the monkey, the tiger and the snake showed their gratitude, but the goldsmith was about to sell him for a few sovereigns, and he was about to be hanged, when the snake came to his rescue ... Abdollah knew *Kalileh o Demneh*, the Persian equivalent of *Les fables de la Fontaine*. He also knew thousands of stories about Mollah Nasser al-Din, a fictional and comical character. He would recite tales by Hakeem Bozorgmehr[11] and Plato. Everyone was familiar with the tales of Abdollah Khan, which were never-ending and never repeated, except when the Empress asked for a particular story to be retold.

The first time I stepped into his inner world was on a balmy summer's evening during our second year in Odessa when Zell, who was in Europe, came to stay before heading towards Iran. He stayed in a palace that the governor of Odessa had allocated but his daughters came to stay with us; a week filled with music and singing in the evenings. On the last night, when everyone had been invited to go over to Zell's, I remained at home as I didn't particularly enjoy such gatherings. So I used my studies as an excuse and asked permission to stay in. Early in the evening there was a clamour and then the sound of shooting. We were aware that Russia was at the time undergoing a revolution, hence the additional guards. From time to time, gunfire could be heard, but suddenly the sound came very close. I was terrified to hear a group of people yelling in Russian below one of the windows, and soon the commotion reached inside the building. Suddenly the door swung open and Abdollah, who had remained behind, threw a *chador* towards me. 'Put this on!'

I dragged on a shabby *chador* and then crouched in a corner in fear. Three or four tall men in riding boots and bandoliers stuffed with bullets entered. As soon as they saw me they started kicking up a fuss. I knew enough Russian to work out that they were revolutionary labourers seeking revenge on the aristocrats and the bourgeoisie. One of them pointed towards me with his rifle and asked me to rise, but Abdollah stepped in.

'My daughter works as a maid here and she is rather unwell.'

The tallest one, who seemed to be their leader, stretched out his arm to clutch my *chador*, which was in shreds, but did not pull at it, and later they let go of me. Abdollah's appearance, with his worn clothes, spoke for itself and indicated the social class to which he belonged, and the shabby *chador* came to my rescue. The next day we discovered that Abdollah had used his genius to prevent the revolutionaries getting into the Empress's vault. They were drunk and quarrelsome but stayed only for an hour, leaving before the Shah and the Empress returned.

Abdollah later beamed, 'I became a father for a couple of hours!'

Though he never mentioned it, everyone knew how much he wished he had a child. Quite apart from this incident, it was as though I was tied to him with a string; he was always anxious for me. Whenever I returned from school I noticed his anxiety for my safe return but he never uttered a word. When I had fallen ill, the only thing I remember amid my delirium was Abdollah standing in the corner of the room murmuring a prayer, his face covered in tears; the face always wore a quiet and motionless mask, and the mask never smiled unless instructed, never wept unless in the evenings during Muharram, when he would sit down in a black shirt buttoned up to its collar.

He would care for the sick but was never sick until the day he finally became bedridden and never rose again.

'What shall we do if anything happens to Abdollah Khan?' the Empress wondered.

As his illness persisted, one of his brothers turned up from Tabriz accompanied by his wife. The Russian physician visited him on a daily basis. A month on and he had become so weak that he could not move, let alone bow when the Empress went to his room, which must have been agonising for him. Instead, he made a gesture with his head and hand to ask the Empress to leave so that he didn't feel so embarrassed.

When no one was watching, I would go to his room and hold his hand. I would pretend that he was going to get better soon, and make it sound as though this was the Russian doctor's belief.

But he gave a meaningful smile and said, 'Pray for me *Khanoum*, my *Khanoum*, that I may soon be relieved!'

Abdollah was a rich man and his brother was believed to have arrived to seek his inheritance. Abdollah, however, announced that whatever he had belonged to the Empress, and the same applied to the plots of land he had earned in the course of some sixty years of service. His most important wish was for his body to be buried in Iran rather than Odessa, and the Empress had asked his brother to stay behind to honour his wish.

One night, I was restless and could not sleep. I was thinking about Abdollah all the time and prayed for him. I got up. It was quiet. I picked up the candelabra and went down the stairs. His door was ajar and his brother and his wife were asleep in a corner. When he noticed the candelabra his face lit up with a smile despite the pain. He beckoned me to get close. I sat by his bed and he looked around, making sure no one was awake. He then removed his agate ring and placed it in my palm. Then he stretched his hand to pick up a small pouch he had placed under his pillow and handed it to me. By putting his forefinger on his nose he was asking me to remain quiet. Afterwards, his lips moved as though murmuring a prayer. He took my hand, turned it to its back and brought it to his lips. I could feel no life in his fingers nor in his hand yet he somehow managed to beckon me to leave.

Two days later the slight corpse of Abdollah was taken to the morgue and, a few days later, the Empress paid his brother 3,000 tomans as travelling expenses. With the permission of the governor of Odessa his body was taken to Tehran.

In the pouch there was a letter addressed to 'Khanoumam', as well as what my mother had given him as a token of appreciation for looking after me. I could barely read his writing, but by the time I had finished the letter it was as though the pain of being an orphan with no one in the world had intensified several fold. He had written about what he had never mentioned to me: the full details of the events surrounding my mother's death. He had written that human beings depended on love for living and that hatred, too, belonged to the family of love. I didn't have to forgo the hatred of the demon who had brought about the death of my mother and Nezhat, and my homelessness, since this was the love of justice that was one of the characteristics of the merciful God. He had prayed for me and left me with a word of advice: he had implored me not to give in to the life in the harem; I had to avoid the establishment of the court and power, as they were both corrupt. He had repeatedly mentioned this to me when he was alive, and in the last sentence in his letter he had written:

> With the killing of Amir Nezam, the curse of thousands of commoners had finally caught up with the Qajars and they shall not live peacefully – do not become one of them. Read my story; the story of my life, and when you are done, discard my diary.

I spent day and night reading his diary when no one was present. He had written about the aftermath of the death of the Vizier and the days that he had followed Malek and her orphaned children from house to house. He was clearly happy that his wish had been granted and that he could spend a lifetime serving Taqi's offspring. As a member of the convoy and away from his homeland, it had, therefore, become his duty to be with Muhammad Ali, the grandson of Amir, rather than 'the Shah'; it made little difference to him whether this Muhammad Ali was in one of the palaces in Tehran or in the Imperial Gardens; whether he was in a military uniform or a sorry sight strolling on the gravelled paths in the gardens of Odessa.

After all these long years I still remember Abdollah's face insisting upon being a nobody. He was like a shadow and the Empress was right: after his departure it was as though happiness had departed from Odessa, something I discovered on the day there were once again shotguns and tumult on the estate. This time, some forty people had poured in. When they fired their guns and a bullet hit the building, the windowpanes shattered. Where was he and the *chador*?

CHAPTER 30

T he city had been in turmoil for some time. For months now, food and other goods had been hard to come by and our kitchen was not as busy as usual. I understood, from the nature of our visitors, that tough days were ahead and everyone's fate depended on the Shah's decision. He was supposed to have left for Europe, but this became impossible as he was pulled off his train. The Russians were even more terrified than us. The general and his wife were too scared to leave the park. We had not received any post from Tehran for two weeks. Our large household was in a state of confusion: the discipline that had for nine years been assiduously maintained by the Empress was now in a state of disarray caused by an unbelievable event: the Russian Empire was disintegrating. One evening, despite our desperate state, the Shah and the Empress, having forgotten our presence, began to quarrel.

'I can't believe this general is incapable of lifting a finger; he could contact St Petersburg, he can send a messenger over...'

'You seem to live in a different world; the Tsar has been captured and no one knows whether he is still alive or not; their country has been overtaken by the Bolsheviks...'

'*Ya* eighth Imam; show us the way!'

Mahmoud, Khadijeh, Etezad and the other children were fortunate; they neither understood what 'Bolshevik' meant nor grasped the implications of the capture of the Tsar and his wife. They didn't even understand that the continuity of the rule of the Qajars over Iran was dependent on the signatures of these same people on the relevant documents, and that everything was going to be in a state of flux. They had no idea about the war either; the war that had broken out three years earlier and had initially engulfed Europe, before spreading across the globe. The Empress, whose happiness depended on her eldest son's well-being, forgot even to enquire what would become of him now that his Cossack guardians were losing their own heads. One evening, when I was alone in my room with disturbed thoughts and confusing questions parading through my mind, the sea suddenly lit up, followed by a terrifying sound reverberating throughout the city.

Someone in the park was yelling, 'The boats are firing!'

We were positioned on top of a hill facing the sea. The shooting had set somewhere in the city on fire; the bells of the fire brigade carriages could be heard fast approaching the site of the incident. We could see from afar that some place was ablaze. We had gathered in Abdollah's room, which, after his departure, had remained vacant. Nadi recommended that we should evacuate the top floor and the Empress agreed. We each held a Holy Qur'an on our heads while listening to the sounds of shooting nearby. We had no understanding of this revolution, or the number of days and nights we would have to spend in a state of terror. We had packed everything and brought it to the reception room, and we all slept in the basement. The barriers had been broken and we would hear the Empress, trying to keep our spirits up. It was she who, one midnight, called the children. There were six of us, and in the candlelight she explained that we had to remain strong and not give up. She then brought out boxes of gold and jewellery for us to wrap around ourselves under our clothes while no one was around. She first wrapped them in fine pieces of material, which we then fastened with a safety pin and, with her help, wrapped round our bodies. It was not clear whether we could take any of the rugs and furniture that we had amassed over the years, but we managed to pack our luggage and listed the contents of each trunk on a piece of paper. The Empress seemed to have the most;

she had put padlocks on some forty European chests while Tal'at checked the contents.

The year before, the guards' lodge had been equipped with a telephone. The Empress had been able to speak to her son a couple of times in the palace in Tehran, and also a few times to Muhammad Hassan, her other son in Tabriz. We could now hear someone yelling in Persian, Russian and Turkish in that hallway. The line was interrupted intermittently. For two days, a group of tramps had replaced our guards and they never parted with their rifles. The Shah carried a pistol and we discovered that the Empress, too, was in possession of a miniature pistol with a mother-of-pearl butt that she kept out of sight in her underskirt.

One dreadful morning they came to take the Shah away; he had hardly any courage left. His wife could no longer stop the sobbing as everyone feared for their own lives. The Empress had collapsed on some wrapped-up bedding and was asking everyone to pray. By lunchtime the Shah finally returned, ashen faced. He was accompanied by four of the same untidy-looking Bolsheviks and looked utterly petrified. The Empress ordered some lunch and a glass of water to be brought to him.

He met our anxious and expectant eyes and said, 'We must leave,' and before we had a chance to ask where, he added, 'Let's leave this hell!'

Later on, when we were on the second floor, my uncle explained to us that the whole of Russia was in mayhem.

'We have to leave somehow – we'll leave for Europe by boat.'

I was the only person who cautiously asked the Empress if we could return to Iran. Any response was taken out of her mouth; I was expecting her to say that in Iran the Shah would be executed, but my uncle quietly said: 'I was happy for us to go back but there isn't a safe route. We can't even go to Baku. If we don't leave aboard the French ship, we'll be stuck ...' And the manner in which he said this put an end to any further questioning.

The Empress, looking more imposing than ever, once again pulled us aside to remind us to take care of what had been hidden under our clothes. The men left with the first carriage and we went in the second one, along with the wives of the general and the physician. Their corpulent figures didn't leave much space for the rest of us. I had Khadijeh sitting on my lap as I took one last look at the building. The window to my room was half open as if, just like I had throughout the preceding years, I was sitting and looking at the sea. Of all the things left behind I missed my paintings, but I was glad that I had brought Abdollah's notebook, which had my mother's letters inserted between its pages. I had slipped a chain through her ring and Abdollah's agate ring, and tied the chain around my neck, hiding it under my clothes. My books were also left behind.

This had been my second home, the memory of which I would preserve in my mind. It was where I grew up and now, all of a sudden, I had to drop everything and flee amid uncertainty and ambiguity. I came to the conclusion that escaping one's home was much more difficult than escaping people!

CHAPTER 31

We spent three days in the harbour, along with thousands of other people. Many of them were princes and princesses whom I had encountered in the past, dressed in their sophisticated gowns. At that moment, however, they were milling around or crouching in a corner dressed like common people. They looked depressed as they anticipated their unknown destinies. Every day and night the revolutionary guards were pulling people out, taking their possessions, and then aggressively pushing them towards the office building. They looked at us a couple of times as well. At such times Khan Baba Khan would go forward and talk to them while we anxiously awaited his return. We were seated on a bench observing the guards, who did not seem to be taking orders from anyone in particular. The only thing that Khan Baba Khan managed to achieve was a telephone call to the Iranian Embassy in St Petersburg, but that proved useless since we later discovered there was no one in the building at the time. The only thing stopping them taking us away was the fact that our travel documents showed that we were Iranians, although this didn't always keep us immune. The general, the Russian physician and their wives used their Iranian travel documents and pretended to be one of us; they were even more anxious than we were.

A French ship had anchored in the port but did not have permission to cast off. Even if it did eventually sail it was not quite clear who could go on board. We had tickets but it was mayhem;

tickets or travel documents were not much use. Complaints were dealt with aggressively or by shooting, followed by yelling and wailing. And we, the children, having wrapped ourselves with all that jewellery, didn't dare make a move. There was nothing to eat either. We had consumed everything we had on the first day: stale bread, some minced meat and chick peas, which had been prepared at the last minute thanks to the foresight of one of the servants. We had assumed that we were going to board that very evening. Up to then we had always thought of our previous exodus, some nine years before, as the worst possible such experience; over the years we had recalled every moment of the journey from Tehran to Baku many times over, thinking that anything worse was highly unlikely. Every time we looked back I remembered all the spitting and cursing that we had endured in the course of our journey across Iranian soil. The constitutionalists had launched a few attacks in revenge against the deposed Shah and his family for those who had perished. The final delay had been caused by the demon's attempt to take me away.

It was dark, and the commotion and fear in the harbour had not calmed down. Khan Baba Khan kept going off and coming back with news. It was preferable for us to separate, with some of us going in different directions so that we were not recognised. We were particularly concerned for the former Shah, and it was a worrying time for the Russian general since he stood the risk of being caught and executed by the revolutionaries. Our appearance did not seem aristocratic enough to ring alarm bells. The women were better off in this respect since the Empress had asked us to take some *chadors* with us so that we were not taken for Russians, though it was obvious we were no ordinary folk either. In the morning the Shah was yet again taken away for questioning. Meanwhile, the Empress and the rest of the women kept praying, looking in the direction of the large door through which the Shah and two tall Russians had just passed. We did not relax until his return.

Meanwhile, one of the servants arrived carrying a bag full of bread, which he had managed to get with great difficulty. We were busy munching when the Shah returned looking more pitiful than ever. He informed us that they had searched him and confiscated whatever he had on him. He bade us farewell and once again disappeared somewhere on the harbour amid the thick of the crowd. The guards kept arriving and taking away the refugee men one by one. Those who returned did not have the strength to move. We had by then laid down a kelim and placed the trunks and other cases around it. We could finally sit somewhere. It's beyond me, but somehow I managed to fall asleep briefly amid the surrounding commotion until Nadi's voice woke me up.

It was time to leave. A rather hefty bribe seemed to have persuaded the captain to let us on board. Carrying our entire luggage without any help proved very difficult, and we had already lost two cases. It took them all morning to check the passengers and their luggage. When we were climbing up the steps, I noticed that as soon as the Empress leaned forward she fainted. The clamour and shouting of the armed revolutionaries then engulfed the motionless body of the Empress and us. This, however, turned out to be a blessing in disguise as we ended up not being searched too thoroughly!

We were finally on board, but had been wrong to assume that our cabins would be ready to accommodate us, some in first class, others in second. There was such a crowd on board that all the cabins were full: every cabin accommodated tens of people. By midnight, the twenty-six of us had managed to find one another and to take a nap seated on our luggage in the corridors. Everyone had ended up leaning against each other or on someone's lap. The Empress suddenly came up with an idea: we all made a circle around her so that she could open one of her wrapped bundles. Two travel documents fell out from inside. These were long sheets of paper bearing my uncle's photograph and the name of Haji Baghdadi, all of which bore stamps of one kind or another.

So, what we had a few years before read in the papers was true: the deposed Shah had, under this name, arrived in Astarabad armed with the weapons he had purchased in Europe. This had prompted the parliament to put a price on his head and on that of his brothers. Now those travel documents had become useful once again and Khan Baba Khan took them with him. A few days later, we discovered that the same travel documents had at the last hour rescued my uncle from being detained by the Bolsheviks. A new search party arrived and, yet again, checked everyone's papers and forced some men to go with them.

At night, two people jumped in the sea to escape; or did they want to commit suicide? Nobody knew. The thousands of people who were milling around only thought of themselves, and nothing else held their interest for long. The children and the elderly were in the worst possible state: many had simply collapsed on the floor. Two young nuns were busy attending to the sick, dressing wounds and trying to console wailing children. In the middle of the night, the ship's horn made a loud noise and we all chanted *salavat*;[12] many also made the sign of the cross on their chests. My mind seemed to have stopped working. Every time one of us wanted to go to the lavatory, it was quite a task to unwrap the jewellery, but under the *chador* anything was possible.

When the ship finally left the harbour, there were still some Bolsheviks milling among the scattered crowd. A few minutes later, a shot was heard and we discovered that we were being shot at from the shore; a few people who had just arrived from around Odessa were angry that so many had been allowed to flee – as far as they were concerned, all the passengers aboard the ship were aristocrats, the wealthy, and all with the blood of the Russian people on their hands. We had by then heard their speeches and slogans over and over again. An hour later, my uncle and the other men managed to get through the crowd with difficulty and join us. We then realised that we had embarked on a journey with no particular destination. The French captain was himself in flight from the revolution; as he explained to one of the men, 'We'll have to keep going until someone is prepared to let us in.'

However, no one was particularly bothered about our homelessness; the fact that we'd managed to escape the Bolsheviks was enough to make everyone jubilant. At that moment we caught sight of the gardens of Odessa looking at us from the hilltop. The lanterns were still on and I assumed that, like any other large estate, the revolutionaries had by now occupied that one as well. I closed my eyes momentarily to go over all the years I had spent in that place.

Even though there were some four thousand passengers aboard, the ship was slowly forging through the waves, though it wasn't making much progress from the shore. A boat would occasionally approach and shoot at us. We saw at least one naval officer fall from the deck into the sea. The French captain was heard to say that he was not going to stop under any circumstances, even if they threw a bomb to sink the ship. The fear we'd all felt during those few days spent in the harbour was such that they were not prepared to risk being halted.

On the second day we ran out of water and everyone was gasping. Even a gold imperial could not buy a jug of water and we couldn't work out how and when someone would finally manage to get some. Then, a boat carrying water approached the ship and the naval officers took the flasks and used the ladders to get them aboard. There was a kerfuffle over a bowl of water, but we managed to get hold of a canteen and pour a few drops down our parched throats. Nonetheless, by the time we passed under a vast bridge with minarets reaching to the skies, I could hardly see. The ship came to a halt in the middle of the sea and a few boats approached carrying people wearing fezzes; we had reached the land of the Ottomans. Everyone who had spread out on the deck gave out a joyful yell; alas, it was for nothing. The only thing we achieved by our stop was to get more water and some thick black bread that was hard to swallow.

I can't recall anything else; I can only remember the Ottoman officer who came aboard for inspection receiving a few imperials from Khan Baba Khan, in return for which he took my uncle's letter to town and promised to present it to the Iranian Embassy. The deposed Shah, using his son's title, had written to the embassy saying that the parents of His Majesty were prisoners aboard the ship and did not have permission to get off; they were about to collapse.

The ship was about to embark, but on our group's insistence and Khan Baba Khan and the general's pleas, they decided to hang on for another hour until a large boat with the Iranian flag fluttering aloft finally appeared. When one of the women lifted me so that I could sit somewhere on the boat, I caught sight of the flag and tears rolled down my cheeks. It was as though I had managed to find a cool, shaded place in which to die. Someone handed us a bowl of water. My head felt hollow and my stomach was so dry it ached. The water I drank was as wholesome as the water we had pulled out of the well in a bucket in the middle of the night in Nanny's house and which Mother had poured over my head. I told myself that Mother and Nezhat were fortunate; in the past two days I had repeatedly wished for my own death.

With the little strength we had left we managed to get off the boat and once on shore we got into a carriage with drawn curtains. We then passed through steep streets, eventually arriving at the Iranian school. A room was swiftly prepared for us and as soon as a rug had been spread on the floor I lay down in one corner with Khadijeh by my side. I hardly noticed the passing of the night or the arrival of the morning.

The next day we found out that although the fireplaces were all in use, the rooms in that school were bitterly cold because they had no insulation. In any case, we were not really safe because the Iranian management, mostly from Azerbaijan, the compatriots of Sattar Khan and Baqer Khan, recalled the pain and suffering of two years of fighting and starvation which the same Shah had forced upon them, and were not prepared to give him and his convoy shelter.

After a couple of difficult days, one of which was rainy, we finally ended up in Beyuke Ada.[13] Compared to Odessa, the mansion was modest, but for a group of people having just escaped death and starvation it was pleasant enough. The small marble *hammam* was particularly enjoyable and we could finally wash after ten days. As we unwound ourselves in the warm pool it was as though we had survived a nightmare and we splashed around idly and full of giggles. It took the Empress a few days of talking to us and restoring discipline to bring some sort of order back to our dishevelled convoy and to remind everyone of their duties; after the week spent at the harbour and aboard the ship our behaviour was all over the place.

Three days later we took a boat and went to Istanbul. This was my first ever outing in a city; until then I had not even gone to the *bazaar*. Strolling in the magical *bazaar* in Istanbul, wearing Ottoman *chadors*, heralded a new beginning. I felt I had been born again to live a different life in a different city.

CHAPTER 32

We were in the reception room at Beyuke Ada when Malakeh Jahan managed to have a private moment with me.

'There won't be enough time so I'll arrange for you to have a moment alone with His Majesty on Sunday or Monday, and you, my dear daughter, need to be direct and explicit with him so that you can finalise the situation with him personally.'

When the Empress stopped talking, and saw my puzzled expression, she realised she had to explain a little further.

'Look Khanoum, you are nineteen; when I was your age I already had two sons and was expecting Khadijeh as well. It is not in your interest to wait any longer. I am not aware of what goes on in your heart, all I know is that your situation needs to be clarified. Whether you'll become my daughter-in-law or remain my daughter, as you are now, makes no difference to my feelings for you. You are no less to me than Khadijeh and it shall continue this way as long as I live. Though you'll have to clarify the situation directly with His Majesty himself – as you know, like you, I haven't seen him for ten years.'

As usual, whenever she talked about her son, tears would roll down her cheeks. I was grateful that she seemed to value my opinion and wanted me to decide. So I bowed and kissed her hands.

'Wouldn't it be better if *you* were to conduct such a conversation?' I said, at which she shook her head, indicating that she could not accept such a responsibility.

I curtseyed and went to my room. She was right, I was no longer the little girl who had fled Tehran but older by ten years. Abdollah had already loosened my remaining ties to the fantasy that Nezhat had shaped by warning me not to seek happiness in the palace. The thought of being a prisoner like my mother terrified me as well. At the same time, the thought of living with a rotund man who, in my mind, was always affectionate, had long left my head. The Empress was right: I had to clarify my future.

It took an entire week for the mansion in Beyuke Ada to be redecorated. The Shah was supposed to stop in Turkey en route to Europe, his first foreign tour, so that he could see his parents after ten years. Every day the embassy staff came to speak to my uncle about preparations. The Ottoman Sultan had proposed a palace for the Shah's visit, but the embassy had leased a hotel near our house so that during his two-week-long visit the Shah could be on the same side of the waters, close to his parents.

Everyone woke up early on the day and there was commotion in the house. We were wearing new clothes and, despite the scarf and *chador*, we had our hair done. All the men except my uncle had left earlier to attend the welcome ceremony. The Empress was clearly impatient and she kept pouring *espand* into a brazier to ensure the Shah's good health.

The Iranians living in Istanbul had hired a couple of excursion boats; both were flying paper flags in the Iranian colours. The guards went through a formal welcome ceremony and a military band struck up on the dock, but it was late afternoon by the time we sighted the carriages. Looking even more obese, Ahmad Shah, who wore a dark suit, managed to get off the carriage, walking-stick in hand. The Ottoman guards had cordoned off the area surrounding the mansion. The Shah, accompanied by his two brothers, arrived in the front yard with his uncle Nosrat us-Saltaneh, as well as Nosrat ud-Dowleh, the Foreign Secretary. The latter was my cousin, Khanoum Nanny's son, whom I had met as a child. My uncle opened his arms and the Empress flew to him: the three of them were in tears. Khadijeh and I, who were watching everything from upstairs, were in tears as well.

The next day the Empress fulfilled her promise and took me to the room by the entrance where the Shah was talking with his sister Khadijeh. I was wearing a green *chador* and I shall never forget how hard I tried to contain my excitement.

He rose from his chair and when the Empress and Khadijeh left the room he sat down again, and the first thing he said was, 'Dearest cousin, would you not sit down?'

So I sat down and, without further delay, began to ask him about his journey. He was brief and then began to approach the subject.

'Would you permit me to talk without formalities?'

'I wanted to say the same thing.'

'I am aware of how you spend your time, and I know that you like reading and drawing, not much like the ladies in Tehran. The truth is that monarchy is nothing but trouble: one has no private time and at times it feels like being a mere captive. Do you recall that ominous day at the Russian Embassy? Well, rather than placing this cup in front of me, I wish everyone had agreed with my mother and put someone else in my place. Alas, it didn't happen. Though I am not trying to wriggle out of all this, I don't wish to share this tragedy with someone else, either. I have vowed not to repeat what went on in my ancestors' establishment: the harem and the way the martyred Shah and Shah Baba went about their lives. Moreover, I think it unbecoming for a knowledgeable and talented lady like you to lead your life under such circumstances. What do you think?'

He was looking down while making some sort of pattern on the floor with the tip of his walking-stick. I rose and tidied my *chador*.

'I am grateful that His Majesty has made it possible for us to put formalities aside so that we can talk with sincerity. I have for a long time been looking forward to such a moment.'

I could by then feel a sense of relief in him. He moved his walking-stick and asked me to sit down, and continued to speak very quietly so that no one could hear.

'I consider you a sister and very dear to me. Your sensibility has made it possible for me to speak openly. So, please allow me to discuss something else as well. I am very pleased that your life has turned out in such a way that you have come to be with my mother and I beg of you, whatever happens, stay with the Empress and do not return to Iran. Let me reveal a secret to you: I shall not stay either. I shall leave Muhammad Hassan in the palace as soon as I can and leave for Europe; your convoy will join me as well. No one needs to know this. Until then will you promise to remain with the Empress?'

'I have no one but the Empress, and in all these years she has been both Empress and parent to me. The thought of spending a single moment away from her is unimaginable for me.'

He then giggled childishly as though someone had just given him the happiest news of his life. He got up and, before leaving the room, adopted the manner of a sovereign once again.

'I shall reward your kindness,' he said, but I did not expect a reward.

We left the room and I looked in the Empress's direction and smiled – she was talking to some of the princesses in the corridor. I went up the stairs. I already felt lighter, as though I had shed a responsibility onto someone else's shoulders. As that corpulent figure, looking prematurely old, was leaving I felt he had become a brother to me. I pitied him for being so sincere, yet he struck me as weak, and though I didn't have a clue about politics I had no doubt he could not run a country. Moreover, I didn't think he was even capable of managing himself. At the time I had no idea that his tour of Europe would alter his destiny as well as the path that the monarchy was to take. It was not unreasonable that Qajar princes such as Nosrat us-Saltaneh and Nosrat ud-Dowleh shared the same concern and followed him wherever he went. He was letting go of the throne his forebears had won in battle a hundred and fifty years before.

The following week he left for Europe with the same pomp and ceremony with which he had arrived. His arrival had opened the doors to the homes and palaces of the Ottoman rulers, a reminder of the *One Thousand and One Nights*. The palaces were located on either side of the Golden Horn – Dolmabahçe, Topkapi, Cheraqan, Beilarbi, Yildiz – overlooking the Bosphorus and the Galata Bridge, which connected Europe to Asia.

CHAPTER 33

I can't quite recall my first visit to an Ottoman palace, but I have kept a vivid memory of the day we went to meet the mother of the Ottoman Emperor, Sultan Reshad. A charming and beautiful Turkish woman who, upon lifting her Turkish *chador*, revealed her heavy makeup, came to visit the Empress the day before, and went through the customs and formalities of Bab Ali Court, including the *tamannaa*, similar to the 'reverence' or curtsey Madame Francis had taught to me, Khadijeh and her other pupils at school. We had to bend one knee and lift the two sides of our skirts and then kneel slightly, lowering our heads when encountering kings and queens. Here they placed one hand on the eyes and then curtseyed.

A visit to the Sultana in Ortakoy Palace was arranged. We sailed towards the jetty of the palace aboard a boat with ten 'Royal Ethiopian' oarsmen dressed in white tops and puffed scarlet trousers. At the jetty, some ten or twenty eunuchs, each of whom was in charge of looking after us individually, bowed and led the way. Once we reached the steps, a tall woman dressed in red satin with a long row of buttons running from the top to the bottom of her dress and covered in the same material welcomed the Empress. She had the traditional Turkish women's headgear ornamented by a row of pearls round the top. Khadijeh and I were introduced as princesses: she was the sister of the Shah and I the niece of the former Shah and granddaughter of the noblest Shah, Shah Baba.

When we went up the stairs the eunuchs took our *chadors*. We then checked our appearance in the mirrors in the hallway.

Turkish women in the inner sanctum wore hats but we had white scarves fastened under our chins with a jewelled pin. The enormous chandelier hanging in the parlour enhanced the glow of all the jewels and gold that adorned the heads and necks of the women; the elaborate woodwork on the walls, the magnificent doors adorned with patterns of flowers picked out in golden nails and the columns of mirror-work were imposing. Sultana, who was referred to as the Great Kadin, was leaning against a large stiff cushion; though not as charming, she resembled my mother when she was sitting in our sitting room. Surrounding the room were lounging sultanas who rose to their feet as the Kadin got up and we had to greet every one of them with a peck on the cheek. Their scent filled the air. There was a purpose to our visit, which the Empress had talked us through the day before. During Ahmad Shah's visit, Sultan Reshad, the Caliph, had expressed an interest in the two imperial families becoming united through marriage, meaning that one of the sultanas was to wed Ahmad Shah. A week after Ahmad Shah's departure for Europe, the names of three sultanas were forwarded to the Empress, and now we were going to make their acquaintance, or rather, inspect them. I found the whole thing absurd, but the Empress took the matter seriously and had commissioned each one of us to talk to people and obtain information about the girls. The three of them had been born in the same year and were fifteen years old, which made them four years my junior: Fatemeh Gohareen, Shokrieh, the granddaughter of Sultan Abdol Aziz the former emperor, and Dorryeh, granddaughter of Sultan Reshad, the current Caliph.

It was truly like the slave market, and reminded me of what Abdollah had told me. Each sultana got up and performed a *défilé*; when they approached the Empress or the Kadin they made *tamannah*. They seemed too young for their age and the light colour of their eyes gave them a kind of lamb-like innocence. When they returned to sit by their mothers their smiles revealed their white teeth. Apart from Khadijeh and me, who hadn't taken this seriously at all and were exchanging mischievous glances, the Empress and her four other lady companions watched every move the girls made, and then in their broken Turkish conversed and exchanged pleasantries with the sultanas. Then the Kadin beckoned for the main *défilé* to commence. They rose one by one and circled the room, making an offering of pastries, which they had baked themselves. We had to accept their offering and taste what they had baked so that we could acknowledge their qualities.

I noticed a fanciful expression on the faces of the girls, which I had long ushered out of my head; a fantasy just like the one Abdollah had expanded on in the long nights of Odessa. They were under scrutiny for their wifely duties and qualities in the imperial court. Whenever I thought about these young girls, and the position of women in the harem, I felt sorry for them, though I kept my thoughts to myself. The matchmaking events resulting in our acquaintance with the Ottoman imperial family introduced us to the sultanas and gave us insight into their relationships with one another, their different sentiments and their rivalry. Before we knew it, we felt its impact on our lives as well. But first we moved home, and once again went to live in a palace fit for receiving such visitors.

We had leased part of Sultana Khadijeh's palace, where we could put on display what we had brought with us from Odessa. We had also acquired some furniture, as well as some twenty large rugs, which had been sent over from Tabriz. Our home looked perfectly Iranian except that from the veranda we could see the Bosphorus, which was quite a sight with its buzz and traffic at night. At such times the city hardly resembled a place where the Turks had been fighting for the past six years, the result of which was a city packed with the wounded brought back from the war zone. This was a city where the princesses and inhabitants of the palaces considered themselves to be living in the centre of a vast empire and believed there was no bigger, more prominent and powerful city in the world. In the daytime, however, the city was awash with beggars who roamed the streets by the harbour, on the bridge and in the *bazaars*. They hung onto passing pedestrians begging for money. The women had their goods on display in the most crowded parts of the city and every time they saw someone neatly attired they begged them to buy a rosary, some spice, or cards with prayers written on them to keep bad omens at bay. The money they made was to help them and their families. We heard that most of these people were from decent walks of life. Istanbul and its suburbs were full of immigrants from every corner of the vast empire, which was increasingly becoming hollow, resembling a rotting tree: hollow inside and ready to fall.

On the other side of the high walls of the palaces and stately homes, however, where the Caliph's relations lived, not only was there no sign of poverty; the imperial family, rather, insisted on maintaining opulence and discipline, a reflection of their once-powerful stature. They hardly made any effort to economise, and famine, shortages and the war had barely made an impact on them. This was questioned not only by Khadijeh and me, but by anyone arriving in Istanbul: just how long could this alien existence continue? We read in the newspapers or heard the news that the Turks were commanding different divisions in the military and had the reins of power in their own hands, and that the Caliph was practically a prisoner in his own palace. None of this had, however, made the courtiers lower their grandeur or the scale on which they led their lives. The beautiful nights of Istanbul seemed to be at the disposal of the aristocrats, courtiers, generals and foreign ambassadors, who were fully entertained, but the day belonged to thousands of poor and destitute vagrants who jostled against each other.

Sultana Khadijeh's palace was positioned on the Bosphorus near Galata Bridge. It was a reminder of the Ottoman Empire and filled with tales. The palace gardener had confided in Nadi, the Empress's loyal maid who had accompanied us from Odessa. We understood that Sultana Khadijeh was the beautiful daughter of Morad V, who reigned for only a short time before being imprisoned in his own palace by his brother. When Khadijeh and Naeemeh, her cousin and the daughter of Sultan Abdul Hamid, reached maturity they simultaneously wedded young men from the imperial household. One of the young men was handsome and wealthy but not the other. The more handsome fellow, whose wealth guaranteed his prosperous future, became husband to the daughter of Sultan Abdul Hamid, and the ravishing and charming Khadijeh, whose father was under house arrest in Dolmabahçe Palace, had to wed the other.

There was a debacle when it came to light that Khadijeh had had an affair with Kemal ed-Din Pasha, Naeemeh's husband. When the secret was revealed to the Sultan, everyone anticipated grave punishment for Khadijeh, and it was feared she would lose her life. Sultan Abdul Hamid, however, did not do as everyone had expected; instead, he quietly forced Khadijeh to live with her husband, the person she loved least, in the same palace. This was a harsh sentence for the young sultana. Fourteen years later, when her uncle had to abdicate in favour of his brother, she finally managed to leave the husband who had been forced upon her and put an end to her ordeal.

The gardener described the painful and dispirited life of the proud sultana who had been banned by the Sultan from seeing anyone. She spent her time attending to the garden and the flowers of the palace or in the glasshouse fussing over her flowers. The gardener had explained everything with such gusto that we were all eager to meet the sultana, our landlady. The first opportunity rose when she came to pay the Empress a visit, along with a number of sultanas. From the first moment we set eyes on her we were conscious of every move she made: she walked tall with an air of haughtiness about her. No more than thirty, she hardly gave the impression that she had spent many lamentable years in that palace.

We heard that the Ottoman court's proposal of marriage with the Shah of Iran had been withdrawn. The reasons behind the withdrawal were a mystery to us, but the Empress, who was in a bad mood, explained that the condition for such a match was that when the Ottoman virgin became the Shah's wife, the Shah was not to have any other wives; after choosing one of the three girls he had to divorce his other wives. These were Ahmad Shah's *siqehs*. According to the Empress, the conditions of the match had been reviewed in Tehran and, save the last condition, everything had been agreed to. But Ahmad Shah was not prepared to throw his wives out of his home.

The failed matchmaking, however, did not end the relationship between the two families, and within a short period of time there was a new development. One winter evening, the Empress broke the news to Khadijeh and me: both of us had to perform our own *défilé*. The Empress had to present us and the Kadin, as well as some twenty sultanas, were to pass us under scrutiny before we could be granted Ottoman princely homes.

Khadijeh's situation was not so difficult: she was only twenty whereas I was twenty-one at the time, but she was also sister to the Shah of Iran, which was a great bonus. During our first week a nephew of the current Sultan was proposed. The matter was about to be concluded when it came to our attention that Rahman Pasha was only seventeen; a wife older than her husband was unthinkable, even though he was the son of a sultan. Khadijeh was upset about the news and opened up to me in the evenings, often in tears. She was clearly taken by the thought of living in a palace and being included in the social circle and its glamorous events; she couldn't see that those women were effectively prisoners among the eunuchs and the maids. I, however, was certain that my happiness did not depend on a soulless life in a golden cage. I couldn't work out why the Empress believed that sorting out Khadijeh's life had to be a priority. Since I was not bothered, I was not aware of the difficulties my aunt and uncle found themselves in with respect to the enquiries about my parents. Everyone was told that my mother had passed away and that I was under my uncle's guardianship. My father, however, was a problem, and they could not lie about him. At the same time, they were anxious not to ruin my life by revealing the secret; lying was not becoming, either. I was not aware of this problem until the day we were returning from a social event. The Empress and I were alone in the carriage when she slowly began to talk about my future. She said that my uncle considered it inappropriate to be untruthful and felt that, as was customary, my father had to be informed. I was terrified.

'What if he decides to attend the wedding of his darling daughter?'

I think the Empress said something like, 'So what, we'd tolerate him for a few days!' at which I burst into tears.

'I am not prepared to meet the demon.'

I must then have enquired why she wanted to part with me and whether I had become a nuisance. I said that I didn't really wish to leave her, even for a king's palace. After this conversation there was silence in the carriage, a silence on the subject that was to last for two years. Although I was aware that from time to time my uncle and the Empress talked about this between themselves, no one involved me any more.

CHAPTER 34

It was *Eyd Qorban*, the Muslim festival celebrating God's revelation to Ibrahim. This was by far the most celebrated festival observed by the Turks. Even the poorer families saved all year to celebrate *Eyd* in its full glory, and the entire city had turned clean and new. The *Eyd* prayers in Istanbul were one of the most magnificent events of the year, despite the Ottomans having lost the war, and the French and British generals travelling through occupied Istanbul in their golden carriages. The Ottoman generals had lost their authority and had to take orders from the triumphant victors of the Great War. Friday prayers took place in Haya Sofia mosque and the Empress, Khadijeh and I were included among the imperial ladies, though my uncle appeared only in the formal event, *Salam o Leyke*, as the father of the Shah of Iran together with his young sons.

Having laid out our dresses the night before, the hairdresser, tall and fair, arrived with her black Ethiopian assistant first thing. They first attended to Khadijeh and me, then to the Empress; an hour before the ceremony we travelled on the Bosphorus with Nadi as well as one other servant aboard a boat sent by the court. Its style was clearly that of the Ottoman court, though it could not be mistaken for those carrying the sultanas and the princesses. The sea, too, looked different on this occasion: the jetties had been set with fireworks and the Dolmabahçe resembled a bed of roses planted along the Bosphorus. By then I had learned sufficient Turkish to understand the meaning of the songs the sailors chanted – the lyrics were a tribute to the Bosphorus and the Dolmabahçe. There were many boats sailing towards the Dolmabahçe and the sailors, dressed alike with red fezzes on their heads, synchronised their rowing so that the guests could step out with due regard to their rank. One could scarcely sense the presence of the occupying forces.

Unlike the Empress, who moved slowly and with decorum, Khadijeh and I needed some assistance as we jumped out. We neared the marble pillars just outside the palace, where the scent of the flowers filled the air. We were surrounded by eunuchs and beautiful maids, who courteously directed everyone to the palace. Further up, at the entrance to the terrace leading to the palace, a golden-haired woman greeted everyone. She wore gold and jewellery as well as a wide blue sash bearing some medal over her shoulder. She was the Mistress of Ceremonies and knew all the guests; many sultanas and princesses greeted her with a peck on the cheek. Once again, as soon as my name was mentioned, I had to put up with all the whispers. In the Ottoman court, the daughters of kings were referred to as 'Sultana', and 'Khanoum Sultana Khanoum' if they were granddaughters of the sultans, so, according to the Empress, 'Khanoumi is twice Khanoum!'

Although it was daytime, dozens of chandeliers were lit, making the crystal and glassware, as well as the gold and jewellery on the women, glow and further enhance the light. After climbing up the wide Bakara stairs, we had first to pass through a hallway for our *chadors* to be removed by the maids; the Turkish women's *chadors* were tied above their feet to reveal their colourful Parisian dresses and expensive jewellery underneath. Khadijeh and I had each been given an item from the Empress's treasure chest. We were young and beautiful, and our dresses were quite becoming: I was dressed in green voile and wore emeralds, which matched the colour of my dress. We were completely removed from life outside the palace walls, where the needy were fed on the occasion of *Eyd* and thousands climbed over one another to get something to eat.

There was a band playing in the salon and a woman dressed in an embroidered waistcoat and puffed trousers ushered us in to where everyone was offered strong coffee in silverware – the aroma of coffee mixed with cardamom and rosewater filled the air. Everyone in the salon, except the eunuchs, wore Turkish headwear, which matched the colour of their dresses and was sewn in gold with the customary pearls. At the top end of the salon, the Sultan's mother was seated comfortably on a sofa with a good few kilograms of gold and jewellery hanging from her neck. When she wanted to make a move as a courteous gesture towards the newly arrived guests, two ladies in waiting had to help her. The music hushed as the Mistress of Ceremonies announced the arrival of Malakeh Jahan, 'Sultana Valedeh Fars'. As the Sultan's mother made a move on her sofa, the other women rose in our honour. Khadijeh and I kissed the hands of the Sultan's mother, whose blue eyes twinkled in her deeply wrinkled face. We then approached the sultanas, the kindest of whom was our landlady, Sultana Khadijeh. She was always particularly friendly to her namesake Khadijeh and hugged me as well. Years of living in Istanbul and our participation in social events had resulted in an air of familiarity between us.

We were now absorbed in conversation, pleasantries and whispers. Sherbets and delicious pastries kept going round, just as back in Iran. Bowls of water were then brought to everyone so that the fine, carefully manicured fingers of the ladies did not remain sticky, followed by silver bowls and pitchers filled with an infusion of scents and rosewater.

The sound of music was suddenly interrupted and the Mistress of Ceremonies announced the arrival of the Sultan the 'Caliph of all Muslims'. Since he was related to all, and just as I had seen in the palaces in Tehran upon Shah Baba's arrival in the inner sanctum, everyone circled him. Sultan Vahid ed-Din, with his grey beard, was just as old and weak as Shah Baba had been. As soon as he arrived he went to sit next to Sultana Valedeh and everyone showered him with pleasantries, making the likeness to Shah Baba complete, not to mention his use of the Turkish language. I could now begin to understand how difficult it must have been for my uncle and his wife to forgo the crown and the throne. The Sultan was returning from prayers; tradition required him once a year to lead the *Eyd* prayers, at which point he became Imam for the day. Now he was exhausted and enjoying his first orange blossom sherbet. He didn't stay long; after exchanging a few words with his wives, daughters and other sultanas he got up to go to the inner sanctum, at which point the salon became quite disorderly.

'Pretty Khanoum Sultana,' someone whispered in my ear and I immediately recognised Sultana Fahimeh and gave her a smile; she was placing a small wrapped item in my palm.

I must have looked confused because she said, 'A token of love from Saeed Pasha, prince of …' at which I felt my temperature rise, as though someone had placed a fireball in my hand.

I felt everyone in that room must have heard the whisper and the name, and was aware of the contents of that small parcel in my hand, the thought of which made me even more embarrassed and uncomfortable. For the rest of the time that I was in the salon I felt everyone looked at me meaningfully; even the Empress gave me a smile. I felt obliged to keep my fist closed, since I could not hide the package anywhere else, and when I was putting my *chador* on I had to pass the parcel from one hand to the other so that I could tie it up. The maids tied everyone's *chadors* in the hallway on the way out and made sure they looked right, while the ladies stood haughtily, but I was not used to this.

When we stepped into the boat, I was anxious that the parcel, the contents of which I was still unaware of, might slip and fall in the water. When we arrived home the men hadn't arrived yet and I had hardly released myself from the ties of the Turkish *chador* when the Empress, whose voice suddenly came across loud and clear, asked me to open the parcel so that she could see the contents. So she was aware of everything.

I had been given a fine diamond necklace and everyone was looking at it. However, the news became official in the evening, when the Empress mentioned that she had received an invitation to a *hammam* event in Sultana Fahimeh's palace the following week. We had previously attended such events but with the occupying foreign forces in Istanbul, food shortages and the increase in the number of war refugees in that city, one expected such socialising to be over. That evening the Empress handed me a fine pink envelope embossed with the Ottoman coats of arms that contained a photograph of Saeed Pasha. Sultana Fahimeh had mischievously slipped the photograph in the envelope with the invitation. The photograph was of a young man with a thin, twirling moustache, dressed in military uniform and holding his hat in his arms; his eyes looked sharp, there was a lift in his eyebrows and his dark, sleek hair was combed back.

Before joining the others I spent an hour looking at the photograph. The stranger had been quick to catch my imagination before I'd even had a chance to meet him in person. Later that evening the Empress proudly explained to everyone that Sultana Fahimeh had discussed the matter with her long ago and that Saeed Pasha was Sultan Vahieddin's nephew. His father had passed away two years ago, when he was heir to the throne; had he still been alive, he would have been Sultan, and who knows ... Saeed Pasha had spent two years in a military academy in Paris.

During the entire time that the Empress spoke of Saeed Pasha, I held my head down. Khadijeh, however, was the one who couldn't help but show her excitement and spoke for me. She was delighted that we might be going to Paris since we had the Sultan's permission. The year before, the Empress and the Shah had gone to Europe, spending two weeks in Paris. When they returned they had so much to tell us about the queen of European cities. We had only seen photographs and postcards, in which the Eiffel Tower stood out in its full glory, but we so wanted to go to Paris.

As far as I was concerned, the fact that Saeed Pasha had an understanding of the French language, had read Baudelaire and understood the poetry of Lamartine was illuminating; I could speak to him in that language rather than Turkish. Although everyone spoke Turkish around me all these years, I was more confident speaking French. I had read so many stories and poems in French that the language had become familiar to me; when it came to Persian, I could not recall any other poetry except the lyrics of Hafez of Shiraz.

Two days later we took a boat and went to the grand *bazaar* in the European part of Istanbul, something that I enjoyed very much. We had doubts before making the excursion: Khan Baba Khan and Dr Jarozelski had only a few days before prevented everyone from going to the busy areas. The French and British soldiers got drunk at night and caused problems for women; the insulted Turkish men occasionally lost control as a result and there were brawls. According to Jarozelski, fighting had broken out at the entrance to Galata Bridge and a few people had been killed. The victorious Europeans remembered their defeat on the minor fronts and were now taking revenge. The general and his wife believed the biggest threat was directed at the Russians, who had been defeated in two wars, internally and with the Europeans. He and the Shah held the British responsible, as they did the day we received some news from Tehran that very nearly caused the Empress to pass out; everyone in the household constantly cursed the British.

There had been a coup in Tehran, the news of which distressed the Empress because of her concern for her beloved son, and her sobbing made everyone else burst into tears as well. Khan Baba was later to get news of Tehran via a telephone call to Tabriz.

There had been a heavy snowfall and we saw no movement on the streets. It was late afternoon, and Khan Baba had still not turned up. Two or three other people decided to go to the Iranian

Embassy, which was situated on the other side of the Bosphorus. The evening was upon us and we were still waiting; everyone was anxious and no one spoke. My uncle was pacing the library and kept puffing at the hookah. The Empress was in bed and nothing could help her go to sleep: the thought of the Bolsheviks marching in as they had done in Russia, and later executing the imperial family, was a horrific thought.

Khan Baba finally arrived and we discovered that the news of the coup had indeed been correct but that no one was touching the Shah. The Cossacks had rampaged through Tehran to find the notables and arrest them. The next day we received the Shah's telegram letting everyone know that he and the crown prince were both well. He had also announced that he had made Zia, the chief editor of *R'ad Daily*, premier with full authority.

Two days later we managed to get our hands on the papers and read detailed reports on the Cossacks' full position, the arrest of Farmanfarma and Eyne, who were married to my aunts, and of many other relations and acquaintances. The Shah and his entourage were puzzled; while they believed the British to be the culprits, they could not comprehend the arrest of the pro-British notables.

We assumed that the Shah might have fallen prey to the same destiny to which the Ottoman Sultan had succumbed – his junior officers had carried out a coup against him and he was now under house arrest without any authority whatsoever. Further news from Tehran calmed us down and meant we could actually get on with the task at hand, preparing for the *hammam* event!

Khadijeh and I had to remain vigilant so that unfamiliar people did not catch sight of our faces on the way to the event the next day. The thought of spending a happy day away from the depressing atmosphere of an occupied city was a relief; we were not only further familiarising ourselves with the customs and codes of conduct within the Turkish imperial household; we also found it altogether intoxicating and were drawn to it.

The Empress still missed being in Tehran and at Golestan Palace, and regretted having been stripped off her privileges.

There were no men in sight and as soon as we arrived our *chadors* were taken away, as well as our *hammam* bags. In a round room surrounded with pots of flowers, a maid was sprinkling rose water through a horn-like object while another came to loosen our hair and then meticulously arrange it in some sort of chignon tied with colourful ribbons. Every guest was wrapped in large, colourfully embroidered dressing gowns. By the time we had the embroidered slippers made of sheepskin on we could hardly recognise ourselves. We burst out laughing on seeing our reflection in the mirror, but the Empress's frown reminded us that we should not come across as too enchanted. We then passed through another room with a dome-like ceiling, which allowed light through, and coved walls and beautiful tilework. Surrounding the room were seating blocks where the sultanas were engaged in vivacious conversation. Sultana Fahimeh, who was fair and tall, was dressed in a scarlet dressing gown and greeted us warmly. She then motioned to the maids and a couple of enamelled Russian boxes were brought to Khadijeh and me, which opened to reveal a round mirror and an assortment of cream, perfume and pot pourri. In return, the Empress opened a *termeh*-covered wrapped bundle that Nadi was holding and took out a porcelain comb from a red velvet pouch. The Empress then tucked it into the Sultana's fair hair with her own hands and the diamonds on the comb sparkled. Moments later the comb went round from hand to hand and everyone expressed their approval of the Empress's taste.

The ladies all sat on silk rugs on different blocks among pots of flowers and the incense that filled the air. Everyone seemed happy except me: having looked at the Sultana's box, my mind had flown back to Tehran and landed right in front of Mother, where I saw Morvarid combing her rich brown hair. I was glad to have entered the steam room quickly so that no one could see my tears rolling down. I knew how much Mother would have loved to see me admired by everyone.

Someone carrying a crystal glass filled with a peppermint drink managed to find me in the steam. I barely managed to hear her voice amid the noise, and from what she said I could only work out 'Saeed Pasha's effendi'. Gentle music was seeping through the steam and a few minutes later, while being massaged, rose and purple drinks in enormous jugs were poured into everyone's cups. It was less noisy now and the wife of the French Consul was lying next to me talking of the opulence of the East while the Sultana was admiringly glancing towards us. Our manmade paradise, complete with its milk-filled baths, was a far cry from the Ottoman Empire, which was being torn to pieces by the French and British at that very moment.

Before reaching the room where lunch was being served, the French woman asked me if I had ever seen Paris, to which I replied, 'No.' She added that in Paris one could find poetry, music and beauty but no 'one thousand and one nights'. When she was telling me all this I don't know why but I forgot about my mother and began to think of my father, whose two visits to Paris had meant many souvenirs and presents. That very morning I had read in the papers that the monster, too, had been arrested. His name made my heart race and I could hardly hide my delight at the thought of him being in great agony.

It was late afternoon as we were returning home and the Bosphorus was the colour of molten iron. We felt lighter than when we had set off that morning and we had much to gossip about: a couple of Turkish generals were running the country now, one of whom was Kemal Pasha, who had asked for the hand of one of the sultanas in marriage.

Khadijeh had for the first time overheard one of the women contemptuously referring to him as the 'golden rose', and she could not understand the reference until the Empress murmured, 'Off the rails – homosexual.'

By the time we arrived, there was more news from Tehran. Mossadeq, the governor of Fars, had ignored the Shah's telegram and was not prepared to give in to the post-coup government. We knew him; we had seen him and his family the previous year in Istanbul. Despite his youth and having barely established himself in Tehran, he was to replace his uncle Farmanfarma and become governor of Fars. He had studied political sciences in Europe and I could well recall the monster's envy: my father had so wanted to become governor but he had only got as far as becoming deputy governor in Azerbaijan. Upon hearing the news, while my uncle and his wife admired Mossadeq's resistance, they were filled with contempt towards the notables and the military.

I couldn't be bothered to get involved in politics, something that had engulfed my entire childhood and teenage years. I was at the threshold of a romantic chapter and wanted to be ready. I realised I was no longer interested in the news from Tehran though quite hungry for the Turkish variety. Not having had any choice in the matter, my future seemed to have become connected to Istanbul, Dolmabahçe, the Sultan, the sultanas, Haya Sofia Mosque and Topkapi, and I couldn't afford to remain uninformed. Upon meeting Saeed Pasha I wanted to be in a position to tell him about my future hometown, its customs, people and their troubles.

I had proudly placed the photograph of the young prince in my room and, some nights, whenever I was alone, I would wear the necklace, the very first present from my beloved. I then opened the box that Sultana Fahimeh had given me and looked at myself in the mirror – the bride of Dolmabahçe. Our wedding was to take place in one of the palaces and in the presence of the Sultan.

'Oh Mother, how I miss you! I wish you were here to wrap yourself in your pink tulle shawl. I can still see you by the Russian Embassy, sitting anxiously in the carriage.'

Chapter 35

It was spring by the time Saeed Pasha returned from the front. His sisters welcomed him as a hero, and over the next couple of days they held small social gatherings to which we, too, were invited. We spoke a little during these events, and one day we took the boat to the bridge. The Empress had asked Nadi to chaperone me. Someone called Ezzedin had accompanied Saeed Pasha as butler or guard and, in order not to be overheard, we spoke in French. Saeed Pasha, however, spent most of the time absorbed in animated conversation with Ezzedin, telling jokes and laughing. He spoke about the battlefields in Syria and other related events. Two fez-clad sailors were quietly rowing when Ezzedin wondered if we could get close to the jetty and Saeed Pasha subsequently ordered the sailors to do so. One of the sailors bowed and reminded him that this was not a good idea but Ezzedin was not satisfied. The sailor resisted once again and suddenly things became serious as Saeed took out a pistol from under his belt and demanded that the sailor jump off the boat into the water, which was deep and a trifle turbulent. Nadi and I were terrified and had huddled together with no choice but to watch. The poor man started to beg, but Saeed kept repeating the order. The man was apologetic and explained that he was concerned for everyone's safety since we were in an area beset by riots, which was dangerous. Ignoring his plea, Saeed kept ordering him to jump into the water and threatening him with the pistol.

I was so terrified that he might fire that I covered my face, but all of a sudden I jumped up and shouted, 'No!'

Saeed turned towards me with a cold smile.

'Is the princess mediating?' he asked in his polite French and I nodded. Placing his hand on his eyes he bowed and then addressed the sailor.

'You owe your life to the princess!' The poor man bowed to me and then sat in his place. Ezzedin seemed to murmur something to Saeed Pasha, who came towards me.

'I am glad you mediated; why didn't you say so earlier, it was only a joke,' at which I forced a smile but I was quite shaken. I couldn't believe that his fury had simply been a game, but for my own sake I decided to believe him.

When we heard 'Stop!' from the shore, we realised that the sailor's concern had not been unfounded: a British soldier was warning us not to move. We were rooted to our seats until a boat approached and demanded to see our identity papers. The same sailor went forward and explained to the soldier that our boat belonged to the royal household and then, pointing to us, he added that we were members of the Sultan's family. The British soldier smirked and glanced at us mischievously as he left. We should have known that an occupied city was hardly a place to have fun; Istanbul had for some time now been a garrison for British, French and Italian soldiers. The commander-in-chief was Sir Charles Harrington, who had effectively replaced the Sultan.

On our way back Saeed Pasha explained to me that he had risked everything to return to Istanbul so that he could see me. If the Europeans recognised him he would be in danger. He didn't wait for me to enquire further about his fears but went on to explain that there were pockets of resistance all over the empire, and that the Turks were fighting in all corners to free their homeland from the European yoke of colonisation. He, too, belonged to one of the resistance groups. Although I was worried about his life I admired his courage. I was proud of my future husband's patriotic and brave sentiments. I resolved to read more about Napoleon and tried to picture Saeed Pasha fighting the British.

Saeed accompanied me home and then kissed my hand just before I went inside, asking me to pray for him. He left with a promise to return in a month's time, leaving me to my dreams. Our wedding celebration was going to depend on the Sultan and the state of the country, which deteriorated every day. By the time I managed to see him again the situation had become precarious. Every day there were revolts and clashes in a different part of Istanbul. In the course of our comings and goings to the Sultana's, the Empress and I learned that the Allies had drawn up a treaty, which meant that should the Turks violate the terms of their surrender, Istanbul would be in a state of permanent occupation. However, they had later announced that they had no intention of leaving the occupied territories.

Sultana Fahimeh said that the British were the root of all evil and the Empress agreed with her; according to them, having divided places such as Romania, Bosnia, the Lebanon and Mecca, the British were now planning to break up the Islamic Empire, but the proud and patriotic young Turks were not going to let it happen – or so the Sultana firmly believed. When we returned home in the evening my uncle was suspicious that 'their Sultan' only helped the British achieve their ends, but having frequented social events at the Sultana's, which had incidentally been reduced in dimension, I gathered that the Turks felt their worst enemies were actually the Greeks, for whom the Turks had a particular aversion.

As the days wore on it became more difficult to find food and subsistence. The crate of fruit sent to us from the Sultana's palace was a godsend; according to Khan Baba Khan, fruit and other food was hard to come by in the market, even at a high price. The nationalists had been defeated in one of the cities, and the Greeks were now making progress; when Bursa fell, Sultana Fahimeh was spending the afternoon with us. When I explained that Bursa used to be the old capital of the empire, where a great many sultans were buried, and where there had been many castles, the Empress listened with pride and some satisfaction at her contribution to my upbringing and education. The Sultana was smiling contently, as though she was delighted with her future sister-in-law. Every time she came to visit she brought a token from Saeed Pasha, accompanied by a letter in which he expressed his love and devotion with beautiful and romantic words, saying he couldn't bear to wait any longer. To think that my beloved was busy fighting the enemy in the war zone made me immensely proud, so I never complained, yet I had difficulty understanding why my uncle could not share my sentiments. For instance, he once asked Sultana Fahimeh why the Sultan had not summoned the nation to fight. Sultana Fahimeh took the same line as the rest of the imperial family: 'There must be a very good reason that only the Sultan knows.' She then winked, adding, 'You will come to trust the Sultan's insight,' but he was not satisfied.

Our household was at the time far more concerned about Tehran and Sardar Sepah, the military commander who had seized the reins of power, than the fighting and the revolt in Izmir. My uncle sometimes read the letters that he wrote to Ahmad Shah and the crown prince. Although no one spoke of it, I sensed that Sardar Sepah had become a powerful man in Iran. He struck me as someone like Kemal Pasha, whom the Sultan had made governor of Izmir.

CHAPTER 36

A new arrival from Tehran pretty much confirmed the news we had been receiving here and there. One of the Shah's *siqehs* had been unwell and was now being sent over to receive medical treatment; a member of the Iranian Embassy would collect her at the station. I was keen to get to know her and satisfy my curiosity as to how my life would have turned out if I had remained in Tehran. Ashraf was five years younger than me and didn't have a clue; she was far more naïve than I had been at ten. Khadijeh had to give up her room. The first few nights 'the girl' was in tears; she was lonely and missed Tehran. We tried to keep her mind off her problems by keeping her occupied, and once she began to talk there was much to learn about the hurdles the Shah was facing. I was grateful not to be in her shoes.

I wondered whether or not Saeed was in Izmir, but preferred not to ask until the day I heard that King Constantine of Greece had arrived there. I was relieved to find Saeed back in Istanbul the following day and it was reassuring to know that he was well. As usual, he didn't stay for more than a couple of days, during which we strolled in his sister's garden chaperoned by Ezzedin and Nadi.

I wanted to talk to him about what I had heard in the news about the war fronts. I wished he could tell me a little more about the war and the soldiers' bravery. I took his reluctance to dwell on the subject for modesty. Every time he mentioned something I tried to construct the rest in my mind. Sometimes I was annoyed that he had so much to talk about with Ezzedin and yet when it came to me made do with only a few romantic words. Not that he thought little of women or saw me as unfit to discuss serious issues with; he was educated and open-minded. No, I did not think he was like the men in the East who did not give two hoots about what women thought. I tried to increase my own knowledge of the history of the Ottomans so that I could become worthy of being the wife of a hero. Nevertheless, I would have liked to ask him whether it was true that the Sultan spent his days and nights praying, and whether the Greeks were due to arrive in Istanbul. Was it true that the Greeks were massacring the Muslims and that Kemal Pasha had taken over the forces? And, finally, I wanted to know where my sweetheart was fighting and how many men were under his command. All these questions, however, remained unanswered. Saeed habitually spent a great deal of time whispering and exchanging jokes with Ezzedin, while Nadi and I sat on a bench without talking much.

Ezzedin, who always seemed to know everything, finally broke the news.

'Princess, October is a good month and the wedding should take place on the second Tuesday in October.'

Having encountered Saeed's bewildered smile I just said, 'Whenever appropriate ...'

'We must leave this chaos and go to Paris, to the Côte d'Azur ...'

I broke the news to the Empress later on, and the next day Sultana Fahimeh confirmed what Ezzedin had suggested. Khadijeh had two months earlier got married in a simple, private ceremony appropriate for a war-torn city filled with fear. The foreigners were everywhere and no one seemed happy in Istanbul. The only cheerful part of town was the Fener area where the Greeks had spent many years leading a low-key life in fear of the Muslims, but they were now jubilant. We heard of the restaurants and salons where dancing and live entertainment carried on into the small hours. The area attracted a large crowd, largely as a result of the number of Russian girls coming over after the Bolshevik revolution.

The previous summer the Empress had purchased a house in Nice. I had seen the photograph: a house by the sea where ivy climbed the walls and its terracotta rooftop made it look like the cottages in Odessa. However, I could not see myself living there; I imagined a Topekapi-like home and a salon like that of Sultana Khadijeh's palace. When Ezzedin broke the news, the picture of the future that I had in mind became more vivid. I anticipated that we were going to spend our honeymoon in Europe and then return to Istanbul. The news from the front that reached Istanbul left me in no doubt: Kemal Pasha's army was resisting the Greeks with great force and every day we heard the proud description of imminent victory from the Turks who worked for us. So I quickly pictured my beloved's towering figure going towards the soldiers as people threw flowers at him and he reciprocated their show of emotion.

I carried this image in mind as we went out. On the streets one could sense an air of jubilation; people were embracing one another and large crowds were heading towards the mosques where a service of thanksgiving was in progress and where the *azan* was being chanted from the minarets. The Empress allowed us – Ashraf, Nadi, General Jarozelski's wife and me – to go out to do some shopping for my wedding. We saw Turkish women who had lifted their veils and were directing sarcastic remarks to the British soldiers, telling them to go back home. The British, though bewildered, managed to keep their cool.

Esmaeel Beig, who came from Khoy in Azerbaijan province, had a large haberdashery in the *bazaar*. From time to time he brought us rolls of material carried on his assistant's shoulder. He was greatly excited to welcome us to his shop and was courteous. He took us to the back of the shop where colourful materials were piled up to the ceiling. Jubilant people passed by his shop and Esmaeel Beig was happy to offer them sweets and pastries.

The Turkish military's last offensive had been successful: the Greeks were in flight and important cities were being liberated one by one. On our return we passed by Yildiz Palace, which was guarded by Turkish and British soldiers. The Sultan was known to have preferred this small palace to the great Dolmabahçe and was thought to be praying day and night inside.

Three days later, headlines on the front pages of the newspapers reported the end of the war. '*Allah Akbar*', God is Great, was being chanted from the minarets. The loudest of all was the chanting from the Haya Sofia Mosque, which seemed suddenly to have lifted its head after years of keeping a low profile. The next time the Empress, Sultana Fahimeh and I were going round in a carriage, we saw for the first time a woman who was not veiled and whose skirt was short enough to reveal her legs. We had lifted our veils too.

'Will you not go to Nice now? Are you planning to remain here?' came my anxious question.

There was a pause, after which the Empress responded, 'Whatever is God's will.'

Much as I was looking forward to going to my own home, a palace given to us by the Sultan, as was customary with the newly-weds in his family, I wanted her to stay since I could not imagine living away from her. With this in mind I didn't want to hear about Kemal Pasha and his occupying forces. Yet preparing for a wedding brought happiness, and happiness heralded hope.

CHAPTER 37

T he arrival of the seamstresses meant that everything was ready: the dresses, the presents and the jewellery I was to wear during my wedding ceremony. Given that most of the contents had been deposited two years earlier in a bank in Paris, the Empress's collection seemed to have far more to offer than expected.

I was only two days away from the realisation of my dream; every day a carriage would arrive, bringing Sultana Fahimeh or Sultana Khadijeh. The anxiety that stemmed from reading the papers was palpable but I couldn't understand what had suddenly changed; over the years we had got used to hearing news of war and turbulence. To my mind nothing could alter the plans for Tuesday; my wedding dress was on display in my bedroom, from which I was soon to be parted. The gown, covered with pearl-studded tulle, was mounted on a mannequin that faced my bed. The mannequin was on loan from Katerina, the Russian seamstress, so that her creation wouldn't get creased before the important day. Ashraf admired the gown; she never removed her *chador*, even when she was indoors. We had not introduced her as the wife of the Shah of Iran, nor did she expect us to do so. She spent most of her time in the company of Nadi and the rest of the servants.

The news did not at first seem of any consequence to me, but encountering the bewildered expression on everyone's faces finally brought me back to earth: the parliament in Ankara had deposed the Sultan. I glanced at my uncle who seemed to have become accustomed to unpleasant news. I wanted him to say to me that the news could not interfere with my life, but he was listening to Khan Baba Khan, who was quoting the papers. The Sultan was a mere caliph from then on, and in Ankara people had carried Mustapha Kemal on their shoulders to the palace; he had become the embodiment of power in Turkey, and Rafat Bey, the premier, had handed in his resignation. It took me a while to digest the fact that the Ottoman Empire had just crumbled and I found it hard to believe that at that very moment, the servants whom I had got used to seeing over all those years in the imperial palaces of Dolmabahçe, Ortokuy, Yildiz, Cheraqan and Topkapi were now running away and the soldiers supporting Kemal Pasha were busy plundering the palaces. This meant that all the myths surrounding Sultan Murad, Sultan Salim, the harems and the palaces, which never opened up to the public, were fast evaporating; the sultanas were in tears and the eunuchs in their black Istanbuli gowns were trembling in fear.

The chaotic state of our household was such that I could not ask any questions. My uncle had summoned the Iranian ambassador to seek permission from the new rulers to leave so that our travel documents could be stamped at the French, British and Italian consulates. Our convoy was yet again preparing to set off, once again in the usual hurry that my uncle and the Empress insisted on. But there was the matter of Ashraf, 'the girl'. She was treated like a stranger, and now that we had to leave no one knew what to do with her. There was talk of her going to one of the embassy officials so that a decision with respect to her future could be reached. I was rather vexed that a decision had to be made in her absence, but I had no idea what was to become of my own future either; I had assumed that Saeed was immune in the war against the Greeks as he was with the nationalists. I had imagined him a war hero like Kemal Pasha, Esmat Pasha and other generals whose names were whispered by everyone or appeared on the front pages of the newspapers.

Khan Baba Khan was in charge of organising everything. Our convoy's destination was Nice, and I still didn't know whether I was to accompany them or not. Amid the commotion the Empress summoned me and in the privacy of her room explained, 'Khadijeh and her husband's family are to go to Beirut, but I still don't know what plans Saeed and Sultana Fahimeh have in mind; I assume their situation is dependent on the Sultan.'

'The Sultan is in Yildiz Palace; isn't Saeed going to stay as he is ...'

I was about to say that he was a war hero and was not like the other Ottoman princes who, despite the war, had spent their entire time on leisure pursuits in their palaces. So there was no reason why he had to leave Istanbul.

As though the Empress had read my mind she said, 'I have sent for Sultana Fahimeh. I am even wondering whether it is better for us to go to their palace instead,' and she caressed my head. 'In any case, unless I am assured about your future and Khadijeh's, I am not leaving.'

I was in tears. For the twelve years away from Iran she had looked after me like a mother. She had also told the imperial family that since my parents had passed away I was their daughter: the daughter of Muhammad Ali Mirza and Malakeh Jahan. I knew she had told them that I had inherited rather a large fortune, and as the granddaughter of Mozzafar ed-Din Shah I also received an allowance. Words were not enough to express my gratitude and, as usual, I bowed to kiss her hand, but she would not let me and we set off for Sultana Fahimeh's palace. While waiting for the carriage to arrive, the Empress gave instructions about the packing and everyone was busy; the furniture was to be sold through the Iranian Embassy so that the palace was once again at Sultana Khadijeh's disposal. I suddenly remembered our last days in Odessa and had a vague recollection of our escape from Tehran. I still remembered the things we had left behind in Odessa and I had heard from the Russians we met socially that all the large mansions, estates and palaces in Russia had been confiscated so that the peasants could be accommodated instead. Every Russian aristocrat we met in Istanbul had dreadful recollections and told shocking stories about the executions.

When we were in the carriage I reminded myself that the Turks still respected the Sultan as the Caliph of all Muslims and that his family could not come to any harm; this place was not Bolshevik-ridden. Though it was only a short journey to the Sultana's, one could sense the extraordinary circumstances at the gates: a few military men were standing by the entrance and their manner was abrupt. They hesitated a little on seeing our papers, then searched the carriage and we were finally allowed in. The palace was in chaos and there was no sign of the eunuchs or the maids.

The Sultana came forward to greet us looking pale and embarrassed. We sat on the few remaining armchairs left in the salon now stripped off its magnificent carpets. A eunuch brought some coffee and the Sultana tried to clarify the situation by explaining that the Sultan had arranged for all the palaces to be run by the government and for the imperial family to go to Yildiz Palace, where he was in residence. She then lowered her voice and informed us that the people were with the Sultan, and that there had been uprisings in some places. Kemal Pasha had come to some agreement with the British and was thus betraying his benefactor, but everything would go back to normal since Muslims could not tolerate that godless lot.

What she said was at odds with what we had heard or witnessed: the people saw Kemal Pasha as their hero and considered the Sultan a puppet of the British and French. We had seen Kemal Pasha's pictures everywhere, but there was no sign of pictures of the Sultan and the people on the streets cursed Yildiz Palace as they walked past it. The Empress had to raise the issue.

'I think under the circumstances it is better to postpone the wedding to a later date, as we are going to ...' But the Sultana had clearly predicted the purpose of the visit and apologetically interrupted the Empress, saying that she thought the nuptials should take place that very evening.

'Tonight?' This was my voice coming out of the Empress's throat.

'Yes, this evening!' said the Sultana, lowering her voice. 'We'll bring Saeed Pasha and the cleric to your place and there'll be just us. We must let the young people flee this havoc and be together, but I shall, at a more appropriate time, throw a feast, and the Sultan will honour us with his presence as well. We are still waiting for his decision on a place for these two lovebirds.'

The rest of the conversation that ensued did not matter to me any more. Despite my preconceived ideas about our wedding ceremony, I quickly understood that the extraordinary Ottoman situation demanded a different approach, which I conveyed to the Empress at a glance. All was set for that evening.

On the way back there was silence, and when Nadi posed a question the regal response was, 'It may be for the best: Khanoum will be officially married and then she'll come with us until the situation improves and, who knows, we may well return for a big celebration in a few months. Perhaps Ahmad Shah will come as well. After all, he has been thinking of spending a few months in Europe. Yes, my dear, perhaps this is a good idea and one must leave things to the good Lord.'

And so we did.

My uncle's disagreement didn't alter the situation. The ceremony, which was supposed to have taken place under the chandeliers, in an imperial palace, along with fireworks and festivities, was conducted in our reception room. In addition to ourselves and a handful of others, there was a cleric and a man from the Iranian Embassy. Even the white, pearl-studded gown was left for the 'postponed ceremony'. Saeed arrived late as usual and dressed in clothes that seemed to belong to Ezzedin. We were told that he had to dress in someone else's clothes so that no one would recognise him. According to the Sultana, my *mehrieh*, 'a palace, a gift from Sultan Abdul Majid', was to be included as part of my prenuptial agreement. There was no music either. Nadi offered us pastries and, before night fell, Saeed and Ezzedin were the first to disappear in fear. The sultanas left shortly afterwards.

I was now a woman with a husband who was not at home with me. As ever, I remained alone in the same room and I knew that everyone in the household had questions, the answers to which I did not know. At night, when silence ruled, I felt so depressed that I began to write a few lines in my diary, expressing my love for Saeed and complaining about the circumstances which had forced us to be apart. I wrote that, from then on, wherever I went, I belonged to him and I knew that he felt the same. I wanted to write that I wished I could be in Ezzedin's shoes and always be with him, though I felt such a comment in the current climate was far from gracious; a demeanour that my mother and the Empress had always encouraged. I was not an ordinary woman: I was granddaughter to a Shah and wife to the grandson of a Sultan. I would spend hours at night staring at my wedding gown, absorbed in my thoughts, with little idea of what the next day held.

I woke up to the sound of conversation coming from the floor below. Khan Baba Khan was talking to a few guards and government agents and I noticed that the Empress was listening intently from the upstairs balcony. We had to evacuate the palace as it no longer belonged to Sultana Khadijeh but was now state property. It was finally agreed that the property be leased to the Iranian Embassy for one week. The Iranian flag was raised and a guard was positioned in front of the building.

Our travel documents were now ready, and once we had received a telegram from Golestan Palace and another from Etezad in Paris, our departure suddenly became imminent. On Friday we should have gone to a social event at the residence of one of the Russian generals who maintained an old friendship with the adjutant to my uncle and who had narrowly survived the

Bolsheviks. His son had been killed and he now lived with his fair, rotund wife and their three daughters in a house near Sultan Muhammad Square. Despite losing everything, they always seemed to have an air of *joie de vivre* about them. The women made clothes in their workshop but at home they maintained their regal manner. Khadijeh was anxious that we might one day become like them, but I always reminded her that her brother was the Shah of Iran and that with a guardian such as the Empress we would never have to earn a living by making dresses until midnight, as was the case in General Anreyev's household. I sincerely believed what I told her.

We were getting ready to leave when a messenger arrived with an envelope for the Shah. My uncle read out the shocking news to everyone; he then asked the same messenger to go out and buy the newspaper. The Sultan had fled aboard a British military ship; from his harem and his extensive family the only person to accompany him was his son Prince Ertugrul, together with a handful of servants. We had met his son, whom we believed to be retarded.

'It's shameful,' was my uncle's brief comment, having over the years forgotten he was the first Iranian king to seek refuge in a foreign embassy; no one bothered to remind him of the fact.

More embarrassing was the news in large print describing the Sultan's 'disgraceful' midnight flight. The jubilant crowd danced on the streets ridiculing Vahdettin, who had only a week ago conducted Friday prayers in Haya Sophia where thousands had chanted *salavat* and had called him the father of all Muslims! My uncle had his spectacles on while reading the paper and voiced his sarcasm from time to time. The Ottoman aide-de-camp had noticed Sultan Vahdettin getting into a British ambulance at six o'clock in the morning from the rear entrance to his harem in Yildiz Palace. He had politely asked the Sultan to return to bed, fearful of Mustaphah Kemal Pasha, the chief commander, but the Sultan had closed the door and departed for the harbour, at which point the poor chap had run hopelessly after the ambulance. An hour later, before the *bazaar* had started business, the ship *Rosemena and Malaya* had left the harbour via The Golden Horn and was on its way to Europe.

The Empress, who was listening intently, pointed out, 'Perhaps he would have been assassinated if he hadn't left.'

The Sultan's family had been given two days to evacuate the palaces and leave. But where to? Sultana Fahimeh and her children were going to Beirut but she did not say where Saeed was and what was to become of him. No one was to find out that Saeed had come into possession of an Iranian passport so that he could flee Istanbul. According to the Sultana, Saeed had many friends among the army officers and was, therefore, a wanted man among the Kemalists. I was once again overcome with passion and recorded in my diary that hidden among us was a hero whose existence troubled the British government. I was delighted that, thanks to the Iranian standard fluttering on our rooftop and in front of the car, Saeed had survived. No longer did I have to worry about where he was engaged in fighting and how he was, whether or not he was killed or dismembered. Though not in the same compartment, which had been allocated to women, he was travelling aboard the same train and close to me, and this was a relief. It was a comical sight seeing him in his black morning suit and top hat when we were about to get on the train.

Ashraf, too, joined our group of ten, which didn't please my aunt and uncle, but 'the girl' had gladly agreed to travel in the same compartment as Nadi and the other servants so that she could be of assistance. She was supposed to keep her mouth shut and not disclose that she was Ahmad Shah's wife. According to one of the eunuchs, 'the girl' had unnecessarily imposed herself upon us – she had not been prepared to remain in Istanbul and had declared that she had promised the Shah to go to Europe for treatment. When she realised that such a thing was not going to happen and that her name had not been put up for a travel document, she had threatened to go to the Iranian Embassy and disclose her identity to every Iranian, and then stay put at the embassy. Apparently she had a relative in Istanbul who was a constitutionalist and my uncle's opponent and so the embassy workers were led to believe that she could cause trouble. My aunt was, of course, unhappy, and cross with her own son for the inconvenience, but her name was added to the list and we soon realised that she wasn't as stupid as everyone had imagined her to be. We were thus banned from discussing our private affairs in her presence, specifically financial matters.

During the five years we had lived in Istanbul we had made a lot of friends. Some lived in hiding but many had managed to come to the station. This time our escape was not like previous times: we were allocated three carriages on the train – we had more than one hundred pieces of luggage, which Khan Baba Khan made a note of in his notebook. The Iranian Embassy officials had turned up and did their best to ensure that the customs officers and the police were courteous to the Iranian imperial family, yet there was a constant flow of communication to and from Ankara seeking orders. My aunt kept reassuring us that the shores of the Côte d'Azur resembled the garden of Eden and that there was no sign of misery and upheaval.

Three hours after our departure, Saeed, having spotted his friends and acquaintances, picked up his two suitcases and left the men's compartment. I discovered the next day that Ezzedin was on the train as well. As far as Nadi and the rest of us were concerned, he was a loyal servant who, unlike the other courtiers, had not joined the Kemalists and had not revealed the identity of his employers. Saeed and his sister lamented the situation. It had been the same story with the Russian generals and princes. Ever since we had left Tehran, my uncle, too, kept mentioning names and cursing them for joining the constitutionalists rather than defending the throne. We had heard hundreds of tales about the disloyalty of the people who served the Iranians and the Russians;

now it was the turn of the Turks. However, it was rather odd that Ezzedin had remained loyal, and when we realised that he was travelling on the train, my uncle was suspicious: 'This is not as simple as it seems; everything will soon come to light.'

On the second day, the train passed through green meadows, which made for pleasant scenery. Whenever the train stopped we saw women who were not veiled and revealed their blonde hair, just like my Nezhat, but we also noticed a great deal of poverty. Elegantly dressed men with bowler hats, bow ties and white shirts got on and off the train. Every time we approached the borders, soldiers carrying rifles would get on the train. Khan Baba Khan would present our travel documents and everyone's names would be checked against the photographs. The travel documents would then be stamped, after which the soldiers would get off. We would leave the windows open, but every time we came to a halt we drew the curtains to shield ourselves. The Empress and my uncle kept promising that we were approaching Europe, where there would be no sign of constitutionalists glaring at us with resentment; there would be no repetition of the terrifying experiences we had encountered in Istanbul and Odessa.

As far as I was concerned the start of my marriage also meant discovering a new world. We passed through woods, and every time I saw a large house or even a country cottage I would picture it decorated with rugs and oriental ornaments, and would then imagine my husband and I living comfortably and peacefully. I would even picture a few small children who looked like Saeed. I had hardly spent any time with my husband alone so I was glad we were getting further from Istanbul, a city full of war and unrest, where he was always rushing somewhere.

I managed to trace our route on the map and informed everyone how far we had travelled and how much further we had to go. We were in Bosnia approaching Sarajevo, which, not long before, had belonged to the Ottoman Empire but was now part of

Serbia. This was where the Great War had begun in the first place when a young man shot the Austrian heir to the throne. We were supposed to have spent half a day in Sarajevo, as we had to change trains, and it was at this place that my dream was disrupted.

Saeed had asked permission to have a meeting with my uncle in a hotel near the railway station where we were waiting for the next train. Half an hour later, Nadi came asking for the Empress, after which I too was summoned. Despite his borrowed outfit Saeed seemed happy and relaxed. He rose to greet me as I entered the room. I couldn't read anything from the expression on the faces of my aunt and uncle at the time; later on, however, I discovered that my husband was to separate from us to embark on a task for my uncle and his family. He promised to join us in Nice in less than a month. It took me a week to learn that he had also borrowed one hundred thousand francs from my aunt, which was a considerable sum – rather more than the price of a nice house in the South of France, my aunt thought.

During our meeting he handed me a letter filled with amorous words, though there was no mention of our future together. But having harboured so many dreams, the letter only strengthened my passionate love for him.

CHAPTER 38

Europe, land of our dreams! We went first to the Côte d'Azur, to the house that my aunt had bought a couple of years before. With the flowers climbing up the door and over the roof, the house resembled a picture postcard. Not long after, however, we went to the Italian Riviera, supposedly cheaper and better than France, where we were neighbours with the deposed Ottoman imperial family. *Noruz* was approaching, bringing us happiness and new clothes. Every time I looked through the window I saw the neighbouring houses with their red roof tiles. I imagined, upon Saeed's arrival, one of those houses becoming ours, and yet again I began thinking about furnishing our home.

The magical spring of the Côte d'Azur was upon us and we had gathered around the 'Haft Seen'.[14] We had also placed the photographs of the absent members of the family, the Shah and the crown prince, on the table next to the Haft Seen. Since we were now in a different time zone the Revelation was fixed at around two o'clock in the afternoon. After all these years Malakeh Jahan still insisted on celebrating *Noruz* in its full glory: she had bought everyone new clothes and had placed a few vases of flowers on the table, which was covered in *termeh*, as well as a bowl of water with a goldfish inside. It was not as red as the fish in Shah Baba's tank in Tehran, but very much the same *sekkeh*,[15] *serkeh*,[16] *seeb*,[17] *somaq*,[18] *seer*[19] and even *samanou*.[20] There was also a clock in the middle and its tick-tock resonated in the room.

My uncle, who was by then far removed from his throne, seemed calmer and more at ease than he'd been in Tehran. He put on spectacles, opened the Qur'an, and began to recite. When the clock chimed for the Revelation, we recited a prayer and embraced one another. I was given a peck on the forehead and everyone was given gold coins. Ashraf, too, was given a gold coin. We then got together with the Russian general, Dr Jarozelski, and their wives, as well as with Khan Baba Khan and the rest of the group in a restaurant by the sea; my very first time. We drove in a black car with large round headlights, which took the men first. By then we had abandoned the Turkish *chador* and donned scarves and coats so that we did not stand out. The men and boys wore black suits with red and blue ties against their white shirts. Ashraf and the servants remained behind. The Empress and Dr Jarozelski's wife wished my husband could join us. Indeed, watching the men and women sitting behind the tables with their heads together laughing made me pine for Saeed; I wanted to sit with him at a candlelit table with a polite waiter hovering around.

Everything was a novelty for me; it was as though Europe had to reveal all its beauty to us in a single evening. A woman was playing the piano and the rest of the orchestra were men. Little by little, men and women got up to dance and I translated the lyrics for the others. I felt embarrassed to see the women dressed in their full skirts having their hands kissed by men. The general, and the doctor too, danced with their wives, having asked my uncle's and Malakeh Jahan's permission. I had seen dancing in female gatherings in Tehran, Odessa and Istanbul – in Sultana Fahimeh's social gatherings a half-naked woman had performed a belly dance – but this was different. When Majid, the Empress's son, said he wanted the young people in our group to learn how to dance, the thought of dancing in the presence of men made the blood rush to my face. The Empress pulled a face.

'Khanoum is a married woman now and she has to wait for her husband.'

This was a constant reminder; everyone had to realise that I was no longer the young people's playmate. The next morning, as previously arranged, Caliph Abdol Majid, whose disgraceful escape had brought down the last pillar in the Ottoman Empire, came to see us, along with the Kadin and the sultanas. They arrived in two black cars with a frail-looking eunuch walking ahead. The house was now full of people, with the women sitting on one side and the two deposed kings standing by the fireplace, clearly deep in conversation about the situation in Turkey and Iran. In Turkey, Kemal Pasha had been named Ataturk, and the women had unveiled since he was determined to westernise the country. In Iran, the Shah had finally appointed Sardar Sepah Prime Minister and had himself gone to Paris, though he was supposed to join us in Nice the following week. Ashraf couldn't wait to see Ahmad Shah, but it was nothing like my eagerness to see Saeed. Ashraf, the simple girl who still donned her prayer *chador* with polka dots, was effectively a prisoner in the house; even when everyone was there she was still not allowed to make an appearance. I enquired from Nadi how Ashraf would fare, only to encounter a smile.

Later that afternoon, after the Ottomans departed, the servants were left to clear up the rooms filled with Persian rugs, antiques and *termeh* table covers. Back in my room I sat by the window looking at the busy street from the second floor. Men and women were strolling on the promenade with cars occasionally passing by. There was a vase of flowers, but to me they didn't have the same scent as the jasmines back in Tehran. I had picked a few and placed them in a vase next to Saeed's photograph, which was in a narrow frame on a wooden chest of drawers. I was now a woman with makeup, given to me during the *hammam* event. I also had a box containing a few earrings and a gold necklace, a wedding present. My wedding band reminded me of Saeed, who wore the same on his slender finger. I wrote to him about my dreams but never posted my letters. When I stopped writing, I went to the window to look at the street and the beach, just as I always did in the evenings when I was tired. Years of loneliness and being away from home meant a great deal of daydreaming. Since our arrival in the Riviera there was nothing more enjoyable than drawing the curtains and looking at the view, as though I was discovering a Europe that bore no resemblance to anything I had ever seen in the twenty-five years of my life. It was neither like Odessa nor like Istanbul. The beautiful scene that nature had laid before me filled my eyes; alas, certain events were to mar this beauty.

I used every opportunity to set up my easel and canvas so that I could capture the peaceful scene. But this, too, was interrupted by the occasional unrest on the street, just as on the afternoon when some two hundred individuals carrying a flag and wearing armbands chanted slogans in Italian, which I tried to understand using my French. From time to time they came to a halt and shouted out, '*Il Ducé!*' Mussolini was bald and overweight and his picture was on the front pages of most newspapers. He had been Prime Minister of Italy for the past couple of years and the Italians seemed to like the talkative journalists who used every opportunity to show their solidarity by marching on the streets. Just as they were now, outside the house.

Any gathering of people always terrified me, reminding me of Tehran and Odessa, and of our escapes. I recalled a scene in Tehran when people carried a coffin and chanted *salavat* amid a disorderly crowd, most of whom wore turbans on their heads. They were chanting slogans against my forlorn uncle, the then Shah. I remembered their faces full of hatred and the stones they would occasionally throw at us; at times they cut across in front of our guards' horses. In Odessa, too, I had seen similar scenes in our last months, a horrifying experience which made my heart race, like the day they poured onto the estate.

In Istanbul, until the night the guards had poured into our home, we had spent five years milling among the crowd. But from the moment we were courteously seen onto the train and left Istanbul until we arrived in Europe, it was as though someone, somewhere, had vowed that we should never see resentful crowds again. We were now in civilised Europe, whose women wore lovely hats. People were either on their bikes or in open-topped cars. We had all come to believe that war, fear and hatred were over, and that the Riviera was the playground for wealthy Europeans. No wonder I could not understand why these people were now blocking the streets and shouting, particularly when two black cars drew up in front of a man who was riding a bike, removed a bundle of papers and started to beat him. So there *was* aggression, violence and hatred in Europe as well.

In the afternoons I would read French. I read about Mussolini and, for the first time, came across the word 'fascism'; I tried to look it up in the dictionary but the word was non-existent. Slowly I came to realise that fascists were prejudiced and hot-tempered individuals who marched when Mussolini commanded. The former Shah seemed to like them; although he did not know much about their philosophy, he developed a liking for them simply because they were anti-British, and that was good enough. The Italians respected the plaque on the gates to the garden inscribed 'Iranian Ambassador's Residence', with the sun and lion coat of arms above it. The local police were always around and saluted when my uncle got into his black car. They wanted us not to be alarmed by the crowd and their vigilance was accentuated when my aunt sent them the occasional gift of pistachio nuts or nougat from Esfahan; whenever the chubby Italian postman arrived on his bicycle, as well as letters he invariably delivered parcels too. Every now and then, the Empress's Italian chauffeur would go to the post office and return with a box which contained food and occasionally a rug, which the Empress presented to people, marking her noble and generous nature and prompting everyone's compliments.

One early evening, when the streets were quiet and everyone had gone to the deposed Ottoman Sultan's home, I was upstairs on my own, busy looking at the sea. The sea reflected the lights on the harbour and the young couples strolling. I suddenly noticed Ashraf, her *chador* tucked under her arm, emerge from the neighbouring house situated only a few metres away from ours. Initially I thought she was coming to see me, as she often did whenever she was bored and had nothing to talk about with Nadi and the other servants. When the Empress and my uncle were around this wasn't so easy. Ashraf, however, seemed to be going towards the gates. She looked to see whether she was being watched, as though she had something to hide, so my curiosity was heightened. I felt sorry for her, not because she was a married woman and, like me, separated from a husband who seemed to ignore her – I didn't compare her with myself. It was more her silence and patience in the face of the contemptuous stance the Empress and her family had taken towards her, and the peculiar unease she seemed to be suffering from.

She lingered behind the railings, and when she was sure no one was watching, slipped an envelope from under her *chador* and placed it between the railings. She then cautiously returned to the building. This was odd, particularly for someone like Ashraf. Hard as I tried, I could not forget what I had seen; I couldn't see any logic in what she was doing. An hour later I was still standing by the window, too preoccupied to read a book or paint. It was getting dark but I had not switched the light on. Suddenly, I saw a man in a top hat, on a bicycle, ride carefully past our house, checking around him as he went. The mansion was situated between two smaller properties, one allocated to the Russian general and his wife Maria, the other to one of the servants and Ashraf. The Italian chauffeur went home to sleep and, during the day, when he had done with the car, or if he had nothing else to do, would rest in his room in the house.

The man on the bicycle checked the three buildings as he passed and then returned. He rested his bicycle against a tree and walked towards the gate. The lights above the gate by the statue of the angel made it possible for me to see his face: I was certain he was Iranian. I was hiding by the window while the man stood facing the street to ensure no one was looking. Then he stretched out his hand and removed Ashraf's envelope – he seemed to know exactly where it had been placed. He then got back on his bicycle and disappeared. I was overcome with a sense of anxiety. I had heard that, apart from the two carpet-merchant families and the Turks from Iran's Azeri province, there were no other Iranians on the Riviera, though there was a Bakhtiari family in the neighbouring city. The merchants and their families were kind to us and the day after our arrival had come to greet us with presents and flowers; we had not seen the Bakhtiaris, since they did not seem to care for the former Shah. I was consequently surprised to find that Ashraf was somehow connected to the man on the bicycle; was he one of the Bakhtiaris? What could Ashraf, *siqeh* to the Shah of Iran, have to do with the stranger? The questions raced through my mind until I fell asleep.

The next day I woke up with the questions still unanswered. It was still early and everyone was asleep. I had to inform the Empress but then I didn't think it wise to preoccupy her kind soul with what amounted to gossip, since it would merely worry her. I decided to find a way to get to the bottom of it and to do so immediately.

Nadi was laying the breakfast table when I asked her where Ashraf was. As usual she smiled, saying that she was still in bed, 'busy staring at the ceiling'. I went to the garden as I did every day. I had somehow to get rid of the many disturbing questions that plagued me. I approached the neighbouring building and found one of the servants busy ironing, but before I could ask for Ashraf I saw her coming down the stairs. She didn't seem anxious and greeted me with a dimple in her chin. I proposed to her we take a walk in the garden. She welcomed the idea and we left the building. At the bottom of the garden there was a shed where we kept the chests and excess furniture. A gravelled path by the shed led to the back entrance, which was always locked and chained and only used when Leone, the chauffeur, washed or repaired the car in the back street. It was quiet when we reached the closed door and I began to talk, eventually approaching the subject of the previous night.

'Why did you not let your letter be taken to the post office?'

I didn't have to look at her face as her voice began to tremble and muffled words began to emerge; she eventually collapsed on a bench under the lamppost. I realised that my concern had not been unfounded: she did, indeed, have something to hide, and began by enquiring if the rest of the family were aware of the matter. I did not lie to her. She then looked around and suddenly held my hands. I had no choice but to comfort her, so I sat on the bench and tried to look normal in case someone in the building saw us.

She kept repeating that she was an unfortunate being and that women were born to suffer, but it didn't take long for her story to unravel. Ashraf was a spy! The thought had never crossed my mind; I had assumed she had somehow become acquainted with the man but the story was very different. She tried desperately to whip up some lie to begin with but my expression must have made it clear that she could not fool me. There was a pause, then she insisted that though her future did not matter much the lives of many would be in danger should her secret be revealed.

Her father was a courtier and responsible for the palace archives, where precious manuscripts dating back to the previous rulers, as well as many other letters and antique documents, were kept. He also enjoyed a title that made him an aristocrat, but he was poor and this had tempted him to hide precious manuscripts under his clothes so that he could sell them later to some Jewish antique dealer. Though he was eventually found out, he had, as a result, been able to acquire an estate on the outskirts of Tehran. The antiquarian had been caught and under duress had confessed, revealing Ashraf's father's secret. One night, to his family's horror, the police took him away. They returned before dawn, but they did not talk to anyone. Shortly afterwards, one of the courtiers had proposed that Ashraf should marry the Shah. Her mother had initially opposed such a match but had eventually given in. A cleric had then conducted a temporary form of marriage; Ashraf became the Shah's *siqeh* and moved into the Shah's palace.

Ashraf was a simple woman and began to describe details that I found uncomfortable. It particularly repulsed me to think that I could have been in her place and for a moment I remembered Abdollah's words – I had discarded his letter, though now I wished I could read it again. I began to appreciate the depth of his kindness to me: he had written that having earned an education, and with the artistic talents I demonstrated, I did not deserve to be placed in a golden cage together with light-headed people. Ashraf, however, considered her position a predetermined destiny and didn't seem to regret it. Her only regret was that from her second week in the imperial palace and in the harem of someone who was reluctant to have a wife, she had been obliged to commit something which to her mind was treason; a treason which had been forced upon her. She went on to describe the day the woman in charge of the harem allowed her to visit her parents. She was driven home, where her mother and sisters distracted the eunuch chaperone so that she could go to her father's study, where he was smoking opium. She was surprised to see the head of security emerging from behind the curtains, but was led to understand that she was expected to report everything she observed in the harem. She was to write everything down on a piece of paper, which she was then to hand over every other day to a woman who worked in the palace. Rather than being asked, she had been firmly told what to do.

Once she was alone with her father again he explained the situation and concluded that if the theft of the books belonging to the palace was found out, he would be put behind bars; his reputation would be tarnished and he would end up losing everything. Sardar Sepah's cronies were aware of everything – they had firm hold of the reins and could easily finish the Shah off. Everyone gave in to them since they had no choice. She was told that her family's well-being depended on her, and if she were not prepared to commit herself to what she had been asked to do he would put an end to his life.

Ashraf had, as a result, become a spy, reporting everything that she saw and heard in the harem. She couldn't sleep at night and the thought of the secret of her treason being revealed made her unwell, but the thought of her father losing face and her family's imminent misfortune forced her to do as she was told. In the end she really did become quite unwell. Her illness was for real and she was sent abroad for treatment. The Shah was not keen but his Russian physician had somehow managed to convince him. Until the day she was handed a travel document and was ready to travel to Istanbul and beyond, Ashraf believed that Sardar Sepah's agents had also been behind this. And, indeed, before she embarked on her journey, the head of security had, once again and in her father's home, told her to keep an eye on my uncle and his entourage throughout their journey; under no circumstances should she part with them until further notice. Her orders had been further instilled by her father's threats and entreaties. Ashraf also confessed that throughout her stay in Istanbul she had passed on letters through an embassy agent. After her arrival in Italy, communications had been temporarily suspended. It was then decided that she should place her letters every three nights in a spot in the railings. Occasionally she would find letters from her father transmitting new instructions.

When Ashraf disclosed everything to me, looking distraught and tearful, it was as though I was reading a novel. I had not had any news from Tehran or the court apart from the things I heard here and there or read in the papers. I knew that after we'd heard the horrific news of the Cossacks' *coup d'état* in Tehran, every day had been an eventful day in Iran, including the day we learned that Sardar Sepah was planning to create a republic, just as in Turkey. However, we became aware that the Shah's supporters had interrupted Sardar Sepah's plans and were about to take him hostage but had been unable to do so. I had overheard a conversation, when some foreign visitors had come to visit, that the Shah was receiving medical treatment in France, and that his brother,

Muhammad Hassan, was in charge in his absence. Somehow, everyone was confident that the Iranian people were pro-Qajar and were not supporting anyone else. I recalled what the Shah had told me recently in Istanbul, and the letters that the crown prince had sent from Tehran on a weekly basis, the contents of which only his parents were aware of. They never trusted anyone who came from the embassy or Tehran, and their lack of trust was loud and clear, but little did they know that for the past eight months Ashraf had reported everything they did or said.

I spent the rest of the day wondering what to do. Ashraf had begged me to keep everything between us, and I had reassured her that such would be the case. In the end I tried to help her, but that very much depended on the imminent arrival of Ahmad Shah in the Riviera, when she could be dismissed. In order to calm her down I asked her about her doctor's opinion, to which she replied that she had begun to feel better and she wished she could obtain a divorce. I spent the next hour in my room struggling to find a way out. I knew what I had to do but I also decided that Ashraf should not be harmed.

I went to see the Empress, who was alone in her room reading letters and writing replies. I asked if I could take up some of her time. The timing was good since my uncle was about to take his usual walk with Khan Baba Khan and the Russian general on the boulevard. I closed the door and sat facing the Empress, whom I loved and was confident could find a solution for every problem. She removed her spectacles and watched my face intently. I had spent most of my life with her and, over the years, I had seen how the Empress had managed to overcome crises and hardship by using common sense. I knew she was in charge of our convoy and that from the moment we left Iran my uncle had relied on her to deal with everything, including the political issues involving people who were with us. I was closest to her as far as her immediate family were concerned, and was affected by her more than her own children, and so would be informed of her day-to-day affairs.

I told her I thought, Ashraf's case could not be too complex to deal with. I saw her make a slight move while still seated. She then got up so that together we could go to her bedroom. We pulled out a box, which had been placed under her bed, and took out a bundle of papers, which she began to scrutinise.

'We need to find out what the girl has become privy to and what she has reported, darling. How can we find out?'

I mentioned to her that it was best not to show Ashraf that she had become aware of what was going on. That way, I might be able to find out, through talking to her, what she had already reported back; then we should wait until His Majesty arrived from Paris. But we had to tell *him*. The Empress didn't want anyone to be informed in the meantime, not even my uncle, who, according to her, was already sufficiently suspicious and unwell. The first thing that the Empress needed to know, however, was whether the notebook that we had lost in the course of our transfer from Istanbul to the Riviera was in Ashraf's possession, and whether she had reported the contents or even sent it over. From her expression I gathered that the notebook contained important information: the crown prince's letters from Tehran were kept inside as well as reports that could jeopardise many lives. She explained to me that she had been looking for the notebook ever since we had arrived in Nice.

There was no way I could find out whether, in our absence here or in Istanbul, Ashraf had managed to get into our bedrooms. We had a lot to do. Our private chats became so frequent that Majid and Mahmoud, the Empress's sons, became curious and occasionally asked me whether there was a problem.

I tried not to change my attitude towards Ashraf and I asked the Empress to let us go out shopping or take a walk on the boulevard. It was rather difficult for Ashraf to part with her *chador*, even when indoors, but she did like to don a scarf and coat. Unlike the first time I had confronted her she had begun to be more at ease.

Two notebooks were missing: one contained foreign press cuttings on the Shah, the other was used to record our annual expenditure. However, the Empress was not so worried about these; her main concern was the letters containing coded information sent over from Tehran, and these were in a red file tied with a black string. I used every method I could think of to find out whether Ashraf had managed to get access to this file. I mentioned to her that this mattered to me and that the Empress had recently been looking for this particular file and that if she had sent this file off she had to tell me so that I could find a solution. It transpired that back in Istanbul she had been instructed to pass on any file, letter or even empty envelopes that arrived from Tehran. She had, however, only been able to remove one of the two letters on the former Shah's bureau when she was helping Nadi to dust and sort out the library.

When we returned home, I handed over a few documents ensuring her parents' immunity; her eyes twinkled and she was grateful. I had the Empress's authority for what I was doing but the planning was mine. An effective strategy because, when we went to the garden the next day, she handed over two files that she had hidden under the boxes in the shed; one was green and the other red – she had not yet been able to send them off. I was in the midst of a case that had put my intelligence to the test. When I handed the files to the Empress, I was told I had performed as well as though I had spent years as a secret agent!

I felt a sense of satisfaction by being of some use to the Empress and the family, but there was something else which drew me to Ashraf. I obviously could not discuss this with the Empress and it was irrelevant to the plans we had devised together. I was eager, however, to find out how the members of the convoy, with whom I had spent years going from one place to another, regarded me, and Ashraf's naïveté was a useful tool in this respect. Unfortunately, what I learned was far darker than I had imagined. I'm not sure why I had assumed that everyone took me for an adopted child. This was how I had been presented over the years to new acquaintances, until I, too, had come to believe that people regarded me as such, but I was unaware of what went on behind my back. When I found out that to everyone around me I was a long-suffering relation whose father had robbed her of her innocence and whose mother had terminated her life to end the shame and misery that she had to suffer as a consequence, I had to try hard to contain my emotions. I somehow managed to come across as nonchalant and simply said she had been wrong in her assumptions.

Later that evening I wrote yet another page in the diary that contained my innermost feelings towards Saeed.

'Please come immediately and take me away! Let's go to a place where there is only you and me and no one else.'

Despite my attachment and the anguish of parting with the Empress and her family, I had for some time found it difficult to remain in that house. I yearned to leave with Saeed; I didn't know where but I couldn't care less.

Ahmad Shah arrived on the eve of *Sizdeh Bedar*, the thirteenth day of the Persian New Year, and decided to stay in a sumptuous hotel. Ashraf dressed up in the evening and went to greet her husband and to seek his permission to leave. A few days later she left for Iran accompanied by two members of the Turkish families. She was delighted with her newfound freedom, particularly since she no longer had to return to the palace but could go to a house that had been given to her.

I, however, could not wait for Saeed to take me away. Obviously not to a palace in Istanbul or Tehran; I merely wanted to go to a small house in a quiet place, in some corner of the big wide world.

CHAPTER 39

We moved to San Remo in the spring, and the Ottoman imperial family followed suit. It was there that I saw him, in the corner of some square in the centre of San Remo. We were standing around the Empress, dressed in black and wearing dark glasses. A representative of Mussolini's government was paying his respects to Ahmad Shah, who had the last Ottoman Sultan by his side, together with a few others. I could see Saeed from afar – he had arrived the previous week and I had managed to see him a couple of times, but my uncle's illness kept him and the rest of the men at the hospital bedside. His death finally meant that he was no longer there to frown or shrug his shoulders, demonstrating his suspicion as soon as Saeed's name was mentioned.

A year had passed since the fall of the Ottomans, and their unveiled heads and Western clothes were telltale signs of a past era – and of exile. Having spent a lifetime behind palace walls, arriving in Europe meant freedom from all ties, yet they still missed their extravagant lifestyle back in Istanbul and seemed to have been more content in their golden cage. Their degraded financial situation had become noticeable since Sultan Abdul Majid, who had spent his last years imprisoned in Yildiz Palace as Caliph, had not been able to bring with him any of the riches that his forebears had amassed; or perhaps, as we were told, he did not want any of it.

I was aware that having arrived in Europe, and living near the exiled Ottoman family, the Empress was careful not to display her wealth. She even went so far as appearing not to be content with life in general. I, however, was aware of the immense wealth that my aunt and uncle possessed. In addition, they received an income from her estate in Azerbaijan as well as the properties on the outskirts of Tehran. After her husband's futile trip to Iran in the hope of regaining the throne had resulted in the killing of so many, the parliament had decided to confiscate my uncle's properties, but the Empress's were left intact. I don't know why, having seen the Ottoman's impoverished state, it never dawned on me that Saeed must have shared the same fate; I never even gave any thought to my lost *mehrieh* or the non-existent palace in Istanbul that had been part of our prenuptial agreement.

The Empress, however, seemed to have understood the situation and knew that the money that Saeed had taken on loan in Sarajevo was never going to be repaid. One day, when I embarrassingly discussed the matter, she smiled and said that she had paid that money from her own reserves; she always said to everyone that my parents had left me a considerable inheritance, but I knew that she was too kind to me, and I felt ashamed that she never deprived me of anything during my sixteen years with her. Was she going to pull the strings now that her husband had passed away? It didn't take long for me to get an answer: she not only kept Dr Jarozelski, the Shah's physician, and his family under her wing; they were given a house next to ours in San Remo. When Ashraf's case came to light, the Russian general, Khanbayev, and his rotund wife left us a few months after arriving in San Remo. The Empress had insisted that the deposed Shah's adjutant should carry on guarding the family but the old general retired himself and bade us farewell, at which point a young officer, who was also Russian, replaced him.

Smirnoff, a member of the Russian nobility, had managed to flee Bolshevik Russia. I can't remember who had made the recommendation but he seemed to perform his duties well enough; dressed in his military uniform, he always sat next to the

Italian chauffeur while the Shah or the Empress sat in the back. During the funeral procession for my uncle, his display of medals and his very presence added to the occasion; on the day of the funeral he stood behind Ahmad Shah.

My uncle's body was taken to Karbala to be buried next to Shah Baba in a mausoleum belonging to the Shahs of Iran, and every year some cleric joined us in the memorial service. Saeed had volunteered to escort the body all the way to Karbala; this had endeared him to the Empress and made me proud. Meanwhile, I remained with the Empress in her house. We were going to be married officially on his return, which meant that we could go to our new home: mine and his. During our second year in San Remo I commenced my studies at medical school.

CHAPTER 40

A s soon as the memorial visits were over the Empress began to sort her life out, which meant that every morning, while Nadi was busy at work, she would search through the papers in her husband's study with my help, throwing the unwanted material into the fire. Ever since Ashraf's deeds had come to light, everyone had become vigilant; we hadn't discounted the possibility of another spy among us and the servants were not allowed in my uncle's study for some time. Contracts, political documents and various handwritten notes were placed in a box, as well as medals and personal effects, which were housed in various boxes each bearing a different son's name. There were a few diamond cufflinks, a pair of which was put aside for Saeed along with one of the gold fountain pens.

My aunt picked out one of the letters that my uncle kept in his desk, and began to read. She was about to throw it into the fire but hesitated. The letter was from my father at the time of his effort to block my departure – the memory of him repulsed me. In his fine script he had talked of 'the light of his life', who might possibly have been included in the 'Crowned Father's convoy' without my father's knowledge. My resentment was at its height when I noticed that he had made a mild threat to take the matter to the Russian embassy should my uncle not consider it. I gave a wry smile; we had not talked about my helpless mother for some years now. Though Abdollah had unravelled what I already knew, this seemed a good opportunity to hear it from the Empress. The expression on my face must have revealed my desire once I had finished reading the monster's letter and passed it back to her. Perhaps she was reminded that back in Odessa she had promised to discuss Mother, and that now might be the time to honour her promise.

'Your poor mother,' she said, and she was about to pass over the painful memory when I caught her skirt. The tears began to roll down my face and, as I was sitting on the floor, she placed my head on her knees.

'When we return to Tehran, we'll first go to your mother's grave next to the martyred Shah, her grandfather …'

Then she got up and removed a file from the second shelf of the bookcase. I knew that resting on that shelf was a file for every one of the twenty-odd people who had travelled with us from Odessa. My file was thick. The Empress put it aside and promised to go through it with me one evening.

'I should really let you have this file to take with you, to your own home, God willing, as I, too, shall one day pass away, and you must keep these with you. You must know what belongs to you and where things are.'

I couldn't work out what was going through the Empress's mind; I wasn't after wealth, and at that moment I was hardly thinking about money and property.

The next evening I opened the file and found my unfortunate uncle's script in English, 'KHANOUM', and underneath he had written 'Her Grace Khanoum, my niece'. I then found the bank receipts and invoices that related to what Mother had wrapped in the wrapped bundle she had handed to the Empress on the last day at the Russian Embassy. There were share certificates and letters. One was from my mother, on top of which was written in large letters, 'The Will of Monii us-Saltaneh, daughter of Mozaffar ed-Din Shah Qajar', and underneath, in the same childish handwriting, she had asked her crowned and benevolent brother to look after the 'light of her eyes' like a father. She had written that first and foremost she left me in the hands of the Almighty, and then to him, and that she was leaving this world content but sinful.

I looked at the date at the bottom of the letter: it was written four months after our last meeting and underneath there were a series of signatures and stamps. She had written that she was leaving her estate and that of her unfortunate sister, Nezhat, which had been left in her guardianship, to His Majesty, 'so that Khanoum may never be in need of funds from unscrupulous individuals'.

'Mother, you were anxious for me not to see him again, the one whose punishment you left in the hands of God. What good was wealth to me? When you wrote this I was ten years of age and the only thing I wanted was you, and that you took away from me. I wish you had left me your own self instead,' I lamented.

When my aunt noticed I was indifferent to money and wealth, the thought of which brought me no delight, she asked Nadi to bring her the hookah and I poured us tea. She explained the extent of Father's frivolity: having lost a great deal in gambling, he had reached a stage when he was going to sell our home, left to him by his father. When Shah Baba was alive, he did not dare to be cruel to Mother, but after Shah Baba's death and his own second marriage he had no qualms. He then sold a number of Mother's properties before leaving for Tabriz when fighting had broken out. It was later discovered that he had embezzled the camp's financial resources and was planning to flee to Russia and then to Europe, but that government agents had discovered his plan and stopped him. When he later returned to Tehran, the Shah was so furious that he wanted to execute him, but until the horrific events of our last days, which had resulted in Nezhat terminating her own life and Mother taking me to the Russian Embassy, the Empress had mediated to prevent the social embarrassment.

Afterwards, he forced Mother to hand over everything she had, threatening that if she refused he would seek the Russians' assistance in the matter, which meant that he could claim me back. Apparently he also presented a document sent from St Petersburg in response to his request, confirming that they could force my uncle to send me back to Tehran. Mother was subsequently so terrified that she had initially been prepared to hand over everything but later decided to devise a plan: first she wrote a letter bequeathing her estate to her brother, witnessed by the Imam of Friday prayers. She then sent her will, along with the other documents, to Odessa.

'When we received the letter we were horrified and began to think of a solution. We sent a telegraph to Azod the Regent to intervene. Our plan was to somehow get your mother to Odessa. Every day, without your knowledge, we pleaded. An agreeable response was received from Tehran and the Regent was to intervene personally. He even wrote that he was going to commission the monster to become governor of Kashan so that everything could be sorted out in his absence. However, a week later, they received the news. Three months later, we found out that the monster had told everyone "her ladyship is away". When the members of the household were interrogated they discovered that she had not been seen at home for two weeks; the reality, however, was that he had hidden her in a vestibule behind his room where he had tortured her for ten days. Finally, all was revealed: one of the servants had found your poor mother's body in the well on the estate.'

While my aunt was telling me this I beat myself about the face and my head; the thought of Mother possibly joining us in Odessa tormented me. I was trying to remember the first days in Odessa, the evenings I had sat by the window and looked at the sea. It was hard to imagine what she must have gone through in those moments. My aunt was not aware that whatever she said had a different connotation as far as I was concerned. I was familiar with the vestibule she was talking about; this opened into the back of the monster's bedroom in the middle of Father's quarters and connected it to the mill. When Nezhat and I fled the house that night we had used that route. Mother was familiar with the route but was scared of its narrow, dark interior. However, back then she had been prepared to step into this cold, dark space in order to rescue us. Halfway through, her heart didn't seem to be functioning and she had leaned on me. Nezhat was wrapped in a blanket and was shaking. Sixteen years later, every step of our escape was now coming back to me: in the darkness, I had noticed some areas of the recess as large as rooms, which were closed off by strong iron doors. I recall, one of those evenings in Nanny's house, asking Mother what those rooms were for. She had explained to me that they were a relic of the days when, at the time of Nasser al-Din Shah, my grandfather, the father of the beast had been governor of Tehran and had to keep an eye on a number of unruly individuals; he had had those chambers built and many had perished inside. The narrow passage was also used as an escape route for the Great Khan. His forebears had all been notables, ministers and governors, and the route had been created years before so that at times of war he could use it to flee the unrest and massacres. It was reasonable to think that many dignitaries had created some sort of escape route in their houses.

Climbing down four steps that evening, I had seen four large barrels of wine placed on either side of the vault. Later we had reached an iron door, which my mother had struggled to open and had then closed behind us.

The thought of my mother spending so many days in that place with no one able to hear her voice, while the monster let it be known that she had gone away, made my heart pound. There were so many nosy servants yet nobody knew what was going on? Or perhaps they had sensed something was afoot but did not dare report him since everyone's well-being was in his hands? But they could have had something written in one of the pamphlets, particularly with the advent of the constitution. Oh Mother, my poor Mother, you must have shouted a great deal; alas, no one heard you. Why did you not give him what he wanted? What good were property and wealth to me?

I tried to complete the story, the extent of which neither the Empress nor anyone else was aware. Mother had been locked up in the dungeon to force her to write and sign something which she had initially agreed to do, but why did she not let the monster know that she no longer possessed anything? Perhaps she did and this was her punishment. And then? He might well have sent her to the dungeon, and when he had found out that the Regent and the government were looking for her, for fear of being discovered he had not bothered to release her until she had finally perished. And what a difficult and painful death: of hunger and thirst. I had read somewhere that people didn't actually die of starvation; rather it was thirst that killed them. It initially blinds one and then makes the body shake. When I was in Istanbul, I had read in the papers the stories the Bolsheviks had written about the Tsar's dungeons: prisoners had actually ended up eating the flesh of their chained cell mates in order to survive!

Sixteen years had not lessened the depth of the tragedy yet my pain had now assumed a new dimension. I began to realise why they had kept everything from me all those years. I recalled what Abdollah said: that Mother had thrown herself into the well just when she was about to come to Odessa. In all my dreams she had not changed: in the evenings she sat on her pink satin sheets in the sitting room and Morvarid brushed her hair and removed her makeup. In my dreams her skin was translucent and, dressed in her lace nightgown, she was floating on the surface of the water with a smile on her face. In my dreams I saw her motionless, floating like a mermaid on the surface of the vast waters of the sea. Nezhat the same, though when she went down the well her tormented body was marked by wounds.

By then I had rested my head on my aunt's knees and was sobbing; I was picturing the image of a traumatised and bruised mother with motionless eyes. Later on, despite the tablets I was prescribed, I was not able to sleep. The house was engulfed in silence and I sobbed while I rested my head on the pillow. Towards the early hours of the morning I had barely fallen asleep when I woke up to the faint sound of an object falling into a well: a motionless and shattered body.

CHAPTER 41

It was a warm summer's day when I finally arrived in the Paris of my dreams. The house which had been purchased for me had two bedrooms and a small garden filled with trees and flowers – it was smaller than Saeed had in mind. We initially took a room in a hotel while the house was redecorated. The most beautiful day of my twenty-seven years was the day Khan Baba Khan handed the key to Saeed, a key that was to open the gates of paradise.

Three months after my uncle had passed away, I sat in the Empress's car and was driven to Paris along the shores of the Côte d'Azur. In the time leading up to my departure the Empress had done her best to help me put my sorrows behind me so that I could arrive in my home to begin a new life. Her constant reminder of the future, and her kindness to Saeed and me, helped me cleanse my memory of the painful past.

By the time I was putting my clothes away in my new home the Empress had arrived in Paris to see her son. These were tough times since Sardar Sepah's stance had dissuaded the Shah from returning to Tehran. He was not prepared to listen to the others but the Empress wanted him to return and guard the crown. Finally, at the last hour, when a ship had been leased and all was prepared for his return, last-minute news from Tehran had changed his mind once again.

I felt embarrassed that amid their worries I was spending most of my time buying furniture and decorating my home. Nadi and Mohtaram had accompanied the Empress from San Remo in order to help me. The evening of my nuptials was spent in a café where the Empress, Smirnoff, a few members of the Qajar family and the Shah's entourage were present, though the Shah himself was not. From Saeed Pasha's side, in addition to Ezzedin, who was always with him, only a few others had been invited. After dinner a dozen cars followed a hired black carriage as far as Place Madeleine. Our house was situated on Rue Pasquier behind l'Eglise de la Madeleine. The only person present in the house was Mohtaram, who was supposed to stay until we found a French maid. Everyone left; for the first time ever I was alone and apprehensive. I had to say goodbye to my aunt, who had never left my side except when she travelled, and was now tearfully leaving me in the hands of Saeed. Ezzedin's goodbye was even more emotional: he kept coming back until he finally settled in the same carriage and disappeared into the darkness.

Tired and a little frightened, I tried to remember all the things that Nadi and the Empress had explained to me about my wedding night, something that Khadijeh had experienced two years before. It was delightful that after two years of knowing each other Saeed and I could finally be on our own. We spoke French, which Mohtaram couldn't understand. I appreciated Saeed's polite and calm manner; it made what might otherwise have been an unpleasant experience easier.

I was tired and Saeed didn't seem surprised when I laid out my prayer mat. I donned my prayer *chador* and stood to pray. He was getting undressed and looking at me with a smile. When I came to the end of my prayer I picked up my mother's rosary, as I always did, and with closed eyes prayed that my mother and Nezhat might rest in peace. Deep down I thanked God for all the things he had given me. My prayers took longer than usual because I had a great deal to tell Mother: I was starting a new life as well as becoming a woman. I had come to my own home and it was my first night and I missed her; I was wearing her necklace, assuming that was what she had wanted.

'I wish you had been here to see your son-in-law: he is a true prince and not like the man you married. Although he does not speak the same language, one has to picture him among the people who prayed in Haya Sofia or when he was carrying your brother's coffin. You would then realise what a good Muslim he is. I wish you could have seen how gracious he is when he stands tall and proud among the crowd. And tonight when he bowed to kiss the Empress's hand you could see how different he was from the beast who shared a home with you.'

I spoke to her and wept. I was subconsciously reminding myself of the hell that I had promised the Empress and myself to forget, but it was a difficult thing to do.

When I finally rose and put my prayer mat away I couldn't hear a sound; Saeed had been asleep for some time. I knew he was tired, and perhaps this was for the better. I tried not to wake him and took a soft new blanket out of the wardrobe to cover him. I then quietly slipped under the blanket on the far side of the bed and soon fell into a deep sleep.

I woke up in the middle of the night and was sweating: I had had a nightmare in which one of the mountain goats whose head was hanging on the bedroom wall was attacking me with its twisted horns; wherever I went it wouldn't let me pass. Its horns had torn my clothes and my screams were tearing through my dry throat, but no one could hear me because there was no one about. When I woke up it took me a while to realise that I was far away from Tehran, oceans apart from the little girl who had struggled in the hands of the monster. The candle by my bedside was about to expire so I got up to drink some water and replace the candle, something I had always done as I was terrified of the darkness; every time the candle expired I somehow woke up.

I was now in a narrow chamber and someone was lashing me. I was blind and in agony, and couldn't see anything except my own blind self crouching in a damp basement suffering great pain. I woke up. When I was in Odessa or Istanbul I would pick up a book at such times and read until my eyes were tired. I would then place my head on the book until the nightmare went away. But at that particular moment I could do no such thing; I had to be quiet so that I did not disturb the one sleeping next to me. His breathing was quiet and calm with the occasional twitching of a muscle in his face. I tiptoed out of the room. Mohtaram slept in the room next door. I helped myself to some water from an enamel bowl. I then glanced through the kitchen window and found the street quiet. When I returned, Saeed was awake; he must have woken up at the sound of the door, and when I slipped under the blanket he stretched out his arm. I jerked as though I had been struck by lightning. I was terrified of my own reaction. I now found Nezhat watching me in the dark; she seemed to have emerged from behind the wardrobe. I couldn't see her but she seemed to be carrying a rifle. I screamed.

In the morning, Saeed's only hint about the previous night was, 'My love, I know everything.'

He was so affectionate and sympathetic that I didn't feel the need to make any connection between his comments and the previous night. To this day I haven't forgotten what he said and can recall every single word. The smell of the warm croissants had filled the house and the cafetière was on the stove. Mohtaram had prepared breakfast but was not around. I had a headache but I didn't want to begin the first morning of my new life complaining; surely it was going to get better. I drew the curtains to let the Paris sun spread its light on the Persian rugs in the drawing room and the dining room. Everything was new. The Empress had seen to it that my trousseau had everything we needed, except the Paris morning papers, which turned up with Ezzedin's arrival. I went to the bedroom to get dressed and when I returned to the drawing room he presented me with a large bouquet – his arrival filled our house with the sound of laughter and happiness.

Mohtaram left just before lunchtime and the three of us decided to have lunch in the Champs-Elysées. We were by the front door when an old Frenchman arrived with a young woman who was to become our maid. She came from Bordeaux and had short black hair; she looked thin and haggard. She had lost her husband during the war and had to work to earn a living for her two sons. After the war France was impoverished and unemployment was high. My aunt had previously explained to me that property and servants had become quite cheap as a result, something she considered a good omen at the onset of our new life; indeed, the house purchased under my name was half the price it had been two years before. Janine was to do all the housework for us for a mere twenty-four francs and return home in the evening.

The Frenchman handed a paper to Saeed to sign, left a copy with us, took his money and left. We returned into the house and, with his usual humour, Ezzedin explained her duties to Janine. As I had not been to Paris before, Janine's presence proved useful, and an hour later we were on the Champs-Elysées with Janine giving us a tour. Saeed and Ezzedine walked ahead of us as usual, busy talking and laughing, and their happiness made me happy as well. Our first lunch in a café by the bridge leading to Les Invalides was delightful. French wine had sparked the humorous side of Saeed and Ezzedin. Janine gave in to us, and after she left in the afternoon to attend to her sons, who would by then have returned from school, we picked her up again in Saint Lazare. She wore makeup and smarter clothes and was now looking more like a Parisian woman. We had taken a rest and were ready to spend an evening *à la Parisienne*.

I missed the Empress and we went to see her the following day in the Hôtel Bonaparte. She had missed me but was content to see that I had finally started my new life. She did not mention her own troubles, but I could read then in her concerned expression; having grown up in their large family I could tell when something was wrong. She broke the news when Saeed and Ezzedin were not in the room, and Mahmoud, Majid and her other sons had gone for a stroll outside the hotel. The news of her intention to return to Iran came as a shock. The telegrams that Muhammad Hassan Mirza, the crown prince, had sent mentioned that Sardar Sepah was hard at work to bring about the fall of the Qajar dynasty as rapidly as possible. The members of the Qajar clan and the parliamentarians had asked Ahmad Shah to hurry back, but he was reluctant and so the Empress had decided to go herself; in less than a week a ship would dock in Marseille ready to embark.

'We shall come too,' Saeed remarked, surprising the Empress, though she had already anticipated we might come up with such an offer.

I added, 'Only if you let us, of course.'

Iran, my homeland, had always been present in my dreams, as the hell I had escaped from, as well as the aroma of the *naarenjestaan*, the jasmines and the lilies. The place I thought I'd never see again was now close to me once more.

We left the house I had decorated so passionately in the care of Ezzedin and Janine, and two days later we were on our way to Marseilles. Was it the sense of revenge that drew me, or my urge to get to Mother's grave? Whatever it was it managed to push my dream of a new life and the beauty of Paris to one side, and we were on our way.

CHAPTER 42

L eaving the house of my dreams was not so easy: it had been tastefully decorated and was perfect, just as I had imagined so often. But I needed time to adjust to my new life and the trip to Tehran was fortuitous; I was wary of the events of my first night but at the same time I wanted to have Saeed with me. I loved him, and the three days spent at sea had drawn me to him more than ever. He was polite and refined, and I felt proud that the Empress could rely on him, leaving him in charge of the arrangements. I was also pleased that the Empress treated him as her own son-in-law and preferred Saeed's suggestions to those of Captain Smirnoff.

In Marseille, an hour before boarding the ship, we received a telegram from the Shah which upset me, though I didn't let it be known. Bearing in mind the relationship between Iran and Turkey, the Shah had written, he did not think it sensible for Saeed, a member of the fallen Ottoman imperial family, to accompany us. Initially we were hesitant, but Saeed reminded us of the diplomatic obligations and said that he had been concerned that his fake passport issued in Istanbul granting him an Iranian identity could cause embarrassment in Iran. The Empress decided that I, too, should forget about the trip.

Saeed, however, said that it was better for me to accompany the Empress, adding with his usual humour, 'It is I who has to put up with the agony of being away from Khanoum, but I shall look after everything until all is sorted out.'

As far as we were concerned either we were going to make it possible for the graceful return of the Shah, in which case Saeed would accompany him, or we had better return to Paris and stay where we were.

'You will join us very soon, you will see,' said the Empress with confidence.

We were standing on the deck in the harbour in Marseille. The captain and the naval officers, dressed in their whites, stood to attention. We waved to everyone who had come to see us off. Saeed offered a military salute and then blew a kiss from the jetty, at which point I tried to hide my tears from the Empress and the others. Earlier, when Saeed bowed and kissed the Empress's hand, I noticed that the Empress gave him a cheque, presumably to cover his expenses during our absence. Apart from Nadi, all the servants and the Empress's companion were delighted to return to Iran.

The Empress's sons were also on board – the Shah had issued a decree commissioning Majid to become governor of Esfahan and Mahmoud governor of Fars. We were supposed to disembark in Boushehr, a port south of Iran, and then go on to Fars, followed by Esfahan and finally Tehran. Dressed in military uniform, Smirnoff and General Khanbayev stood behind the Empress and her children at all times. Dr Jarozelski was also travelling with us and held medical files for each of us. His presence was reassuring when, as usual, the Empress and a few other people were seasick. I, along with a couple of others, felt feverish from the vaccination against the diseases common in the Middle East. Though Jarozelski looked after us, the British ship was equipped with everything, the same enormous ship that had taken us from Istanbul to Marseille. In the salon, a grand orchestra played Western music whenever lunch and dinner were served, and men and women would dance to the different tunes. Seven years after the war, life was still a struggle in Europe, but aboard the ship we seemed to be on a different planet and the passengers, especially those who, like us, were in first class, didn't seem to have been affected by the upheaval at all.

The Empress felt better by the second night and the side effects of the vaccination seemed to be subsiding as well. I missed Saeed when I saw men and women dancing together since he was quite adept on the dance floors of Paris. I did not have a clue how to dance and had I stayed behind, Janine was to have taught me.

In the day we would gather in the small cabin next to the Empress's while she conferred with her sons like some formidable commander, discussing the latest developments in Iran; the governors of the provinces had given an account of the situation in Tehran and also the extent of the authority of Sardar Sepah in their letters. Mudarress, the representative of the clergy in Tehran, had sworn allegiance to the Shah and had further reassured him that, upon his return, the parliament, which opposed the Qajarieh, as Sardar Sepah claimed, would unite against the man and bring about his downfall.

'His Majesty must know that it is impossible to bathe in the sea without getting wet; Iran must not be compared with France or England ...'

The Empress prompted her sons to exercise utmost authority on settling in their respective seats; they were to unify the local khans and set about dismissing Sardar Sepah's supporters. I was anxious: did the Iranian people really want the Shah? Nezhat's talk of the people's uprising had indicated that no one was happy with the Shah, and I had also heard that the people resented my uncle, who had fought against them and let the Russians manipulate him. At the Russian Embassy it became clear, however, that the constitutionalists did want the continuity of Qajar rule and were insisting on keeping Ahmad Shah on the throne.

The further we got from Europe the hotter and more humid the weather became. We would generally stay indoors, but as soon as the sun went down we would get dressed and go on the deck like everyone else, retiring to the sumptuous dining room in the evening or taking supper on deck. One evening I was still reading when someone knocked on the door around midnight. I leapt out upon seeing my aunt in her elaborate red dressing gown. She sat on the edge of my bed and began by asking how I felt now that I was returning to Iran after seventeen years. She hadn't returned to Iran either, since she was reluctant to leave her husband alone. I did feel happy but I was also preoccupied with leaving Saeed and our home behind. Had he been with us I would have been far more eager to return. The Empress, though, looked at life from a different perspective; she explained to me that when she thought about the Ottoman Sultan's family who, after their downfall and escape, had lost respect and were as a result snubbed in Europe, she felt her blood boil. She thought her eldest son had not appreciated that the courteous treatment he received in Europe was simply because he was still considered the Shah of Iran, but should, God forbid, he come to the same fate as Sultan Abdul Majid, then he would find that the French servants and San Remo's mayor would not hesitate to stand up to him. Worse still, his own family would treat him contemptuously as he had let a few hundred years of monarchy slip through his fingers. I understood that the Ottomans were financially hard up, almost destitute, having lost all their wealth and glory back in Istanbul.

It made me think of Saeed, who had frequently accepted my aunt's generosity; wouldn't we become equally destitute if the Empress did not succeed in removing her son's enemies and helping him return to his palace? I had no notion of poverty. To be more precise, I had not the faintest understanding of money matters, and despite the many calamities that we had gone through I had never anticipated that we might one day experience the same fate as the Russian princes, let alone the Ottomans. I recalled the daughter of the Russian general who made clothes for us when we were still in Istanbul or, worse even, the man in Aati Bahçe, who wanted to exchange his medals for food, not to mention the Russian princes the Bolsheviks had executed and whose estates they had confiscated.

The pomp and ceremony around my aunt, however, was reassuring, and she was adamant that when all was sorted out, Saeed and his family could go to Tehran and lead better lives. Everything that she said, coupled with her wish to return and succeed in regaining what was not yet lost, had sparked my excitement, particularly as I sensed that she was determined to put the monster in his place. I had never imagined myself with such a thirst for revenge but, listening to the Empress, I was once again filled with resentment and ponder what one could do to him.

'I have so far made life difficult for him through His Majesty's intervention – he has not been offered any posts; "the man" had the audacity to introduce himself to one of the ministers as "His Majesty's father-in-law"!'

I suddenly remembered that it wasn't long ago when I had thought myself the future queen. Abdollah had prevented me from falling into that trap, otherwise I, too, would have shared the same fate as Ashraf. Poor Ashraf, what was she up to now?

'His Majesty released her while in Istanbul and now she is married to one of the Cossacks, which is what she deserved.'

I was listening intently and was keen to know how exactly the Empress was going to take revenge. I had read in the Italian and French newspapers that people could be taken to court, where justice prevailed; years after their original crime these criminals could still be prosecuted. One such was a French general who had killed his valet and was subsequently guillotined. Could the same thing happen in Iran? We kept dreaming during the moonlit nights to the sound of the waves and the seagulls. Meanwhile, a group of people in Tehran were working day and night to thwart our plans.

We finally received news as we were approaching Bombay. We were due to change ships here before heading for the Persian Gulf, but the first boat that approached our ship to deal with customs delivered a message from the Aga Khan. He was inviting us to break the journey by staying in his home, and to continue with our journey aboard his personal ship. The invitation had come from Bibi, the Aga Khan's wife and cousin to the Empress and my mother. I had heard a great deal about her but did not see her until later that evening.

Bibi was overweight and old but extremely kind. She received us in a palace larger than any of the palaces in Tehran, its tall columns resembling those in Aati Bahçe. We were driven to the Aga Khan's palace escorted by British and Indian guards. I had previously seen the British in Istanbul, where they always travelled in carriages or on horseback and were invariably accompanied by a turbaned and bearded Indian or Nepalese officer, who aggressively pushed people aside to clear the riders' path. Here, however, rather than occupiers, they were very much at home, and the Aga Khan was one of the most powerful and richest individuals in India; no wonder the Empress believed that as long as her family remained in power we would be treated with respect everywhere we travelled.

Our one-week sojourn in Bombay turned out to be quite eventful. When we drove around escorted by a number of Indian officers the paupers would climb on top of each other and hang to the car begging for money or even some bread. This, of course, terrified us at times, and I don't know what would have become of us had it not been for the guards; it was only too evident that we were strangers here. Back in the palace everything sparkled, a far cry from the poverty outside the walls. We felt thoroughly pampered. Dr Jarozelski and our Russian entourage made the most of sightseeing and shopping, always returning with innumerable bags. They were immensely grateful for the generosity of their host, the leader of the Esmaeeli sect. For the first time in years Bibi had her relations around her and was able to show off the Iranian imperial family to the Indians; indeed, her husband's relations insisted that we should extend our stay. The Empress, however, reminded her that we were pressed for time and had a mountain to climb. We decided to leave by the end of the week since the news coming from Tehran obliged us to expedite our departure; she regretted the delay caused by our extended stay. Majid, who was a contemporary of the Aga Khan's children, had found good friends and wanted to stay, but the Empress promised that, God willing, Bibi would return the visit in Tehran.

We ended our visit with a magnificent gala to which some two hundred English women and Indian grandees were invited. The Empress's sons had many tales to tell of their experience in the other quarters: the gold plates, the chandeliers, the gold and silver powder-covered meals. In Bibi's corner we saw Indians dancing to the tune of a sitar and a small *tonbak*.

Back in Istanbul we were still veiled but after two years in Europe we had grown used to seeing women who never covered their heads, and in San Remo we had even seen women who bathed in the sea together with men. Here in Bombay it was quite something to see half-naked dancers who twisted and turned with their bellies uncovered, not to mention women clad in their colourful saris revealing their shoulders and midriffs. We were astonished to hear the next day that the dancers had also performed in the men's quarters; though not all the guests were followers of the Aga Khan's sect, the thought of these women before their eyes was unbelievable.

By the time we boarded the Aga Khan's ship our luggage had somehow doubled. I, for one, had received many sumptuous presents for my home – Saeed was going to marvel at the sight of all the statues and the silver dinner service. I had even received presents for Ezzedin and Janine. We had truly been overwhelmed by India's riches and beauty during our short visit. When Bibi kissed me goodbye she said, 'I am the granddaughter of Nasser al-Din Shah and you are the granddaughter of Mozaffar ed-Din Shah,' something which I had not been reminded of for some time. By the time the ropes were cast off and the horn had blown we were keener than ever to reach Iran, the Empress far more impatient than anyone else.

Chapter 43

I had posted the letters to our house in Rue Pasquier on reaching Bombay; by the time we left I had posted ten more to someone whose love had stirred my enthusiasm to write, to say that I could not enjoy the beauty the world was offering me without him. I described some of the wonders I had seen in India and I ended my letters with the words: 'I enjoy the moments by thinking of you; the moments are not without your presence,' something he used to say, something I had heard for the first time when he was going away just after our nuptials – the most amorous thing one could possibly hear.

I always carried the lyrics of Hafez and Saadi with me and had many a time tried to translate them into French but I knew they could not sound as beautiful. I did, however, translate the following verse by Molana:

Endure I may, away from everyone;
But the unbearable is to be away from you.

When the ship reached the waters of Iran, where the Iranian flag flew on the mast in Boushehr harbour, I missed Saeed; I wished he could be there in his military uniform standing next to the Empress. The boats came to greet us and the cannon fired to mark the arrival of the Empress and the brothers of the Shah. The British captain and the naval officers stood to attention and a little while later the governor's agents came on board to pay their respects. I wanted to get off there and then; having been away for sixteen years I never thought my encounter with my homeland could be so moving and exciting.

'Praise be to God,' were the Empress's words.

Our Iranian servants and entourage, male and female, were all in tears. We did not disembark, however, and the ship began to sail after about an hour.

With its tall masts, Abadan resembled a European harbour, but we had hardly taken in the sight of the refinery when the cannon began to fire from the fort belonging to Sheikh Khaz'al, one of the Shah's supporters. Despite all the pomp and ceremony we did not disembark in Abadan either; the ship then entered the wide estuary of the Tigris and Euphrates, and when Basrah's palm trees came in sight we could not wait to disembark; we had come a long way from Marseille to Bombay and from Bombay to Basrah.

We had to pay our respects at the holy shrines, where the Empress and her sons had to attend important meetings, so once again we were veiled and taken by car on the arid roads. Once in Najaf, we stayed in a relatively modest house and the Empress and her companions set out to visit the religious leaders we had encountered in Odessa and Istanbul during *Ashoura*. It was apparent that the clerics were not happy with Sardar Sepah either, and although they supported the Shah, they reminded his brothers always to think of God when holding the reins of power; they feared that living in the West and socialising with the Europeans might have prevented them from performing their religious duties. They were, however, aware that, despite the many years in exile, the Empress had preserved her beliefs and had kept up all the traditions related to Muharram and Ramadan. They were also aware of what was going on in Tehran.

And so our convoy headed towards Karbala where the Qajars owned property. The tombs of Shah Baba, Muhammad Ali Shah, the great-grandfathers, uncles and acquaintances whose burials had taken place in Karbala lay next to the holy site and, in addition to offering various facilities, were cared for by people who were paid for their services. The set-up made matters easier for the Empress, who had come to seek the religious leaders' seal of approval for the democracy in Iran and her son's reign. Supported by their authority she could confront Sardar Sepah. Though she knew she was short of time she was not in too much of a hurry.

The day we were supposed to pay our respects at the holy shrine of Imam Hussein, the Empress made everyone wash and put on new clothes. She had brought along a very large rug to donate to the estate. The doors to the shrine were temporarily closed to the pilgrims so that we could spend an hour praying in private. A cleric recited prayers and we followed suit. For a moment I felt I had become empty of any thought, my past and all the resentment I felt. I asked for forgiveness and compassion for everyone, hardly thinking of Saeed and our home in Madeleine at the time. 'God save Ahmad Shah!' we chanted during the three days of the same ritual. Every time we left the shrine, a number of Persian-, Arabic- and Turkish-speaking beggars pursued us, but the guards ensured that we were not harmed. The Empress would stop from time to time to give them some coins.

The run-up to our visit to Baghdad was a happy one, and the Empress took every opportunity to send telegrams to Ahmad Shah in Paris, as well as a coded message to Muhammad Hassan, the crown prince, who was at Golestan Palace in Tehran. The notables of Najaf, who saw it as her religious duty, were urging the Empress to get to Tehran without delay. Despite advice to spend a few weeks in Baghdad to think her plans through before setting off for Kermanshah, she was determined, no matter how exhausted we were, to embark on our journey as soon as the means of travel were available.

The vehicles that took us from Najaf to Baghdad were not in good shape and we were forced to stop several times. When we reached the gates to the city of Baghdad we encountered a car bearing the British flag and were delayed while the Russian officer went back and forth. Our travel documents were all with

Khan Baba Khan, who was still with us. Meanwhile, a tall Arab, whom we discovered was Farmanfarma's butler, had turned up to deliver a handwritten note: Nanny, my aunt, was insisting that we should go to her house. The Empress did not much care for Farmanfarma.

'We shall go to the Iranian Embassy – the Shah's mother has not come on holiday.'

A telephone call revealed that the Iranian Embassy was closed since Iran had not yet sent an ambassador and the consul general was not in Baghdad at the time. The government of King Feisal had barely established itself and the British, who were evidently in charge, had only just recognised him. We had no choice in the circumstances and finally, with the British military escorting us, we passed by the shores of Dejleh and arrived in a tree-lined street. We stopped by a rather extensive establishment flying the Iranian flag; we had arrived at the Iranian Consulate. The only person present was a warden, who initially had no idea what to do with us, but who finally relented and unlocked the doors. Staying at the consulate would enable the Empress to make contact with Tehran and Kermanshah to forewarn the governors. She wanted our arrival on Iranian soil to be with such pomp that Sardar Sepah couldn't help but back off. The enthusiasm with which I had embarked on that journey was now waning; the task we had embarked on was not so simple and not without risks.

'Would they kill us?' Majid asked his mother, to which the Empress retorted: 'But they are nobodies my dear!'

A room was swiftly prepared for the Empress and communication with Tehran and Paris was established.

The operator had difficulty making contact to begin with and kept repeating, 'I can't find the line.'

Hours later, when we finally succeeded in establishing contact with Golestan Palace, we heard Khan Baba Khan shouting across the line, demanding to speak to the crown prince, informing those at the other end that Her Majesty, the most honourable and beloved Empress, was on the line, but the response didn't seem clear. Several hours passed and the sound of the constant yelling down the line was bothering everyone. The kitchen was not fully operational but we managed to have some tea and hookah, and an English soldier arrived to deliver some telegrams. My aunt seemed preoccupied, as though she had received bad news. By then, a group of Iranians had gathered outside the consulate; every time someone emerged from the building they would circle him to find out more information.

We spent a couple of days in a state of uncertainty. I spent the night in one of the rooms where the Empress, accompanied by two servants, lay on a camp bed. Everyone had found a corner in the consulate to rest and the warden tried to be of some service while looking apprehensive; tips and the promise to repay his efforts didn't seem to relieve him of his anxiety. The Empress kept asking him about the whereabouts of the Consul and the staff, only to meet with his reluctance to respond.

On the third night we were woken by heavy knocking on the door. A lantern was brought out and the building suddenly seemed to fill with noise. Given the hour, we got up, terrified that we were about to receive horrific news. A group of Iranian and Arab men poured inside and Smirnoff was about to shoot to prevent them from approaching our rooms. Hearing Smirnoff's yells, my aunt, clad in her *chador*, made an appearance and demanded that the men explain the commotion in the middle of the night, at which point a man came forward and replied in Persian that he had orders from 'His Majesty' Reza Khan, Sardar Sepah. Looking comical in his pyjamas, Khan Baba Khan, who was clearly petrified, entered into talks with the invaders. They disappeared behind closed doors and no one knew what was going on until Khan Baba Khan emerged with his robe on his shoulders apologizing as he broke the news.

'Today, the parliament voted to put an end to Qajar rule. The crown prince has been thrown out of the palace and he is under close watch on his way to Kermanshah as we speak, and …'

I was sitting on the bed listening to Khan Baba Khan.

'They have their orders and are not prepared to let us stay here any longer. We have an hour to evacuate the consulate building...' And then we suddenly heard the sound of something breaking; a portrait of the Shah, which had hung on the wall of the main salon, was now on the floor with the glass shattered.

One of the women was beating her head; thinking that the Bolsheviks had arrived in Tehran she was concerned about her family. My aunt was sitting on the edge of her bed more composed than everyone else. The door suddenly opened and an armed man entered. The women pulled their *chadors* on their heads.

The man kicked the nearby chest and shouted, 'Out! It's over.'

Was it really over? It was four o'clock in the morning on the last day of October and we were thrown out like discarded paper into the cool air of Baghdad. Smirnoff's hands and feet were tied and no one paid any attention to our pleas. The noise had drawn the Iraqi police and people to the building. We were out on the road and my aunt was sitting on one of the chests in the middle of the street. Mahmoud and Majid looked petrified and were busy dressing themselves in the middle of the street. The intruders were now closing all the doors and we could hear one of them yelling at the warden, admonishing him for letting us inside the building without seeking permission.

'Do go to Iran, people are waiting to deal with you,' a man said sarcastically.

The Empress murmured, 'People!' with a wry smile.

The people's will, or the force of Sardar Sepah and the Cossacks, whatever it was, had forced us onto the streets with nowhere to go. The intruders didn't even take any notice of the maids, who pleaded, 'You are Iranians; you must be ashamed of yourselves treating us in such a manner, leaving a bunch of women and children on the street,' but my aunt motioned them to keep quiet, as it was useless.

Perhaps she was the only one who could comprehend the magnitude of what was happening: our delay had granted Sardar Sepah sufficient time to hold a meeting in the parliament, forcing the members to vote. According to one of the men, the whole world now recognised the new government.

Then someone among us mentioned 'Republic, like the Turks,' and the same man shouted out, 'Long live His Majesty Pahlavi,' a name we were hearing for the first time.

Everything was racing through my mind: our escape from Tehran, the invasion of the Bolsheviks at our home in Odessa, the time on the harbour and the day we were thrown out of Sultana Khadijeh's palace two years ago. Yet none of these events had been as abrupt as the one we were experiencing now in Baghdad: we had been thrown out in the middle of the night with broken trunks, the contents of which were strewn on the street! Khan Baba Khan urged my aunt to send for Vahab, Farmanfarma's butler, which the Empress accepted; it was only two days since he had insisted on taking us to the princess's house. Though the house was nearby he was nowhere to be found.

In the depth of our desperation, seven cars approached and two men stepped out. They were heavyset and clad in formal attire with fezzes on their heads. Khan Baba Khan went forward to talk to them. It transpired that Raouf Nasri, head of the cabinet to His Majesty Malek Feisal, the King of Iraq, was to take us to one of the palaces. At this point Majid suddenly burst into tears.

'They want to terminate our lives, just the way Tsar Nicolas and the Tsarina of Russia were treated.'

His mother retorted that he should contain himself, but she didn't think it improbable. Smirnoff, having by now freed his hands and just about got dressed, spoke to me in French.

'Princess, this place is run by the British and there is no reason why we should be fearful,' which I translated to my aunt.

She forced herself up from where she was sitting, muttering, 'Lord, we are at your mercy!'

We had received orders to make a move and it was daylight when we arrived at a palace in Kazimayn, situated in a palm grove, where an English woman greeted us. While travelling with them in the car, the Iraqi minister had reassured the Empress's sons that they had nothing to worry about; he had asked them, however, not to make contact with anyone while the government took time to think of a solution. We were effectively respected prisoners left to deal with our anxiety; alas, Dr Jarozelski's expertise was not of much use this time!

Four days later, the crown prince arrived having been thrown out of the palace immediately after the parliament vote. He was frightened and shut himself in his room, spending hours talking to his mother. The Shah's *siqehs* and household servants had not been spared either, and were brutally thrown out of the palace. The crown prince kept cursing the traitors, among whom the monster's name was also mentioned; my father, like many others, had become a supporter of Sardar Sepah.

I found it hard to believe that I was encountering the same fate as the members of the Russian aristocratic families, not to mention the Ottoman sultanas who had had to adjust to their new lives in different parts of the world. The Iraqi and European papers were filled with tales of the families whose lives had taken an unexpected turn within ten years of the Great War. One such tale happened in Beirut, where Prince Nadim, the son of the Ottoman crown prince, had shot his two-year-old daughter, followed by his beautiful wife, and had finally terminated his own life.

CHAPTER 44

I received Saeed's first letter two weeks later. The family with whom I had grown up were now so preoccupied with their problems that there was no time for anyone to listen to my dilemmas; my problems were different from theirs.

Since the terrifying events of that autumn night, something seemed to have shattered within me and I began to feel distant from the aristocracy. I had no more space for the turmoil that came with such a life. My only hope was Saeed, who I felt had also given up on monarchy. I spent hours listening to the ordinary people whom I met on a daily basis. I remember the day that a representative of the Pahlavi government arrived in Baghdad; everyone was anxious to ensure that the splendour of the family shone as brightly as ever. The Empress received the man in the reception room of a mansion she had leased along the River Dejleh with Smirnoff standing to attention behind her. I sat in the room and adopted the role of Malakeh Jahan's lady-in-waiting with another woman seated on the other side of the room.

The representative arrived alone and announced that he needed to deliver a message to the Empress in person. He came with a proposal: the Empress could return to Iran and take up residence in Golestan Palace. The government would then agree to fund the education of Majid and Mahmoud in a military school in Europe; three million tomans were also to be disbursed to take care of our expenses.

The Empress dismissed him and arranged for another meeting two days later. After further discussion and soliciting advice, it was concluded that Reza Khan had intended to take the Empress hostage to prevent her children claiming the throne. Accepting the proposal would mean the Qajars recognised the Pahlavi regime. However, before responding, the Empress gathered everyone, plus a handful of new arrivals from Europe, as well as Muhammad Hassan and his entourage from Tehran. She tried hard to hold back her tears.

'My children may return to Iran at some point in the future but I don't have much time,' she said.

She then left everyone to decide whether they wanted to remain with her or return to their homeland.

'This is a good opportunity since we can now obtain passports and assurances of everyone's safety,' she added, at which some people burst into tears saying that they were not going to leave her. In the end, eight decided to return with their families.

Finally the Empress turned to me. She didn't feel as anxious for me as she did for the others since I had a husband, a house of my own and the funds that Mother had bequeathed to me. When I asked her when I should return to Paris, she said it would be more appropriate for Saeed to meet me in a month's time in Beirut.

During our sojourn in Baghdad, we also received visits from a few members of the Ottoman family. Sultana Fahimeh delivered Saeed's letter, in which he mentioned that he wanted to sell the house in order to acquire a larger property somewhere in the suburbs of Paris, 'So that there is enough space for the children' – a comment accompanied with a wink.

When the Empress heard Saeed's message her analysis was as gracious as ever.

'Clearly, with the events in Tehran they have understood that they need to economise. This is a good thing and shows their wisdom, unlike some thoughtless families!'

So I picked up a pen and wrote to Saeed, wondering as I did so why he had not responded to any of my letters. I gave him power of attorney to enable him to sell the house but I asked him to take care of my seemingly worthless belongings, such as the box containing my letters, drawings and childhood souvenirs, and reminded him that they were more valuable to me than a box full of jewels.

Having given up the thought of returning to Iran entirely, Muhammad Hassan and his family had by now joined our low-spirited convoy. Unlike his elder brother he was married to a Qajar, Malakeh Jahan's niece by her sister, and they had two children. For some time to come the family bickered over which brother had brought about the loss of the throne; some thought Ahmad Shah had demonstrated a common touch and honesty, some were critical of Muhammad Hassan's inherited arrogance, which had brought about the people's uprising in Tabriz. Others, however, stood by Muhammad Hassan and believed that if the Shah had abdicated in favour of his brother, he could have whipped up a discontented crowd to fight Sardar Sepah, together with the support of the local khans and other supporters. The never-ending debates went on for the next eight months until we embarked on our journey to Beirut.

Beirut resembled a small paradise, the Empress renting a large property there that would accommodate her sizeable entourage. Some sultanas and members of the Ottoman ruling family, who outnumbered us, were also based in western Beirut at the time. The residential district was high up in the mountains overlooking the sea, just like our park in Odessa and Sultana Khadijeh's palace on the Bosphorus. White houses with terracotta rooftops, however, gave Beirut a particular charm. By the time we settled in Beirut Saeed had arrived. He stayed with one of his sisters in Rostam Pasha Street and very soon the round of socialising began. Beirut's high society, in particular the Muslims, regarded the Ottomans with respect and were eager to mix with them, even to marry into them.

Soon after Saeed's arrival we were invited for the evening by one of his friends in Soursok, an elegant part of the city. The music and dancing continued well into the night, after which the men started to play cards. There were three other young women whose husbands participated in the games. French wine kept arriving on silver trays, and I felt embarrassed that I could not join in, though I was not prepared to break the habit under any circumstances.

We carried on partying over many evenings, and at the end of every evening I was driven home feeling tired and sleepy, only to end up in bed alone. One evening, I accidentally found out that Saeed had lost a fair amount gambling. I wondered how he could access funds if he lived on borrowed money from Malakeh Jahan. I was, nevertheless, still drawn to him, and this attraction and affection blinded me to any faults. He told me that he had got together with two Frenchmen and invested heavily in a project to build a casino in West Beirut. I had seen the men he was talking about. Whenever there was talk of my estate I found that Saeed tended to boast and exaggerate the extent of it. I did not know what belonged to me or where my assets were; all I knew was that whatever I had rested with my aunt.

One Friday, when Saeed's French friends, his sisters, and Majid and Mahmoud were present, Saeed suggested that his friends should involve me in their plans. They had the drawings and had already registered a company. The drawings were marked with an area in Beirut where the hotel and the casino were to be constructed. I, however, loved Paris and wanted to live there.

'How could we continue living in Paris?' I asked in a hushed voice.

'One month a year in Beirut in princely fashion,' he burst out laughing.

In the end, Saeed decided to discuss everything with Malakeh Jahan since he now felt close enough to discuss his ideas openly. I was to become a partner in their hotel and casino corporation. The Empress didn't see anything wrong with this but she wanted *me* to decide. She had, on our last evening in Paris, passed on to me all the relevant documentation on my shares and whatever she held for me. I didn't want to take them, but she reminded me that in no time I'd be thirty and that she preferred me to be in charge of my own affairs. At the same time, she mentioned an organisation in Paris which had, up to now, been in charge of running everyone's finances, including mine. The company she was talking about was an affiliate of the Banque de Paris, and she recommended that I should seek their advice in future financial transactions. I discussed everything with Saeed and he agreed that the Empress was sensible and far-sighted.

'Without her, God only knows what would have become of the Qajar imperial family,' he said, something I agreed with since I had already experienced her wisdom on my account.

My farewell to my aunt was harder than I had imagined; we were all in tears.

Saeed kissed the Empress's hand and promised he was going 'to guard Khanoum like a jewel'.

I didn't want to leave but soon found myself seated next to Saeed in the back of the vehicle. I watched the balcony, where the Empress was still waving, through my tears. Sitting next to Saeed gave me a sense of security, though momentarily I felt him let go of my hand, which he had held up to then.

While sailing towards Marseille, I kept saying how much I missed my aunt, and when I was on my own I couldn't help my tears. Saeed was kind and helped me wipe my face. The Empress's last present to us was our first-class cabin, where I could get changed and apply my makeup. We would then step into the salon as prince and princess. With a cigarette in the corner of his mouth Saeed looked clever and proud every night he gambled. Having already sailed to different countries as a member of the family of the former Shah of Iran, this was by far the happiest sea journey I had ever taken – the prince and princess.

When we disembarked in Marseille, the captain and the naval officers were standing to attention to say goodbye. I was touched when the captain proudly presented me with a signed photograph of himself standing next to us, in a beautiful frame. The porters had already taken my luggage to the harbour and Ezzedin, dressed in a white linen suit, was expecting us. Later on that evening we celebrated my independent arrival in Europe in a café in Marseille. We spent three nights in a spacious suite in the Hôtel de Paris, the largest and grandest hotel in Marseille. Everywhere I looked I found flowers in our suite, as though we were in a greenhouse. This was Ezzedin's idea, to ensure that his friend and his beloved had a good time. Since there were two bedrooms, Ezzedin also stayed in the same suite.

When it came to settling the account, Saeed said to the receptionist with his usual humour, 'We are guests of the princess,' and the three of us burst out laughing.

He knew very well that, having been through a great deal, a young woman like me needed to keep her self-respect and pride; indeed there was no reason why I should not have felt proud.

CHAPTER 45

Nine-thirty in the morning, 22 August 1927, Gare de Lyon, Paris – a day I would remember, though at its start I had no idea how significant this day was to become. Two hours later, when I was clutching my handbag in the middle of the large station and looking at people rushing from one place to another, I began to see a hazy image of the future.

Saeed, Ezzedin and I emerged from the first-class compartment. I then had to wait for them to deal with customs and luggage collection. The other passengers had already been greeted by their families and acquaintances and had left. It was 11.30am and a different group of passengers arrived and scattered on different platforms. I was by now concerned by their delay though tried to distract myself by looking at the departure and arrival board, the station's high ceiling and the traffic of people. From time to time someone shouted out a passenger's name or held up someone's name on a board, but no one was looking for me. I couldn't understand what had taken them so long. By noon I had approached the officer in charge; he checked my name against his book as well as the train number. He informed me that my luggage, consisting of four suitcases, had already been collected and that everyone had left.

'But I am still waiting.'

'Whatever you wish, Madame.'

He didn't strike me as particularly concerned.

I was then motioned to go the central hall. I sat on a bench under the departures and arrivals board. I had pins and needles in my feet and was exhausted. I decided to read the newspaper I had picked up earlier on the train. Alarmist headlines announced the workers' strike and clashes between the communists and the extreme right. There had been demonstrations and clashes on a daily basis, mainly near the Panthéon, where Jean Jaurès, the founder of France's Socialist Party, had been buried. The Communist Party had summoned people to more extensive demonstrations in Paris. It was warm and I could hear a group of people shouting 'Down with Sarraut' in the main hall. I knew Sarraut, the Prime Minister, had referred to the communists as 'the enemy of the nation' in parliament the previous week.

Angry young people waved their fists in the air and shouted out slogans. Their voices reverberated under the iron-structured dome of the Gare de Lyon and heightened my fear. I kept craning my neck for a sight of Saeed or Ezzedin. It was four o'clock and I was still hovering around the Gare de Lyon. Fear and anxiety had crept over me. A police officer approached me and asked me if I needed assistance. I explained anxiously that I had lost my husband, at which he smiled.

'It's he who should be concerned and not you,' he responded and then left.

I had to put pride aside and approach the same officer, who, in the circumstances, was the only person I could rely on. I explained to him that we had arrived from Marseille and that I had been waiting around since that morning. Meanwhile, I suddenly remembered that I was hungry; I had had a sumptuous breakfast on the train but nothing since. He took me to the central police bureau at the station and reported the matter to his superior. A thick moustache marked his face. I was then asked to present my passport. I began to search in my handbag and it suddenly dawned on me that, on arrival, after the police had stamped it, Ezzedin had kept Saeed's and mine. I didn't even have the train ticket and had no other form of identity papers on me. He forwarded a sheet of paper so that I could write down my details.

How little I knew at the time that by doing so I was entering a tunnel the end of which was out of my reach. I wrote down the address of my house: Rue Pasquier in *quartier* Madeleine, behind the church. I also wrote down where I had come from and the address of the Hôtel de Paris. The police officer had given the case a job number and was now walking ahead of me. We got into a black police car; nothing like the Rolls Royce that had driven us to the fabulous cafés in Marseille. Had I been dressed differently, the people passing by could have easily taken me for a communist who had been arrested on the street.

While we were passing by the Trocadero, I tried to convince myself that this was some joke, that Saeed Pasha was going to open the door to me and I could tell him how tired and hungry I was. I was going over events, now registered somewhere in my memory forever. The officer asked me some questions while we were passing through the streets. I explained to him that I was the granddaughter of the former Shah of Iran, hence my being well versed in French. He raised an eyebrow, looking incredulous; I had only spent a few days in Paris and I need not have told him how much I had enjoyed those days. We arrived in Rue Pasquier, and when I saw the lights in the house on, I suddenly didn't feel tired any more.

I smiled to the police officer, 'My husband is at home waiting for me!'

But when we knocked on the door a young Frenchman appeared in his dressing gown. In the hallway, a woman of similar age to me looked curious as soon as she saw me. The police officer asked the man whether he knew me. The man looked bewildered, eyed me head to toe and then shrugged. This could have come as a shock but I was trying to keep calm and explained to him that he was standing in my house. The man, however, explained that he had only the previous month purchased the house. I asked him from whom he had purchased it.

Within a few minutes part of the story began to unfold. My house had been sold as well as all of the contents. I asked the man whether I could take a little more of his time. The man had a tête-à-tête with his wife and reluctantly allowed the police officer and me to enter the house. My Esfahani rugs were still lying in the drawing room, and I even saw the *termeh* tablecloth on the mantelpiece on which my photographs and personal items had once rested. Once the woman had ascertained that I was indeed the previous owner of the house she went to fetch the letters she had found in the letterbox. Those were all the letters I had written to Saeed when I was in Beirut; letters filled with love and expectations of future happiness; a future that was fast fading away. I remembered that Saeed was indeed supposed to sell the house but wondered why he had sold the contents as well. The final stroke came when the man mentioned that at the time of signing the contract, Saeed and Ezzedin had been present, and they had explained to him that I had returned to Iran and that they were to join me later on, hence leaving everything behind. He had told him to discard anything he did not need.

'And you did?' At which the man nodded.

This was unbelievable; by doing so Saeed had effectively discarded every reminder of my past. Why did he not discuss this with me in Beirut?

The woman brought me coffee in one of my Russian cups. I could not sit there forever, thinking about all the incredible things that had happened. When we left the house, the police officer asked me where I wanted him to drive me to, but I couldn't say anything. I suggested that I should stay in a hotel – the Hôtel Royal Madeleine was a few yards away – but he explained that it was impossible for a single woman to be offered accommodation without identity papers. He then politely explained that until my identity was proven I had to stay with them.

'In any case, where else would you go?' said the officer, indifferently and perhaps somewhat sarcastically.

I couldn't respond. We stopped outside a café so that he could use the telephone to ask his superior's advice. Meanwhile, I tried to think of a solution. I thought of running away in his absence, but where to? I searched in my handbag and found a few gold coins, a purse which contained some Lebanese bank notes, the value of which I did not know, Saeed's photograph and a letter in which he had so eloquently written about love. I read the letter twice. No, there must be a mistake. I recalled the evening in Paris when we, Ezzedin and Janine strolled around town. Janine... Where was Janine? I had brought her some presents but they were all in the suitcases that Saeed and Ezzedin had gone to fetch. The thought of Janine was like the key to paradise and I suddenly felt relieved. When the officer returned I told him that I had the address of a friend who could help me. He hesitantly agreed to take me to St Lazare. It was a long way but he had no choice.

I tried hard to remember where Janine lived. Twice wrong, I finally found the alleyway where Janine's house was. I still remembered the shoe shop at the beginning of the road and I knew that Janine was in one of the nearby buildings. I got off and spoke to an old man sitting outside one of the houses. He couldn't help but decided to call his wife. The old French-woman looked at me curiously. When I told them about a young woman and her two boys she pointed to the upper floors of the neighbouring house.

As I climbed the stairs I braced myself; I even anticipated that someone else might open the door and present me with a similar sort of story as I had encountered earlier in my own house. The doorbell made a loud, hideous sound and I could hear voices from inside. The door opened.

Janine hesitated at first but then screamed, 'Princess!'

The police officer took a step back. Janine was transfixed to see the man and looked puzzled and a little frightened. The young woman seemed to have guessed everything at first glance. I asked Janine why she had left the house and who those people were. It transpired that Saeed and Ezzedin had three months earlier informed her that I was not planning to return to Paris and that they intended to sell the house and leave France to join me in Tehran. Later, at the commissariat, Janine explained the same to the commanding police officer.

I was wondering what I should do. Having listened and found out that I had no identity papers and nowhere to go, he was filled with fury as though the enormity of the injustice had suddenly become clear. He raised his voice and asked the officer what legal provisions there were in France for a princess who had been subjected to such a crime. Janine talked with such clarity and sincerity that the commanding officer began to ponder. He asked me whether the Iranian Embassy in Paris held any files on me so that I could prove my claim. I was bewildered.

When Janine described how two corrupt men had mercilessly planned to rob me, I found it extraordinary. I found it hard to believe that the past three years were nothing but lies. We filled in a questionnaire, which was filed together with Saeed's photograph, which I found in my handbag. They were busy talking when I suddenly felt dizzy and fainted as a result. When I woke up I was lying on a bench with Janine standing by holding a glass of water. She signed a paper acting as guarantor and then took me to her house. I was hungry.

Janine's house had a bedroom and a living room. There was a kitchen in a corner and a small bathroom by the entrance. When she removed my shoes I felt my feet were burning; I remembered that I had been standing all day. I shared her bed and when I woke up it was daytime. I couldn't recall any dreams. All the questions in the world suddenly rushed into my head. Janine had already left early in the morning to buy a toothbrush and a comb for me. When the children went to school she insisted that I should have a wash. There was a shower with a tub beneath it. I felt embarrassed that I was bothering her but she was very kind and kept telling me that the law was going to protect me. She refrained from discussing my husband, preferring to let time unfold everything.

We had to go to the police station, but before doing so she fetched an old bag from her wardrobe with her entire savings of some two to three thousand francs. She put it all in front of me and I felt my eyes well up with tears. I suddenly remembered a novel by Tolstoy that I had read in Odessa. It was the story of a thief who stole things in order to care for his sick neighbour and her young child. I told myself that I had no right to shed tears in the presence of a woman who had to work so hard. I remembered the Empress, who, despite difficult and uncertain times, had taught me and her children not to lose hope since the sun might suddenly shine from an unexpected corner. But where from? I tried to hold back my tears and told Janine that perhaps this was meant to be so that I could get to know her a little better. I declared in earnest that we were going to sort everything out that very day. We ate the freshly baked bread she had bought and drank café au lait. I asked her whether she had to go to work. She explained that she had not been able to find a full-time job but that for the time being she worked two days a week in a hospital; that day and the next she happened not to be working.

When we arrived at the police station we did not resemble the women who had left the station the night before; a year seemed to have passed since then. An old man, who also worked for the police, offered his services as a lawyer. He seemed interested in the fate of a woman who had been caught in some sort of conspiracy. As he listened to us he cursed the monarchy, the monarchists and the aristocrats. He was a socialist and a republican. While he interrogated me I suddenly remembered what the Empress had mentioned to me during our last meeting, about an office in Paris that managed the Qajars' financial and legal affairs, including mine. The old man clapped his hands with joy when he felt he had suddenly found a solution. Once again, Janine acted as guarantor and we left the police station.

Monsieur Gaston, the lawyer who was to help me, explained everything on my behalf to one of the partners at Établissement

Gaspard. He kept repeating 'fraud' and 'abuse'. I was not yet ready for my husband to be referred to in such terms. But they could not confirm my indentity, and without identity papers they were not prepared to discuss anything. After making a variety of threats, Gaston managed to convince them not to make any decisions about my estate until further notice. Having filled in a questionnaire which Monsieur Gaston and I signed, we left.

We were now sitting in a small restaurant in the Boulevard Haussmann. Monsieur Gaston wanted me to think hard. The great difficulty was to prove my identity. According to him, as far as French law was concerned I was non-existent. I asked Janine what had become of our furniture and belongings in the house, and she said that as far as she remembered everything was left as it had been and she did not think that Saeed and Ezzedin had removed anything.

A few minutes later we found ourselves outside my house once again. From outside, I looked at the curtains I had made with such attention to detail. This time, the woman let us in and we went upstairs. The rugs, the *termeh* that the Empress had given me, the pictures, everything I had purchased were all in place. The framed photographs, however, had been replaced: rather than the photographs of my mother, the Empress and her family, and that of the Ottoman Sultan that Saeed had added, pictures of strangers were now filling the same frames. The new owner listened to our story in astonishment. She had thought Saeed a true prince, a gentleman who fulfilled his promise and had not removed a single item. Was this true?

Janine and I looked at each other. I was now thinking of my books, a small trunk which contained the photographs, letters, my mother's letters, my childhood clothes that my mother had made, all of which I had brought with me when I left Iran and had kept all those years, not to mention all the documents that the Empress had handed to me before I left San Remo. Yes, I had many documents to prove my identity. If I could, I would immediately have run towards the bedroom where I had only spent three nights. My suitcase was inside a wardrobe on which I had placed a mirror, but we had to wait for permission from the owner of the house. She said indifferently that she had taken the trunk to the cellar and got up to accompany us. It was wonderful that amid the desperation my mind still worked.

As we climbed down the stairs Janine winked at me as if all was going to be sorted out. In the basement, not only could I see my green suitcase, there was also a pile of clothes along with my personal effects: Persian and Turkish books piled up in a disorderly fashion. I first caught sight of the Qur'an and the book of Hafez. When I opened the green suitcase, however, I was stunned: it was completely empty. The photographs, the letters and the documents, everything that could prove my identity, had disappeared. Looking at the tragic expression on my face Janine rushed to search among the books and my drawings. I was standing there searching for a solution; I had to find a solution.

Gaston, by then resembling a pauper's advocate, found some papers and asked me to translate their contents. I was impatiently searching in the dark basement. I was confused and began to think that I was to experience the same fate as Jean Valjean. Janine touched my shoulder from time to time to reassure me that everything was going to be all right. More than worrying about the future, I was thinking about people's capacity for good or evil.

As though he was about to discover the clues to some crime, Gaston asked the owner to leave everything as it was in the basement. Having briefed the woman on events, he had roused her compassion. Consequently, Gaston discovered a paper that he confidently thought could help us sort things out. The paper the new owner handed over was the deeds of the house. These were proof of my identity, passport number and my details as the seller of the property. However, Saeed had signed on my behalf using his power of attorney!

The following day, the same document helped Gaston to acquire from the town hall the power of attorney I had given Saeed. Later, at Établissement Gaspard, he was told that Saeed had signed papers transferring my estate to Ezzedin. More important, he also discovered that Saeed and Ezzedin had left Paris the day after our arrival. This meant that while I was a wandering soul in the Gare de Lyon, and all the time that the police and I were driving around, they were still in Paris. The transfer of the estate at Établissement Gaspard had taken place before noon on 22 August. This coincided with the time I was waiting at the railway station wondering what had taken them so long. I had missed Saeed and anticipated his imminent return with a smile; he never complained about being tired.

After numerous visits to Gaspard's, I finally came into possession of an identity card proving that I was Iranian and had permission to remain in France for one year. I was relieved that I did not have to present myself at the police station on a daily basis. Despite Janine's protests I sold two gold coins, my only assets. I still wore a ring but asked her to hide my necklace.

After receiving my identity card I took Janine and the children to a small restaurant, where Janine tried to pretend that everything was going to be all right. I first had to relieve myself of some of the burden, so I decided to write to my aunt. I spent some time thinking about what I wanted to say. I put my whole heart into my thanks for all she had done for me and promised to write to her again. I put Janine's address on the back of the envelope and nothing else. At the time I was too embarrassed to describe my misfortune to a woman who had looked after me for eighteen years and who, everywhere she went, boasted about my wisdom and maturity. I didn't want to upset her. I was only too aware of her problems and the heavy burden of responsibility since my uncle had passed away. Since the crown prince had left Iran her responsibilities seemed to have doubled. She had to manage a large family of some thirty or forty, who were not prepared to live anywhere but with the trappings of imperial grandeur, and this had made me laugh. I recalled the demands of the Empress's grandchildren and the families that I had encountered up to then. I also thought of the small things that made Jacques, Janine's elder son, happy. When I took my clothes to Janine's home I found a top that I had bought in San Remo; it fitted Jacques and pleased him immensely.

Every day Janine and I queued up to buy food and other goods, which we stored in the cupboards of her modest home. I remembered that in the most difficult days of my life, save the four days spent aboard the French ship taking us from Odessa to Istanbul, I had never had to worry about food; I had only read about poverty. I couldn't understand why Janine tried so hard to prevent my learning about the brutal realities of life. I saw how she made a mattress for her children so that we did not have to spend money on a new one. She wanted us to arrive home as late as possible so that we did not have time to see the poverty in her small apartment.

Now that I look back, I realise what really gave me the strength to continue, rather than go ahead with my initial instinct on first arriving in Janine's home, was the resentment I felt after hearing what Janine had to say. I felt beholden to her, due to her immense kindness, although I wanted to relieve myself of the burden of her compassion that had enabled me not to choose Pont Neuf. I had read in books that those who didn't want to live threw themselves off this bridge into the River Seine. I came to think that not everything ended up in a *cul-de-sac* and one did not have to carry such a heavy burden. I imagined for a moment that I had gone to Mother and, like Nezhat, was floating on the clear water feeling light and calm.

Janine didn't seem to be in a hurry to tell me what she knew, but my questions made it increasingly difficult for her to keep her silence. She finally decided to help me to get to grips with the reality. At the end of my first week in her home we went for a stroll one evening. It was still warm and humid and I was feeling low. For the hundredth time I spoke of what was going through my mind.

I asked, 'Why?' and added, 'I shall, eventually, find out.'

I told her that I had difficulty believing that Saeed was so evil, and that there was perhaps something else that I was still not aware of. I said the few days that I had spent with Saeed had been filled with love and I could not believe that he could lie to me. Once again I opened my heart to her; I was rather hoping that he had fallen victim to some conspiracy. What if Ezzedin had conned him? I explained to her how much I wished to spend my life with Saeed, even in a humble servant's room, because he was my first love. For hours she listened to me talking, in tears.

When the rain became heavier we took shelter in a tram stop and resumed our conversation. I finally confessed that I might as well end my life if I were not going to find Saeed. I said that I was even prepared to assume that at that very moment he himself was a wandering soul and was too embarrassed to return. Perhaps he was under the heavy burden of gambling debts. I was confident that sooner or later he was going to return and, if it were not too late, I could even direct my questions to him. But what would I do meanwhile?

We were sitting on the edge of a bench, watching the pedestrians come and go at that late hour, and Janine suggested we have coffee. As we sat in a bustling café my eyes still searched for Saeed among the people who were seated at the bar smoking and drinking. Janine finally decided to open my eyes. Later on, she confessed that she had fought hard with herself before finally coming to her decision to wake me up, or rather put me in the hot oven – burn me. When I had lost everthing, I would then, perhaps, be able to tolerate my life better and believe that evil did exist. I was seated, looking mute and bewildered. I tried to show her that despite my pain I preferred to hear the bitter truth, which was still sweeter than the lies that could keep me up in the clouds.

She gave a simple account of the day Saeed returned to the house without me; the realisation that there had been no love from the very start was unbearable. He had never intended to go to Iran. Had it not been for Ahmad's note to his mother advising her against taking along a member of the Ottoman imperial family, Saeed would have found another excuse, since Ezzedin was expecting him in Paris: he effectively saw us off so that he could borrow more money. I felt a tremor within me as I heard how the two of them had mimicked me, and how my immaturity and gullibility had been a subject of their jokes.

'I don't understand; he could have had me and all the wealth he wanted.'

It was not easy for Janine to tell me the truth, so she lowered her voice in shame when she explained that Saeed did not love anyone in the entire world except Ezzedin. I remembered how back in Istanbul I had heard and even seen men who loved other men, yet I found it hard to believe that Ezzedin and Saeed would sleep in my bed! Janine found it embarrassing to tell me everything she had seen, but she mentioned that there were other men who frequented our house.

I suddenly began to see the past three years in a different light: his sisters whispering to each other and his discomfort at staying alone with me when we were engaged. I was glad that he had never touched me; I would have felt even more repulsed at the thought of such a nightmare. My resentment was at its height when I came to realise that all the mementoes, letters and beautiful words were nothing but lies; such pettiness, such callous creatures. My agony was compounded when I realised how naïve I had been. I remembered the day after our wedding, when I had to lie to satisfy Nadi's curiosity and had told her that I was too embarrassed to talk of something so private and personal.

Janine had even caught Saeed wearing my clothes and going to the Pigalle hand in hand with Ezzedin. I found it hard not to look back at the happy times that had been so short lived;

the ugly truth was fast unravelling. Why did I go along with his plans? Why did I lie to the Empress? Why did I believe the Sultana when she said that Saeed wanted a house where there was sufficient space for our children, only to repeat the same to the Empress? Why did I resent my uncle's distrust of Saeed, whom I loved so much, and his scepticism that Saeed had ever been to the war fronts? My uncle was quite suspicious in those days, but I had fooled the Empress: every time I was alone with Saeed I would later see my aunt and offer a somewhat exaggerated account of our meetings. I could, like Khadijeh, have left it to the grown-ups, but I didn't.

The thought of hearing so many lies over the years tortured me far more than being left alone and destitute in a foreign country, a sentiment which prompted me to go to Gaston's office the next day. I asked him to help me find Saeed no matter what, since I believed there was a way.

'There are many ways, Princess, but they are going to cost you and you have no money,' he said.

While I was confident that I would be able to cover his expenses, I didn't actually know how!

When Janine went to work I tidied up her modest apartment and prepared something to eat. The rest of the time I lay in bed staring at the ceiling. I went through every hour of my life from the moment we left Iran. When Janine returned in the evening she was completely exhausted and eventually collapsed into bed. I then spent hours looking through the window. I was so confused and so deeply buried in the past that I could hardly dwell on the future.

Thirty-seven days later the postman knocked on the door one morning; a large envelope was addressed to me and I noticed the Empress's name and coat of arms on the outside. My heart began to race and I was apprehensive. I rushed to open the envelope, just as I had when I had eagerly expected my mother's letters back in Odessa. The envelope contained a letter and a large parcel. In those days I always read my mother's letters instantly, so I began to read this one while I was still standing by the door. Her words did not communicate motherly affection; in fact they hammered my head. It was unbelievable: was this some sort of conspiracy?

The letter began with 'Ms Khanoum' and there was no 'light of my eyes', 'my darling', or 'how I miss you', or 'I hope the world revolves around your dreams'. There were only a few lines and some words had been crossed out. It was incredible: for years the Empress had been everything to me, mother, father and everyone else; now she had become cold and ruthless. She asked me to forget her and her family, never even to mention their names. She wrote that she was not going to remain in Beirut, but failed to mention a future address. There was no explanation other than that she had never imagined I could end up behaving in such a way, reminiscent of my father's character. I could not have imagined a more hurtful insult; the Empress knew only too well how much such words would torment me, so she must have written them intentionally. I could not understand why her words were so resentful.

I hit my head against the wall and the impact was so hard that my vision blurred. This was a much harder shock than the one I had received a month earlier. Although this letter meant that I had no one in the world and everyone had let go of me, what mattered to me was to discover what had made her write in such a way. I kept hitting my head against the wall and the door, screaming. I can't remember how long it took but I suddenly noticed Pierre, Janine's younger son, calling me. I jumped as though someone had just woken me up. I tidied my hair and splashed some water on my face. I then heated some milk so that the little boy could satisfy his hunger; despite his youth, he clearly understood I was in a state of shock, so he resorted to sitting quietly in a corner, where he opened a book and peeped at me occasionally.

Janine and Jacques arrived a little later looking happy. She was carrying a bag full of bread, vegetables and perhaps a little meat, something she always did in the late afternoon. Their happiness evaporated on seeing Pierre and me. The poor woman hardly deserved this on top of her own worries. As though no one as needy as the miserable auntie existed, she let go of her bag and came to me to find out what was wrong, at which point I exploded. I was crying my heart out and she knew that she had to let me be. She fed her children and took off her uniform. Then, I was handed a coat and, holding my arm, she motioned me through the open door. I was in a horrible state and found it difficult to speak of my pain in such a small space, so we went to the Boulevard St Lazare. But not before I had placed the Empress's letter, by then much the worse for wear, in my handbag. We sat somewhere, ordered coffee and began to talk.

When I translated the contents of the Empress's letter, I felt the words were beating in my head: she had no desire to see me and I was now in receipt of every document that she had kept for so long, including my 'beloved' father's letters. My demeanour meant I had made her feel she had let my mother down.

Janine was vexed and asked me questions that I could not answer. She was as perplexed as I. She stroked my hair and wiped my tears with a handkerchief. She felt I must have been a fool to admire the woman, with my tales of her wisdom and kindness. She thought I was a gullible fool who had made the wrong assumptions about the Empress as well as about Saeed, and that it was time I learned people were not as nice as I thought. I retorted that she was wrong: the Empress was an angel, the like of whose wisdom I had not encountered elsewhere, so what could possibly have happened?

We hurried back. When she realised I had not bothered to open the parcel she said, 'The clue must lie in the contents of the parcel.' It was still sitting on the small table we had dinner on and where the boys did their studies. Inside the parcel there were a few photographs of my mother and me, and a few bank statements, on the corner of which was written 'Khanoum's account' in my uncle's script, and the figures had been underlined. It was a list of my assets kept in the Empress's guardianship but now in my possession. There was a bank order of 100,000 francs, a figure reached by adding up certain figures in small print. There was only one other paper, which I wish had never been included. It was a letter from the monster, my father, in which he had offered his condolences on the occasion of my uncle's demise, obviously a recent communication. In his distinctive script, which I recognised with loathing, he had reminded my aunt of his old age, his loneliness and his wish to see me. I couldn't read everything that he had written because his writing was not clear. What I did manage to read, however, was his happiness in bequeathing his entire estate to me, his only offspring. I was so furious that I crumbled the paper and threw it aside. I then started to inspect the rest of the items in the parcel. There was also a letter addressed to Établissement Gaspard, which I passed to Janine to read.

I could no longer understand anything and needed time to put my thoughts in some sort of order; too many questions were racing in my head and Janine's words were of no consolation. She sat next to me feeling useless, and I was so buried in my thoughts that I almost forgot that the poor woman was about to expire after a hard day's work. It was midnight when I came up with an idea: I asked her whether it was possible for her to ask for a day's leave. She did not question the idea and said she would do her best.

By the time I woke up the next day I had experienced many nightmares, none of which I could recall. Janine had left a note by the mirror indicating that she was going to be back before 10 am. There was no sign of the parcel and the other papers. I could, as usual, overhear the noise from the neighbouring flats – the sounds of people and the water in the pipes. I struggled to find an answer to my many questions: why did the Empress want to drive me away from herself? I didn't think she was aware of my predicament. I knew her well and thought if she knew my situation she would already have sent someone for me. By the time Janine returned I had made up my mind: my most pressing thought was that I must pay Janine back. We went to her bank to deposit the bank order in her account and I kept back only a few hundred francs for the rest of my plan. By lunchtime we had managed to find lodgings with three rooms on Boulevard Haussmann, near the Champs-Elysées; I knew this was what Janine had always dreamed of. But she was not prepared to accept my offer. I had come to know her as a gracious and open-handed woman.

'I thought you wanted us to be together, but perhaps you, too, want to drive me away!' I said, which made her smile, revealing a great deal of affection.

Two days later we were ready to move into our apartment on the second floor and we went to collect the books, suitcases and the two trunks from the house in Madeleine. The French man invited me to take whatever belonged to me. I agreed to pay a certain sum and took away the two *termehs* covering the chimneypiece and the table. He folded them and handed them to Janine. He was then hesitant; he wanted to ask me a favour. He wondered whether it would be reasonable if he asked me to sign the deeds of the house so that there would be no further problems. I understood his concern and without bothering to read the document, accepted his word and went ahead and signed the deeds. The husband and wife looked bewildered, at which Janine declared proudly that they shouldn't be surprised since they were dealing with a truly noble person; 'princess' was particularly highlighted. I was speechless; she was such an optimist. If I had not been close to tears, I would have described to them how, in the past forty days, this woman, who except for a couple of days in my service was by no means connected to me, had so graciously put up with me. I should have described to them what I knew about aristocracy, the princes and princesses, but I decided not to do so since I didn't want to embarrass Janine.

I now possessed a birth certificate, a bank statement and the documents my aunt had sent over; the documents without which, that first evening, had it not been for Janine, I would have been abandoned to my fate in a foreign city. I recalled what the police officer had told me as he tried to save me from the only option open to me: prison or a state-run hostel; I would not have been able to put up with prison conditions. If I hadn't thought of Janine, or if she had in the meantime moved homes, I couldn't imagine what might have become of me. I suppose I *would* have gone to Pont Neuf and done what I had thought of in those first moments.

The new home and the task of furnishing it kept us busy for a few days and it didn't seem to matter to me that I had lost half my estate. Three days later I looked for Monsieur Gaston and we went to Établissement Gaspard. A senior official received us in his magnificent office. He handed the file to Gaston who had, by then, officially introduced himself as my lawyer. The file was my aunt's record and it consisted of details of my estate and a balance sheet, including the money spent, for example on the house in the Madeleine, the stocks and shares; as well as the interest gained. At the end of the meeting we were told that their organisation had received instructions that I should no longer have any dealings with the Empress. By doing this, she was effectively punishing me. Gaston thought the balance sheet was the perfect document to help us file a formal complaint against Saeed.

When we were leaving Gaspard's, Janine explained to the lawyer that I possessed a letter proving that my father had bequeathed his estate to me, and asked whether we could pursue it. The lawyer explained that I could only pursue what belonged to me in France and the rest of Europe. I turned to Janine and said, 'No!' so vehemently that she did not insist any further, though she had no idea why.

The money that the Empress had sent over rescued us from absolute poverty. After the war the French economy was not stable: unemployment and inflation were sky high, and every day revolts and industrial action added to the tension. I constantly worried about the state of my finances, which I kept an eye on without stressing Janine. I was concerned how on earth we were to carry on given the ever-rising prices. Despite our economies and Janine's overtime, nothing could prevent the accelerating rate at which my funds were diminishing.

I spent my days keeping the house clean, looking after the children and preparing meals until early evening, when Janine returned exhausted and miserable. We were both embarrassed and nothing could improve the way we felt. When she collapsed into bed in the evenings, I looked at her and the photograph of Maurice, the children's father, which she always kept on the mantelpiece. I felt uncomfortable that I could not help lift the heavy burden off her shoulders. Every month that the rent was paid Janine thanked me by words or occasional letters left on the dressing table; she clearly felt uncomfortable, as though she were indebted to me.

Autumn was upon us and the evenings were getting cold, but we still managed a stroll. Our haunt was near Place Trocadero, in a large, busy café where hundreds of people stopped by in the late afternoon to drink, smoke and discuss world events. The daily newspapers hanging there reported political upheaval, the most active element being the socialists, whom Janine tended to support. We usually spent only an hour in the café because I felt bad that she had to go to work the next day. Had it not been for our usual anxieties, life in the Paris of the late-1920s would have been interesting; we would occasionally join in the debates of people there, mainly office workers or labourers. This helped us momentarily to forget that we were two young women leading lonely lives with no future to look forward to. God only knows what kept us going!

Saturday nights were the only times we could peacefully remain in the cafés, although the children generally kept us too busy. Pierre was sweet and climbed my shoulders, referring to me as 'Auntie'. We would have a light supper somewhere and then go to the theatre or some place with entertainment that suited the children. In the park we would meet other talkative French mothers who chatted to Janine. I would also occasionally join in, though clearly I could not fully understand their day-to-day dilemmas since I was not a mother. Ironically, by then I should have been living in my 'large home' with rooms dedicated to my own children. I sometimes pretended that Pierre and Jacques were my own children, something they seemed to like.

The reality, however, was harsher than one could pretend. I was far removed from my usual hobbies of playing the piano, painting and reading. We didn't have a piano, and the papers, easel and canvas that I had managed to bring over from Madeleine were redundant. I finally gave them to Jacques and, from time to time, helped him to paint. I couldn't be bothered with reading either; I had spent a lifetime reading a few hours every day and the number of titles I had read, together with my resultant knowledge, astonished the women who participated in the debates in the café. What I did manage every night before going to sleep was just a few pages of Montesquieu. However, the next day I couldn't remember what I had read because my mind was elsewhere. I effectively spent some seventeen or eighteen hours a day thinking vicious and destructive thoughts. I took up Edgar Alan Poe's new novel to occupy myself but that didn't work either. I alternated between thinking and nightmares. The carefree days of my thirties were slipping away to be replaced by tough times, a constant presence, and the painful moments that filled my thoughts.

CHAPTER 46

Not far from our apartment there lived an old journalist and his wife; the old woman was from Nantes and, as I was to discover many months later, suffered from a mental disorder. During the day she would sit on a step in the small garden and watch the pedestrians passing. When I sat next to her she would describe who the passers-by were, where they were going and what they were thinking about. I would spend hours listening to her. Madame Jineau could, indeed, foretell the future.

During the cold days of winter her friends and I would get together in her home. It was always in a state of chaos, books and newspapers strewn all over the place. When she got together with her friends I would make coffee for everyone since I was the youngest. Sometimes I would even buy her cakes from the patisserie in the Trocadero. Madame Jineau would draw the curtains and then hold a mirror and look at it. She would begin to talk of the past and the future. Sometimes what she said would even reduce them to tears.

Once, a young woman wanted to know whether her husband was having an affair. Madame Jineau would occasionally involve me as well, and when it came to this particular young woman, Madame Jineau asked me whether her husband was tall, at which point I thought of Saeed, wondering where the demon could be, and answered: 'Yes.'

'What is he doing at this moment?'

'He is holding hands with someone of medium height …' and I described Ezzedin.

'What are they doing?'

'They are laughing out loud.'

My responses gave Madam Jineau a sense of triumph, and the young woman looked depressed but left satisfied. The women insisted on paying Madame Jineau but she always refused. She was not prepared to charge people for the gift she believed Christ had bestowed on her, and she strongly believed if she accepted money she would fall from his favour. I often wondered whether this was really the case.

Every night I was determined to have my fortune told as well, but by the time I woke up in the morning I would have changed my mind and, when I climbed down the stairs, Madame Jineau would already be in her usual place. We would spend an hour chatting, in which she talked and I listened. I would talk about my life and she would speak of her mother, who was a strict Christian and did not get along with her godless and carefree husband. Someone would invariably arrive before noon and greet her from behind the railings, then we would go up to Madame Jineau's apartment.

One day, however, Monsieur Jineau was unwell with fever and at home. He usually left home first thing. He was stooped and had long grey hair and a pair of spectacles hanging from a black piece of string around his neck, which rested on the tip of his nose. Whenever he was unwell I would prepare some soup and, while his wife was in a huff, the old man would kiss my hand and invite me to sit down. The only thing he knew about me was that I was Iranian and that everyone called me 'Princess'. He always showed an interest in my life and one day he even asked me if I would be interested in writing a column for the newspaper, to which I responded, 'No,' to his wife's delight.

I had this desire for Madame Jineau to tell my fortune and I mentioned it to Janine, at which she burst out laughing; she found it hard to believe that an educated person should believe in superstition, but I explained to her that I had recently purchased two books written about the sixth sense, supernatural powers, miracles and predicting the future. As I understood it they were not completely unfounded. Janine raised her eyebrows, as if to say, 'Perhaps that is the case, but I don't believe in such things.' She didn't have time to think about anything but work, her children's studies and how to make ends meet.

One day my wish was finally granted, but in an unexpected way. It was cold and we had had a heavy snowfall. As a result, Madame Jineau had remained in her room. When I went downstairs she knocked on the windowpane, motioning me to go to her room. She drew the curtains and lit a candle. No one else was in the room and I felt alarmed. She took her time and then asked me to sit down. She then asked me to pick a knitted green scarf off the armchair and place it on my head, and so I did. Then she began to recite a prayer from the Bible, in Greek or Latin, which I couldn't understand; I only managed to work out familiar words such as 'Solomon'. 'You detest men,' a quiet voice said and I nodded.

There was a pause and then she said, 'There are two evil persons and one angel in your life; all of them are men, though the angel has flown away or has not yet arrived.'

I knew which two monsters she was talking about, and indeed they were men. The angel, however … I didn't move.

She then asked me if I wanted to converse with the monster in my life, to which I immediately replied, 'No!'

'He wants you to forgive him.'

'No!'

'He is in tears.'

'No!' and my tears rolled down.

There was a pause as though she was talking to someone.

She then asked me, 'What do want to ask your angel?'

I couldn't think of an angel at the time; I thought only Janine worthy of being referred to as such; she *was* my angel and right then she was working and sweating, yet in the evening I was confident she would arrive with a smile nonetheless.

'Do you want to hear about the past or the future?'

I thought for a moment and responded, 'Tomorrow.'

'I see light but it is hidden behind a wall which is thick and high, a bit like a church. Pray and believe in God; your angel is next to Jesus. Kneel down and repeat whatever I say,' and I did kneel by the flickering candle.

I couldn't see her any more but I heard her pray, and I repeated her words without knowing what I was saying.

'You can now release your tears,' but I didn't need to be told that, since tears were about to roll down my face.

My face became wet, and I can't remember how much time passed before she drew the curtain and daylight was allowed in.

'You can go now. I shan't see you for a few days but you needn't worry.'

I didn't ask why and where she was planning to go; instead, I went upstairs and fell on my bed. I can't remember how much time passed; all I know is that when I woke up I felt I had no strength, as though all my energy had gone.

The children returned, followed by Janine. She was acutely anxious to see me in such a state and thought I was unwell. I felt a chill so she covered me with a couple of blankets and then helped me lie down by the fire. I was shivering. She wanted to call a physician but I refused.

I later woke up sensing someone touch my forehead. I opened my eyes to see a masculine hand. I pulled back and started shivering again. A monster passed by; no, it wasn't a monster, he was the physician Janine had asked home. I caught sight of Jacques and Pierre, who looked anxious; they were my angels. The physician listened to my heart. He then took my pulse and examined my eyes. The smell of alcohol suddenly filled the room and I realised he was about to inject me. The only time I had received an injection was in Marseille harbour, on the last day of our journey. I clutched Janine's hand, buried my head in the pillow and clenched my teeth; not that I was in pain. Janine was the only person aware of my phobia about a man touching my body. She was the only person who knew my secret and now she was talking to me while the liquid began to travel in my veins. She then dipped some cotton wool in alcohol and rubbed it on my flesh, before pulling the blanket over me.

I spent two weeks in bed, during which Janine administered the rest of the injections in the presence of the physician. I had fallen ill in Odessa but nothing like this. During the second or third week I saw a bundle of dark hair on my pillow, not to mention the bundle in my hand. I was frightened; the whole thing seemed like a nightmare; every time I touched my head I ended up with a bundle of hair. Janine tried hard not to look terrified; she told me stories of patients who had experienced the same thing but who had ended up with new, thicker hair the following week. I looked at her as though I had no strength or hope.

In less than a week the wall that Madame Jineau had talked about appeared before me. It was a new church and, having wrapped my head in a thick scarf, I had gone to ask whether being a Muslim prevented me from working there; a wall but no angels! Father Wilfred had dark eyes and was dressed in a black robe, which was not as dark as his eyes. The first thing he asked me was to think whether I was sure of what I was saying.

I wondered whether he meant my working there, to which he said, 'No, the fact that you are a Muslim.'

'No, but I have throughout my life believed in God,' I said after a pause, looking at the floor.

'Have you ever tried to call Him?'

'I suppose so,' I said, upon which he asked whether He had replied to me.

'I think He did.'

'Can you come back on Monday and explain to me *when* you called Him and *how* He responded?'

I could not get his words out of my mind. I don't know how, but that very evening I began to pray once again. When I did the *Vauzu* ritual, cleansing myself to do my prayer, I felt very different, just as in Odessa, when I would at times spend an hour praying for my mother. I began to remember the nights of Ramadan when Abdollah woke us up to have *sahari*. He worked out the timing by checking the time against a Russian alarm clock, and when the sun began to rise, Khadijeh and I stood facing the window overlooking the sea, in the direction of Mecca, witnessing the onset of a silver dawn. I was delighted that Abdollah's compass had been bequeathed to me. It was one of the items I had managed to find in the vault in our former house and it enabled me to find the direction of Mecca.

Before Monday, however, something else happened: Madame Jineau died peacefully in her sleep. Everyone went to church, including those who used to come and consult her. Monsieur Jineau was standing in front in the church, his spectacles hanging round his neck and still tied to their black string. He was as quiet as a lamb, as though he were writing the story of a woman who happened to be his wife and who was reputed to predict the future. Everyone believed in her except her husband, who didn't believe in fortune telling. On the way back Janine explained to me that she had heard from the neighbours that Madame Jineau had been mentally ill and repeatedly hospitalised in some mental institution. The neighbours also said that she knew she was soon to die, something she had disclosed some weeks before. I wondered whether that had been the reason why she said I was not going to see her for a while. She had been right: I had not seen her any more, as though all those months that I had chatted to her daily had merely been a prelude to that day, and the beginning of a long chapter of my life.

CHAPTER 47

T wo months later I left Avenue Haussmann and the children amid tears and Janine's doubts. I went to live in a room in the new church, away from the nuns, in a place where I could experience a different world. I spent the days in a hospital wearing a white scarf – which, from a distance, made me look like the nuns – and a long gown brought to me two weeks after my arrival. I had lost my hair entirely but it hardly mattered to me; I felt as though someone had removed me from a tumultuous and stormy sea and dropped me in an oasis, where the water seemed like a mirror, reflecting the skies where there were clouds but no breeze to create waves in the sea.

In the daytime I dedicated my entire time to the patients who were in pain. I would remove pan-fulls of blood, urine and faeces, change their clothes and linen, help them get down from their beds, sit by their bedside and chat or read to them, administer their medicine, feed them and, when their health was improving, help them stroll in the garden. I could not sit down and rest. It felt as though I had broken away from the past; I felt lighter every day, a state Father Wilfred helped me to achieve. He would always ask a couple of questions, and then leave me to find the answers for myself.

After I had talked about the second evil in my life, he arranged for me to move to a little room in the pentagon-shaped garden. He asked me whether I was sure there were only two evils in my life, and I was not. When he wondered about the angels I knew of, I talked about my mother, Nezhat, Janine and even my aunt, the Empress. Despite my having become *persona non grata* for the moment, she still was an angel to me, and so was Abdollah.

'These have become angels in your eyes; and you, what do you think *you* have become, are you an angel or …'

'I am not an angel.'

'Be an angel!'

And I endeavoured to become an angel and worked hard at it. Every other day Father Wilfred would guide me back to the calm and peaceful oasis, making me feel lighter each time. Many weeks passed. Now and then Janine and the children would come to see me. Janine had anticipated that I would eventually return. Every time she came to see me she brought along my favourite homemade tarts; I used to have these for breakfast, and would also offer them to the nuns, except the ones filled with peach or apricot jam. She occasionally brought me some news, as when she mentioned that Gaston had succeeded in rescuing some of my shares from falling into Saeed's hands. She was cautious in mentioning his name as it had previously made me tremble, but she noticed that it no longer did. Father Wilfred had helped me destroy 'vengefulness' within me and it was as though I was hardly acquainted with Saeed. I signed the document Janine had brought me entitling Gaston to one hundred shares to cover his costs and bequeathing Jacques and Pierre the rest. Janine was about to contest this but then understood that she was relieving me from a heavy burden, and by shedding it I was getting closer to becoming an angel.

The next day I confessed to Father Wilfred that I felt I still needed to cleanse my soul because I had been momentarily delighted that Gaston had managed to rescue some shares from Saeed's clutches. Father Wilfred, however, did not seem to have heard what I said.

'When you bequeathed your shares to your angel, did you look down at yourself from above and see yourself as the angel, or did you look up to see the angel?'

I didn't know what to say. I was about to reply when Father Wilfred smiled and placed his forefinger on his lips, motioned me to keep quiet, and then left. He used to do this to stop me answering a question without thinking. He left me to think, and the thinking took place every time I sat on my prayer mat and went on until I felt I had found the true answer; only then could I lie under my blanket feeling light and calm as though I had been able to step into an oasis. Up to then, for the past two years I had not spent a single night without going into a spasm. I now spent two years sleeping calmly every night under the blanket, and every day I became more peaceful than the day before. Though Janine was giving up on me returning, she would still come to visit and had no intention of letting go of me. I spent two years in that calm oasis.

I was getting close to the angel until the day I asked permission to go to Father Wilfred's office because something was not right. I felt as though a stone had fallen in the middle of the calm oasis and caused a ripple, though not any waves. The priest sat me down, then left the room to deal with something, before returning immediately afterwards. He first told me a story: the tale of a fisherman who prayed to catch two fish so that he could give one to the poor man he happened to pass by every day. When he threw the hook into the water he caught two fish. He was surprised. The second time round he caught two more. He became greedy and threw his hook in yet again, only to catch one fish. He went to check his basket but saw only three fish inside – one was missing. He threw the hook in once more and caught two large fish. When he came back to his basket there were only two fish. So he decided to be content with those and left. He realised that his catch corresponded only to what he had prayed for and no more. However, he could not understand why he could no longer see the poor man. He searched for him but to no avail.

After Father Wilfred had finished telling me the story of the fisherman, he sat down and waited for me to tell him why

I felt my oasis was no longer calm. I began to explain that when I was walking in the corridor that morning I had heard some men and women conversing in Persian. I had almost lost control of the pan I was carrying. I then understood that the patient in the large room, which was usually given to important people, was the former king of Iran, Ahmad Shah, whose engagement to me, I was told, had been bound in heaven. The engagement had for years been the subject of my dreams: my life in palaces, my becoming the Empress of the land of legends and ...

Father Wilfred laughed, 'The large fish!'

'Father, please send me somewhere else.'

'So that you can escape God's will?'

'I am scared.'

'Of yourself or ...'

'Of myself, Father.'

'If the ship takes a sharp turn while the wind is blowing, it can capsize.'

'And if it doesn't, Father, its sail may break!'

'One can reach the shores with a broken sail but not in a capsized ship.'

I asked permission to go, but, before I left, Father Wilfred calmly said, 'I shall see you first thing tomorrow and then we'll make a decision.'

I felt calmer having spoken to him though I was in turmoil. After two years of calm a cloud was marring the blue of my sky and disrupting my oasis. I did not want my inner calm to be disturbed; I felt light, as if I had no weight. But now it felt as though a burden had suddenly fallen from above and was resting on one of my shoulders. I felt it and prayed that I might not lose my angel. At night I wondered why this had to happen and I resented myself for being doubtful. I felt scared and the questions kept racing.

My life had become so structured in the course of two years it was as though I had been programmed from birth. Lately, I was not even thinking of the familiar people of my past. I got up at dawn, did my prayers in my room and recited from the Holy Quran. In fact, I had got used to taking my Qur'an to the chapel; everyone was busy praying and I read my own holy book in a quiet corner. Each morning I took a light breakfast, which consisted of a piece of bread and a cup of coffee, all consumed in a hurry. I would then walk the distance between the church and the hospital, passing through the carob and pine trees, hearing the birds sing. There were usually three or four of us walking together but we never conversed. Dealing with the patients' hygiene and their beds were the first tasks of the day; these I carried out without the slightest distaste. At times I would go up and down the stairs in between the two floors ten times in order to take the dirty linen and clothes, occasionally stained with blood, and pans full of urine to the utility room. On my way back I would take fresh linen and clothes with me. Afterwards I had to distribute the patients' medicine and administer injections. I had gone through the initial medical training while in Beirut; as a result I was confident in my knowledge and carried out my duties with diligence. I was at times so occupied that I completely forgot about my lunch hour – in those days the nuns and I ate together and our simple lunch consisted of lentil soup, broad beans, a piece of meat and a loaf of bread.

I had an hour to lunch, pray and spend a quiet moment in my room, where I usually lay down with my feet slightly higher than the rest of my body so that the blood flowed to my head and helped me relax. By the time I was back on the wards I wouldn't feel tired at all. I was on call three nights a week, which gave me the opportunity to read, and I read a great deal. I was slowly beginning to read in English and also in Italian. Every other day I would take the day off, which I would use to attend to my room and launder and mend my clothes and linen. In between I read medical books recommended by our tutors as well as books I had on loan from the library.

My work was so menial and hard that, apart from one other nun, only I was permitted to take a shower twice a day if I wanted to. The church bathroom was in the basement and its entrance was covered in ivy and passion flowers. There were various vestibules, vastly different from the opulence of the *hammams* in the palaces in Istanbul. There was a little tank in the middle with clean water. During winter there was no heating mechanism to warm the air in the bathroom, only a large boiler where boiling water could be released by turning a tap. We were then able to pour warm water into cast-iron pans and use it to wash ourselves.

During the previous two years I had not touched makeup; my sole toiletry items were a comb, a small mirror and an ointment made from paraffin, without which my hands would become completely dry and flaking. I kept a few items of lingerie and two dresses in a bundle, one for winter and one for summer. I also had two white scarves so that I could wear one while the other was being washed. Instead of a coat or rainproof covering I wore a large, thick, navy scarf, which kept me warm in the winter months. I had two pairs of comfortable black shoes and four pairs of white socks. These constituted my entire possessions. Once a year we could use our allowance to acquire a new dress, a pair of shoes, or underwear through Sister Céline, who was in charge of a kind of shop, somewhere in the church, where one could find soap, toothpaste and a few other items neatly arranged on the shelves. Whenever we took something she registered it in a book.

I had looked weak the day I moved into the church and had lost my hair, not to mention having a body that periodically went into spasm. However, by now I had copious black hair and a robust physique which had grown immune to disease. All I did was work, pray, listen and read, mainly medical books. Father at times joked and called me 'Doctoress' when the other priests and nuns were present. I was confident I knew as much as a young intern. I was particularly good at plastering broken arms or legs, bandaging and administering injections, but I still continued with my menial duties such as cleaning and looking after the patients. These were the most inferior of tasks at the hospital, though I never regarded them as such and managed them as though they were the best of jobs. I attended lectures for two weeks and managed to complete my training successfully. Those two weeks transformed me.

Now that I look back, I am amazed how easily I managed to part with earthly possessions and attachments. I find it unbelievable that during my two years at the convent I never came across any money; I had a few hundred francs on arrival, which I handed over to Janine, along with all my clothes, the following month. After that, as far as I can remember, I had no dealings with monetary matters nor did I feel the need to. When Janine came to see me I never asked how she coped and how she got along with André. André was a milkman, who, a few months after I left, asked for Janine's hand in marriage. My sweet Janine only made up her mind after she had discussed the matter with me. On the day of her wedding I was not ashamed to present her with only a few flowers since I had nothing and didn't want anything.

I really enjoyed reading and by the time I went to the convent I had read hundreds of novels. However, once in the convent, I began to feel no association with the world of fantasy and stories. I didn't even dream any more unless I sat listening to patients who told me about their lives. When I read a story to them nothing seemed to register in my mind; I had become a different person. Occasional scenes from my past life would appear before me but I now knew how to dissociate myself.

Of all the things that had happened in my life all I had managed to retain was the memory of my mother and Nezhat, of whom I had a vivid memory. For instance, the day I was busy washing my clothes and sheets in the laundry room when my hands felt cold and numb, Mother suddenly appeared. She held my hands and began to rub them. She was using the warm water in which rice had been cooked. I then immersed my hands and feet so that I didn't get frostbite. I did the same thing for the patients who felt feverish: I used warm water and sometimes paraffin. That day, I felt so warm and comfortable that I closed my eyes so that the thought of Mother couldn't escape me. I did not notice at the time that one of the nuns was looking at me in astonishment. Whenever Mother came to my dreams she wore a long gown as well as a white matron's headdress pinned under her chin. She reminded me of when we went on pilgrimage, or to Tekyé Dowlat for mourning, or for the *Ashoura* rituals. All the men conducting the rituals in my dreams were dressed in long black gowns and recited prayers quietly, just like Father Wilfred.

That evening, when I returned to my room after meeting Father Wilfred, I spent some time thinking everything over: myself and the calm, and my concern over the renewed turbulence. Before I fell asleep I decided to go to him again the next day and repeat my request to be sent to a different convent. However, by the time I went back to the office to see Father, I didn't seem to have any fears left; on the contrary, I had committed myself to God, believing that was the best thing to do. I found Father Wilfred behind his desk looking pleasant as usual. When I sat facing him I felt light-hearted. He asked me if I still felt the need to go away.

I said, 'No, but ...'

He continued speaking while he got up, and together we passed through the corridors. We came across Mother Theresa, who supervised me and everyone else. She kissed Father Wilfred's hand and said that she had asked one of the nuns to cover for me. Father nodded, she left and I followed him. He stood in the middle of the garden and gazed at a flower in the middle of the flowerbed. We were all aware of Father Wilfred's love of gardening and knew that he was also passionate about music. While we were walking he spoke to me about the Christian ritual of confession and explained that, by confessing, people were relieved from the burdens they carried with them.

'That is why you see us enclose ourselves in the confession box; we believe no one should take the thought of their sins with them to bed, no matter how private or small the sin may be.

Only then should one kneel before God and greet Christ feeling cleansed and free from sin.'

He then asked me whether when I went to church I lit a candle like the other nuns and whether I knelt and prayed, and if so, whether I did it for the sake of following the others or ...

I explained to him that as a child I had been used to going to *Saqqa Khaneh*, the place where one lit candles and prayed, in our local *bazaar*. I also explained that after our daily worship we always prayed, and that I had not done so merely for the sake of copying the others.

He then motioned me to enter the church. He picked up a candle and so did I. We placed them in the holders and then fell silent. Later he asked me if I felt the need to confess. I thought for a while. Yes, I did. So he proceeded to his place, and I joined him in the confession box. He opened the little hatch and I began to speak. I recounted things from the very beginning: my father, Nezhat, my escape from Tehran, what went on with my mother and my marriage to Saeed. He asked whether I had annulled my marriage. I said that I hadn't. Was I aware of the reason behind the Empress's hostility? Up to the previous year it had mattered to me but I had not thought about it for some time. Did I deep down still question myself? I believed so. Would he help me to erase this from my mind as well?

He didn't respond and closed the hatch. It seemed we had done enough for one day. On the way back he explained that from then on I was in charge of the ward and the large rooms, and that I had to help with their upkeep. I had to ask Mother Theresa about my duties and should use my own initiative. He added that, since I was not a Christian, I was not considered a nun, rather an employee of the hospital and therefore entitled to a small wage. I was about to say that I did not need an income and was happy with my situation, but he asked me not to say anything and left.

I had to supervise two nuns who carried out ward duties in that section of the hospital. I also had to confer with the physicians on a daily basis. I did not have a great deal to do: I had to attend to the fresh flowers and supervise the cleaning and the state of hygiene in the rooms. The physicians' instructions had to be followed with precision: the medicine, injections and all else.

I was looking through the medical papers when I first came across his name: 'His Majesty Ahmad Shah'. I saw 'tuberculosis of the kidney', but there was no mention of the duration of the treatment. I knew the critical state of health he was in; was he also aware? He had been accommodated in the largest room. His team of physicians consisted of eight specialists. As a patient of some stature, fresh flowers were to be placed in his room daily. The same applied to his linen and hospital gown – he was fastidious. The three nurses administering his food and medicine had to wear gloves, and I had to supervise them.

I can't describe how I felt the evening I set foot in his room. A nurse was sitting in the corner busy reading. The 'large fish', as Father Wilfred had it, was lying in his bed. I knew that he had taken his sleeping tablets and was not awake, but I lowered my voice to speak with the nurse. On his bedside table there was a book with a pair of spectacles inside. There was also an expensive-looking leather briefcase embossed with a familiar image: the lion and the sun, which I had completely forgotten about. This brought back many memories, and I recalled my engagement to Saeed Pasha, when he was given a medal with the same crest, which he always pinned to his jacket.

I looked at the vase full of white flowers by his bedside. The flowers in one of the other two vases looked withered so I decided to take it away; the card by this vase read, 'From the Empress to her beloved son'. I knew how much my aunt doted on the large fish and that her well-being depended on his. I had seen her weep many a night for the one who was now sleeping soundly on this bed. Once upon a time, when my head was full of dreams, I, too, had missed the large fish. Looking at him now I began to remember him as a child: the day he came to the country, the letters he wrote to me; in the gardens of the Russian Embassy where he was wailing about not wanting the throne; everything that Abdollah had described; his affectionate letters that Saeed stole; our last meeting in our home in Istanbul; his wife Ashraf and her tales ... Dear Lord, why did I have to remember it all? I had tried so hard to forget!

Later on that night, back in my room, I blamed myself for my fears; I could not understand why all that I had managed to discard from my memory was suddenly rushing back now. Every painful moment in my life had surfaced; even my father, the demon, had resurfaced. Why did these thoughts have to come back to me? I prayed to God to help me and, despite my restless mind, managed to fall asleep. I must have had nightmares because I felt rather rough when I woke up.

My days seemed to have become long and exhausting. I tried to keep myself away from that particular room and took extra care not to see any of his entourage. Nevertheless, I once bumped into Mahin Banou, wife of the crown prince, who was walking with two other women who could well have been my aunts or cousins. None of them even glanced at me; I must have looked like a nun and unrecognisable. This reassured me and I felt more at ease.

I went to his room every night while he was asleep, changed the flowers and read his medical report. I was in his room one evening when his condition became critical, demanding injections. Having read his report I discovered that he had just survived a near-fatal episode. The nurses in charge of him were delighted so I assumed the Empress and her entourage had tipped them handsomely. In the nearby rooms there was a countess and another Muslim, the latter some notable from Morocco who always had visitors.

I was slowly regaining my peace, which had been disturbed by the arrival of Ahmad in the hospital in Neuilly, when it all happened. I was in Mother Theresa's office when I heard his voice: he was in the corridor talking to someone in French. Initially I found it hard to believe; before my eyes could see, my ears had heard the voice. I was petrified: it was no mistake – Saeed was chatting to the Empress!

Mother Theresa realised I was not feeling well. Making sure no one was in the corridor I left her office and rushed to the library on the first floor, where I managed to take refuge. I found Father Wilfred sitting behind a pile of books, busy reading as usual. I couldn't disturb him so I picked up a book and sat behind a table, but I felt feverish and short of breath.

'Father, I must speak with you!' I was standing by him when the words left my mouth.

He was surprised but remained gracious. He rose, placed a piece of paper as a marker in the book, and then walked towards his office.

'Can you try and translate for me one of the prayers that you recite every night before going to bed?' he asked.

I closed my eyes and forced myself to calm down. I recalled the words and slowly began:

'In the name of God, the Benevolent, the Merciful; who forgives our sins; who is beyond Man's understanding and who is able to do all things. Give us your favours; enlighten us and don't abandon us. Give us light and knowledge so that we keep in the right path; the Healer of Pains, the Saviour of prisoners; the One who resurrects the dead; the Creator of Heaven and Earth, the Sun and the Moon, and the changing of the months and the years ...'

When I paused I found him on his knees with his eyes closed.

'Amen,' emerged after a long pause.

He then sat behind his desk, and I stroked my face with the palms of my hands as I always did.

He smiled and said, 'You hadn't taught me this one; you are not a good teacher!'

'Nor am I a good pupil, Father,' at which I received a wry smile and the reply: 'Are you complaining about your creator?'

'I am complaining about my weakness.'

'Didn't you just say everything is God's will?'

I was about to say something when I remembered that in his presence I had to be cautious and only mention what had been well thought through. I hesitated for a moment, unable to find a response, yet I wanted to talk with him, something I enjoyed.

'Father, help me!'

'God will help you; have you asked him?'

'Help me find out what is best for me.'

'I may be able to help you with this.'

I calmed down and then, releasing my breath, asked him, 'Can you remember the second evil in my life?' and I began to speak of Saeed.

He nodded as though he remembered.

Then, while struggling to hold my tears back, I said, 'Father he is here, in this very place!'

He thought that he was one of the patients, so he said, 'You are going to be tested and you must demonstrate that you've become free of any resentment and are filled with God's love. Today he is unwell and needy and you must forget the evil in him. Perhaps he was the means of bringing you to this place, you never know,' to which I gave some thought.

I had to explain that Saeed was not a patient and that he had come to visit Ahmad Shah, along with the rest of my family. Father Wilfred fell silent for a moment as though going through the events in his mind.

'Does this mean that your family have preferred him to you? Perhaps they don't see the evil in him, perhaps ...'

Though I had answers for every question I simply said, 'I don't know, Father.'

'What do you want to do now?'

I didn't know, I had come to ask him.

I decided to say, 'Father, please send me somewhere far away.'

There was a long pause. He then began to search for something amid the pile of papers on his desk. He found it and began to read. He then picked a book from the bookcase. It was a large book.

'Do you know where Jamaica is?'

No, I didn't and it didn't make any difference.

'Do you want to say that you are ready to go and leave everything? This place is far away!'

'It doesn't make any difference, Father.'

He stood up, which meant that I had to go and wait for him to call me. I felt relieved.

Later, I was in my room thinking about Jamaica, a place I knew absolutely nothing about, not even where it was. I had come to accept that this was the only way I could survive. When I looked up Jamaica in the atlas, I understood that it was in the middle of the Caribbean, in the continent of America, the other side of the world. I was initially apprehensive but then I calmed down and thought it a good idea. This place was so far away that nothing could stir my oasis. Marvellous!

I was deep in thought when one of the nuns came in, motioning me to Mother Theresa's office, where I found Janine deep in conversation with Mother Theresa. I had not seen her for a few weeks; her new life had transformed her – she looked happy and prosperous. It gave me satisfaction that my beloved angel was no longer sad. When I had seen her last she had announced that she was expecting a baby and she was now in her maternity dress, carrying a basket with a few tarts inside as usual. I said that I didn't want to trouble her.

'But I wanted to. I am not working at the moment,' and then she handed me the letters that Pierre and Jacques had written to their dear auntie.

I always replied to them and posted the letters. As soon as Mother Theresa left, Janine asked me if I was ready to hear some news.

'What news?'

'Monsieur Saeed,' and she explained that Gaston had been to see her the night before. Saeed had arrived in Paris and, during a meeting, Gaston had accused him of robbery. Saeed had shown him some papers, threatening that he was planning to take him and me to court, and that soon enough he was going to put us in our place. Now Gaston wanted to know my thoughts.

'What documents? What claims?'

Janine, who was clearly shaken, explained that Saeed had claimed that I was a thief and had robbed him and others of their estate by forging documents, claiming that though he was married to me I had a relationship with another man.

'Bastard!'

I couldn't help the word and I was glad that no one but Janine heard it. She, however, was terrified and said that Gaston was in no better state. He had told Janine that perhaps we should return to Saeed all the money we had taken so that he would leave us alone.

'Dearest Janine, I am going far away, further than you can imagine. It's over!'

'If Monsieur Saeed finds us, what shall we do?' She was quite anxious.

I said I couldn't imagine what business he had with her.

'He knows everything. He has told Gaston that I am your ally. He has even mentioned André.' He was a simple man whom I had met only once.

I murmured a prayer; I didn't like seeing my dear Janine anxious. I held her hands.

'But Janine, you know everything,' to which she nodded agreement. 'So why are you concerned?'

'I don't know. I am only scared of Monsieur Saeed; he's capable of anything, otherwise Gaston wouldn't be so terrified. You do remember how fearless he is?,' But I took the tarts and said a few calming words, which I myself didn't believe, and then sent her away.

Chapter 48

I did not go to Jamaica. Janine's visit and the news she brought meant that I went through three sleepless nights; it was as though sleep could not find its way through to me. No matter how hard I tried I could not rid myself of the thought of the monster: Saeed kept creeping back into my head. Evil thoughts had buried their anchor so deeply within me that nothing seemed able to uproot them. I did not discuss this with Father Wilfred; it seemed he had decided to let me fight the inner evil on my own.

I shivered at night and in the daytime tried to do the best I could while keeping my head down. The large room on the second floor was always full of visitors, and when visiting time was over, his family – or rather my own family – would gather in the adjacent room or somewhere in the corridors. I felt their presence wherever I went, but they failed to recognise the nun who was withering away and hardly resembled the young woman they had abandoned. My loose clothes were a better indicator of my gradual loss of weight than the looking-glass; indeed, I had not looked at my reflection for some time.

On the third night, once the visitors had disappeared, I did a ward round in the quiet of the hospital. I checked on the nurses and then headed for the gardens when I felt my legs wobble. While walking on the quiet gravelled path towards the convent, I stopped a couple of times to look around me: I initially took the sound for the impact of my shoes on the gravel, but it was more like heavy, monster-like footsteps. The sound of my breathing had also changed, as though it, too, was that of a monster. When I reached my room I drew the curtain. I was worn out by lack of sleep so I pulled off my scarf and removed my long uniform. I would normally have folded my clothes on a stool in the corner of my room and then done the *vozu* ritual followed by prayers in the direction of Mecca. That night, however, I had no strength and could barely switch the light off. I collapsed on the wooden bed without even bothering to fold back the covers.

I jerked as I felt a hand touch my shoulder; it hit the wall as a result. Was I experiencing a nightmare? The faint light coming through the curtain revealed his figure and then I suddenly felt I was being smothered by a jinnee. His hand had covered my mouth to hush me. I heard him; it *was* him.

'You are my darling.'

I felt my body go into spasm but then struggled to release myself from his clutches like some corpse.

'Why can't I be dead?' left my mouth in Persian.

Mother Theresa and one of the nuns who were by my bedside did not understand what I meant. They drew back the curtain, and the sunlight flooded the room, hurting my eyes.

'Khanoum, why did you not let us know you were unwell?'

I was confused and had nothing to say. My eyes closed and I didn't notice as a nun entered my room with a tray of food. The sound woke me up, however, and I was sweating and shivering. She suggested I should eat something and not go back to sleep, since a physician was coming to see me. She helped me tie up my scarf and then tidied my room. I was about to stand up but my weight was too much for my feet to bear. I didn't need to look at myself in the looking-glass to know I looked gaunt. The nun folded my uniform and put it away, together with my shoes which were strewn all over the place. She then stood outside waiting for the physician and Mother Theresa. I answered the doctor's questions briefly. He examined me and then left, together with Mother Theresa. I could vaguely hear them talking behind the door.

I spent the day mostly sleeping and thinking about the nightmare. I kept telling myself that I was going to leave very soon; that I'd go to Jamaica and rid myself of everything. My bones were aching and the nun reported that the physician said I was experiencing fever and shivers as a result of exhaustion, and that I was going to recover after a couple of days' rest. But I was certain I had caught some terrible disease from one of the patients. The nun spent the entire day sitting by the window reading a book. She occasionally handed me a glass of water, and I once managed to step out to go to the bathroom only a couple of doors away from my room. It was around midnight when I heard the nun leave; when she returned she asked if I had the strength to sit and talk to Father Wilfred. I was delighted. Father came in and the nun left. He sat and prayed.

He fiddled with his beard a little and suddenly asked, 'What do you want to do?'

'I am going, Father. With your permission, I am going to Jamaica, whenever you see fit, today even!'

He said no and then rose. I followed him with my eyes. He paced the room once and then stood by my side. I didn't notice him releasing his hand from behind though I did notice him holding something in front of my eyes.

'What is this, my child?' He was referring to a leather briefcase.

It looked familiar.

I searched in my mind and hesitantly said, 'This belongs to the king of Iran who is sleeping on the second floor.'

'What is inside?'

I was still seated and many thoughts were racing in my mind.

'Father, how am I to know?'

'This bag was found in your room, my child. Police officers are coming here in a moment to ask you the same thing. Do you wish to confess?'

'I don't have anything to confess, Father,' I sobbed. Then it suddenly occurred to me. 'So it wasn't a nightmare, in that case ...' and I felt a sharp pain run through my body.

Rather than the police, Muhammad Hassan arrived, and with his arrival everyone left the room.

I had been trying to forget the devil, and the belief that he was trying to rob me of my material wealth, in the hope that this would better enable me to hang on to my real life. I was forgetting about revenge, but now the devil himself had called me to a duel: he had made an accusation against me. I should have known that every evil thought would home in, including the desire for revenge.

When I described to Muhammad Hassan what Saeed had done to me I was filled with anger and renewed desire for revenge, and kept sobbing. He, like Father Wilfred, paced the room, and after a while kept muttering, 'The damnable man.'

Finally he came to a halt and said, 'It's enough, you shameless creature,' and I knew he was not addressing me.

Shortly afterwards he left. It wasn't long before I heard Janine's voice. She came in, followed by Father Wilfred. Janine was quietly getting my clothes together and packing them in a suitcase pulled out from under my bed. The room was quiet; I was expecting either of them to interrogate me but neither of them did. I was bursting with pain. I wanted to fall at Father's feet and ask him to send me to Jamaica as he had promised. I stood while Janine put the few items of clothing I had accumulated in those two years into the suitcase.

Father Wilfred must have read the expression on my face as he said, 'This was God's will. Have you ever heard that Satan lays hundreds of traps but God destroys them all in one go?'

He was standing, the kind father who had, in the past two years, slowly entered my conscience and taught me to lean on only one being: the good Lord who was always present.

He had taught me to embrace my loneliness and, in the end, he reminded me, 'Do not forget,' but he didn't say what and whom I should not forget.

However, when I sat in the black car with its leather interior, and rested my tearful head against Janine's shoulder, it began to dawn on me what he had meant.

We were drawing away from the stone palace – my paradise – which Madame Jineau had talked about. The bells began to chime and, for a moment, I wondered, 'Have the patients taken their medicine?'

I was fearful of stepping back into the chaotic world of human beings. Two days later Janine finally began to talk.

'When the crown prince returned to the room upstairs he was furious and instantly described to his mother and sick brother the way that evil man had treated you. To avoid scandal they decided to announce that the king's precious bag had been found and that the contents were intact,' though, according to Janine, the pearl-studded pocketwatch and the antique cigarette holder alone were worth hundreds of thousand of francs.

What had mattered to her most, however, was the way the Empress had reacted.

'When she had heard everything she nodded with regret and said some things in Persian which I couldn't understand, but somehow I knew she was referring to you. She finally embraced me and wanted to know my address. She then asked me to spend a few days looking after you.'

'A few days?' Janine was now stroking my head and I thought just how much the poor soul had to put up with.

She nodded and said, 'Only a few days.'

A few days had become a month when Janine said, 'We must go.'

I put on a black dress. We now had to see off the body of the large fish. Having spent a few months on the second floor of the hospital, his spirit had finally slipped through the white sheets and left the large room. I had to go and look after the Empress; I knew only too well how much his death was going to torment her. I didn't know how to face her for the first time, what to say and what she was going to say.

'My darling, how thin you've become; my poor love,' she said, as she embraced me fondly amid the sea of black gowns and laces, wreaths and elegant Parisian men and women.

I had so much to tell her. Life did not only belong to monsters; I had just come from three years in the city of angels.

The following month Janine gave birth to an angel: a little angel with golden locks resembling my Nezhat. Had my aunt been born again? I was thinking of her once more.

CHAPTER 49

T hree months on, my was life transformed; its brilliant colours took me by surprise. The Empress had established herself in a large building in the middle of a park she had bought outright. Upon arriving in St Cloud, she informed me that I was going to be accommodated in a building to the east of the fathers' quarters, the construction of which would be complete in a couple of months. I was about to say that I had been accepted at the medical school, was going to rebuild my life and that I had no intention of being a burden to her, but she seemed to have read my mind.

'Janine and her family will join us here as well.'

I then realised that she had spoken to André, Janine's husband, and he was to become my aunt's chauffeur; she had recently purchased a Packard with blinds. Janine was given certain responsibilities as well and was now in charge of the entire household staff in St Cloud, a compound to which family members, who used to live in Beirut, had been added.

I asked the Empress for permission to go to university, at which she smiled and said, 'Dr Jarozelski has retired and will leave next year and there's no one better than you to replace him; your hands don't tremble either!'

While the building work was in progress I remained with Janine and her family. It was then that the truth behind the Empress's unkind letter became clear; a tormenting letter received at the height of my poverty and hardship that had driven me to my sickbed. I had made a pact with myself that I had to find the culprit before I died. I discovered that, a few days after having abandoned me in Paris, the monster had asked his sister to inform my aunt that I had colluded with Ezzedin, sold my home along with his estate and then fled with Ezzedin. I could just imagine how the embarrassment must have infuriated the Empress; she must have wanted to disappear from the gaze of the Ottoman clan. The idea that her protégée had committed such an unscrupulous act had brought her and her entourage such shame that when, after a while, Saeed Pasha turned up, they tried to make it up to him; they kept him in their circle because they felt responsible for his destitution. Thus he was able to benefit from the Empress's largesse until they moved to Paris.

Établissement Gaspard and Monsieur Gaston made the first strike during their first meeting with the Empress and the crown prince. My name was mentioned, as well as the details of my claim, the court case and the verdict. When the devil discovered that all was about to be revealed, he went to Monsieur Gaston and then Janine, to find out my whereabouts. I knew the rest of the story.

One day, when the workmen were busy at St Cloud, I was sitting on a bench next to the Empress, translating her instructions to the French architect. When he left I was alone with my aunt for the first time. Without beating about the bush I asked, 'Would you mind if I ask you about something?'

She was holding a cup of tea, and as though anticipating such a moment said, 'I wanted us to talk when all is ready, so that we could have more time to ourselves, but go ahead.'

'Please talk to me about the days I became such an evil being in your eyes; did I make you suffer a great deal?'

She closed her eyes. 'Yes …' And after a long pause, 'I could only blame myself because I felt responsible for your upbringing and thought I must have been far too preoccupied with my own situation and must have neglected you as a result. I agonised over this; what this boy did was nothing compared to all that we've gone through.' I wanted her to carry on and tell me why she had written that I was like my father, the evil man that he was. However, I sensed that the reminder might cause her enormous pain. So I decided, despite my many questions, to close the chapter. I paused, but the Empress continued.

'Thank God it's over, though I must tell you about the last episode. I knew the contents of that bag mattered a great deal to His Majesty and he never parted with it. I still don't know what was inside. In any case, when Muhammad Hassan Mirza came and explained everything, His Majesty, despite his severe condition, said, "This was the price of Khanoum's freedom. Let it be!" His brother insisted that the police should pursue the case but His Majesty said, "This will ensure he never returns."'

While the Empress was talking to me she had tears in her eyes, and the memory of the rotund, polite boy who used to come to our park and write me letters came back to me.

The pinnacle of our conversation was the Empress's reassurance that the devil was never going to return, something which made me immensely happy, though I still experienced the nightmare of that night in my room in the convent. I would wake up in the middle of the night and scream. The thought of never having to see that demon restored my peace of mind. I had to remember Father Wilfred's words and give in to my destiny, which I did.

CHAPTER 50

T he summer of 1930 was a new beginning for me; I celebrated
the demon's departure with no one but myself. One evening I left Janine to her family and decided to go out. I was in
awe of the magnificent buildings in Avenue Victor Hugo and the
sumptuous cars that passed by from time to time. I wondered,
having learned so much in the convent, whether I was still drawn
to luxury and the aristocratic way of life. I searched for an answer
but realised that large homes and aristocracy were not what
I was after. I lingered at the bus stop, and when the bus arrived
I got on with no particular destination in mind. A couple younger
than me, seated close by, seemed not the slightest bit bothered
with what went on around them. For a moment I thought about
love, but the idea of a man placing his arm on my shoulder, as the
young man was doing with his companion, repulsed me. So what
was my dream? I was now free to choose.

I was so late back that Janine had become anxious. At home
I continued to search, as though I was determined to bring
everything to a head, which I did. But let me first tell you about
the state of the world when my new life began. The Great War
had ceased but Europe was in ruins. Millions had been killed and
the disabled had poured onto the streets. Our hosts, the French,
had been on the winning side and had seized Alsace and Lorraine
from Germany. Poverty and unemployment were widespread in
the defeated Germans. In France, too, poverty and unemployment
were at record levels and the communists were becoming more

powerful; there were demonstrations on the streets every day, with the communists shouting out their slogans. In August 1927, in the days preceding my taking up residence in the convent in Neuilly, thousands of students and workmen had participated in a demonstration, waving scarlet flags, shouting slogans against the government, accusing the communists of being the enemies of France. There was talk of the Soviet Union and Stalin, who had replaced Lenin. Before I left for the convent, I took an interest in the debates printed in the newspapers, and the debates in the Parisian cafés. Every day there was news of the communists' victories in different parts of the world.

Such was the atmosphere, that I found myself recalling our last days in Odessa and some thousand princes, wealthy Russians and Ukrainians, whose possessions the Bolsheviks had seized, becoming wandering souls in Istanbul. Having heard the full, horrifying extent of the execution of the Russian imperial family, I found it hard to believe that the cultured French could have set their hopes on Lenin, Stalin and Trotsky. The day we learned the news of Lenin's demise, the Champs-Elysées was full of people wearing black armbands. The atmosphere of Paris was such that even Janine and I had practically become communist sympathisers.

It was the same story at the medical school in the École St Martin. Like the other students, I wore a white coat and attended lectures on medicine and anatomy in the lecture theatre, but I hardly had to step outside to be engulfed in the debates as the walls were covered in slogans. Unlike China, Japan, India, and the uprising in Algeria and Tunisia, the latter both French colonies, there was no news of Iran. I then discovered that in the previous year important events had taken place in the United States. America had long been a safe haven for many people and was a symbol of prosperity and freedom, but now we were hearing of the crisis in Wall Street. I couldn't comprehend what was going on, and by the time I got to grips with the phenomenon, thousands had lost all they had overnight and many had committed suicide as a result. The Empress's wealth was literally halved and the rest of the imperial family, who had invested heavily in American financial institutions, now found their fortune almost wiped out. I was told that when Ahmad Shah received news of the economic crisis in America his state of health deteriorated, and that, in the first few days, the thought of poverty and distress had left the Empress in a state of confusion.

The summer of 1930 in Paris, for a woman embarking on medical studies, was most exhilarating. I was once again drawn to books and began to read works by Marcel Proust. I managed to follow the news of a busy world by listening to my newly acquired radio, and when I had more time I listened to music and events in the art world. The news of the latest book by André Gide, the daily analysis by French intellectuals, political parties and philosophers, and various other new discoveries were particularly appealing, since I had a good command of the language. I was young once again, and not only did I feel nothing was amiss; my past and what I had been through also put me in a better position to deal with things than everyone else. No wonder I was elected head of the students' union of our college. I would leave home early in the morning and not return till late. I would prepare myself for *Agrégation*, search in the library, attend lectures, explore in the lab, or munch a piece of bread among the crowd while reading. I felt like a child who had just opened her eyes and was constantly exploring the world. My friends, many of them from different corners of France, were often younger than me and they had no notion of what I had been through.

I was glad I had not gone to Jamaica; having lived my new life of the past two months, the thought of living like a nun in a remote and depressing convent in Jamaica made me uncomfortable. In the early days I had every intention of paying Father Wilfred a visit once a week; he had come to my rescue in the days when I was a recluse. In the end it was he who had set me free and, despite my being adamant that I would continue with that life, he had encouraged me to leave. I seldom went back to see him, but Janine remained a loyal visitor to the convent, paying her dues on a monthly basis.

Meeting Françoise and Brigitte was the most important event in the new chapter of my life. No one made decisions for me and I was step by step taking the reins of my life into my own hands. The two girls, originally from Normandy, were down-to-earth and had abandoned the lives that their fathers had predetermined for them: marrying a local chap, having children and, according to them, leading a so-called 'normal' life. Brigitte was my contemporary and had been married once before. Françoise, however, was a few years younger than us. She was a petite, typically French woman. The outbreak of war meant that she had to leave school and attend to her father's farm while her father and brother fought on the front, but she was determined to leave their village as soon as the men returned. Françoise and Brigitte were both poor and wanted to use their meagre savings to build their future and be free. They had initially imagined that, as a 'princess', I was wealthy, but soon enough they discovered that the weekly stipend that I drew from the bank, an account set up for me by the Empress, meant that I was no better off. Two months after the start of the term, I began to share their accommodation in what would originally have been a maid's room in an old building that had been turned into a nursing home. We did our work and chatted well into the night. I finally made an important decision, which I thought was the best solution in the circumstances. The three of us rented a studio flat in the basement of an old building for eighteen francs a week. Janine was taken aback to see the conditions we lived in. Despite having three children she managed to keep her home clean and orderly; no wonder she was taken aback to see the chaos and asked me how I could bring myself to live in such squalor.

I paid the rent and, in return, Françoise and Brigitte provided food. The two of them worked a couple of hours a day in a nearby hotel. I had left my belongings in Janine's home and André brought only a few items in his car to put in the room in the basement. No doubt Janine, André and perhaps the Empress never imagined I would last in that basement for three years, but I did.

My more radical decision was to leave medical studies to the younger women and men, who couldn't wait to be called 'doctor'. I had other things to do: I was once again doing what I liked best, delving into literary works. Françoise was of the same bent, but Brigitte was a born artist and she had left Normandy to follow her dream. She played the violin and, when she practised, our small home was filled with the sound of her gentle music. We had so little space that I had to place my easel at the bottom of the stairs.

The people who strolled in the Bois de Boulogne on Sundays were getting used to seeing the three young women, two painting and the other playing the violin. From time to time, passers-by threw a coin; at other times they let us have some of their lunch. We were happy and never idle. Occasionally, remembering her father who had been killed in the war, Françoise sank into depression. There was a host of other issues that also made her unhappy, but my experience had prepared me to help someone in her situation. I knew how to let them be and when to hold their hands and pull them out of the bottom of the abyss without their knowing it. The most enjoyable days were when Professor Alain, who lectured on art history, took us to a museum, as well as the days Janine came with a handful of food and the three of us played with her young child, Christina, our doll. Janine was motherly to us and felt the urge to look after us from time to time. She once brought us three coats she had bought in the sales so that we could keep warm during the winter months. She was concerned how we managed in a room with no heating at night, and we told her that we would wrap ourselves in a blanket and let our body heat warm us.

Every day, on our way home, we would pass by the shops filled with goods and clothes. They attracted quite a crowd during the sales at the beginning of every season. Paris was slowly shedding the image of war but we were oblivious to it. The biggest event of the first year was that the three of us passed the *aggrégation* and could now go to our respective colleges. Françoise came out second from top and got a scholarship that paid her fees.

The next day, after college, we made a plan: we took some seven or eight paintings to Sacré Coeur and wondered if anyone would buy them. This proved quite an experience, and later on that evening we went to La Coupole and had duck for dinner. Brigitte loved wine and so made the best of her evening. We then decided to travel south – the South of France where all the respectable and wealthy French families spent their holidays – by selling some more pictures.

Before we set off, however, we decided that Françoise and Brigitte should give up their part-time jobs at the hotel since we had found better ways of earning money. If we secured a good position by getting to Grand Chevalier on the Seine very early in the morning, the pictures that Françoise and I painted would sell by the end of the week. After so many years of painting, I had now abandoned my realist style for a more modernist genre. The customers on the Seine, however, wanted portraits, and so, with the help of our course books, we began to copy pictures of men and women. We even copied Michelangelo's work, and soon, instead of following the models in our books, we began to draw lightning portraits of people; at fifteen minutes a time we made good money. This, however, had nothing to do with our studies: at art school we were getting to know Picasso and Salvador Dalí. Françoise was passionate about the Belgian René Magritte and would create pictures in the same style, which would later hang in the studio at our school. I liked the Impressionist school, and we dreamed of going to Holland or Haiti, following in the footsteps of Van Gogh and Gauguin.

We enjoyed our Sundays when we sold pictures while also having fun, and when we got back home in the evening, we would laugh our hearts out looking at men and women whose pictures looked far more magnificent than they were in reality. We then decided to pack our easels and Brigitte's violin on the back of our bicycles and head towards the Côte d'Azur. What we didn't think about, though, was our expenses. We had hardly any money to stay in a hotel on the azure shores in the South of France, but we had self-confidence, which made us fearless, and we sincerely believed that we could do whatever we fancied, which actually materialised with little effort. However, by early evening on the first day, we had only managed to ride forty kilometres to Vernon, at which point an old man mentioned the train. Considering that the journey was going to be much quicker, I don't know why we'd never thought of the train. So we went to the railway station early the next day, left our bicycles in the luggage van, and sat in the second-class compartment like ladies. Trees and farms whisked by along with the birds perched on the power cables, which inspired our next pictures.

Later that afternoon we arrived in Juan-les-Pins. We decided to carry on with the rest of the journey on our bikes through the fields, and to spend the night in some farmhouse. The women of the village were stupefied to see three slender, medium-height young women, a dark-haired one called Princess and two French and fair. We looked healthy and cheerful and so they offered us food and their produce for very little. We spent another three days in a château where a young woman, Maréchale, lived by herself and was happy to receive us. Her only problem was loneliness, as well as her dislike of village life and the wish to go to Paris. In the daytime, she would take us for a stroll in her gardens and spend hours watching us paint while listening to Brigitte's music with us.

'Our presence makes Maréchale feel like some philanthropist princess who has given shelter to three promising young artists,'

Françoise said once at bedtime, while mimicking her hostess, and we laughed.

In fact, it didn't take a great deal to make us laugh as though we had heard nothing so hilarious in our entire lives. Madame Maréchale would usually turn up in our bedroom at night in her lacy pink nightgown. Having wiped off her makeup she looked prettier and always carried reading material, a novel or some magazine. She liked participating in our nocturnal feasts and explained to us that she had inherited the estate from her husband, who had left four years before for Algeria to do business. However, he had later informed her that he had fallen for a dark-haired Muslim girl and was not coming back.

Despite her preference for life in Paris, Maréchale had remained in that village. She had nothing but the estate, and in the difficult post-war economic climate no one was prepared to buy it so that she could lead a middling life in Paris. Like us, Maréchale enjoyed going to museums and the opening nights of concerts and galleries. Sadly, she had to make do with a library of some three thousand books, a gramophone and some sixty records by Beethoven and Bach. Brigitte had become particularly attached to Maréchale, who was happy for us to spend the rest of our holiday with her. Françoise and I pretended we would return after a week.

When we came to say goodbye we gave her three pictures we had painted during our stay with her. She insisted on paying for them but we could not accept payment and accepted instead some bread, some excellent cheese, mulberry jam and some tarts to snack en route. She stood on the balcony and waved to us; her eyes followed us until we disappeared at the turn of the road. We realised that the world was full of lonely but good individuals who could not attain their dreams. For restless souls, becoming a prisoner like Maréchale on an estate in the middle of nowhere was an unbearable thought.

Our first encounter with Cannes was much more exciting for Françoise and Brigitte than for me. Having spent months on the

Riviera and at San Remo, I didn't feel any particular excitement; however, this was to be an experience of a different kind. Cannes was a buzzing city of casinos, cafés and wealthy people who had come from different parts of the world, among them the many young men who would invite us to join them in a café. Whenever we gave in to such invitations I would always insist on leaving early, or bury my head in a newspaper. Françoise once asked me just how long I was going to avoid talking to men and, when we were sitting on the balcony of a hotel where we had taken a small room one night, I explained to her that I did not feel any gap in my life and didn't feel these was anything unnatural about me. At the same time, I did not consider it wrong for her and Brigitte to keep male company, just like everyone else.

While going from place to place we would sometimes get off our bikes and have lunch. At other times we would snack while on the move. We spent most evenings in our small room talking about our experiences. We didn't share each other's opinions, and each of us had different aims, but we enjoyed each other's company. We would go over everything that had happened during the day; while Brigitte and I painted we chatted, but we became quiet when she played her violin.

Nothing could have been more amusing than what took place in Nice. We had run out of money and ended up looking for work. One afternoon, when we were taking great care in eating our prawns and fries, purchased with our remaining money, the owner of the café offered us a job. He was getting a restaurant ready and needed cheap labour to decorate it on a low budget. He even proposed that Brigitte should play on his old piano for his wealthy and often elderly customers – piano and violin, it couldn't be better. We left our bikes in storage, put on the uniforms he had provided and began to paint the chairs and tables. Meanwhile, we also painted a couple of pictures, which were framed and then adorned the walls. It was initially hard to entice Brigitte, though little by little she put her reserve aside.

When we stopped in the afternoons, Brigitte's work would begin. Her playing appealed to the customers at the Café Deauville far more than we had anticipated. It was apparent that the owner of the café wanted us to remain there for the rest of summer; we, however, had other plans in mind.

On the fourth day, a black man in a turban made a sudden appearance at our table. He bowed, and with both hands presented a card addressed to 'Princess'. I thought he had taken me for someone else, but the man insisted that I should open the envelope. The note was from Bibi, the Aga Khan's wife, whose hospitality had extended to a week in her sumptuous palace in Bombay. She had spotted me earlier while looking through her binoculars and was confident that it really was me. An hour later we found ourselves standing in the Aga Khan's magnificent villa, a completely inappropriate sight in our unsuitable clothes.

Up to this point, Françoise and Brigitte had assumed that Janine called me 'princess' just as a nickname, but now, having witnessed a woman with such status and wealth call me her niece, they were astonished yet proud. The majestic Begum was sitting on the tens-of-thousands-of-francs-worth handmade wooden-framed sofa, and it took us a while to convince her, using her companions' assistance, that we were not poverty-stricken and that we did not have to commit to some lowly and unthinkable work. We had come purely to tour the South of France on our bikes, and there was no need for her to be in such anguish. She was anxious for me and felt my disastrous marriage had resulted in my present situation. We spoke Persian, and Françoise and Brigitte didn't have a clue what we were discussing.

Later on that evening in our magnificent bedroom on the upper floors of the Aga Khan's villa, I was filling them in on our conversation and Brigitte, being her simple self, agreed with the Begum. She loved aristocratic life and wished she could one day marry a wealthy prince and have servants and ladies-in-waiting.

I described our stay in Bombay – the Aga Khan's main seat – and the pomp, sophistication and princely receptions, which only fanned her enthusiasm. Françoise, however, thought the whole thing was some fairy tale and was more interested in the antiques and pictures adorning the villa.

The Begum insisted that my friends and I should stay on, as the Empress and her entourage were due to arrive in two weeks. She was determined to sort our lives out, but we decided not to stay more than three days. The next day, the Aga Khan's butler took us to the shops to buy some clothes since we were to attend a cocktail party later that evening. A Muslim Rajah and the French ambassador to Delhi were among the distinguished guests. There were more than a hundred guests and Brigitte had the opportunity to display her talents. Once we had our expensive Parisian dresses on, we looked different and no longer resembled the labourers who had been painting the Café Deauville the day before; our only reminder of that was Brigitte sitting behind the piano, with the guests enthralled.

We had to bid farewell to the Begum, who was reluctant to let us go, but we explained that we had to go back to Paris and to our studies, and then kissed her hands. As well as the expensive outfits that we had purchased for the party, each one of us received a gold necklace and matching earrings. Bibi also gave me four thousand francs as well as first-class train tickets to Paris. These were worth twice our annual expenditure and a hundred times more than what the owner of the café had paid for four days' work.

We were then driven to the station in the Aga Khan's limousine. The expression on the Indian man's face upon seeing our bicycles, which had been stored in the café, was quite something. I was glad of the money, but I felt bad at having delayed our plans by four days. It took us only a few hours to put the magic of the past four days behind us, and we were once again our usual selves fooling around. We were in the luxury compartment covered in red velvet, and Françoise once more had the opportunity to exercise her skill in mimicry – something she was rather good at – and we were in stitches. Françoise told Brigitte to be happy that she could join the harem of the Aga Khan and spend a lifetime leaning on the sofa covered in gold and jewels, only having to lift a finger to have the slaves bow before her. Brigitte did actually seem to like the idea of such a life, and the Aga Khan appeared to have taken a fancy to her as well!

With our bicycles parked among the elegant cases, we were complete misfits among all those ladies and gentlemen stepping out from the first-class part of the train. I looked at the women in their elaborate dresses and large feathered hats, a reminder that I, too, had dressed like that once upon a time and still had such clothes stored somewhere in Janine's home. We had only had to sell two fur coats to keep us going during our poverty and destitution. I now found it hard to believe that I had walked hand in hand with that evil man from the house in Madeleine before getting into the car and heading for the Moulin Rouge. I was actually content to have discovered the truth. Had I not, I would still be living that ridiculous life. Now, I wouldn't want to give up a single moment of my happy and carefree student life, or of my hunger to discover the world, to go back to my former life.

I had enjoyed reading Exupéry's *Little Prince*, and was enthralled to see a play by Beckett – directed by the man himself – in a small theatre. For me, the films that we saw in Salon Wagram and the debates at the Louvre were more than a match for all the jewellery and sophistication of the aristocratic life; nothing could be more delicious than when we sold a picture and could cover yet another week's expenses.

The three of us were finally offered places at different colleges but we remained together. Brigitte had met a young German by now, Gerhard, whom we called Garry, and the end of this chapter of my life began when the four of us went to Germany.

We had heard a great deal of French propaganda about Germany, about its horrifying poverty and inflation, and when we crossed the border and reached Düsseldorf, we realised that whatever we had heard was true. Garry's parents had a bakery in a small suburb of Berlin and lived with their other son Michel in a house with a small garden behind the bakery. Work started very early in the morning and stopped at midnight. We stayed in a guesthouse in town. Brigitte and Garry discussed their decision to marry with their families and us, and soon a date was determined. We were then taken to their house, where Françoise and I were put in Michel's room. He was two years younger than me, played the guitar and filled his room with pictures of musicians and music journals. Since he spoke good French, Françoise and I spoke with him most of the time.

During the ten days we were in Berlin, Françoise and I visited a number of museums and galleries, and Michel occasionally came along as well. He was shy and worked very hard in the bakery. He played folk music on his guitar, and when everyone gathered in the orchards of Wiesbaden, Michel, who was an obedient son, played his guitar while the guests drank wine or beer, and sometimes exceeded the limit.

At the end of our short visit, Françoise and I were taken to the railway station. Brigitte was in tears and we were already missing her. We bade her farewell as we left her behind in Berlin. This could have become just one more passing event; but that wasn't the case. I knew Michel was taken by me but I had decided not to let any man into my life. On our return, Françoise mentioned to me that Michel had asked Brigitte whether he could propose to me and she had warned him not to even think about it since anyone could predict the response. Whenever a fellow student showed any interest in me, my reaction was always abrupt and unfriendly. I would then be unable to sleep, as I experienced the tormenting nightmares of the old times. This sort of interest was quite natural for young, unattached women, but as far as I was concerned, it was as though someone had knocked an already cracked glass and shattered it into fragments. Françoise and Brigitte were quite used to this.

Parting with Brigitte, the most gentle of us, was hard, and also affected our financial situation. We had very little food, the winter nights were too cold to bear and we didn't have the strength to talk. We had to sleep with all our woollies on. Françoise finally got fed up and decided to work in a hotel. Although André gave me some money in addition to my stipend to help us pay our rent, our poverty affected our happiness. Brigitte was no longer there to entertain us by playing her violin and sharing her peaceful and simple conversation. We would lose our tempers easily but made up soon afterwards. When Françoise borrowed my bicycle so that she could go out with one of her classmates, Fred, my loneliness became unbearable. Fred came from Paris, and was an active member of the Communist Party. He had taken us to a few heated revolutionary meetings of left-wing students, but I could not conceal my distaste for the Bolsheviks. Fred, however, insisted upon us going, and Françoise was so drawn to him that she followed him everywhere.

The first Saturday that I went to our usual pitch by the Seine and took a couple of pictures to sell, I realised I couldn't do it on my own. On my way home that afternoon, I was fed up and threw the pictures into the water. I almost threw away my easel and unused canvases as well. I hadn't been to college for the past week as I didn't feel up to it, and I wrote about it in a long letter to Brigitte later that evening. Brigitte had written a couple of letters from Germany but I had not written back.

That evening, however, I suddenly decided to write; I needed to talk to someone and to describe how bitter and negative I felt. It must have been well into the night when Françoise turned up and I was still writing. She looked lovely and exuded passion. She described their clashes with the police while they were distributing Party pamphlets. She carried on chatting but, as she found me uninterested, she gave up and went to bed dreaming about her man, to whom she was becoming more attached every day. Before she went to sleep, however, she asked me if I would be going to college the next day since there was going to be a lecture about Western cinema, which I was passionate about. Had this been taking place two months earlier I would definitely have gone, but I had to decline. I would never know whether my depression was a result of loneliness or some premonition of what was to happen a couple of weeks later.

One evening I was yet again on my own reading Marcel Proust's latest book. I couldn't concentrate and had to keep returning to the beginning. It was at this moment that I heard the sound of footsteps. Someone opened the cast-iron gate and was climbing down the steps. My heart sank. I could only think it must be Françoise and Fred. But when someone knocked at the door, I could only think of André or Janine, or even the landlord who lived above. Why was I overcome by anxiety? I had read somewhere that before someone appears in our lives, whether they are good or evil, we can sense their vibes, which impinge on our inner consciousness before we actually see them. My heart was by then pounding and I was confident some evil person was at the door, but which one?

A few firm knocks were repeated, then a pause and silence. I could hear his footsteps and see his shadow. I had huddled behind the easel and might even have been shaking. I didn't feel any less scared with his departure and didn't dare make a move. What if Françoise arrived just now? Then again, she couldn't do much on her own. I hoped Fred would be with her. Alas, I knew this was hopeless because Françoise and Fred had taken to returning home very late, much later than it was now. Sometimes they even went to Fred's place.

I was deep in thought when I heard the footsteps again. This time I was able to glimpse his top hat. My fears were not groundless: it was Saeed, but how, just how had he managed to find me? Surely not Janine's doing as she was only too aware of how resentful I felt; she had witnessed the many nights I had been unable to go to sleep when she had remained awake so that she could talk to me. Even *she* had come to despise that evil man. But no one else knew where I lived.

Every time that evil man's fist knocked on the door, it was as though someone was knocking every tendon in my body. My hands and feet had become numb. He was shaking the door and calling me. What could I do? After a few minutes I heard him climb back up again. I decided to get up and go to Françoise's room in the rear of the flat. It was dark and I had not turned any lights on because of my fear: the thought of him entering my home at that hour of night terrified me. Once in the courtyard, I tried to call the neighbours on the floor above. They knew Françoise and me, and we knew the middle-aged couple who lived above us. They were pleasant people.

I was now so fearful that Saeed might catch me when it became dark that I decided to make a drastic move: I'd leave my place and go into the street; he wouldn't be able to harm me on a busy street. So I put my coat on in the dark, wrapped my neck with a scarf and, at a speed my numb feet tried to keep up with, emerged from the basement. There were a few pedestrians and from time to time a car passed by. Paris had been swallowed by night, and if I went through Rue Fortuny I would to reach the busy Wagram Metro. Someone, however, called me; it was his voice, very soft.

'My darling …' At which I froze.

'Let's go to the Plaza.' As though he knew I was trying to get him away from my place.

I was powerless and did not say a word in the taxi until we reached Montmartre. Save a few words, he didn't say much either. We stopped by a busy café in Montmartre. The Plaza was, as usual, busy. The waiter heard him and, after receiving a tip, directed us to a small table with two chairs. Unfortunately, Janine did not have a telephone, otherwise I would have called her from the café so that she and André could come to my rescue. He began to speak with the same hand and neck movements and his effeminate voice uttered the same old romantic words. He spoke of college, my lecturers and even my trip to Germany; he knew everything. He said how hard it had been to find me and, as a result, he had delayed his trip by two weeks.

'Where are you travelling to?' I spoke for the first time.

He said he was going back to Turkey; he had managed to get a passport and the new government had even agreed to offer him a job. But he was suspicious; this could well be some trap and they might kill him, though he had no choice but to return. I asked the reason he had to go back there.

After a pause while he drank his second glass of wine, he said, 'I am quite helpless, Khanoum! Don't think everyone in this world is as good and forgiving as you. The sisters whom I loved so much have now taken everything and have abandoned me ...'

This was something new! I recalled the Sultana with all her dignity and haughtiness. I reminded myself not to believe him and adopted an expression which clearly demonstrated my indifference to his fate and to that of his sisters, but he didn't seem bothered. Apparently, whatever he had done was as a result of his sisters' persuasion. They had conned him, the Empress and everybody else; they had even taken Ezzedin from him!

I can't remember whether I imagined it or whether it really happened, but when he mentioned Ezzedin's name he looked as though he was about to burst into tears. I was aware of his affection for Ezzedin; not only had I witnessed it, Janine had mentioned it to me as well. I did believe that the only thing he wanted in the whole world was Ezzedin. Nevertheless, I remained indifferent; I didn't move except to pour water down my thirsty throat. He spent hours talking to me and in the end said that he merely wished to be forgiven and that was why he had remained in Paris. He wanted to be sure I had forgiven him and then leave. After that I would never have to see him again. I was confused and needed to be alone. I needed to talk to Janine, but how? I could never adopt Saeed's charm and soft manner when it came to telling her everything he had said to me. No doubt, Janine was never going to believe him again.

But what about me, had I believed him? I picked up my gloves. He called the waiter, paid the bill and, as usual, observant of the etiquette, let me go out in front of him. I was concerned that he might want to come to my place, though he seemed to have read my mind and said to the taxi driver: 'We'll first drop Khanoum and then return ...'

Once we were outside my modest home he looked embarrassed and said, 'Why should my princess live in such degrading basement lodgings?'

He looked down in embarrassment and asked if I could reply to him the next day. I did not reply and carried on walking so that I could be as far away from him as possible, but he called to me: 'My darling!'

I did not shudder as much as the first time; I paused without looking at his face.

He said, 'We must pay a visit to the mosque as well so that they can annul our marriage and take this honour away from me since I was not worthy of it.'

And then he left.

I became more perturbed than I had expected. I turned the key inside the lock. Françoise had returned home. The light was on. I said hello and she replied in a hoarse voice.

That evening I felt I couldn't sit and listen to Françoise, who explained tearfully that she had parted with Fred. It wasn't the first time I had seen the romantic Françoise in that state; I was only too familiar with her tears and complaints every time she came to the end of such episodes. That evening, however, I wasn't in the mood and wanted to think about my own situation. I had to relive the past few hours, with many questions racing through my mind. This distracted Françoise from her anguish and she managed to forget about her own sorrows. As soon as I began to speak she lifted her head and looked at me. A few minutes later she wiped her tears and an hour later we were sitting on our beds in our nightgowns chatting and we hardly noticed the arrival of the morning. She could not believe the things I told her, and kept asking questions. She was aware of my saga, as I had on occasions mentioned to her, Brigitte and Janine the evil deeds that Saeed had committed. Now she wanted to know whether everything was true, to which I said I didn't know. I can't remember the rest since we must have fallen asleep.

The next day I took Françoise with me since there was no time to call Janine. The three of us went to La Coupole. The waiters knew Saeed. He didn't wish to discuss everything in Françoise's presence and simply moaned about his sisters, with Françoise listening in astonishment. He handed me an envelope and a bunch of flowers as soon as he saw me. When we parted outside our place I noticed that inside the envelope there were all the documents, the absence of which had put me through so much trouble – I had almost ended up being imprisoned.

Before I fell asleep Françoise quizzed me and insisted that I should believe Saeed. How could I? Yet again we chatted till dawn and I cannot remember who fell asleep first. In the morning we woke to the sound of Janine bringing croissants and warm milk, as she so often did. She had brought Christina, my little angel, with her. For once in many weeks I woke up feeling happy. Françoise, too, seemed to have forgotten about Fred. An hour later we were standing in Parc Monceau, next to the other mothers who had brought their children to play. Janine and I talked while the children ran around. I realised that I had not been wrong in guessing that Saeed had managed to get my address from her, though not easily. He had first convinced her of his innocence, and Janine had come to share the same opinion as Françoise.

'We were too suspicious of him. He was misled as well. It was clear that one individual could not become so evil entirely of his own accord, let alone such a man who is even more delicate than a young girl!'

I wanted to scream. How could she have forgotten so soon? It was only five years ago. She had no right to forgive Saeed so easily. Had it not been for her, my angel, I would have drowned in the Seine early on, or I would have gone to prison and come out a different person. I was pouring my fury out at Janine, and with tears rolling down my face was remembering those difficult and unpleasant times.

'Anyway, just what sort of a tale did he manage to whip up for the Empress? He separated me from her, knowing that I had no one else in the world but her. Did he not for a second think that he was fooling around with my innocent feelings?'

By then Janine, too, was quietly weeping. I had succeeded in convincing her and she was finally in agreement with me.

'You must see the Empress and seek her opinion too. She is waiting for you.'

CHAPTER 51

I t was a year since Janine and André had taken up residence with the Empress and her family. During this time I had been to St Cloud only twice, for *Noruz* and Ahmad Shah's memorial services. I felt a certain embarrassment, which prevented me from seeing them, but I was aware of events in St Cloud. For instance, I knew that despite losing a good portion of her and her husband's wealth in the 1929 stock market crash, with the wealth she had inherited from Ahmad Shah and her own skill in such matters the Empress had managed once again to bring everyone in her immediate family together. By now, two of her sisters and their families had joined the compound as well. With a dozen grandchildren and daughters-in-law Parc St Cloud had become crowded. The estate had been designed just like those in Tehran, where every family was housed in different sections. In the middle, my aunt lived in a beautiful fathers' quarters with a red sliding roof. I noticed the passage of the years whenever I went to see her.

The residents of St Cloud treated me as if I were the little Khanoum who had been brought to them in the gardens of the Russian Embassy in Tehran. I knew that employing Janine and André was a means of repaying part of Janine's kindness to me, and I knew where the money Janine brought to me from time to time came from. I was certain that whenever I saw Janine she would give my aunt an account of her visit the following day. I wanted to finish my studies and make something of myself to make her proud. I knew how much she suffered seeing the daughters of the family getting married early and behaving like aristocratic ladies rather than finishing their education.

'I wish I had come to France when I was younger so that I could have studied,' she once said to me.

When Janine told me that I had to go and see the Empress, I could never have guessed what she was going to tell me about Saeed and his resurfacing in my life. I wished to God he had never come. I had got used to my poverty-stricken student life, my bicycle, and the food that we made and took with us to college. I had even got used to putting up with the cold weather when I stayed in the library. I enjoyed the atmosphere of the tight space that I shared with Françoise after Brigitte left. Why did everyone think that a single young woman had a sad life? Why did Françoise insist that I should accept Michel's proposal? I wrote to Michel that I found him a pleasant enough man but had no intention of getting married. Michel did not believe what I said and wrote that he was going to wait. I hadn't lied: the thought of receiving a man in my solitude tortured me. Even if I trusted what Saeed had said it made no difference.

Before I went to St Cloud, I did something I should have done the first time Saeed returned. I had thought about it already, but the days went by so fast and in such turbulence that my whole being trembled.

When I entered Father Wilfred's office his face opened in a smile. I had seen him no more than a couple of times since I left, yet every time I saw him I drew strength from talking to him, and that kept me going for months to come, and now...

'I am glad to see you happy again.'

I was about to say something but I thought he was placing his finger on his lips, which meant that I should not answer just for the sake of it – you must think. I had to think.

'Father, would you give me an hour of your time today?'

He rose. He was still wearing his long gown and nothing had changed except that I was no longer the virtual nun who went to see him on a daily basis. He had remained the same and hadn't grown any older. He called Mother Theresa and handed over the tasks he had to attend to and the letters and notes he had read, and then began to walk. The oak trees were there waiting for me. The room where I had spent two years was still in the corner of the garden. I began to talk when he stopped. He lost his smile but then found it again.

'Father, I am scared. I can't believe him.'

'But you do, you do want to believe him.'

I paused. Did I really want to?

'Humanity's innocent nature demands innocence. Pray that you remain this way; remain like a spring so that when the others look to you they come to purify themselves and become ashamed of their deeds. But do not become arrogant; it is not you who purifies them, they are meant to come.'

'But why did he come? As you said, I was distancing myself from evil and I was not even thinking of the monsters; I had forgotten them.'

'But even when you do not think of them, evil, angels and the spring never die, nor does it rain only once. They are all there and one day they turn up. Every story has an ending; but the looking glass is still there, even when you are not looking at yourself.'

'You mean even that monster ...'

'All monsters are restless. The angels may achieve calm but that is not the case for the monsters, and until they shed their façade they shall not die.'

What an analogy! What was he trying to say? I wanted to confess to him that the evil in Saeed had almost driven me to my death, and that during the time I spent in the convent I repeatedly told myself that had it not been for the evil in him I would have missed something so worthwhile. I would not have appreciated the meaning of life and would have become like thousand of others who never did. Since then, my resentment of him had diminished. The main monster, my father, however, never parted with his status and never shed his façade in my mind, which meant that I never forgave him. I had blamed myself for it nights on end, but I had lived resenting him. Every time I remembered him, the faces of my mother, and of Nezhat who had fallen in the well in Nanny's house, came to my mind. Perhaps only Abdollah could comprehend what I went through in my lonely nights in Odessa, a young, lonely girl who could not carry the burden of resentment on her own.

'But, Father, let me confess. This is why I am scared: ever since Saeed has turned up the thought of the other monster has returned to me as well, and I dream about him.'

'Meaning he has come close to your inner spring!'

'Don't, Father.'

He laughed. In the days that I had lived in the shadow of his kindness and his teachings he occasionally asked me to recite a Persian poem and translate it for him. He then memorised the verses and recited them back to me whenever he thought it necessary.

'Can you remember, "God can direct the ship to wherever he wishes"? But now you take yourself for the Captain!'

'No, Father, I am sure now.'

'So why are you waiting? Be grateful and go! I do feel it: I can't say anything but I feel you are approaching land.'

And he would not let me tell him about Saeed and the questions that plagued me. As usual, he talked to me about life, Man and the Lord, whose presence was everywhere and we only had to call Him. As ever, I left him feeling lighter than when I had arrived. I passed through the oak trees. Neuilly hospital and its robust walls were still there, and so was the tall spire of the church, reaching up into the blue sky. I could now feel a happy resonance within me, and only me.

CHAPTER 52

André arrived driving that magnificent car. I was sitting in a café near my college with Brigitte, her husband and Michel. The large black car, which had a glass panel between the driver and the rear seats, bemused the Parisians. André wore a cap and white gloves, just as the Empress's old chauffeur had done. As I was leaving, Michel got up. I knew how much he loved me but didn't know why. I had repeatedly spoken to Brigitte about it and we had nothing more to say on the subject. She and her husband Garry were looking at us. Michel followed me to the car.

'We may not see each other again,' he said.

They had managed to obtain visas to France with great difficulty and he wasn't sure they could come over again in the future.

'Perhaps it is better this way.'

'No, not unless you promise to come to Germany.'

'Michel, please don't.'

I went and sat next to André and looked at Michel from behind the windscreen. I knew he had come purely to see me; what a pity I didn't have the opportunity to sit and listen to what he had to say and, as on previous occasions, go to the park or the cinema. The thought that I was not going to see him again saddened me, but I had to think of what was awaiting me in St Cloud. I didn't know why my aunt had summoned me. By the way, Michel, I don't know why I have never told you, not that I wanted to hide it from you but even *I* had forgotten: I had a husband. He has recently turned up to set me free though I had not given it any thought all these years. So now, it is best for you to go back to your life; leave me with the monsters. You are too good and simple to be caught up with my monsters and angels.

I was talking to myself while André was talking about the children: Jacques, Pierre and Christina, the china doll. Until we reached St Cloud he talked and smoked, which was forbidden in my aunt's presence. I, however, was thinking of Michel, Saeed and the other monster, thoughts of whom had been resurrected since Saeed had turned up. Perhaps something was afoot. I was happy that the monster was miles away. While André was driving I reviewed my life from a thirty-five-year-old woman's point of view. We were passing through the spruces and the poplars, which were touched by the magic of autumn colours, bringing back distant memories of our home in Tehran and Shah Baba's *naarenjestaan*.

Did you know that, when I was born, Shah Baba was here, in Paris? For a moment I imagined his eternally sick-looking face, riding in the imperial carriage, visiting the *exposition universelle*, just as I had visited the Eiffel Tower. When Saeed and I had our picture taken by the Tower, it was as though Shah Baba was standing next to me. We passed by *Le Petit Palais* and I imagined riding in the same carriage as Shah Baba when the nihilist youth shot at him. He was so frightened that he 'had nearly passed out at the thought of being shot'.

Paris now was as tumultuous as my heart: the previous year there had been unrest everywhere, and Françoise and I had not been able to leave our place for four days in a row during winter. We kept warm under our blankets, bundled in all our warmest garments. There was talk of Maurice Thorez and his picture could be seen everywhere. We were in Avenue Wagram when he was speaking of fascism and Nazism and inviting people to form a common national front. This took place only two months after Hitler had become the *Führer*. I remember I had asked Michel whether his *Führer* was as dangerous as everyone described. His smile revealed his healthy white teeth.

'No one is as bad as his enemies wish to portray, nor is he as good.'

I knew Brigitte admired Hitler, as well as the German sense of discipline. She described how he was rebuilding a nation. I never had the time to discuss politics, people, literature and art with Michel as I used to do with Saeed, but I knew he was much better informed than Saeed or anyone I knew. His reserve and modesty, however, prevented him from revealing his knowledge. The only thing I could remember was that the previous year he had written a letter to me at the time Hitler and Mussolini were meeting in Vienna.

'These two are the representatives of two nations proud of their philosophy and art, yet none of them knows much about philosophy and art!'

He was anti-fascist, yet I could sense his discontent with Germany's current state. So why did he say that they might not be able to return to Paris?

André was one of Maurice Thorez's devotees, and once, when we were caught in a traffic jam caused by a demonstration, he explained to me that soon France and perhaps all of Europe would have to brace themselves to fight Hitler and Mussolini. France's survival depended on Thorez and the socialists; the rightists were hopeless. Whenever André discussed such issues I remembered the Bolshevik revolution with bitterness and invariably launched into a heated discussion. At the height of our debate he would sympathetically remind me: 'You must defend the rights of your class, princess.'

I would always sense a tinge of sarcasm in his tone; he knew only too well that, living in the basement of that old building, I hardly resembled a princess!

As we were passing through the busy streets on our way to St Cloud, he suddenly used the opportunity to tell me what he thought of Saeed. His opinion was different from that of Janine and Françoise. He still wouldn't explain why he did not much care for the Turkish prince. I asked him whether he couldn't understand or didn't want to say. He tilted his cap and politely asked whether I wanted to hear his honest opinion. I reassured him that it didn't matter to me; why would it, since I found it hard to trust Saeed anyway. André said that although he belonged to the working class and did not much care for the aristocracy, he did respect nobility with a backbone. Not only did he not detest the Empress and her children, he cared for them enormously and was happy to be kept in their employment. He added that he was never a practising Christian; nevertheless, having seen the Empress commemorate Muharram the previous month – as she always did – he raised his hat to her for maintaining the customs that demonstrated her pedigree. With this prelude he concluded that he did not think that Saeed had a single noble bone in his body and didn't think he held any beliefs, and that, moreover, as far as he was concerned, he came across as a fascist.

I asked André whether he had mentioned his opinion to Janine as well. He smiled.

'You know Janine; she's so kind she only sees the good in people. I shan't be surprised if one day she manages to discover the good in Mussolini as well.'

He then laughed and his laughter made me laugh as well. He was right in thinking that Janine was such a positive and good person that it took her a long time to arrive at the point where she would concede that there were any evil minds around.

I felt I was going to hear certain news; news that was going to overturn my life for days to come, so I preferred to arrive as late as possible and carried on chatting to André. Both Janine and André represented all things heavenly as far as I was concerned. Yes, heaven; a place where not many people could be received.

When we entered the Parc St Cloud I felt autumn had done wonders: it was as though a yellow screen had separated heaven and earth. In the glasshouse, however, the red and white flowers were happy in their shelter. The Empress and her sister and grandchildren were in the glasshouse. I went to kiss her hands and, as always, I found my lost mother in her embrace. Though I was fast leaving youth behind, in her presence I became a child once again.

When Janine arrived dressed in blue and beaming, it was as though she had blossomed. I would have never imagined that having started a pleasant day in a café in the Champs-Elysées, followed by the warmth in St Cloud, I would end up feeling anxious, but I did. I can't quite remember how my aunt went about breaking the news; I can only recall a few sentences mentioning Saeed and these came from an angle I least expected. She said that if I did not wish to live with him, now that he had come up with the suggestion, I ought to endorse our formal and religious separation as soon as possible, and she showed me how to go about it: I had to go to Sheikh Shafei, a cleric from Tunis at the Muslims' mosque in Paris, whom I had already met. I then had to go to the Registry Office in Paris.

I was expecting the Empress to pry into my renewed acquaintance with Saeed, say a thing or two about the past, or recall the days that, according to him, 'she abandoned me and didn't want ever to mention my name'; or at least to say he had squandered my wealth, not to mention the disgrace at Neuilly hospital. But she didn't; I should have guessed that she was far too gracious to put me in an embarrassing position. She was a truly noble woman.

When lunch was over, the Empress's sister and the children went to take a rest, and Janine was asked to take our tea to the library, which also served as the Empress's office where she usually conducted her formal meetings. She sat on one of the armchairs by the fire and began to talk about Iran and how Reza Khan had brought some sense of order to things. He had rooted out the rebels, and had at the same time executed a great many landowners and notables. Lately, Teymour Taash,[21] who had been so firmly on his side, or the children of Farmanfarma, who believed 'this man is our servant', had all eventually had to bow to his command. She carried on until she finally got to the point.

'The borders have now opened up and many travel abroad, many come for treatment as well. "That man" arrived just last week. He even expected us to go and visit him. He keeps asking for you ...'

I must have looked shell-shocked. I had become as still as a statue but my heart was pounding. Once again I became the child who was struggling at the hands of the monster. Once again I fell on his large bed with the tiger skin at the side and the heads of the hunted animals on the walls. To think that the monster was so close to me ... I felt I was passing out.

I got up and, with a voice sounding like mine, said, 'If you permit,' and that was all.

I wanted to get away. I wanted to go far away.

She seemed to have sensed how I felt and said firmly, 'Do sit down.'

I paused for a moment before I sat down, trying to keep quiet. She began by remembering my mother and I burst into tears. I don't know how I managed to sit down on the coffee table, but I found myself sitting next to her with my head buried in her skirt, weeping. I had done the same in Odessa and Istanbul whenever I was overcome by sadness. I had not wept this much for some time; my whole being was in pain recalling all the events of the last week in Tehran. I was being beaten for my mother, was suffering for Nezhat and was dying.

The Empress stroked my hair as she had done in my childhood and youth.

'He is dying,' she said in a voice devoid of emotion.

Why was she telling me this? Was she hoping to make me feel happy, or relieved? Then, two days later, I was going to the mosque in Paris, along with Saeed and Houshang, the Empress's nephew, when Saeed completed what my aunt wanted to say.

'Your father wants to bequeath his estate to you, and why should you not accept?'

No ominous thoughts crossed my perturbed mind at the time; he talked about the monster and it never occurred to me how he knew, nor did it really matter to me. I just didn't want to hear any more about the subject. Even when Françoise and Janine talked about it, reminding me that I wasn't a child any more and that I had no money, and that I shouldn't ignore what was due to me, I screamed my reluctance at them a couple of times and they were hushed. Saeed, however, was more diplomatic than everyone else. He stood in front of the mosque and, having spoken a little and encountered my reluctance, he suddenly decided to adopt a severe and more serious tone.

'You must leave him to me since you detest him so much. You'll just need to come along to the hospital with me, today and just once more. You can then leave *me* to deal with him.'

Oh God, how evil we could all become! I could not believe that I could become so wicked and have it within me to become so spiteful. His suggestion delighted me for a moment; yes, he was quite capable of making that monster suffer, for he was like him, actually he was *him*: tall, with a thin twisted moustache, and more or less the same age as the monster had been in Tehran; just like when his drunken body collapsed on my mother's mattress where I was asleep under the blanket. How could I have missed such a resemblance? I suddenly felt a certain excitement creep over me at my revelation, at how the devil had boosted my energy.

'What reward do you want to carry out your task?'

CHAPTER 53

The cleric recited the appropriate verses from the Qur'an and our marriage was annulled. I had little appreciated how easy it would all be. Over the years I had never given a single thought to the fact that I was still Saeed's wife and that a divorce had to be legally obtained. I looked at the ceiling of the mosque and in the cleric's office there was a large painting of Mecca hanging on the wall and a frame exhibiting 'Allah' in hammered gilt calligraphy. When the sheikh looked at the marriage certificate and read out the terms of my *mehrieh* – a palace, a gift from the Ottoman Sultan – he smiled and looked at me from above his spectacles. He asked me whether I had received my dowry. I gave him a sarcastic smile.

'Of course!'

Saeed lowered his head, and I didn't show any particular emotions.

When we left the mosque, Janine and Françoise were waiting for us. Saeed jokingly suggested celebrating my freedom and so he invited everyone to a restaurant. He initially wanted to take us to Café Moulin Rouge but, since we were reluctant, he agreed to go to a newly opened café by the Pont Mirabeau overlooking the Seine where an Austrian played the violin.

After describing the café, he turned to me and suggested, 'We'll go to the hospital.'

I was about to resist but, as though having read my mind, he said, 'Tomorrow we'll have to go to the registry office and you'll be free,' meaning that I had to honour my promise.

'Why today?'

With a tone that was clearly put on he said, 'The old man is waiting. Who knows, he may not be alive by tomorrow.'

He took out a piece of paper handed to him by the sheikh, then put it back in his pocket. It was quite clear by now that his return, his kindness over the past few days and all his sweet talk were directed to gaining the monster's estate, but it hardly mattered to me; the thought of thus regaining my freedom and not seeing Saeed any more made me happy. Janine kept saying that with the money from the monster's estate I could buy a house in Paris and put an end to my worries about paying rent, and that I would no longer have to stay up till late going from one house to another teaching idle children. She insisted that perhaps I should retain a portion of my father's estate, but the thought repulsed me. In fact, had it not been for Saeed I would never have gone to see the one who had murdered my mother and Nezhat. Why did I have to make the demon happy?

'Just go and see him,' she pressed, anticipating that by finding him on a hospital bed I might become compassionate and forget the past. After all, hadn't I just done so with Saeed?

When we entered St Rafael's Hospital through the large doors, Saeed seemed already familiar with the set-up and went directly to the office. I stared at the large bouquet of flowers that he was holding in his hands, and could see from a distance that he was charming the nurses. I answered the nurse's questions with regard to my name and my relationship to the patient. Saeed explained the rest. I signed the book and we climbed up the stairs. It looked like Neuilly Hospital but it was a more recent construction, so it felt smart and fresh. My heart was racing; I was cursing myself for giving in to such a game. The door opened and a young nurse carrying a tray of food and medicine emerged. An ageing physician was examining the monster and a nurse was writing down his instructions. We waited outside until he emerged in his white uniform; with his stethoscope hanging from his neck he somehow resembled Dostoyevsky. Saeed greeted him and walked with him a few steps, making his inquiries. Everyone already seemed to be familiar with him. I had no doubt now why the evil man was behaving as he was; nevertheless I was content, as the sweet taste of revenge had filled my entire being.

I can still recall the details of that tormented hour. I can even remember biting my nails, and at times clenching my fist so hard that my nails pierced the skin.

When the monster opened his eyes, our eyes momentarily met, which made me shudder and I stooped my head. Saeed was speaking to him in Turkish but he kept looking at me. He said something I didn't understand. He seemed weak and was more like a skeleton under the sheets than a person. He struggled to stretch out his arm, which resembled a narrow line emerging from the white linen. It was unfair of him to want to hold my hand. I motioned to Saeed that I couldn't.

Saeed murmured, 'I beg you!'

And then he took hold of the narrow line, pulling my hand at the same time. When my hand touched his I had a desire to pull it so hard that he would fall off the bed. And when he placed my hands on his lips I no longer felt anything.

When I was conscious again, I was lying on a bed and the eyes of the young nurse and Dostoyevsky were staring at me. I could hear Saeed explaining to them that I was meeting my father after thirty years. I had no strength, otherwise I would have shouted that that was not the case, that I detested the creature and that I had been forced to come.

The reconciliation Saeed had wanted did not happen and Janine took my weak body to her home. Françoise stayed till late, and listening to the story of my past reduced them to tears. I told them I had suddenly felt dead at that moment: I was finished and saw my spirit leave my body. I then seemed to be reliving my life and my childhood pains came back. I saw my mother,

Nezhat, our home in Tehran and the man who was beating my poor mother.

I wish I had withstood it that day and hadn't lost consciousness; I had to return to the demon one more time. Two days later, Saeed came again and put me under a great deal of pressure. He made threats, he begged; he was planning to leave for Switzerland for good and I was not to see him ever again.

I saw two other Iranian men in the hospital room this time. At first I didn't know who they were, but I later understood that one of them was an Armenian currency broker who received Iranians' funds and ensured their transfer. His name sounded something like Johannes. The other man had brought the demon to Paris, as he had difficulty travelling on his own. They had been in Paris for the past month searching for me. The Armenian began his flattery and explained that the Khan had left his house and his other lands to me, not to mention all that he had in Paris, which I could receive at any time. He further explained about the rental income I was going to receive and that it was advisable for me to go to Tehran and take control of my assets.

I wasn't listening. He was asking me to sign some papers, and before I could say a word Saeed came forward and took the pen from the Armenian so that he could sign them, but when he understood that the Armenian would not accept his signature he took a piece of paper out of his pocket and handed it over.

'The power of attorney is a valid document but Khanoum is here in person!'

They exchanged a few words, the outcome of which was my signing a document I didn't even bother to read. I knew this was yet another paper giving Saeed power of attorney to sign all papers enabling him to receive, on my behalf, all the money and shares. I could imagine the torment I would bring upon the monster and his friends just by signing the paper. I turned a look of resentment on Saeed as though I was rediscovering the monster that *he* was, and paused. This, however, did not unsettle him; he gave me a smile and motioned me to the corner of the room so that he could have a word with me.

He handed me a certificate bearing the seal of the French government, which I understood to be the document pertaining to my freedom that he had talked about. All the torment and hardship had now made me appreciate the value of the certificate: I placed it in my handbag and returned to the bedside. I then sat motionless on a chair and was beginning to look like someone who had lost her father. They gathered around the monster's bed. He was half alive and could barely be heard, as he was clearly in agony. I didn't know what Saeed had done but they all seemed to be in it together. They took an envious and contemptuous look at me sitting on the chair. I didn't care what they said; I just wanted to leave immediately. I intermittently heard Saeed talk about me, perhaps just for the monster to hear. He was saying that seeing him in that state had made me unwell, and was further describing my deep affection for my father! I secretly made a quiet derogatory smile at all the deceit, the pretence and lies aimed at securing the money. At that moment there didn't seem to be anything dirtier than money as far as I was concerned; it brought out all the filth in people and placed them all in Satan's hands.

I didn't say anything until I heard the man who had accompanied the monster to Paris – he was called something like Esfahani or Kashani – say something in broken Turkish.

'You'd promised to bring the children. Khan woke up a few times during the night and spoke of them and said that you'd chosen his name for your son. Where is he now?'

I could not put up with this one, so I made a move to say 'Which children? Which son?' but Saeed silenced me with his look. I was frightened; there was something terrifying in his eyes. He then apologised to them, saying that I wasn't feeling well and that he had to take me home. The monster directed a yearning look at me once again and his hand sought mine. Saeed took his hand and then turned to me.

'Say goodbye to Khan, Princess.'

I looked at him, turned and left the room so that I would not experience the same trauma as the previous day. Saeed took a few more minutes before joining me in the corridor. He was clearly elated and I knew why he felt this way. We climbed down the stairs and left St Rafael's hospital.

All I then asked was, 'Is it over?'

I meant that I did not wish to see him or the monster ever again. He did not say anything until we had left the building. The large black vehicle that he always hired – and the black chauffeur – was parked on the other side of the road. He offered to give me a lift but I said that was not necessary as I wanted to walk a little. I could no longer maintain my reserve and seemed to gather the full force of the resentment I felt; I told him I was thrilled that from then on I was going to see little of people like him and the monster lying upstairs.

I was about to take my leave when he called, 'Princess!'

I did not stop but he rushed to me to say that I was a miserable being and not worth a thing, 'just like all the other women who draw their worth from men'.

He then added that the filth of the half-dead creature lying up there was worth more than we women because he had lived life to the full and enjoyed it. It was as though he was determined, even at this final hour, to reveal his vicious nature. My silence and graciousness had made him angry. He seemed determined to rouse my hatred, from which he also seemed to derive enormous pleasure.

He asked me to take a look at the large car. I turned and caught sight of Ezzedin, who was sitting in the rear waving to me and beaming. Saeed had, by then, lifted all his masks; he looked through me and said that he had resented me ever since he set eyes on me. He had put up with me for Ezzedin's sake because he was his *raison d'être* and he would do anything for him. I never had believed him when he claimed to have lost Ezzedin to his sisters, but why did he want to torment me so much? I kept quiet until he said: 'He is waiting for you; go to him and spend an enjoyable hour with him. I am busy as I have to carry out your duties for you and take care of the man while he is still alive.'

I was so taken aback by his suggestion that I used all the strength I had left and slapped him so hard that the passing pedestrians came to a halt.

I was about to go when he said, 'My Ezzedin is even better than that man,' and while he held his hand on his slapped cheek, he somehow let go of his reserve and displayed his effeminate side.

'How could you surrender to him?' he said. 'Who is all the pretence for? Do you imagine I do not know?'

'You filth, you animal,' and then I remembered my mother saying the same to the monster: 'animal'.

But Saeed wouldn't stop.

'You miserable thing, neither I nor Ezzedin have a pleasant memory of you; the poor chap had to tolerate sleeping on that filthy, coarse bed of yours in that church, just for your sake.'

No, it can't be true! I had been dreaming it all: the convent, my room, and Ahmad Shah's briefcase ... I rested my hand on the wall so that I did not collapse. The realisation that is was Ezzedin who had planted the briefcase in my room all those years before had completely thrown me. Saeed had effectively returned my slap and now was walking away, leaving me behind in Rue St Rafael. My tendons seemed to be tearing apart. I was trembling, not from the cold winds of Paris but at the thought of what he had awakened in me. Up to then I had woken in the middle of the night having experienced nightmares – the monster's bedroom in the fathers' quarters – when I sweated heavily. Now, however, I had to harbour yet another nightmare: the one who walked hand in hand with Saeed, with their *tête-à-têtes* back in Istanbul when I heard them whispering amorously in each other's ears ...

When I came to my senses I was still leaning against the wall. The black car was not there any more. Oh Father Wilfred, how could I bring myself to disclose *this* to you? You never wanted to accept how helpless your innocent princess was.

CHAPTER 54

I wondered why when troubles came they crowded together at the same time – my life in the cold basement apartment was tearing apart. I had got used to being a student who read books, economised and bought bread before going home, and I was content. I ate only one proper meal a week, when I saw Janine, and I had as a result lost weight. I also received a meagre income through tutoring. All that I did brought me happiness; having killed the thought of ever having a family of my own, I contented myself by seeing Janine's children and occasionally bought them presents. When they climbed all over me my happiness was complete. I bitterly regretted the evil man having climbed down the stairs to my modest nest and finding me. Did the monster have to come all the way from Tehran to die at my doorstep? Had *he* not come, the other one would not have turned up either. If I had not given in to such spite, I would never have found out about what had taken place in the quiet of my room in the convent, and for the rest of my life I would have taken the intruder for my lawful husband. Was this some nightmare? I decided to turn up outside Father Wilfred's office the next day so that I could hear in his own words that it was over, that this was yet another nightmare and another test.

I climbed down the stairs. The light was on but I wished it wasn't. Françoise was in but I wished she weren't; I wished she hadn't come to help me to bed having seen my state.

She made some coffee and poured it down my throat saying, 'People from the East have so many tales, and *we* are so unfortunate to lead such uneventful lives.'

She then poured her heart out and lamented that if she had remained in Normandy she would by now have been married to a fellow countryman, had children, gone on the farm, milked the cows and never learned about life's ebbs and flows, and the many kinds of people she had encountered. Françoise seemed happy but confused as to why I had not been prepared to take what my father had bequeathed to me and become prosperous and happy. She then reminded me of the long waits for a customer to buy one of our pictures. For the past few months we hadn't even bothered to paint any. She found it ridiculous and yet fascinating that we had run out of money; the economy was in a state and, bearing in mind the number of industrial actions, it was not so certain that even the current state of the economy was going to last, and now she couldn't get over the fact that I had rejected millions of francs.

I was in tears and asked her not to discuss the matter further. She wondered why I was weeping as no one had forced me to make such a decision. Though I had no intention of telling her everything I had no choice but to explain the events in Rue St Rafael. I then told her about Ezzedin sitting in the black automobile and waving. She said something that I initially thought I had not heard properly, so I asked her to repeat what she had just said.

She laughed, 'He is an interesting person.'

'How do you know?'

She went quiet as though she was uncertain how to continue, but then, as though there were no reason why she should feel that way, she explained that she had seen Ezzedin a few times during that week. I couldn't believe it. How?

'He came over a few times and we went to the café to dance. We had a great time. Saeed would occasionally join us and at the end of the evening they would give me a lift. But when we were on our own ...'

'You fool! How could you? Why?'

She was taken aback by my reaction to something she considered pretty normal, so she just said, 'Because it was fun.'

I held my head in my hands and perhaps even cursed her, which was unsettling for her.

'Very well, I'll tell you everything. Ezzedin loves you. When I was with him and put your clothes on he wanted me to wear your perfume as well.'

I felt a spasm, until she said, 'When he came here, he would ask me to put your dresses on. I'm sorry but I did. The night that you were unwell and stayed at Janine's, Ezzedin came here and slept in your bed. He was sad that you, a princess, were living in such a place. I think you shouldn't have turned him down. If I were you ...'

I yanked the blanket and glared at her, 'Shut Up!'

She was agog. I then rushed to get dressed, picked up my handbag and stuffed my papers in it together with my toothbrush, and that was that. I knew that I was never going to return to that place. I had somehow to come to terms with the end of this part of my life as well.

Chapter 55

When I arrived at St Cloud the next day I was in the same state as when I had been left in the hands of the Empress twenty-six years earlier. The difference, however, was that I was no longer an innocent nine-year-old girl, nor did I have my mother's wrapped bundle to provide for me. Everything I had, and every memento of my mother and Nezhat, was gone, and I had given away one monster's estate to another. The Empress was giving Janine instructions on which room should be made ready for me and then she turned to me.

You are no longer the little girl. You've tasted life and have experienced every aspect of it, and now you have grown and are a woman you could share some of my responsibilities with me. You haven't made me suffer as much as my other children and have hardly been a burden to me.'

I didn't know how to respond to such kindness and magnanimity, bestowed on me without expecting anything in return. I was actually quite fortunate to have a place in which my weak body and tormented soul could recuperate.

The Empress said, 'Tomorrow we'll go to Paris to do some shopping. It'll all be back to normal after a few days. We've got a lot to do.'

I was slowly beginning to fit into that kind and noisy compound once again. The Empress had enlisted her household of thirty to help me forget all that had happened to me over the years. I had to let 'water under my skin' and rid myself of my anorexic appearance. I had registered with some agency to find a job, which didn't prove difficult since I had a university degree and some experience under my belt. It was nice to be able to see André and Janine – and occasionally their children – on a daily basis. Jacques was by now an adult and the thought that I, too, might have had a son like him depressed me. The thought of sharing my life with a man, however, made me forget about my craving for a child.

A month later I found a job in an art gallery, which offered me the opportunity to get to know artists, intellectuals and literary critics. The economic situation in France and in Europe, however, was dire, with ever more revolts and political tension. Hitler's presence in Germany meant that there was talk of Nazism, which was fast taking shape. Having started off with black armbands in Italy, fascism was slowly infecting the world. Gatherings took place in different corners of Paris, where such topics were debated – Paris was, at the time, the capital of political debate as well as of literary and artistic innovation. And I saw the leader of all this the evening I went to see *The Threepenny Opera* by Bertolt Brecht in St Michel: I saw André Gide. For me it was a dream to meet Gide, as I had read his works and heard that he was a great author. However, no sooner had I seen him than all that attraction and importance seemed to evaporate. The tall and slender André Gide, with his wire-framed spectacles, looked just like the photographs of him that were displayed everywhere in those days. When the play was over he was the centre of attention, as though people had come to see him rather than the play. The director rushed to him to thank him in a princely fashion. As usual, at the end of every première, be it a play or exhibition, the majority of people – the authors and intellectuals – went straight to La Coupole, the hub of intellectuals. The great André Gide was now draping his arms over the shoulders of two young men who were with him at all times. The author of *The Fruits of the Earth* no longer lived up to my expectations and to my mind was no different from Saeed or Ezzedin, the ones I had assumed had vanished from my life. This, however, was wishful thinking; there was no end to my nightmares.

One day, in *Galérie Mission* on the Left Bank, I was busy grouping samples of works by a Belgian artist so that the selection committee could decide which ones to exhibit. A young man suddenly towered over me, introduced himself as a police inspector and asked me to present myself at the police station in St Rafael the next day with my lawyer. He didn't answer my questions and said that I was not to leave Paris for the time being. I was anxious, so I finished my work earlier than usual and took the metro to St Cloud. I had to take the bus afterwards, on which I usually read a book or newspaper. That day, however, I couldn't stop thinking about having to go to the police station. I hadn't the faintest idea what the problem was or what was once again in store for me. I tried to remain strong and to remember that somehow, in the darkest hour of my life, some hidden force seemed always to protect me and pull me out of horrific whirlpools.

The Empress contacted Établissement Gaspard. The following day I had a young lawyer, dressed in a well-cut navy suit, with sleek hair and a black folder under his arm with me when I went to the police station. Mahmoud, the Empress's son and my cousin, came along as well and André drove the car. I later found myself sitting in a room with three chairs and nothing else. I was murmuring some prayer and trying to remember what Father Wilfred had told me. I was reminding myself that I didn't have to worry about anything. The police inspector started by explaining to my lawyer that he was investigating a murder that had taken place the previous month in Paris. I don't know why but I didn't feel particularly perturbed. The inspector then took out a photograph and held it in front of me.

'Do you know this man?'

It was the monster's photograph, with bruised eyes and a wide, twisted mouth. He looked thinner and more translucent than when I had encountered him in the hospital bed. I didn't feel sorry and did not tremble.

To the lawyer, who was staring at me, I said, 'Yes.'

The inspector explained that the man had been strangled and asked me whether I could think of anyone who might have wanted to kill my father. The lawyer motioned to me and then whispered a few things in my ear. He insisted that from then on I must take extra care as to what I said. The inspector picked a couple of papers from the file and handed them to the lawyer to read. The young lawyer took some careful notes while reading and, when he had finished, turned to me and said: 'The inspector wants to know your whereabouts from the thirteenth to the sixteenth of June. Did you, during this period, go to St Rafael's Hospital?'

I had to think. I took my diary from my handbag. On the thirteenth of June I had scribbled down the name of some film, which helped me to recall that I had worked in the gallery all day and then gone on to the Louvre with a female French colleague, and from there on to the great library in Paris. I could not remember the other days and there was nothing else in my diary for the period.

I insisted that I had not been to the hospital for the past three months. The inspector asked whether I was sure I had not been to the hospital. My response was firm. He asked how come I had not been to the hospital to see my father despite his having been on the point of death. When I explained that I was hearing about his death for the first time he raised his eyebrows. Had his death upset me? My lawyer objected that the question was irrelevant as it concerned my opinion. He said I was not going to answer the question, but I ignored the expression on his face and explained that I had not become upset because nothing about my father's demeanour had helped endear him to me, and that until I went to St Rafael's Hospital on 24 April, and again, for a last time a few days later, I had not seen him since I was nine.

The inspector gave a sly smile and declared, 'You have inherited thirteen million francs!'

I didn't say anything. This time, it was the young lawyer who raised his eyebrows. He then asked the inspector to grant us a few days.

'In which case we'll have to detain Madame for a couple of days,' said the inspector, as he showed us the judge's orders.

I was confused and felt I was slowly slipping into a hole. I began to think of Saeed and Ezzedin but was advised not to mention that I suspected anyone. So when the inspector told me that I could lodge a complaint, and that by signing a paper I could prompt the search for the murderers of my father, I declared that I knew nothing and had no complaints. I then had either to give in to a few hours of questioning or go to jail. The thought of going to jail, which Janine had helped me avoid six years earlier, terrified me. The lawyer had a word with Mahmoud and when he returned he mentioned to me that I had no choice in the matter and must go through with the inquiry, but that I should be cautious in my responses.

It was hard to retell a story I so badly wanted to forget: I had to open the parcel that had my nightmares wrapped inside. I talked, my lawyer wrote and I signed: tens of pages, and it was over by the afternoon. By then, Houshang, the Empress's nephew, had also joined us. The noise in the corridors had died down. My main concern was my embarrassment at putting Mahmoud through all this. I once even asked him not to stay, but the Empress had sent him to take me back to St Cloud.

Some time in the afternoon Mahmoud Khan asked Établissement Gaspard to provide the bail of twenty million francs the inspector had demanded. Their representative turned up and my lawyer questioned the necessity of such a large sum. The public prosecutor, who had by then joined us as well, offered some explanation. When we were returning to St Cloud I had a pain in my midriff and was tired. I was right in thinking that Janine and the Empress were anxiously waiting for me. While on the road I kept asking myself why the monster had to come all the way to Paris to die. I found it hard to believe that he had a guilty conscience and regretted his shameful deeds, and now wanted to find his only daughter to see her before dying. How egocentric of him to assume that, not having looked him up all those years and having ignored his pleas, I was now going to put it all behind me; that by paying him a visit his conscience was going to be saved from suffering in the last days of his life and that I was going to exude affection. I could be and wanted to be of service to a great many, to help better their lives. For that evil being, however, I was not prepared to spare a single moment, even if millions of francs, with which I could be leading a comfortable and peaceful existence, were coming my way as a result. Perhaps his wealth had actually become a burden to him, who knows?

I was confident that Saeed, whom the monster had taken for a prince and was so proud to have as his son-in-law, had strangled the wretched soul when he had no strength left. I told myself that if that monster had been in Saeed's shoes he would have done the same.

The following week the court was in session and I was anxious. After having put a number of documents together my lawyer had been to St Cloud the previous day. He had presented each of them in the Empress's office and was confident that we were going to win the case. The Empress was up earlier than usual on that day to say some prayers, and then I passed under the Holy Qur'an seeking the Lord's protection. I suddenly remembered Nanny and the last days together in Tehran: whenever Mother had donned her *chador* to leave the house she had murmured some prayers and blown left and right. I had seen Father Wilfred the day before and confessed that when Saeed had said he was going to make the devil suffer I had experienced a pleasant feeling. As a matter of fact, I had had no other choice but to concede to Saeed's proposal. However, I couldn't help feeling happy about it. Father listened to me with kindness.

'You want to say that you decided to take your revenge, and didn't believe that there was a God.'

'No Father, I did believe there was a God. When I saw my father yearning on the hospital bed I was confident he was paying for the pains he had brought on my mother; however, I could not keep my vengefulness at bay.'

'So you set one against the other.'

I hesitated; this was the reality. At the end of our meeting Father Wilfred stood up, patted me on the back and said that he was confident I was not guilty, hence in no danger, and he asked me to believe in what he said.

When we entered the courtroom, the first person I caught sight of was Father Wilfred, who looked confident; he had come to prove what he had said to me. He wanted to say that I should lean on the righteous Lord, but it was hard. The judge and the public prosecutor called me twice to the witness box. Question after question I tried to keep calm. My lawyer had brought with him some documents, including the power of attorney that I had signed, and the evidence of the representative of Établissement Gaspard and the Armenian dealer, who looked even more anxious than I did. The climax was when my lawyer asked Father Wilfred to go into the witness box. In response to the first question he began a sermon that I wish I had had a means of recording word for word.

He spoke of a little girl who had fled a father's tyranny only to be embraced by her destiny, where God had been her only guardian. The devil had reached me at the onset of my youth and he had, with utmost deviousness, sucked my entire wealth. Then he spoke of his own experience of the day I arrived at the convent and of the devil's last strike. Throughout his speech the judge, the jury and all my family who had come from St Cloud were listening intently and there was no other sound, except for my quiet weeping. At the end of his speech Father Wilfred addressed the judge and said that he was confident and had no doubt that the court was going to find me innocent since this was God's promise: that the innocent experienced short-lived punishment yet the outcome was victory.

At the end of his sermon, as though he were in church, he read out verses of the Bible demonstrating that God in His mercy did not leave the most innocent of the innocent alone on the cross. I could not help my tears; it hardly mattered to me what the verdict was going to be. When he was returning to his seat, Father Wilfred turned his compassionate glance on me as though to reassure me. And I *was* reassured: I suddenly had a newfound courage that had not been there previously, and I believed that even if the judge passed a harsh sentence I would not be harmed.

While awaiting the verdict, Janine whispered in my ear that Jacques had not been allowed inside and that he was waiting outside to embrace his auntie. Alain Terres and a young man called Jean Jaurès, who were literary critics and wrote short stories, were both in the courtroom. More excited than them was Clara, André Malraux's wife, whom I had come to know recently and with whom I had formed a close friendship. Ever since they discovered that I was Iranian, she and her husband had kept in touch. They always had something to say about their visit to Iran and enthusiastically described Esfahan, which Malraux was passionate about. I felt embarrassed that, despite being Iranian, I had never been to the city they talked about.

By the time the courtroom bell rang, Clara whispered in my ear her regret that André was in Spain at the time.

'I am certain he would have written an article about you.'

She, too, was transfixed by what Father Wilfred had said about the story of my life.

When the judge announced my innocence, I first heard Janine's scream and then Clara shouting: 'Long live justice!'

I was, however, sworn in to attend as witness should the police find Saeed and Ezzedin, the main suspects in the murder inquiry. I didn't know whether I really wanted that day to come.

A reporter approached me. I did not have to see Mahmoud biting his lip to realise that I had to avoid any publicity surrounding the former Iranian imperial family.

Retelling my life had rekindled a certain resentment in me, which was apparent when I went to see the representative of the Iranian Embassy. He asked whether I preferred my father to be buried somewhere respectable in a specific cemetery and whether I was prepared to undertake the expenses.

'Wherever,' was all I had to say.

I struggled not to say anything worse; even his death had caused me torment.

I still remember the man with a squint in his eyes and a pipe in the corner of his mouth. I saw him a few nights later in La Coupole. He was quite sharp. Clara Malraux had told him about the case. 'Jean Paul Sartre,' he introduced himself as. He wanted to know what I had dreamed of at night. I described the dream I had had after the first day of the hearing. In my dream I saw the pool in my childhood house and the cedars. I was sitting by the pool and while Nanny kept an eye on me I put my feet in the water. The monster, dressed in his military uniform and boots, was swimming and roaring with laughter, but somehow his clothes were not wet. He swam back and forth or jumped into the pool from the edge. The surface of the water was covered in water lilies and he plunged among them yet managing to emerge intact. For a moment I saw his reflection on the water but he wasn't boisterous any more. His moustache was twisted at the ends and he had a black knitted garment on. I could now see his twin, who also had a black garment on, and who was twisting around the monster's feet like the vine of the passion flower.

The monster shot at his feet and roared with laughter and then started beating his twin with a sword, but he couldn't release himself and he was pulled to the bottom. His twin was now laughing away. He kept him down until there was no movement. He then pushed him down further with his boots: the monster's boots were stuck, but he pushed him further until he finally passed through and then emerged from within the well. He didn't actually emerge but his lifeless body floated to the surface of the water. I was looking at him from above. Nanny was careful that I did not fall into the well. In the water I saw the smiling image of a thin girl with golden hair. She was *my* shadow and twin. In my dream everyone had twins who looked like plants. The monster's twin had morning glory twisted around his feet. *My* twin was a cedar or a spruce with its golden branches and needles spreading its shade over me.

Sartre wrote my dream down. He wrote everyone's dreams down. The dream was a chapter of my life but I wonder if the same applies to everyone else.

CHAPTER 56

A week after the court case the Empress asked me to take leave from work and accompany her to Germany for a summer break. I knew her intention was to relieve me from my nightmares and help me get back to normal. I enjoyed our trip, not because I could once again benefit from the luxuries of an aristocratic life – which meant staying in magnificent hotels and seeing the best of what there was – but because I was with my own kind and close to her. I could once again find my identity. Despite all that I had been through, and despite having become acquainted with the French artistic and intellectual scene, I still felt I needed a mother to rest my head on her knee from time to time, and when the Empress said, 'Yes, my darling,' which she always did, I was filled with a pleasant feeling.

Like Shah Baba, the Empress liked bathing in mineral waters for their healing properties to boost her physical strength. Every year she spent a month in the resorts of Baden Baden, Karlsbad or Marienbad. This was a costly visit, as the many family members who lived at St Cloud always looked forward to the event and accompanied her.

We were driven in four cars, the Empress's magnificent Packard with its collapsible roof leading the way. André sat in the front and heard the Empress's instructions through the intercom system. The Packard always attracted French attention, just as the imperial carriage had done back in Tehran – except that André had replaced Heidar Beig and there was a steering wheel rather than reins.

Every now and then we would stop in a place of scenic beauty or for inspections at the borders. My aunt had everyone's papers and André would get off to present them. On seeing her haughtiness and 'Her Majesty' endorsed on her passport, the guards would salute her. Whenever we stopped, be it for inspection or to eat something, André would get off and open the door and my aunt would descend graciously. The hoteliers and restaurant owners, in the hope of receiving a handsome tip, exaggerated their curtsies. At the onset of our journey, however, when we passed over Pont Mirabeau, I turned my face so that my friends and fellow Party members did not recognise me. I had become a member of Parti Populaire Français (PPF) and enjoyed hob-nobbing with artists and intellectuals. I was there when Jaques Doriot announced the inauguration of his Party with his mesmerizing speech. I even once invited Doriot to *Noruz* celebrations in St Cloud when he was mayor of St Denis. I sensed that I was gaining respect in the eyes of my aunt.

As soon as we arrived in Luxembourg we dined and spent the night in a hotel. Early the next day, before we drove to Wiesbaden, the Empress asked me to get in the Packard as she needed to talk to me. I didn't think she was going to break bad news; nevertheless, I was anxious.

'Please ask Michel to come to Berlin during our two-day visit.'

I knew this was Janine's doing; after all, it was she who had insisted that I should accept Michel's proposal. When Michel was in Paris he had proposed again with his usual reserve, and I had rejected him. I hadn't seen him since but still received his letters fortnightly. Brigitte had mentioned to Janine, when they were in Paris last, that Michel couldn't look at anyone but me, and naughty Janine, my angel, must have explained everything to the Empress. I couldn't wait to see Janine. Despite myself, 'If you so wish,' left my mouth. I knew how much the Empress worried about my loneliness and my future. She wanted to put things right, having gone wrong previously, and help me have a family of my own.

'You've learned to fuss like the French; why are you torturing this boy?'

I blushed, which seemed extraordinary for somebody my age, though whenever I conversed with the Empress I was once again the little girl in Odessa. I tried hard to open up to the Empress the way she wanted, so I began speaking of Michel, and by saying, 'I know,' a couple of times she showed me that she was aware of everything. When I said that Michel was three years my junior she laughed and with a tinge of sarcasm said: 'We'll ask him to grow older by ten years so that you don't feel uncomfortable.'

She then said that she wanted to bring the matter to a head in the course of our journey. I wanted to say that I was frightened and that I hated men. I wanted to remind her that Saeed, whom I had loved so much, and had been prepared to go to any lengths for, and for whom I had spent years longing, turned out to be such an evil creature. How could I now bring myself to trust someone else again? I wanted to say that I was enjoying my life as it was and didn't feel anything was amiss, but her reply surprised me.

'Aristocracy breeds corruption as a norm. Think of our own family, the Ottomans and the Romanovs: it was as though their palaces were built with cursed earth and stone. Just imagine how our own forebears acquired their wealth and power, and what exactly they achieved for their country. Bless your uncle; he didn't know anything beyond giving orders! Do you recall how helpless he became when he could no longer lean on his right-hand man, his military and the Cossacks? As though when one is born a king or prince there is no need to acquire knowledge and use one's brain. You've read so much history and know that the same applied to Louis and Marie Antoinette and the others: there is little space for intellect and ethics.'

I couldn't believe that it was my aunt, the Empress, talking; what she said sounded like what was said during the debates in highbrow circles in the Paris cafés. She had not read *The Outlaws* by Ernst von Salomon, neither had she heard about Maurice

Thorez and Doriot, yet she had managed to reach a similar conclusion from a completely different angle. But how? She had always lived in palaces and even when she had to wander around the world, she had done her best to recreate the same atmosphere, so it was odd now to hear her express such an opinion. She must have suffered. I tried to think back; the ten years spent in Istanbul, the Riviera, San Remo, Beirut and many other places. I thought of all that Saeed and Ezzedin had done. I wasn't sure whether she knew anything I didn't know.

'Perhaps you haven't realised in all these years how much I have tried to raise my children to be sensible individuals like everybody else. I believe it was God's will for the Cossacks to rise and for us to wander around to see the world and wake up. I have tried my best not to let my grandchildren become like us. I did everything to rid them of the ridiculous pride that one develops by living in palaces. And now let me tell you that I received calls from a number of people, including from our own family, who were after you. That includes the Aga Khan's son and Nour ed-Din, Sultan Abdul Hamid's grandson. But I was determined not to let you fall prey to another monster. If I die tonight and disappear from the face of the earth I want you to remember that in the class of princes and rulers, whether they have had their horns severed or not, most of them act like that bastard your father. May God punish him for his deeds! Or the other coward, who didn't even have claims to manhood!'

I felt the Empress was blaming herself for all the calamities I had encountered, but I felt I had only myself to blame. For the rest of our journey to Wiesbaden she tried to convince me that I wasn't as impoverished as I imagined: I owned two properties in Iran, both on the outskirts of Tehran. Her secretary attended to them and sent the revenues over.

'From your mother's wrapped bundle left in my charge, bless her soul, there still remain items which are left in a box in the Banque de Paris, and Mahmoud has the papers.'

Mahmoud travelled with his family in the car behind and, in the absence of the Empress's eldest sons, was the head of the family. In the Empress's absence, he was also to take charge of our group, which had not, after all those years, changed much with respect to the numbers. Although, after the financial hiccup the family had experienced with the 1929 crisis in America, one sensed my aunt's caution and restraint in everything she did, she never made it obvious. Thanks to Janine's generosity, the many years in the convent and in the basement, and having many a night gone to bed on an empty stomach, I imagined that having to 'swallow one's desires' was difficult yet bearable. I knew that some of the jewellery we had wrapped around ourselves as children when we were leaving Odessa had been sold over the years, but I was also aware of the riches deposited at the Banque de Paris, which made the running of St Cloud possible. And when the Empress referred to 'my remaining estate' she was effectively providing for me from her own inheritance. At the onset of my new life she wanted me to have respect and a pillar to lean on. I, however, did not wish to rely on jewels and monetary assets, nor did Michel. He once said that he considered love to be the greatest wealth. I mentioned this to the Empress and at the same time told her that I had heard many charming and alluring words from Saeed. I occasionally became so anxious that I felt I didn't have the strength to withstand the change of faces and removal of masks. I was hurt and preferred not to put my luck to the test once again.

Yet André was to call Michel and ask him to meet us in Berlin; keen for me to settle down, he was only too delighted to make the call to Berlin from Wiesbaden. Two days later a man was playing the piano in the lobby of the Kaiser Palace in Berlin when Michel bowed to the Empress and kissed her hand. The Empress, her sister and her two daughters-in-law looked at Michel intently while he responded to their questions in his comical French. He had charmed them. He seemed elated but

I couldn't help my apprehension and for the rest of the day I remained agitated. André was taking the entire scene in from a distance by the stairs and I was confident he was going to somehow find the means of giving Janine the news that very evening; I could even hear the angel scream in joy.

It took the Empress a while before she raised the issue of Michel's education and career. She already had the information but wanted to hear it from him. I knew that he had studied political sciences but I wasn't sure where he worked. When he said he worked in the research unit of the Ministry of Foreign Affairs, I suddenly remembered what I had heard about Hitler's research units during the debates in the cafés. I was rather hoping that Michel had found a post in a company or at a university. I had heard about the military discipline with which the German government operated and that it was the most organised in Europe. The French, and Europeans in general, were terrified when they spoke of the Nazis' fighting spirit. I remembered the 14 July celebrations two years earlier in Paris, and the thousands who had wanted to form a human shield at the Porte d'Orléans, and how riotous it had become. Although there was no mention of Hitler and Germany, everyone knew that 'fascism' was not just about Mussolini's crowd. I wondered whether Michel was a fascist. Even in France and among the enlightened there were pro-Nazi individuals. They welcomed discipline and the resultant progress, and considered France to be backwards due to a lack of social order and a legal framework.

In the course of that hour I heard my aunt speak like an experienced politician, which reminded me of the debates between Dariot and Gide. I hadn't forgotten how excited Jaques Dariot had been when he described the *Führer's* speech in Nuremberg. He had said that highly organised party activists, in their thousands and dressed in uniforms, had chanted melodious slogans and the atmosphere had been intoxicating. I had, around the same time, read Malraux's anti-fascist pamphlets and also those by Paul Eluard and André Breton, and when Clara Malraux had read them out she had been at fever pitch. My favourite writers and poets considered Nazism to be some wolf with sharpened teeth ready to swallow up humanity.

I went over the debates in my head while Michel dealt with my aunt's questions. This reticent and romantic young man didn't resemble Malraux's portrayal of the Nazis, nor did I find any connection between him and the 'intoxicating slogans' Dariot had described. He was sentimental yet rational, and though I had got to know him, I was never in love with him. I had never given him serious thought until we arrived at the Kaiser Palace Hotel.

The Empress asked whether he would ever consider moving to Paris and joining them in St Cloud. After a pause he replied, 'If you permit, the princess and I would have the honour of your Majesty's annual visits in Berlin.'

'Princess and I', as though he had long been waiting for such a day and now had found the circumstance opportune and was happy to attach himself to me like a safety-pin. It was clear to him that the meeting had resulted in an agreement. And I thought, Janine, the mischievous girl!

The Empress had effectively raised the question of future plans so that she knew where our home was going to be, and though Michel might not have been aware of her intentions, he had said what she wanted to hear. Perhaps her sole intention was for Michel to understand that I was no longer the poor student he had encountered years previously.

Two days later, the car, loaded with our luggage and gleaming thanks to André, was parked by the steps outside the hotel. Michel bowed to kiss the Empress's hand when he heard: 'Come to St Cloud in a month's time, as we have certain traditions that must be observed.'

But he first had to check his availability. The Empress nodded that she understood.

The Empress was bathing in the mineral waters and everyone else was busy doing different things. I sat on an armchair on the veranda with a book. It was useless to turn the pages as I was too preoccupied with the new life I was about to embark on. I was hardly young, and past events meant that I could not get excited enough for my heart to start racing. I had so far lived with a sense of revenge – from which I had managed to free myself during the two years in the convent – but love … I questioned myself whether I was ready to embark on a relationship with someone new, but couldn't work out the answer.

On the way back to St Cloud, the Empress asked me whether Michel was aware that he had to become a Muslim. He was, and had even mentioned it to me months before, at a time when there were no plans for us to get married.

During our month-long sojourn my future was decided. No one ever directly resorted to seeking my opinion, neither the Empress nor Michel. However, when we sat in a café in Berlin or when we strolled in Kaiser Strasse, he spoke about our beautiful future together. I mentioned to him a few times that I was not so sure about what we were embarking on, and every time he asked me not to repeat words which made him suffer. Instead, he invited me to think of the future. And when we were back in the grey Mercedes and pasing under the Brandenburg Gate, I was talking of the beauty of Berlin and he was proud to add: 'The most beautiful city in the world, which is going to become even more beautiful with your presence.'

'How do you know?'

'Wait till you see our home.'

I had seen his father's house and the bakery, and I had heard about the little house where he had lived years ago, not far from where Brigitte and Gerhard lived. However, it seemed he was talking about a better and larger place; perhaps a house more suited to his job. I hesitated to pry any further.

CHAPTER 57

A trip that was supposed to be just like every annual trip transformed my quiet life. It was hard to believe that fourteen years had passed since the day we had been received in the *hammam* at the Sultana's home just before I became Saeed Pasha's wife. Somehow I felt bigger events were pursuing me; once again, the entire universe was at work to ground me while I was suspended between Parc St Cloud and a large unseen house in Berlin. My aunt's proposed one month turned to four months but no one complained; Michel's reasons were always plausible to everyone in St Cloud. He had come to Paris as part of a group accompanying the German Foreign Secretary, Joachim von Ribbentropp. This was an official and important visit during which the Franco-German Treaty was signed. It was reported in all the French newspapers and was the talk of the town.

When Michel was escorted to St Cloud for an hour, everyone in the family felt proud and happy. He was driven in a large car which boasted the fluttering flag of the Reich on its bonnet. The officers remained on guard at the front gates. Michel bowed to my aunt and handed over a box intended for me. A smaller box inside revealed a gold ring mounted with diamonds. I decided to leave the present in the Empress's care as I still travelled on the bus to go to work on the Left Bank, where I spent the entire day in the gallery. The evenings were usually spent in the Champs-Elysées or Saint Michel participating in debates, or at the theatre or the cinema. It was hardly appropriate for me to wear such a ring.

The year 1939 was upon us and the terrible state of the economy had brought Paris, the capital of endless political and philosophical debates, to its knees. The majority of artists and intellectuals I met on a daily basis opposed Germany, particularly with the advent of the treaty signed by Hitler and Mussolini endorsing their unity. It also became clear who supported Franco. Anti-German slogans were everywhere by now and I had to keep my membership of the Parti Populaire and its views quiet and never mention anything about my support of Dariot. Malraux and many other French intellectuals were fighting against Franco on the Spanish fronts. Clara, by then my closest friend, was now living on her own in Avenue Montaigne, and Josette, whose affection for Malraux everyone was aware of, had moved in with him. Clara spent her days collecting money for the Spanish liberals and, in between, distributed anti-fascist pamphlets.

The year began with the fall of Barcelona and Franco's victory. The Italian fascists had now entered Albania. This was also the year that my marriage to Michel was to be formalised. A young diplomat at the German Embassy acted as messenger. My aunt was not prepared to alter the ceremony because of the critical situation in Europe and Germany. Brigitte, Garry and their children all came over to Paris, along with Michel's parents and sister, and on the last day of January, having had a heavy snowfall, we waited inside the mosque in Paris until Michel arrived. He had flown from Berlin and, because of bad weather, was delayed by a few hours. The sheikh observed the preliminary procedures, which meant Michel became a Muslim by reading verses from the Qur'an and adopted 'Maysam' for a name. I had never heard such a name but Michel found it agreeable; from then on, whenever he wrote to me, he signed his letters accordingly. After the religious ceremony we went to St Cloud to attend a small gathering to celebrate our marriage, and by midnight we arrived at our apartment in the magnificent Hotel George V, which the German Embassy had hired for the occasion.

I was forty and no man had so far become intimate with me. It was lunchtime the next day when I woke up to the sound of the bell. Looking through the windows, Paris looked as though dressed in a bridal gown. Before the servants could wheel the tray of breakfast in I looked at Michel's empty place in bed: he had left early in the morning and I still couldn't believe another page in my life had turned. There was a letter by the mirror signed 'Maysam'. The note was written with a refined tone, referring to me as 'My Mary'. He had written that he was happy that his patience had paid off and he thanked the Heavens for his good fortune. He had also written that he was reluctant but obliged to go; his heart was with me and he was counting the moments until he saw me again.

I had mixed feelings when I woke up that fine morning; for I began to remember the days when I had left Saeed in our house in the same city and gone away. Was the same thing going to happen again? I decided to leave it to the gods to decide; even if the same thing were to happen again I had no choice but to give in. In the interim I was to return to St Cloud. A formal wedding ceremony was to be held later – at the same time as *Noruz* – in my future home in Berlin. Waiting was something that I had spent a lifetime getting used to and it didn't seem to bother me any more.

The end of winter meant that my waiting was over as well. Most of my family from St Cloud managed to attend the large gathering at Kaiser Palace Hotel in Berlin. There were also a number of Michel's family, his colleagues and a few Iranians whose names were lost amid the noise and the music until years later when I remembered them. The Empress stayed in Berlin long enough to have lunch in my house, a large building through the windows of which the Brandenburg Gate and a statue of a German army commander were visible. Occasionally I felt unhappy when Michel was not in but, on the whole, everything heralded a pleasant beginning. Michel couldn't wait to see me at the end of the day and so I would wait for him until around midnight when I heard the car, followed by his arrival with a smile.

437

The Persian New Year was upon us and I had soaked some seeds so that I could have the *sabzeh* ready for the ritual marking the beginning of spring the following week. I had also laid out the *termehs* given to me by the Empress. My *Haft Sin* was ready when it all happened. As on most nights Michel did not come till very late. It was past midnight when he telephoned me to ask me to go ahead and have supper without him as he was going to be late. He spoke in such a way that I felt he was being listened to.

Fertisch, a relation of Michel's, helped me to improve my German. He accompanied me when I went shopping and helped me converse with the sales assistants using a mixture of French and German. I had a large radio in the salon, and I used to listen to music. I was listening to Wagner and eventually fell asleep. I must have been having a pleasant dream when I woke up to the sound of the door. It was getting light and Michel was loosening his tie. He seemed exhausted, which slowed his movements, but he had his usual smile. He would adopt my role at times and speak for me.

'How can you leave a beautiful princess alone in this quiet, cold house. Hope it doesn't happen again!' and we would both burst out laughing.

He whispered in my ear to set the alarm for two hours later so that he could get up and go to his office.

'Today is an important day, darling, and though I'm not meant to mention anything, I shall tell you, since you and I are one.'

I looked at him. The news that was so important at such an early hour was that the German forces were crossing the borders as we spoke and Czechoslovakia was going to surrender by noon. But nothing, not even something as important as the start of the Second World War, could mar our moments of happiness.

By the time I woke up, military tunes were being broadcast from the radio with news of the progress the Reich's army was making. Though I could not understand every word of the aggressive slogans, it reminded me of what I had heard in the anti-fascist gatherings in Paris. The words of Clara Malraux and the others began to parade in my mind; they said that fascism was not going to stop and would not contain itself within certain borders. It was threatening civilisations and was going to destroy human beings. I was anxious; by noon, when the telephone rang, my anxiety had escalated. My aunt was calling from Karlsbad and wanting to know whether it was true that Europe was going to be at war and whether it was wise for them to return to Paris. I knew it was Michel she was effectively putting the questions to. Fertisch was sitting at the table and looking at me. I asked the Empress to let me call her a few hours later. I was happy that I could be of some use in helping her make her decision; a decision of such importance for which my Michel had come in useful.

Fertisch finally managed to find Michel on the telephone. As soon as I mentioned the Empress, as though reading from a text he said: 'The Empress must return to her home. France is our ally and we Germans respect all our neighbours and our friends. She must not be influenced by enemy propaganda, and you, too, must prepare yourself for the Persian New Year.'

That was all he said; he then put the phone down. I called my aunt to pass on the message, feeling proud at being able to respond so immediately to her need, and from a reliable source. At the end I asked her to let me know if there was anything else I could do to help. She seemed to have overcome her anxiety and was going to make a move towards St Cloud, though the traffic was heavy and the situation difficult.

The following week we celebrated *Noruz*. According to my aunt's calculations, the Revelation would be in the afternoon of the twenty-first of March. Michel came home. He had brought me a present and I handed him one too: a pair of shoes and a belt. On the table I had placed a photograph of a little girl standing next to her mother, with Nezhat in one corner, along with a few daughters and granddaughters of Shah Baba. This photograph had been taken one afternoon in Golestan Palace and I still had a faint memory of that day. Looking at it then made it seem as though the people in the photograph belonged to a different century. How far I had come. How much older I had grown and what a distance I had travelled to come to this house where from the window I could see a gate on top of which there was a horsedrawn carriage! Was the time galloping away faster than ever? My happiness was so complete in that house that nothing seemed able to disrupt it. I read the lyrics of Hafez from time to time, a book that had come a long way with me and that had been temporarily lost in the basement in Madeleine until I found it. Hafez had also kept me company in the quiet days of the convent; how hard I had tried to translate the verses into French for Father Wilfred.

The days passed and I had nothing else to do except learn German. When I attended social events I was able to speak the same language as the German women and Michel's colleagues. By now I had also received my clothes and books from Paris. Every week I received a letter from Janine. I wrote to my aunt occasionally informing her of my well-being and happiness, which I knew would please her. Michel also arranged it so that I could speak to St Cloud a couple of times.

Some time in the summer Michel whispered in my ear that he was going to spend a few days somewhere close to Iran, my homeland. He left and I only learned about his final destination when I listened to the radio: the German–Soviet Treaty had been signed. I could now picture the tumult in the Parisian cafés and among the left-wing intellectuals, who had formed a united anti-fascist front with pictures of Lenin and Stalin hanging in their offices. What would they make of the news now? Michel burst out laughing. He had brought me a long white fur coat made with polar bear skins from Moscow, and when he opened the large parcel so that I could try my coat on, I said a phrase in German which I had practised.

'Why didn't you bring a Russian doll?'

'Would you have liked one?' he said immediately in Persian; a common Persian phrase that he would use charmingly.

'Not for me but for our children!'

There was a momentary silence; the same silence as in the German doctor's practice when I had heard the news, but Michel soon made such a show of emotion and was so excited that he forgot his usual diplomatic reserve and embraced the chubby maid, Anneh, and jumped up and down like a naughty little boy.

Doctor Friedrich had asked me to move about with care and avoid long journeys. I'd thought I was too old to have children. Indeed, when he heard this was my first pregnancy he repeated his precautionary recommendations. Michel would call me hourly from his office. How could a creature who had barely stepped into this world so transform the atmosphere? Michel was concerned that I should not hear exciting news and so he called on 3 September and asked Anneh whether the radio was on. Germany was at war with France and he didn't want me to hear it.

There was clamour near the borders: thousands of people had, upon hearing the news, begun to migrate; the very route we had taken from Paris to Berlin. When Michel broke the news late that afternoon, I couldn't help but think of my aunt. My heart was in Paris and I was anxious for Janine and her children.

Two days earlier, the German army had entered Poland. Every time Germany made progress people poured onto the streets singing the national anthem. The cafés of Berlin would fill with Germans drinking barrels of beer, and when their faces were completely suffused they would start cheering and dancing.

By the second *Noruz* in Berlin I was heavily pregnant, but my sole concern was the future of my aunt, Janine and her children; I had not received any news for some time. The last thing I'd heard was that they had gone to Spain to avoid the bombing of Paris. I was worried about the convoy, which had got used to being in a state of perpetual homelessness, and also about having to go to the hospital amid the busiest working period for Michel.

It was the day after the invasion of Holland and Belgium, to be precise. The Reich's army had reached Sedan and the radio constantly broadcast how delighted the French were to welcome the spring together with their German friends. I knew the French were not happy but I had to think about the baby that was going to step into our chaotic world. When her cry reverberated in the hospital room it was as though *I* was reborn. Having overcome the pain – which made me wish for death – it was all suddenly forgotten.

'Maryam has arrived,' Michel whispered to me; the very name he had written in his letter on the first night of our marriage.

Brigitte and her children, Michel's parents and many others came to the hospital, but I wished Janine and my aunt could be there as I knew how long they had waited for such a moment. I telegraphed the news to Paris and they finally managed to see the baby when she was six months old: I was holding her sitting next to Michel in the black Mercedes when we arrived in St Cloud.

When France surrendered, the war between the two countries was over; as a result, the barriers had been lifted and it was no longer an issue if I made calls to France. My aunt and her family had by then returned to St Cloud. In the course of the conflict German bombers had targeted factories in Boulogne and Billancourt. St Cloud was hit and the poor old warden, Papa Jean Pierre, was killed.

I followed the course of events from Berlin. Subsequent to his meeting with Hitler in Montoir, France's premier, Marshal Pétain, broadcast a message to the French people in which there was no mention of 'surrender', ignoring the arrival of Hitler in Paris. On his arrival in Paris Hitler went immediately to the tomb of Napoleon in Les Invalides, like a victorious commander. In his message Pétain spoke of the alliance with Germany heralding the end of hardship. I was happy to learn that the war was over, unaware what my French friends must be going through. Maryam had taken all my attention.

When I was driving through the spruces and walnut trees lining the road from Paris to St Cloud, I was sitting next to Michel holding Maryam to my chest. I remembered the day I had gone back to St Cloud after having left the convent in Neuilly in such disgrace. I then remembered the day I left my student life and returned to live there. Somehow, in St Cloud I was able to rid my mind of the memories of Odessa, our home in Istanbul, the villa in Nice and the house in Madeleine. It was as though I was born again in St Cloud. It was at this place that Jarozleski, Smirnoff and even a few Russians had conversed in Persian; it was here that we had celebrated *Noruz*, the bonfire on *Charshanbeh Souri*, the last night of the Persian year, and *Sizdeh Bedar*, the first day of a new year. Every year a cleric would arrive from Karbala and we spent the ten days of Muharram mourning the martyrdom of Hussein and Hassan, the Shia saints. We regularly received parcels from Iran containing food, saffron, caraway seeds and dried herbs. Alas, the backyard of Soltan's was no more, and Nezhat? Nor did Ebrahim and Zahir deliver pamphlets, and there were no monsters ... Then my memory was jogged as though a chain had been tugged. I would eventually come up with the picture of the monster and I trembled. I found it hard to believe that I led a happy life with Michel and Maryam and that there were no monsters. I suddenly became anxious that perhaps ...

Everyone in St Cloud rushed towards us to see Maryam. She was passed from hand to hand until she was brought to the salon in the principal building and into the arms of the Empress, who whispered some prayers into her ear. She stretched her arm under her armchair and out came a small velvet pouch, which was then pinned to the collar of my daughter's cardigan. I was familiar with the necklace. It had come from the safety deposit box and was Esfahani work with two sparkling emeralds.

I spent a week in St Cloud but Michel went to work every day. He also spent a day in Belgium. I decided to see my friends so I left Maryam in Janine's care one day and went to the gallery. Coming into contact with occupied France, where the German soldiers strolled on the streets, felt strange. The people's hatred of the occupiers was predictable but I don't know why I had never thought about it. The headlines in the papers announced the execution of Jacques Ponset of the French Resistance. It was the first execution by the Germans and the Vichy government did not react. The French were shaken; the crime of Ponset – according to my colleagues in the gallery – was that he and his men had planned to sabotage the railway line.

The French were experiencing the bitter taste of surrender, and up to then it had never occurred to me that being married to a German meant that I was alienated even from my closest friends. I fancied going to the Café de la Paix with two of my colleagues from the gallery. It was raining and the gramophone in the café was playing a mellow tune. Though I was in the Paris I knew, the atmosphere was full of gloom and bewilderment, and I was to taste it first-hand when we were having lunch in the café. I suddenly saw Clara Malraux arrive with two other women and as soon as I saw them I leapt with joy. 'Clara!' I had written two letters to her from Berlin and I could now find out why she had not bothered to respond.

She looked at me for a moment.

'I see that the German beef has done wonders,' she said in a tone devoid of any emotion.

It was true. I had gained weight since my pregnancy, but I found her tone sarcastic. To my chagrin, she had assumed that Michel belonged to the Gestapo. I reassured her that he didn't.

One of the other women chimed in: 'But when we kill them it doesn't make any difference to which office they belong! They walk hand in hand with Hitler and that makes them fascists, meaning assassins, meaning ...'

She had arrived together with Clara and had straight hair piled up under her beret. Her tone was harsh, quite unbecoming for such a finely built woman. I couldn't bear such impudence and the threat directed at my Michel. I was about to respond but couldn't; instead, I got up and returned to our table.

I had an even harder time with André. I knew he belonged to the Communist Party but, bearing the union of Hitler and Stalin in mind, I had never imagined that he might think like the idealist French intellectuals. I never thought he would be such a ruthless judge of people.

'Oh *ma chère princesse*, I only wish Monsieur Michel were not a German working for Hitler.'

'But André ...'

'I know you, and I know Monsieur Michel a little. Please don't say anything. You were not the decision-maker and neither was Monsieur Michel. Life has placed us on opposite sides.'

'Why oppose each other? Why André? Janine, please say something ...' I felt helpless. Janine took Maryam from her husband and, while holding her tightly to her chest, chose to fix her gaze on me with tearful eyes. She was in no better state than me. Jacques however ... Janine's eldest son had cared for and sympathised with me in my darkest hours ever since he was a child, and I was his 'dear auntie'. It no longer seemed to matter that I had once upon a time parted with the meagre funds that I had in my possession, depositing them in a bank account in his and his brother's names. At night he had slept next to me in the modest *chambre de bonne* in St Michel, and despite his tender age he had tried to console me. He was now eighteen but looked much older in his scarf and hat. When he arrived he saw me in the drawing room sitting with his parents.

'I shall go to work soon and reimburse you for the loan so that I can tell you without embarrassment that I resent every German alive!'

'Jacques!' Janine roared like a lion.

I felt my entire being was suddenly filled with sorrow. I got up so that André could take me back to St Cloud. I decided never to return to Paris again. Damn the war and those seeking power, who had turned my angels against me, I told myself.

CHAPTER 58

'Not returning to Paris' was wishful thinking; we were in Paris when we celebrated Maryam's third birthday. Michel was no longer a mere employee of the Ministry of Foreign Affairs and was overloaded with work. He was now a managing director in charge of all French-speaking countries. Michel was informed of his new posting while we were living in Brussels. We'd been assuming we were to return to Berlin after a year, but Michel came home one day looking quite excited and announced that he was going to work in Paris. Though we had never quarrelled before – he always gave in to me in the end – we had a heated discussion that day. I had never disclosed to him what had gone on during our last visit to Paris, and now it was difficult to reveal to him the reasons behind my reluctance to go to a city where my family and friends were. Michel was staring at me with his blue eyes and wanted to know what lay beneath it all.

'It is difficult to live in a city where people dislike us, and how are we going to protect ourselves?'

'Surely your friends can't be more patriotic than Pétain ...' Sitting next to me he was calm. 'The situation is very different from what it was two years ago. The French have come to appreciate the benefits of uniting with Germany. They don't want to waste their lives in Stalin's camps and are aware that once the last mission has been accomplished and Russia has fallen we'll have a better world, without the Zionists or communists.'

Perhaps it was his love rather than his logic which convinced me to put my anxiety aside. I could not let him go on his own so

I had no choice. I just hoped that he was right and that everything would work out according to plan. After all, not all our French friends were like Clara.

My second child was due to be born in two months; as soon as we arrived in our home in Avenue Foche I had to rest. Our house was large, with five bedrooms, and there were a number of tall spruces and poplars in the garden. A nanny and a maid were employed on our arrival. But we had barely settled in when two German officers were shot; one died on the spot and the other lost his eyesight. The papers only touched on the incident. I learned the details when I was resting, something I had to do a great deal. I overheard our nanny speaking to the man who came over to clean the house. I was not going to mention anything to Michel to begin with, but then I decided there was hardly any difference between Michel and the one who had been killed. What if tomorrow … I shuddered at the thought.

I was carrying a creature that moved and kicked from time to time and I couldn't afford to get emotional, but, given the news, it was impossible not to be anxious. The fact that there were two armed German guards stationed just outside our home didn't alleviate my anxiety either.

Janine and André came to see us the day after we arrived. André was visibly agitated by coming to a house which belonged to a German, particularly a high-ranking one, but he had come for my sake and for Maryam's, whom he adored. So when he said that he had to run an errand for the Empress I was not surprised. Janine, however, was so patient and kind that she treated Michel as usual.

My aunt and her family were now living in Fontainebleau and Janine worked for them only a couple of hours a day. A few families were still living in St Cloud. After the outbreak of war between Germany and Russia, the Russians in my aunt's entourage left France and my aunt had to make do with fewer people in Fontainebleau. André, however, was still in charge of the Packard. The first question that sprang to my mind as soon as Janine arrived was about Jacques. Janine's eldest son was so dear to me that I had put his abrupt manner during my last visit down to his youth. I had brought him some clothes from Brussels and I wanted to hand them to him personally, but he had gone to Marseille, to his aunt.

Janine came over the following day to take me to Fontainebleau. When we sat in the black Mercedes I found her exceptionally depressed; it didn't take long to find out the reason since she was not a good liar. She was holding my arm as we walked slowly around the grounds of the mansion in Fontainebleau. She mentioned to me that Jacques had joined the Resistance. I was terrified since he was still a mere child as far as I was concerned: though he was twenty, he was still *le petit* Jacques. Later that evening I found myself telling Michel how much I liked Jacques, his intelligence and how he had cared for me when I was in trouble.

I felt my aunt had suddenly aged. She also seemed heavier than ever. She was firm but kind as always. The arrival of the Allies in Iran made for exciting news since it had jeopardised Reza Shah's position. Muhammad Hassan had become active at the prospect of the return of the Qajars to the throne and the recovery of what had been lost to the clutches of Reza Khan for the past sixteen years. Muhammad Hassan was in London at the time and couldn't visit because of the occupation. My aunt was now wondering if Michel could do something. She was also using the subject of revenue from my properties in Iran as a pretext to give me some money, but I asked her to hold on to it as I did not particularly need the money at the time. We had no expenses and Michel's income was sufficient. The government paid for our lodgings and our expenses were taken care of.

I felt embarrassed at having to lie on the sofa and my aunt was particularly careful to ensure that unpleasant matters should not be discussed, but it was not so easy to control everyone else. One cousin believed that with the Americans joining the Allies German victory was highly unlikely. Mahmoud believed that America was a wealthy country and, had it not been for the Pearl Harbor incident, would never have joined in. With Germany, Italy and Japan declaring a state of war with America, Churchill, 'the rascal' – he always referred to the British Prime Minister as the rascal – had reached the outcome he wanted. Britain was fighting alongside the Russians and using Iran to transport artillery. I was learning for the first time that earlier, in Washington, twenty-six countries had united against Germany.

When I mentioned some of the discussion to Michel later that evening he asked me what my aunt and her family thought of Germany now that they knew what the British had been up to. I said that a German victory was desirable because they neither liked the communists nor the British.

He laughed and said, 'I know, pity we couldn't convince Berlin.'

This came as a surprise as I never knew Michel had been involved with current affairs in Iran. I even discovered that the Iranians – the ones who attended our wedding reception – were anti-Pahlavi, and that, at the time, Hitler was busy conducting negotiations with them in order to set up a pro-German government to succeed Reza Khan's.

Michel got into his civilian clothes and then explained that when the allies had invaded Iran on 25 August the previous year, he had made several trips to Berlin to try and bring the Qajars to his superiors' attention. Though some had favoured the idea of promoting them, the *Führer* felt Reza Shah was a trustworthy ally and would withstand the enemy. It was unusual for Michel to discuss his work but he was being humorous now.

'I tried to return you to the imperial palace so that perhaps I, *too*, could become an aristocrat!'

'But I prefer our home in Berlin.'

Aware that the conversation was about to enter sensitive ground, he touched my swollen belly and asked, 'So when is this prince going to make an appearance?'

'You've always said that you are an ordinary citizen. How can you now expect to have a prince for a child?'

'No matter what you say, he is still going to be noble, like you.'

I told myself how happy Michel would be if we had a son, which prompted me to make a *nazr*. Should we have a son, I had always wanted to call him Ali – as far as we Shias were concerned, it was Ali who should have succeeded the Prophet Muhammad.

We were still talking about the same issues the following day when the telephone rang in the evening. We had got used to Michel being summoned late at night. Now that I could understand some German I could tell it was not good news, but he tried to appear calm.

He approached me and said, 'Your family are in trouble,' and before I had time to become anxious, he explained that my aunt's nephew, Houshang, was discovered to have been involved with the Resistance and had been detained.

Houshang had remained by my side during the court case involving the monster's murder. I was now concerned for him. I asked Michel what was to become of the poor man.

He seemed indifferent, 'But wasn't it André who said when the Gestapo suspect someone and get hold of him they execute him? Well then, Houshang's fate is quite clear!'

I knew he was teasing me but I couldn't help my anxiety, particularly as he was aware of André's sentiments.

When the telephone rang Michel joked, 'It must be for the princess!'

He had guessed the call must be from Fontainebleau and so passed the receiver to me. My aunt wanted to know how she was going to face her sister. I glanced at Michel; he was still beaming. I reassured her that I would ask Michel to deal with the matter.

Houshang was released the next day and we were subsequently invited to dinner in Fontainebleau. I knew the idea was to thank Michel but I was not so sure I could participate. Michel had to attend many social events without me because of my confinement and that evening, which turned out to be quite eventful, was no exception.

The doorbell rang and the guard informed the nanny that two ladies had come to see me. I said I was not expecting anyone, but was told Janine wanted to speak to me.

'Indeed, do show her in,' I said in haste.

I propped myself against the pillow wondering what could have brought Janine to our house at that hour of night in occupied Paris where pedestrians were stopped at random and asked for their identity papers. I couldn't think who the other woman might be. When they arrived in the room Janine looked quite pale. The other woman had covered her head with a rather large, thick scarf, which made it difficult to see her face. Janine had barely arrived when she asked me in the broken Persian she had managed to pick up from us over the years to ask the nanny to leave the room. As soon as the nanny left she threw herself at me and started weeping. They were after Jacques.

'The Gestapo are going to arrest him!'

She was trembling. I embraced Jacques who looked comical in the woman's outfit.

'My dear boy, whatever have you done?'

He was quite composed when he spoke.

'Auntie, they have killed my friends,' but he didn't seem fearful at all.

I knew to whom he was referring by 'they'.

I was a little impatient. 'What have you done?'

He dropped the scarf and I noticed that his lips were bruised, and once he had described everything I realised how troubled he was: they had recognised him and had gone to search for him at his place. They couldn't find him and were now looking for him.

Janine was tearful. 'Can we spend the night here? I shall take him to Normandy tomorrow.'

I felt sick with anxiety. Why did I ever come to Paris? I should have known I could never have a peaceful life here. Michel was aware of my close friendship with Janine. He even knew how attached I was to her children, Jacques in particular, but would he be able to do something? Janine begged me not to mention a word to Michel, but how could I not?

By the time Nanny returned, Jacques had the scarf on again. She had brought some coffee.

So that she did not suspect anything I said to Janine, 'Why don't you spend the night here? Both you and your daughter,' then I rose with difficulty and showed them to their room upstairs. I was speaking Persian now, 'Don't worry,' and I told myself that perhaps it was best to pretend I was asleep rather than lie to Michel or keep it secret, but by the time I heard a car in the garden I felt such a sharp pain that I was in agony.

Michel was in the bedroom removing his shoes when I screamed and then let myself fall on the bed. He rushed towards me, lifted my head and called Maryam's nanny. She appeared in her nightgown. He then grabbed the telephone and made a call to the military hospital, before helping me to get dressed, but I insisted that I was all right.

'My doctor said that I was going into labour next week so why the hospital?'

My sole concern at that moment was Janine and Jacques, who were in the room above.

Michel came and sat next to me and sent the nanny to check on Maryam.

'Don't worry about your guests,' he whispered.

I looked at him and he soothed me with his smile.

'They should stay here for a couple of days.'

Janine was now coming down the stairs. My angel couldn't bear hiding in the room while I was in pain.

'Please help her get ready and don't bother waking your daughter up. Stay in your room until I return.'

My head was resting on his shoulders. I felt Michel was the most reliable person in the world. I knew how precarious his position was with Jacques' presence in our home. I would have kissed his reliable hands had it not been for Janine's presence. The pain, however, had doubled me up. We heard the sound of a car outside. Michel said it was time to leave. He was just about to put my shoes on when we heard a knock. Michel gestured to the nanny to open the door. Two men were standing at the threshold. They were not wearing uniform. 'Gestapo' was the only thing I heard and then didn't feel anything any more. Everything was dark …

'Where …?' It was as though my voice was coming from the bottom of a well. 'Where am I? Michel?'

I could just about work out the white shadows, and among them I could distinguish some faces, but nothing was familiar. I opened my eyes but the light disturbed me. I could now hear voices around me and finally heard Michel's. I reached out and a hand held mine. I called for Michel. He responded with love. Tears started rolling down my cheeks. His hand was now touching my hair.

'My princess …' he said; he sounded tearful.

I touched my tummy but there didn't seem to be anything inside.

I struggled to say something. 'Michel, where is our son?'

There was silence.

Then I heard a couple of people converse in German, 'Anaesthetics …'

Janine and I both lost our sons on 4 May 1942, and it took us three days to find out. The Gestapo had killed them both. A year later we were both standing by Jacques' grave. Maryam insisted that Auntie Janine should not cry. Madeleine Cemetery was only a few hundred metres away from Rue Pasquier where I had met Janine for the first time, something she reminded me of when we were leaving the cemetery.

CHAPTER 59

There is nothing like war for revealing the heights and depths of human nature. The events of that night of 4 May brought us even closer than before: Michel, our daughter and I became inseparable from André, Janine and Christina. My infant son, whom we referred to as Ali, and Jacques, who had shivered in his mother's clothes as he was dragged away at the hands of the two Gestapo agents, were gone and nothing but love could fill their empty places. That is why, when Paris was being bombed, Michel decided to take us, along with our small suitcases, to André's house. He wanted to leave us there and flee a city in turmoil. Maryam and I had spent the previous two nights in Fontainebleau. When Paris was bombed my aunt asked Michel to help her obtain permission for her and her family to leave for Switzerland. Michel had even travelled to Berlin, but von Ribbentropp had rejected the request. Instead, he wrote to my aunt that no member of the Qajar family was subject to the same mandate as the other Iranians and the French, as they were not considered the enemy.

'But the German bombers are not going to read von Ribbentropp's mandate when they are about to drop their bombs,' was my aunt's response.

The turn of events, however, changed everything at a much faster pace than either Hitler or von Ribbentropp had imagined: the Allies arrived in Normandy by the summer and the Germans began to evacuate Paris. With the Nazis' departure in early August it was not safe to remain in the house in Avenue Foche, and when the

Germans surrendered in Paris on 25 August 1944, we were stuck. I did not want Michel to turn himself in as I had seen how the Germans and French collaborators were treated. We therefore sought refuge in Fontainebleau, but my aunt and her entourage were not immune either; their two Czech servants, having failed to blackmail their wealthy employers, informed the cleansing committee that their masters had been friendly with the Germans and Gestapo, and they poured in one evening. They were all young and armed. Michel, Maryam and I were on the top floor at the time.

'We must search everywhere and take everyone away,' shouted the young man with a cigarette in between his lips and a beret on his head.

I was shocked, and my poor aunt, by now very overweight, looked stunned. I had never seen a stronger and more level-headed person in the most trying of situations. To see her in that state was depressing.

Mahmoud stepped in, having adopted the role of head of the family. 'But my dear boys, you had no right to enter this place. This house belongs to the Iranian Embassy, which effectively means we are on Iranian soil, and therefore have immunity.'

Michel beamed upon hearing this fabrication. We all knew it was a bluff but it was said with such assurance that the men seemed convinced. The *Ministère des Affaires Étrangères* decided not to take any risks given the chaotic state of the country, and the youth militia put the telephone down on hearing they had to leave the house. Mahmoud, however, believed they would soon return and that it was not sensible for us to stay there.

Driving in a car flying the Iranian flag we passed by the Champs-Elysées, which looked jubilant despite the chaos, and there were celebrations taking place on every corner as we drove towards Janine's place.

Michel, standing in the middle of the hallway, asked André and Janine to look after me and Maryam. Janine was staring at André, who was watching us with a gun in his hand. When he saw

Janine's imploring expression he marched firmly to the door and closed it.

He then told Michel, 'Please come in,' somehow managing to bring himself to take in a German family.

Two days later, we were sitting in a van driving to the German border. We were carrying papers which identified us as Janine, André and Christina. Michel had to speak as little as possible so that no one heard his accent, and Janine and I had dyed his hair brown. Before we said goodbye, I left some jewellery and gold – my meagre valuable possessions – with Janine. I then concealed a few items around my body. I didn't know whether I was going to see Janine again and I tried to swallow my tears so that Maryam did not notice anything.

A week of hiding in a room had destroyed Michel's spirit; he repeatedly decided to turn himself in and relieve everyone from the burden.

'Why should I trouble André and Janine since they dislike the Germans so much?'

I made an imploring gesture to Janine and André to stop him. They did not really have to wait for me to ask, as they would not have let him go anyway. Nothing made an impact as much as what Janine said to Michel: 'You, too, put yourself in danger; that night ...'

She wanted to say that he had given her and Jacques shelter in his home but she could not.

Michel, however, heard it and said with embarrassment, 'But what was the point?'

Then she revealed for the first time what Michel had said on that mournful evening of 4 May. As soon as the guards had been informed, Michel had returned home immediately; he had already known about Janine's presence at home before arriving. He even knew the identity of the other woman.

'But the guards had no reason to call the Gestapo in. In the days that followed I was summoned twice by the Gestapo to be questioned, but the trust that von Ribbentropp and Hitler personally held in me meant I wasn't caught.'

'You did what you had to do.'

'But what you are doing now is a hundred times more than I managed to do then. I don't know whether I'll ever be able to repay you. I hope you are not going to be harmed.'

The van arrived and we got in. Janine handed me a bag with some food for Maryam and then she hugged her tight. She was still standing there as the van turned the corner and I lost sight of her, my anxious angel.

It took us three days to reach Strasbourg. Vast numbers of people were following the same route on carts, horses and in decrepit cars. Our identity papers were sufficient to get us to the border. From there on we did not need fake identities: we were Germans in German territory. We had sent a message across to Brigitte and Gerhard. If they received it they would meet us in Karlsruhe, but it wasn't as simple as we had imagined. Throughout the journey across France, Michel was silent for fear that his accent would reveal his true identity, so I had to do all the talking. The driver had come to know us as a couple who had no interest in politics. I had told him that André, aka Michel, was a gardener in St Cloud and was not feeling very well and as a result spoke little. I was in the business of selling pictures and we were on our way to my parents in Switzerland. Apparently our driver had used the same route to drive a number of wealthy Jews over to Switzerland and he explained to us how to cross the border.

Michel and I could talk to each other only when we got off the van from time to time. He kept saying that if he were caught I should go to our house in Berlin. I knew his parents' address. He felt Maryam and I would be safe and his parents would look after us. I, on the other hand, was concerned for him and wanted to see him cross the border with us. Back in the van we would keep quiet, and when I called her Christina, Maryam would wink.

We had to divert from our route and spend the night in Dijon. The town had been bombed an hour before and was still burning. Pockets of resistance were still firing aimlessly. We were shaken to see the execution of Germans and collaborators in every town or village we passed through. I was exhausted but couldn't afford to fall asleep as I was in charge of my husband and daughter. The driver said that he had a cousin who lived in Dijon and he was going to look for her place so that we could spend the night in her house.

We drove by a great many ruins, with groups of people shouting and wailing, until we reached the house, but the only section left intact was its garage. The woman didn't seem able to help us, but when she saw Maryam sleeping in her father's arms she reluctantly allowed us to spend the night in the garage, while she went to a friend's house.

We found a radio and Michel was keen to listen to Radio Berlin but he was concerned that the sound might be heard so changed his mind. Instead, I listened to the French news and heard de Gaulle's voice accompanied by patriotic anthems. General de Gaulle had arrived in Paris the previous day and had gone to the Champs-Elysées. The French people welcomed him as a hero. According to the reporter, the crowds stretched from the Arc de Triomphe to the Grand Palais. I could just picture how happy my French friends would be and I wondered what Clara was up to. I had not had any news of my colleagues in the gallery for some time.

No matter how hard it was, Michel stuck his ear to the radio at night and managed to listen to the *Führer*'s voice. Hitler invited people to persevere, informing them that life had become difficult for the British and that the Jews and capitalists were collaborating. It was so cold I couldn't sleep. I was terrified and shook with every sound. We had huddled together so that we could talk amid the furniture in the garage.

'Michel, is it true?'

'What, my darling?'

'The gas chambers?'

In the past two months I had been hearing about the chambers and for me this was no longer the casual, unfounded discussion of intellectuals in the Parisian cafés. While en route the driver had described these and, according to him, most of them were in Germany and Poland.

'Michel, I can't believe it.'

'You can't believe what?'

'Burning human beings; using their fat to make soap and their hair to make blankets and dusting tools.'

Despite all the misery, he had not lost his sense of humour.

'Watch your buttons, they may be someone's spine you are touching!'

'Don't! Just tell me it is not true, just tell me ...'

'Why should I?'

'Because it can't be true, they must have made it up.'

'But not everyone lies. The truth is even worse.'

'What do you mean?'

I could see he was tense, as though about to burst into tears.

'I mean, damn power, damn the war ...'

He was about to get up but I wouldn't let him, and I then regretted having the conversation. Moments later we were fast asleep.

The van did not go beyond Dijon. There was nothing else, either, to take us to Strasbourg. The driver abandoned us with a couple of pieces of luggage. Maryam had a cold and was feverish so we hopelessly knocked on doors. We frequently bumped into groups of young people from the cleansing committee who checked our papers. They occasionally became suspicious and took us to a room and searched our bags. My familiarity with Paris helped us; everywhere we went I said that Michel and Maryam were sick and that they had lost their voices.

Night fell and we were still on the street. Maryam was still feverish and she had fallen asleep while Michel was holding her. For a moment I remembered the four days we had travelled from

Odessa to Istanbul aboard the French ship, but here I was in a far more miserable state. A member of the Resistance came to our rescue and, after some interrogation, directed us to a medical team to treat Maryam and Michel. The physician agreed to let us stay in the shed in his house, another desperately cold place.

In the morning I went out to fetch some food and medicine. People were sleeping in the parks and around the bombed-out buildings; and it was cold, so cold. A man directed me to the town hall to register for food. There was a long queue of people stretching from the town hall, past the church and ending in a square. It was snowing and all sorts of people were queuing, from beautiful, elegant young Parisian women who, despite the troubles, still held on to their charm, to old men. There were armed young men watching everyone. A couple of young women behind me reminded me to register my name in the book just outside the town hall and then queue up. They promised to keep my place. My legs had no strength and I knew I had a cold as I was not feeling well, but I could not afford to be ill. I had to take some food to Michel and Maryam, whose papers I was carrying in my pockets. When I crossed the street I heard someone call, 'Princess'. I was about to turn but soon remembered the situation and reminded myself that I was Janine. I carried on but the voice was close, in fact right by my ear. I did not take any notice until someone caught my arm.

'I beg of you, Princess!'

By then I was confident it was Saeed; he looked terrified and was imploring me.

My face was drawn with fury and the words 'You bastard,' involuntarily left my lips.

The beast was shaking and he was trying to speak quietly. He begged me for some money. I pulled my sleeve from his hand and headed for the queue. I wanted to escape the situation and vanish. I knew if he discovered that Michel was with me and that I was travelling with Janine's papers he would cause me trouble. I was terrified.

He followed me. I quickened my pace. He carried on and, when he caught up with me, pulled at my sleeve and begged me to listen to what he had to say. We both came to a halt. I had lowered my head so that the snow did not get down my neck through my scarf. We were now just outside a narrow alleyway. He asked me to go into the alleyway and I did. I stood by the porch of an old building and leaned against the pillar so I could avoid the snow.

'Give me some money. If I don't get to Switzerland they'll kill me here.'

I ignored his pleading and kept repeating that I had no money. He was now holding my weak hand and I pulled it away with disgust. He wanted to search my pockets but when that failed he decided to threaten me.

'Where is that German husband of yours?'

My heart sank. Though he seemed far too desperate to be of any threat to anyone I still panicked. I found my hand inside my pocket touching a bundle of banknotes. I wanted to take a few but my fingers were too numb. He suddenly caught my hand and removed the bundle.

I shouted, 'Not everything ... I don't have any more money,' but he was running away and couldn't hear me.

Perhaps it was my imagination and the sniggering I heard was not his. I was leaning against the pillar when I heard shouting, followed by a shot. I stepped forward and saw two young gunmen chasing Saeed, ordering him to stop. One of them pointed his rifle at him and fired. I saw the beast come to a halt and then turn towards me. He was raising his hand. He had a gun and I couldn't believe he was pointing it towards me. I froze. He pulled the trigger and I fell but it wasn't me who was hit, rather one of the young men. The other was taking shelter behind a large tree. He yelled and others came to his rescue. The sound of shooting filled the street; having fallen on the ground I was so terrified that I closed my eyes, but I managed to see him fall. The hood of his cape went back revealing his soft, lush hair, now grey in front. He was then dragged across the ground. I wanted to run away from the scene but the young man wanted to help me and insisted on taking me to the police station as he had seen the beast take my money. I was about to say that he was a murderer – he had murdered the other beast that was my father – but I was so overwhelmed with emotion that I burst into tears, occasionally laughing amid my tears.

'*Vous n'allez pas bien, Madame.*'

Maryam was worse off than me. When I returned to the shed that afternoon Michel was holding her and she was burning with fever. Michel was looking at me with apprehension and asked me to take Maryam to the doctor. He said that he had been planning to do so himself if I hadn't returned, despite the consequences. The doctor advised us to go to a building by the town hall. This was a large hall with several fireplaces burning with logs or coal. There were more than a thousand men and women milling around. Some had covered themselves in the blankets and huddled around the fire. It was hardly the Hotel George V but the warmth coming from the fireplaces made it as enjoyable as though we were surrounded by luxury. We took it in turns to sleep.

The year 1945 was upon us and we spent a week in that hall. Our situation remained the same. Saeed was executed on New Year's Eve. He had not only killed a young man from the Resistance but had forcefully directed another young man to a desolate warehouse and had made a certain proposal to him. The young man had not accepted his proposition and was subsequently attacked with a sickle. Saeed was charged with a number of crimes, but no one in Dijon was aware of the full extent of his deeds. When he stood before the firing squad he was neither the grandson of an Ottoman Sultan, nor the murderer of an ageing beast in St Rafael. He was put on trial with a false Lebanese identity. I had had no reason to be frightened of him and lose all my money. I shouldn't have been; in his miserable state he was hardly a fearsome creature. I could even have gone to the police station the next day and retrieved my money, but how could

I have done such a thing with false papers? To let go of so much money at a time when there was a shortage of everything, with no certainty about our situation, was something that I had not considered carefully enough.

My only ray of hope was the weekly calls I made to Janine, though we had nothing to exchange but sorrow. Worst of all was to see Michel not sleeping and deep in thought all the time. He didn't seem ever to have considered the war's outcome, as though he could never have fathomed that Germany was going to be defeated one day and the entire world would become its enemy. Everyone in that hall, whatever their nationality, shared one desire: to catch a Nazi German and kill him. The men spent hours sitting together and going over the events leading to the occupation of France, Belgium and other European countries. I was far too concerned to leave Michel to himself. When dealing with curious women I pretended that my husband was unwell.

Once, one of them said, 'He must have had German ancestry, as he looks so German,' at which point my heart sank.

There was plenty of petty robbery in the hall and one of us had always to remain behind. We couldn't move freely in that place and in our nightly whispers Michel always went through what I should do and where I should go without him, something I did not want to hear. One evening I lost my patience and retorted that after forty-six years I had finally managed to find happiness with a man.

'And you cannot take it away from me.'

But he would become abrupt and say that I needed to be realistic and reasonable. Sometimes he came out with something which set me on fire, like the day he said: 'Two years ago I wanted to go to Paris rather than enter the Foreign Office, but you did not agree; if you had, the outcome would have been different.'

Every other day an inspector would come to check papers. He would occasionally take the new arrivals from Paris in for questioning. The worst thing was the news of the war: after the retreat from France the good times seemed to have turned their back on Hitler: there was news of defeat on all the remaining fronts and the war had intensified. Hitler's speeches, however, kept Michel's hopes up. The bombing of cities was also another worry.

A call to Janine meant that we set off on yet another journey before January was over. Janine managed to use whatever language she could to tell me to go to Switzerland. Michel was not prepared to do such a thing and wanted to get Maryam and me to our home as soon as possible. Maryam was feeling better and, as a result, keeping her indoors had become difficult. The departure of the first groups and arrival of new ones, however, meant that there were a few children with whom she managed to amuse herself. Every day I went out in search of some means of getting to the border. We had been in the hall for a week and a half. Hunger and uncertainty were about to take their toll when, finally, my efforts bore fruit. After much haggling I managed to persuade a man to take us in his van to the Swiss border, provided only one person sat in the front. Michel was still adamant that we should head for Germany, but the man explained that it was going to be much easier to go to Germany via Switzerland. He added that crossing the Franco-German border was to embrace one's death. He had a barber's shop in Basel and was over in Dijon for some work.

We were about to leave when Michel started talking to the barber, who spoke German quite well. Michel asked him whether he was prepared to sell his van to us but the man refused. Michel went on proposing an incredible sum but the deal was still about to fall through until Michel proposed offering him half the sum in advance and to drive the van himself to Basel, where he would hand it to whoever the man had in mind. I was not sure why he was making such an offer but I trusted him as I always relied on his wisdom.

We were in a café, sitting by the window admiring the arrival of spring. The barber had had some wine and the proposal seemed to have loosened his tongue. He suddenly stretched out his arm to shake Michel's hand. He had agreed to the compromise and launched into giving Michel instructions on how to drive the van. He then felt so reassured that he even let us have the address of his shop and house so that we could take the van to his son. Michel then asked what would happen if we were not able to cross the border in the van. The man glanced at him and laughed. He mentioned Frieman, a village close to the border, and then wrote down his sister's name on a piece of paper. He asked us to leave the van with her and then nodded his head as a sign of trust. I had to sell a few items of jewellery so that the funds could be made available. This didn't prove difficult as some Jewish antique dealer purchased my diamond earrings – for half their value – and we managed to set off.

I asked Michel why he had gone about striking such a strange deal as it was much easier and more practical for the man to take us to the border himself. It was simple.

'I wanted us to be alone so that we could talk, as we may never have such an opportunity again.'

He asked me to memorise a five-figure number and the letter K. He said that this was the code for a Swiss bank account in the Geneva branch. A sum of US$300,000 had been deposited in that account and Michel wanted me to access the money after January 1946 should he not be around. He insisted that I should go about it in a year's time since the funds were not his before then. I was not happy to take part in such a worrying conversation but he promised not to talk about such issues from then on, which we did not.

Spring was upon us. Once, we were listening to Radio Berlin, when an officer approached us for inspection, and we quickly tuned the radio to a French station. From then on, we decided not to take the risk of listening to Radio Berlin more than twice a day; the rest of the time we listened to music or the French news, although I knew it was hard for Michel to listen to the news broadcast from the French side.

We were driving along a road we hoped would never end. Maryam was sleeping on my knees and Michel was driving calmly. We were looking at the fields and gardens slowly emerging from their winter cover, and the people who were clearing up the remains of the war. The ruins of the aftermath of bombing could be seen everywhere. We occasionally diverted from the busy main route and from the many men and women walking and begging to get on the back of the van. We stopped halfway and spent the night on a farm. We bought fresh milk for Maryam. The farmer, who lived with his elderly wife, did not want to give us shelter anywhere but in the stables. However, when he realised that our only other option was to spend the night in the van, he agreed to let us stay in his house. Later on, he told us that his sons used to work with the Germans and now they had escaped to Switzerland as they feared the cleansing committees; the old couple occasionally received their letters. We agreed to visit his sons in Geneva, which made him more hospitable. The room we stayed in was clean and belonged to the boys; signs of their youth were everywhere.

When I got up in the morning I saw Michel through the window. He was coming from the cow pen in front of the building and was carrying a bucket of milk. Looking at him from above I told myself, 'What if one day he is not there …' and I quickly brushed the thought aside. He brought some warm water and we gave Maryam a bath. He was so filled with affection that I trembled with fear. I sneaked a glance at him.

'Could there not be a place in the world where we could lead our lives without fear?'

'Yes, in Berlin, my homeland,' he said laughing.

Alas, we were unaware that the Russians had already entered Berlin from the East and that the city had been bombed incessantly for the past two weeks. We put on fresh clothes, bade farewell to the old man and woman and drove off. Not far now until the border, we thought. We then wondered whether we could drive into Switzerland, but we could not: we had to drive back to Frieman. Michel insisted on honouring our promise and handing over the vehicle to the owner of the van at the place he had mentioned. How quickly time had passed: we had managed to drag out the few hours' journey to a day and a half.

It didn't take long for a car to stop near us. Someone was yelling, motioning to us. It was the owner of the van. He kissed Maryam, gave her a tart and then thanked us and took the key. We took our two pieces of luggage and arrived at the guard's outpost, where we sat on a bench and waited. We both referred to Maryam as Christina and kept reminding ourselves that we were Janine and André.

André/Michel went forward. A quarter of an hour passed. Maryam had climbed the bench and was looking through the window.

She suddenly cried, 'Papa!'

I got up. Papa was being forced to get into a black car with his hands tied behind him. I rubbed my eyes; surely this must be just a nightmare, one of the so many which crept into my sleep every night. No, it can't be real. I had to keep touching Maryam to remind myself that I had to be strong and persevere.

Just before getting into the black car Papa turned momentarily, as if he knew we were standing behind the window. He said something I couldn't hear.

He waved at us as if he were saying farewell: '...Carry on and don't forget what I said,' and the black car made a U-turn.

The name Janine was shouted out and I entered the room. There was only one chair and, when I sat on it, I could feel his warmth. I burst into tears. My sobbing made Maryam cry too. The man was holding our papers and asked for my real name. I did not say anything because I did not know what to say. He, however, helped me out by mentioning Michel's name and details. He talked about his position as advisor to the Nazi Ministry of Foreign Affairs and Deputy Commander in Paris. He said it all to make me understand that there was no point in denial. I could only just about deny that I had any acquaintance with Janine and André.

After about an hour he asked me to return to Paris. He said that without my true identity papers I would face the same ordeal wherever I went. He insisted that since I was French I had to present myself in a Paris court to be exonerated.

I suddenly thought of something and said, 'No Sir, I am not French.'

He laughed.

'I am Iranian!'

CHAPTER 60

He was gone; rather, he was taken away, just like that. For a moment I imagined myself dragging my fragile body along the street in the same direction as the black car, but as soon as I reached the street the car had disappeared. I had run for so long that my feet got tangled with each other and I fell down. A number of men and women were towering over me looking curious. I suddenly remembered my little girl. When I was myself again I found Maryam standing on the same chair by the window. She threw herself into my arms and I pressed my forehead to her head and began sobbing just as when I had parted with my mother.

'I shan't leave you alone! Don't be frightened, my darling. Papa shall return tomorrow.'

'Papa André,' she whispered in my ear; little did she know that all the secrecy had been to save the very person who had just slipped through our fingers.

The Frenchman sitting in the room at the border no longer looked so kind. There was an air of resentment in his expression and his first question was: 'How could you bring yourself to this disgrace and sell your homeland? Were you not ashamed? Can you imagine what they would do to you if I told the people who gave you shelter who you were? Can you imagine?'

Yes, I could imagine: in the past couple of months I had seen women with shaved heads who were insulted on the main square. Sometimes they were hit by ripe tomatoes thrown at them. Just outside Paris I had seen a father slap his daughter on the face and people pat him on the back. Now this man was threatening me and I was staring at him, but it hardly mattered to me. I wanted to know where Michel had been taken.

I spent an hour in that room not knowing what was to become of me until the same car, or one similar, returned with three grim-faced people. They went to the room next door and then called me in. Maryam did not want to stay on her own as she was frightened. However, I insisted that she should and she remained standing on the chair looking into the street so that she could, perhaps, spot her father. I was accused of treason, collaborating with the enemy and forging official documents. After two hours of interrogation, during which I had burst into tears, they asked me to return to Maryam while they consulted together. I was desperate to know where my husband was. The youngest man, who happened to be tall, replied with resentment, 'We threw him into the very chambers where he burned human beings.'

'Michel is not a murderer!' I wailed.

Half an hour later they called me in yet again. They were wondering what to do with Maryam. I said that she was to go with me as I did not have anyone to leave her with, and truly I had no one. I managed to keep any acquaintance with Janine and André quiet to save them huge trouble.

'We'll leave her in the care of the state orphanage, though they hardly have any more space,' was the grim-looking man's response.

He then asked me about my family. I said that I had no one, and I was not lying – except that up to then I had never thought about it. My pleas were of no use, and Maryam once again witnessed the black car leaving. I was thinking what was to become of her and the two items of jewellery I had wrapped to her body. What if they decided to execute Michel and me? What would become of her?

An hour later I was sitting on the edge of a bench next to a few German, French and Austrian women in a school that was being used as a prison. The room was noisy, and I kept thinking about Michel, and Maryam, who still coughed. Where was she at that moment? A woman who worked in a village bakery had set herself up to run errands for everyone: she would take some money and shop for them. Another woman said that she had even managed to deliver a message through her so I felt there was some hope. And thus my message was transmitted to Janine.

The next day I was called in the afternoon, as I had visitors. I had no idea who they might be. There was the unfamiliar face of a man and then Janine's. The expression on her face was full of sympathy and my first question upon seeing her was to enquire about Maryam's whereabouts. The man sitting next to Janine was a lawyer. He was erudite and quick.

I felt so reassured to see the two of them that when I returned to the prison cell I asked my cellmates to pass their messages to me, confident I was going to leave soon. And so they did; one wrote a letter and asked me to put it in an envelope and post it, another wrote her bank details down and asked me to pass it on to her sister. An hour later I was called to the office. I had to write a letter to the city council giving Janine power of attorney to enable her to collect Maryam. I was relieved and felt I could now concentrate on Michel's situation. Whilst in prison I had heard about the bombing of German cities, except in Berlin, where the Russians had entered from the east and the Americans from the west. I wondered what state our house was in.

I cannot describe how I felt when I was released the following morning. I only remember that I could see 'Khanoum' written on my papers. I was now referred to as 'Iranian', whereas elsewhere I had been treated as a French national, despite my protests. Later on, I learned that I owed my freedom to that lawyer.

Maryam was confused as to what she should call me in Janine's presence! The lawyer drove us to the lodgings where he and Janine had spent the night. We had a wash and when I was dealing with Maryam I realised that the two items of jewellery wrapped to her body were missing. I did not say anything; in the circumstances I was better off not thinking of anything but Michel. We went to the dining room. Janine and the lawyer were obviously pleased; my angel had once again come to my rescue and wanted to take me back to Paris. I said that I had to get news of Michel. I insisted that the young lawyer should pursue his case so that we could go and see him that very day. I had assumed that Michel was in prison somewhere close. Janine seemed to be hiding something from me, and after a little wrangling she finally said that Michel had been sent to Germany.

'Then I shall go to Germany, since it is possible to do so now,' but she said that this was impossible as the borders were closed.

I said that I had every right to enter German territory since I had a German child. Janine tried to make me understand that if I went over I would be arrested as well, but it was no use. Janine looked melancholy. She took Maryam's hand and left the room to let the young lawyer break the news to me.

'No, that can't be right!' I shouted out, and everyone in the room turned towards me.

What I was not supposed to know was that Michel had managed to steal a gun from one of the young men and shoot himself the first night he was taken prisoner. No, this was impossible; life could not be so ruthless. He had no right to do this. He had promised to take me along wherever he went.

Maryam was playing with Janine in the garden. I remembered that I had become an orphan at the age of nine, and Maryam was just four. I wished I had Michel's courage. Why on earth were these people dancing and offering each other wine? A chubby Frenchman had come to the entrance via the garden and was making Maryam dance with him and my daughter was laughing. Moments later, the owner of the lodging broke the news. She was in her apron offering everyone some wine. I said that I did not drink.

She said, 'But you must drink this one, don't you know what's happened?'

I did not know that in the past hour the radio had announced that Adolf Hitler and Eva Braun had committed suicide. The Frenchman said that Goebbels had his family of seven had terminated their lives: his wife, their children and himself. I leaned back while the news went around. All the senior Nazi officers had committed suicide. In prison I had heard that Mussolini was hanged upside down by the Italian militia while trying to escape. The Frenchman told the young lawyer that Pétain had committed suicide as well.

The shrewd lawyer said, 'The French needn't have done this,' and then added with a touch of humour, 'The Germans *should* terminate their lives, as they don't have Bordeaux wine!'

They both laughed, and Janine's face searched mine to discover if the lawyer had broken the news to me. I said to her that he had; yes, my angel, I did hear. Something else I did not know was that Michel's watch, notebook and his gold fountain pen were in Janine's handbag.

CHAPTER 61

I was in Berlin on 7 May when the German surrender was signed. Janine could not persuade me to go to Paris and Maryam and I managed to get to Berlin with great difficulty. Everyone en route tried to dissuade me from going to the war-torn city. We walked half the distance and managed to get a lift with British army trucks from time to time. The British were jubilant and responded in kind to the people whom they had bombed up to the previous day. The world war was over, but not my war with life.

Finding Brigitte's home was not difficult. They lived on the southern outskirts of Berlin, which had been less affected, but their house and the two neighbouring houses had been completely destroyed by the bombing. Michel's parents had been killed while they were in a shelter. Finding Brigitte and her family alive and well was the best thing that could have happened in the circumstances. Getting close to the Reichstag, where Michel and I had lived, however, was only achieved with great misery and difficulty. No building had been spared during the bombing and it took quite a bit of wrangling with the Russian soldiers to allow us finally to search the ruins. I mentioned to Maryam that we used to live in that place; the place where she, along with her sister and brothers, were to grow up: the house of Michel's and my dreams.

There were seven of us including Brigitte's children. We pushed the rubble aside, hung a cloth from the window and spent the night amid the ruins. Our food consisted of water, some biscuits and tinned food. A Russian truck would arrive from time to time and distribute water. The bulldozers made a lot of noise and people were still hoping to find someone alive in the rubble. We, however, were not searching for anyone.

The sound of shooting could occasionally be heard. American aeroplanes would drop parcels of blankets and cold food and we would eat the tinned food that came down, using the forks that we managed to find in the remains of our kitchen. People begged on the streets for a piece of bread and desperately searched the large houses for food. The house next door belonged to a German colonel and, not long previously, had been guarded by a couple of soldiers. On the third day of my return to Berlin, however, the Russians dragged a man from the basement. I knew him: he was the colonel and he still behaved with his customary hauteur. His wife was old and looked dusty in her elegant attire. The colonel pulled the trigger right in front of our eyes and shot the Russian officer. This was met with a volley of shots from a young soldier. He shook with the impact and then fell to the ground. The old woman began to sob. I was trembling with fear and held Maryam tight so that she could not witness the scene.

It made perfect sense when she asked where her Papa was. Perhaps at that moment, like me, she was thinking that, had Michel been alive, he would have faced the same fate; his wounded body would shake in front of our eyes, and then what would we have done?

It was spring and we were still clearing the rubble. In the daytime Brigitte and I went out in search of food and Gerhard remained in the house. He had hired a couple of people to do the repairs and I admired his efforts in trying to resurrect the house where Michel had wanted us to stay. My bedroom was the least damaged, and by the time Brigitte and I returned with a few items we had so desperately wrested from other's clutches, it was being sorted out. The children were crying and one workman had been left behind to look after them until we returned; the Russians had taken Gerhard away. I cannot begin to recount what we went through during the four weeks that Gerhard was detained by the Russians. Stefan, Brigitte's eldest son, who was twelve, was more impatient than the others. The thought of Gerhard facing the same fate as Michel weighed down on all of us.

I was slowly running out of funds and had begun selling my jewellery on the black market for half its value. I occasionally thought of contacting my aunt for help but this was not so easy; she no longer enjoyed her former prosperity. Janine had informed me in a letter that they had all returned to St Cloud. André was still in charge of driving the Empress around and Janine worked in the compound a couple of hours a day. They had moved somewhere close but Janine also had to work part time in a restaurant.

The economy was in chaos, not to mention the political disarray. France was struggling with unemployment and poverty. The national hero, General de Gaulle, saw his efforts undermined by the different parties. Germany was still occupied by the Allies and was slowly trying to shed the image of war, as we had done in the six months of hard work it had taken to restore the house to its former glory, as I had promised Michel. In the process, we had been forced to sell everything else.

Such was the state of the Europeans: searching for life amid the ruins and suffering the wounds of war, as we did ourselves. One summer's day we pulled out our trunks from the basement. Before leaving for Belgium we had packed away all our letters, documents, and the mementoes of my childhood, along with those of my mother and Nezhat, and stored them in trunks in the basement. I became so engrossed in my past that I had no intention of leaving it. I really should not have delved into the bitter reality: in Michel's trunk I came across his childhood photographs and all the letters that I had written to him after meeting him for the first time. I had a pang of regret for all the days of my youth I could have spent with him. How cruel to say that I had no intention of forgoing my carefree student life. He, in return, had written that he was going to wait for me. I had replied

Masoud Behnoud

with such indifference: 'let time resolve everything'. At the time I had no faith in his staunch love and, alas, he had so easily slipped through my fingers.

I had taken a job in a medical centre, where I used my nursing experience from my days in the convent and the hospital in Neuilly. Brigitte had also got a job in a factory producing flour, and Gerhard worked all day; nevertheless, we could barely keep our heads above water. We just about managed to feed ourselves and get the children to school. I had registered Maryam in a nursery school connected to the medical centre and left her there until late in the afternoon, when I picked her up. While we were slowly adjusting to the new life, Europe was changing before our eyes. The wartime coalition between America, Western Europe and Stalin came to an end when Churchill announced in Washington, for the first time, the beginning of the 'Cold War'. After the bombing of Hiroshima and Nagasaki the state of the world was worrisome.

Brigitte and Gerhard eventually relocated to West Berlin, where the Americans and their open-handedness provided a better life for the people. Having stayed behind to look after Michel's memory I was still in Reichstagung, by then part of East Berlin. Eventually, though, I was obliged to leave the house of my dreams when the Russians dumped two German families to share the house with us. Maryam and I packed our suitcases and took the first train for West Berlin and then on to Frankfurt, where we rented a flat on the sixth floor of an old building.

The court proceedings in Nuremberg kept everyone engaged for months to come. Everyone followed the news of the trial of prominent figures in Nazi Germany in the tabloids or on the radio. The impotence and feeble manner of some made us furious, yet we laughed at the tenacity and fury of Göring and, more important, Joachim von Ribbentropp, Michel's boss. I had seen him twice and knew of his affection for Michel. I did not know whether he had heard of Michel's suicide or not. The Germans

480

then whispered rumours about Göring having committed suicide with a razor blade his mistress had managed to smuggle in. In fact, it was potassium cyanide tablets that were smuggled in, Göring taking his own life the day before he was due to be hanged and only a day after he mocked the Allies, calling them enemies of humanity.

Most of the remaining war criminals were finally hanged, save for Rudolf Hess.

Amid the strenuous work – beyond my capacity at fifty years of age – with no future and no identity, half French and half German, I received Janine's telegram. She had sent Maryam and me plane tickets for a week's trip to Paris, along with the news that the Empress was unwell and wished to see me.

This was Maryam's first time on an aeroplane. When the plane landed at Orly airport I saw my angel in the hall. Her hair was loose, now with many grey strands running through it. I understood that my aunt, my shelter, had finally passed away. I did not possess a black dress and had to buy one in Paris. In St Cloud we received everyone who had come to the Empress's memorial service. When I was laying some flowers, I said to Maryam, who was now seven years old: 'She was my mother; my real mother, who for forty years became everything to me.'

The day I was due to return to Frankfurt I saw Mahmoud in the room which served as library and office. In the absence of his mother and other brothers, who had also passed away, he had become the head of the family. He gave me a folder and read out the part of the will concerning me. My aunt had honoured her promise, made at the time of my wedding to Michel, and had enclosed the title deeds of a village in Saveh and a ten-thousand-square-metre estate in another village in the vicinity of Tehran. The date on the documents was 1939. There was also a banker's draft in the folder, which enabled me to access the income generated over the past years from Mr Mamaqani in Tehran. In her will my aunt had asked me to take some flowers to my mother's grave at the first opportunity I had to return to Tehran. She had also asked if it were possible for me to live in the same house – the whereabouts of which Mr Mamaqani was to tell me – and to hold on to it. She had prayed to God that Maryam might grow up in Iran and remain Iranian, something everyone knew the Empress had wished for her and her own grandchildren. She had always wanted to die in Tehran and be buried in her family's mausoleum in Qom.

I asked Janine and André whether they wanted to go to Tehran with me, even though I had no idea about the city I had left in fear and doubt some forty years before. When, a month later, I had an appointment to see the Iranian Ambassador in Bonn, the new capital of East Germany, I never imagined that Maryam and I would spend the summer of 1948 in Tehran. Entezam, the ambassador, nodded when he learned who I was and then left me in the care of his head clerk, an elegant young Iranian called Hoveyda.[22] When he heard that I wanted a passport to return to Iran after forty years, he laughed and advised me not to burn all my bridges. Little did he know that I hardly had any bridges left and that I was counting the minutes until I reached my mother's grave.

CHAPTER 62

M r Mamaqani was there to greet me at the modest airport in Tehran, which was a far cry from the European airports. He took me to the Park Hotel, where he had booked a room for me and Maryam. He also let me have 2,000 Iranian tomans, a currency I had not seen until then, and we arranged to meet the next day.

Late that afternoon I stepped into a city I hardly knew and was driven in the hotel's large American car in search of my house. We drove to a district which was still named after my grandfather and was a reminder of the monster. When Mr Mamaqani gave me the address I did not know I was effectively heading for Nanny's house. The well had no water but, at one glance, I could see the image of a young girl whose golden hair was floating on the surface of the water.

Mansoureh, the youngest daughter of Nanny, lived in that house with her family; and said she had been the same age as Maryam when I left Tehran. Though she looked older than me she was more vivacious. We were surrounded by her two grand-children and four children. Here were my newfound relations, in my birthplace, in which I felt alien. Later that evening they accompanied me to where the hotel car was waiting for me in the alleyway illuminated with gas lanterns. Every step I took in that house was as though I was retracing my own steps.

Later that night I looked out of the window from our room on the fourth floor of the hotel and saw a city filled with plane trees. I opened the window so that the familiar breeze of my birthplace could caress my face.

I told myself, 'I belong here, a city familiar to me.'

While I was on board the plane flying towards Tehran I had delved into the lyrics of Hafez to see what the omens had to say; it was not promising:

> *Our faces are marked with sorrow,*
> *Can't bring myself to tell you what I can see in your sorrow.*

I marked the page so that I could read it at my mother's grave the next day. Maryam was sleeping and she seemed peaceful. I looked at her and thought, 'Tomorrow we'll go to see my mother.'

Mansoureh and the children had come to the hotel earlier than we had arranged. We got into one of the American cars and set off. Maryam and I were looking around us as though we were discovering a new place. We were passing by the farms and fields of clover. There were still many horse-drawn carriages on the streets and we could also see the chimneys of brick factories as we made our way to the cemetery. Mansoureh and her children helped me choose some flowers and rose water. Oh Mother, I have finally come!

> *We have come a long way,*
> *With days and nights filled with happenings;*
> *Who are we to know of the passer-by,*
> *And what has been.*

I was reluctant to leave her grave and was filled with a sense of revenge for the monster lying in the cemetery in St Rafael. Mansoureh and the children took Maryam for a stroll. In that empty chamber, where there were only two antique candelabra covered in dust and two chairs, which the warden quickly dusted, I spent an hour talking to her. I had to tell her what had gone on for the past forty years. Among all the things I had lost I could only remember

Nezhat and Michel. In the silence of that space it occurred to me that my mother was an only child, and *I* had been her only child, and Maryam was *my* only child, something I had never given thought to previously. Then I remembered my son, Ali, who had left us before he could even see the world.

That evening I wrote everything in a letter to Janine. Two months later I wrote that I had bought a house in north Tehran, on a street lined with plane trees overlooking the mountains near the summer palace of the imperial family. The mountains were usually covered in snow. Further to the north of the district there was a green palace which Shah Baba had been very fond of and which was now inhabited by Reza Khan's children.

Mr Mamaqani had helped me buy the house with the proceeds of the sale of the estate given to me. There was a tank, and an arbour in the middle, the entire grounds surrounded by walls covered in honeysuckle. It hardly resembled my modest student accommodation, being even larger than our house in Berlin. I had enrolled Maryam in Tehran's French school, which was situated near a church. The cost of living in Tehran was low, and life was easy, even though the drinking water was an issue for me. The water we drank came from the streams that flowed on either side of the streets, before being directed into the tanks. I therefore had to boil it before letting Maryam drink it.

Mamaqani advised me very early on to sell the house where Mansoureh and her family lived, but I immediately expressed my reluctance, as the house was a reminder of my mother, a reminder of the last nights we had sat under the *korsi*, imprisoned in a room. After my return to Tehran, whenever I set foot in that house I could picture Asdollah, Mansoureh's father, leaning against his walking stick on the veranda and keeping an eye on us.

Poor old Mansoureh had assumed I wanted to sell the house and one day told me that her son-in-law was prepared to pay part of the price in cash and the rest in instalments. I embraced her and said that I was never going to do such a thing, that the house belonged to her. I said *I* felt indebted to her for letting me sit on the rug laid in the garden so that I could be next to her and she could pour me a cup of tea from the samovar. She had looked after the house and my mother's memory; how could Mamaqani now bring himself to assume that I would want to sell that house!

Mansoureh's daughter and her husband, an army officer, came to live in my house so that we were not alone. Mansoureh would visit occasionally. The first night I slept there was the day after the young Shah, Reza Khan's son, had survived an assassination attempt. My furniture was delivered amid the curfew. We had no curtains yet and Mansoureh had covered the windows with sheets and blankets. Maryam was asleep when I took a stroll in the garden. The moon was reflected on the surface of the water in the tank and I felt I had been away from myself for forty years. Heaven seemed more compassionate over here, and I only wished Michel had been with me so that we could stroll together on the gravelled path, immersing ourselves in the intoxicating aroma of the stocks and honeysuckles. I felt his absence more than ever now that I was more settled, and couldn't help my tears.

Before I purchased the house, I had asked Mamaqani to help me change my family name, as well as Maryam's German one. This was sorted out within a few days. I did not wish to carry the burden of a name which was a reminder of a monster of a father. Moreover, I wanted my daughter and me to become one entity. The day I went to collect our new birth certificates I was directed to an office. A distinguished-looking, grey-haired man was sitting behind a large desk. He glanced at me, introduced himself and then asked for some tea to be brought in. I was perplexed when he said that he was the grandson of one of my aunts, and then he asked me whether I wished to see my extended family. I didn't know what to say.

The following week I met some hundred people in a social gathering in his house, in a district close to the imperial summer

residence. They were all close relations and I was immersed in
the waves of memory. The older people had met my mother and
knew, more or less, that I had left as a child, and what had become
of my mother, though they did not mention anything. I cannot
describe Maryam's happiness when, two weeks later, I invited
them back to my home; she was immersed in a strange yet happy
world where she found herself amid children of her own age.

I could never have imagined such vivid memories when
I went to see my Aunt Fakhr: when I entered Amin Park through
the gates, everything seemed familiar. It was as though I had
dreamed it the night before. My memory served me well as far
as the bombing of the parliament was concerned. I knew exactly
where the Ayatollahs and the members of the parliament had
gathered when the Cossacks poured in. I had heard it from
Ebrahim and Nezhat, and now the image was as vivid as though
I had been there when it all happened. My visit took my aunt to
the past and she also helped me to remember. It had been the
same evening that Nezhat's gathering had been in session in our
house. They'd been saying '*Ho Ya Ali*' and someone had been
playing our Iranian drum, the *daf*. I could remember every detail,
but had never thought of it for years.

My aunt Fakhr had aged. She was seated on a wooden frame
under the shade of a willow tree, wearing her white scarf, and had
wrapped her prayer *chador* round her waist. She was listening to
me with a smile on her face. She then turned to her sons telling
them off for not remembering the events, whereas, despite the
length of time away from Iran, I could still remember every
detail. I did not say anything, nor did she know anything about
my years in lonely exile, an exile during which I had relived
my childhood so many times that I had managed to preserve
everything. Only the ten-year period in Odessa had somehow
escaped my mind.

Every week I delved into my identity a little more by going
to different corners of the city. I was particularly enthralled by

the older generation, who remembered my mother, and having been brought up away from my homeland, everything they said filled the gaps in my memory. A visit to Dr Mossadeq's[23] house was one such occasion. He lived in a beautiful house and his wife Zia embraced both Maryam and me. I knew he was a great man; he was a member of the parliament and had for years served as a minister and lawyer. I did not see him that day but his pictures were everywhere in the papers, like other members of my newly found extended family.

When, a year later, Janine and André came to Iran, and when Brigitte and Gerhard were our guests for the month, all were bemused by the sheer number of relations that I had discovered. They had always seen me as a loner and never fathomed that back in Tehran I could be so settled. It was a pity that Janine and André were busy with their children and grandchildren, otherwise they would have found Tehran a good place to set themselves up. I was now working at the French Embassy, dealing with translation and administrative work.

On the second day, Janine insisted on going to the cemetery. I had told her so much about my mother that I found her by the grave speaking to my mother in French. She told her that her daughter had at all times remembered her, which compounded my pain.

In 1951 Mossadeq became Prime Minister. Janine wrote that he was very popular among the French. Pierre, who was an adult by then, asked me to obtain his autograph, as he collected autographs. When I asked Zia if she could get this for me – she was praying surrounded by her grandchildren – she laughed and said that I should ask Mossdeq myself. He arrived in the inner sanctum at lunchtime and I rose to greet him. He looked much older than his pictures. He picked up a paper and put crosses all over it, looking just like Monsieur Gaston who had looked after my affairs in Paris for the past twenty-five years; thin Monsieur Gaston. He asked me what the French thought of the nationalization of oil and I explained. He then wondered why I had never thought of working for the government, given my command of several foreign languages, as the government was in need of such individuals. I said that it would be an honour and I would be happy to offer my services; I also knew how to type. The job never materialised, though, as three months later a coup took place. I had gone to see a sick relation who lived on the same street as Dr Mossadeq. We climbed to the roof and noticed that there was shooting directed at his house. A jeep had crashed into the gates and a group of people were busy looting; just like the scene I had witnessed in Odessa, except that in Odessa a revolution had been taking place. I could not understand what had brought this about here.

That incident withstanding, peace and calm seemed finally to have nestled in our lives. It was summer 1958 and I was at work. I picked Maryam up from the summer school in the afternoon and headed home. Although I could afford to buy a small car I preferred to economise. As the taxi neared home I felt something was not right. When I knocked on the door Yadollah immediately opened it, as though he had been waiting for me.

He took Maryam's bag and said, 'There is a foreign gentleman waiting to see you in the garden,' which was surprising because the embassy staff would call in advance if they needed to see me.

In any case, I had just left work, so I wondered what might have happened in between. I followed Yadollah and glanced at the arbour. I don't know why I was so anxious; no event of major significance had taken place since my return to Tehran more than ten years earlier. While I was moving towards the arbour I asked Yadollah whether he had offered the man something to drink, to which he muttered something. Through the railings of the arbour, well hidden among the trees, I saw an old man with grey hair – or rather, completely white. The presence of that unknown man had, for some reason, unsettled me. I could not understand why Yadollah had let a stranger in, let alone some foreign man.

I had to climb up the steps to the arbour. The old man, who was sitting on the bench with his back to me, turned towards me. Unbelievable! There must have been a mistake ... it just could not be! I let him speak.

'Princess!'

And the voice did it. I rested my hand on the arbour and, before I collapsed on the ground, managed to sit on the bench.

'Michel?'

I could hear his silent laughter. He was my Michel but old, grey-haired and stooped. I called Maryam. Michel was now kneeling before me, holding my hands and kissing them. I stroked his hair. I had lost the familiarity of touching a man; ever since Michel had been taken away I had never been intimate with another. The collar of his white shirt, which had twisted slightly; his brown suit; his green and beige striped tie: I was taking it all in. I can't find the words to describe how I felt. I just kept shouting, 'Maryam', as though she was the only one who could shed light on this charade. She had to come and see: thirteen years after his death, her father was breathing again, right in front of me in the arbour of our house. He didn't say a word; he just held my hands, rubbed them on his face and smelt them.

Everyone was speechless except for Maryam's tears and screams. My darling daughter did not say anything; she was agog with wide eyes and then glanced at me, glued to the bench.

'Maryam, *mein Schatz!*' and she went to his arms weeping copiously.

Surely she could not remember anything except for the photograph above her bed and another above mine. Yadollah and Mansoureh were standing by the tank, looking at us in disbelief. They were able, finally, to put a triangle together having just discovered the third side. It was not a dream: Michel *had* arrived that afternoon. But the reality of his story was far more painful than one could have imagined.

It transpired that he had managed to con the officer while in prison in Dijon. The officer took him a few kilometres out of town and then released him. Michel then managed to reach the German border, while I was being detained and my little girl was in an orphanage. He finally managed to reach Berlin by climbing the mountains and eating leaves from trees. However, he was eventually shot in the foot by Russian soldiers and caught.

When they were about to kill him, he introduced himself and said that he was privy to a large amount of secret information held by the Nazis, and that he was von Ribbentropp's deputy, and so on. This changed the Russians' minds and, as a result, they flew him to the Soviet Union shortly afterwards, where he spent four years in some camp, before eventually being transferred to Siberia, where he stayed for the next eight years. Once released, he managed to reach East Berlin, thinking we were still there. He began a desperately search for us after he ran into his brother Gerhard in Frankfurt quite by accident.

The account of the unbearable torture he had been through in Kyrgystan and afterwards in Siberia sounded more like fiction than reality, but now Michel was sitting in front of me and Maryam was not prepared to leave him for a moment. Michel asked me why I had not returned to our house in Berlin and I explained everything. He asked me whether I had claimed the funds from the bank.

I asked, 'What funds?'

I then began to recall the numbers that he had tried so hard to help me memorise on the way to the border from Dijon. The only numbers I could remember after all that time were '1' and '8'. More interestingly, during all the years of hardship and poverty in Germany the thought of the coded Swiss bank account had never crossed my mind. It seemed that with Michel gone and news of his death, the numbers had subconsciously escaped my mind. It was unbelievable.

Michel was with us, and was once again Maysam. He limped as a result of a broken bone, the pain of which made him groan in his sleep. He seemed to be suffering in body and soul. At night, when I was woken by his cries of pain, I would look at him and suffer with him, but I could do nothing for him except stroke his grey hair. He smoked a lot when he was on his own, and at night he drank, as though drinking could heal his tormented body. Although the alcohol did not quieten his pain it helped him to lose himself. Yadollah would help him to bed and he would collapse into it like a stone falling to the bottom of a well.

CHAPTER 63

I had turned sixty. Maysam and Maryam decided to throw a feast and invite everyone, all our newly found relations, now amounting to a hundred, though Maryam proposed a private celebration later on. Janine and André arrived from Paris as a surprise. One late afternoon Maryam used an excuse to visit her friend so that she could keep me away from the house. When we returned, I did not even glance at the arbour where preparations were underway. I took a shower and got changed so that the three of us could dine, until I heard Mansoureh. It was not so strange to see her at that time as she occasionally came to see us and her daughter, but...

When I stepped into the garden the whole place was suddenly illuminated: there were hundreds of lights everywhere, in the trees and in the flowerbeds, as well as tall candles, which lit up the path to the arbour where Janine and André were expecting us, and my favourite old song was playing on the gramophone. I was speechless: you Janine, wherever have you come from! Maysam was there in a navy suit as well as Mansoureh and her children. We were awake well into the night.

Maysam's state deteriorated as the evening wore on and he could no longer remain seated or dance. He struggled to perform a Russian dance – something he had learned to do in Siberia or Kyrgzstan – due to his disabled leg. We had a barbecue as well as a large birthday cake, but when the evening was over Janine, André and I, having been through so much together, sat in the arbour and talked about Michel. His arrival had brought life to our home but he was fading away; he no longer resembled the young man who was capable of concealing his fatigue with a smile when he returned home late. Sitting in the black Mercedes, immaculately dressed, he had been the epitome of youth, as though old age and death were non-existent. Janine and André remembered him from the days back in Paris and Belgium, and I recalled the wonderful nights in Berlin.

A couple of days after his arrival I took him to be examined by a number of physicians. His eyesight had weakened and so we bought spectacles, as well as a new set of teeth. He had a brief spell at the hospital in Tehran to have his leg seen to and the dysfunctional kidney removed. I had bought a Ford; we were not poor and I wanted to spend everything we had to help him get better, but it seemed useless. Worst of all, he was an alcoholic, unable to live without drink. This made him lose control towards the end of the day and in the mornings he would wake up with a headache, feeling anxious and guilty at what he might have done or said the previous night.

I was beside myself when I saw Maryam's anxiety over her tormented father. As a result I spent many hours walking in the garden alone with my thoughts when everyone else was asleep.

'Janine, what should we do?'

At the end of a delightful evening Janine and I were sitting in the arbour chatting. Her daughter Christina had become a doctor and had set up a practice in Besançon. Janine suggested that we should take him to her. And so we followed Janine and André to Paris.

Towards the end of his life Michel seemed much older than his fifty-seven years. His leg had turned much darker and he was in agony. By the time we climbed the stairs to the bank in Geneva he found walking unbearable, but he insisted on it. Claiming the funds from the bank was not easy; the bank manager had a document claiming that Michel had been executed. To prove his existence we had to travel to Germany. He did not wish to go to East Germany, being clearly terrified by the prospect, but he ignored my plea to let go of the whole thing. He was adamant and at times aggressive and abrupt, determined to resurrect the account.

We finally resorted to seeking the assistance of a Swiss lawyer. After four months, when we climbed the stairs to the bank yet again – by this time armed with papers obtained from the German authorities – we managed to collect US$240,000. After twenty years, not only had the money failed to accrue any interest, it had diminished. I took the banker's draft to the hospital just outside Geneva. When Michel saw the draft he smiled, something he had not done for some time. He said he wanted to use the money for Maryam's higher education, but I wanted to use it to have him completely cured, and to do so I was even prepared to go as far as America. He, however, was reluctant and dismissed the idea of treatment. He lost his leg at the same hospital.

Our visit to Germany had proved fruitful as we managed to sort the paperwork for the house in Berlin. The originals had been completely destroyed in the course of the bombings and we had to obtain duplicates, which, as far as I was concerned, were of no consequence. I could not understand why he insisted on this, considering that he did not even wish to go to East Berlin; in any case, even if he had done, all private property ownership had been declared null and void.

When we were flying back to Tehran seven months later he said to Maryam and me: 'This won't last. You mustn't think that Hitler was the only person to commit horrific crimes; he was an oppressor and we didn't know what went on in the concentration camps. These people won't last either; no oppression can go on forever. I want to live to see the day the Soviet camps are opened up and thousands, whose suffering no one can fathom are released. It wasn't merely in Buchenwald and Auschwitz that mass murder took place; there are places where every day one repeatedly wishes for death. I cursed myself so many times for escaping the clutches of the French and not having been executed.'

He had not talked about his life in the camps of Siberia and Kyrgystan much, only hinted at it. I could begin to see how deep his suffering had been. When he was talking to Maryam he said, 'You must develop a profound belief in humanity and justice so that when you have the reins of power in your hands you'll never take a step forward except for the well-being of mankind.'

It was as though he were making his will in the aircraft; finally he fell asleep. He was returning to Tehran with only one leg and from then on he spent the days in his room smoking and writing. He worked in a hurry for some seven or eight hours a day. I would occasionally spend the night in his room; since our return we slept in separate rooms. I knew he was too proud to move around with someone else's assistance and he preferred to be alone.

During this period, one of Maryam's school friends, who had gone to France to continue her education, became engaged to the Shah. I had seen Farah Diba at school and other social events. Like Maryam, she had been brought up without a father, and after her departure for France I had heard no news of her. I did not attend the dinner given in her honour at the palace, though I encouraged Maryam to go. My resentment of the Pahlavis was in my blood and had been transferred to Maryam as well.

When she returned from the event she sneered at the pomp and ceremony, and it seemed she had aired her opinion to her friend as well, telling them, 'It'll be sorted out!'

Farah was placed where I could have been, as the Shah's wife, the thought of which was always present in my dreams. The passing of time, however, had driven it from my mind.

I wanted to send Maryam abroad to continue her education. She had completed secondary school and was studying law at university. She, however, did not wish to leave; it was as though she knew she was about to lose her father once again.

496

Six years after his return Michel used our absence to commit suicide. He had helped himself to Yadollah's opium, as well as a whole lot of sleeping tablets, which he consumed with the contents of one of those bottles he drank every night. At the end of two days, slipping in and out of a coma, during which time Maryam and I were in his room and spent the night with him, he opened his eyes around midnight and called me, 'Princess, Khanoumi.'

I was happy to be woken up as I was experiencing a nightmare: the three of us were under siege with incessant bombing. I looked behind the railings and there were many heads, which in reality belonged to the same person: that of the demon, my father. They were getting ready to shoot us. Someone was giving the go-ahead when Michel's voice woke me up. He first tried to say something in French but could not. He finally resorted to German.

'Life could be so beautiful had it not been for vicious people. *You* are so good, Princess; why did you have to suffer so much?'

And he tried to hold my hands in his trembling ones, but they loosened, became ice cold and dropped. I looked at him; it seemed as though he had already been gone for years.

I buried him in our mausoleum. He was now Maysam and, having adopted my family name, he lay next to my mother. I also ensured that I would eventually be placed there to rest as well. Maysam was the only male angel I had known all my life. Ever since I met him as a reticent young man, his shyness had always prompted him to drop his gaze.

'I love you.'

He was sincere and never lost this quality even in the worst possible circumstances. From the day we became husband and wife until the day he was dragged to the border he was always busy with work and never had the opportunity to break away from the rigorous discipline that ruled his life.

Every time I complained that I did not see enough of him in the four years we lived together he said, 'In a few years the world will calm down and we shall have plenty of time. We shall sit and watch our children grow.'

For fifteen years I had kept his watch and fountain pen, which Janine gave me. She had wanted to help me believe that he had been killed. Looking at the items from time to time reminded me of the happy days, albeit short, spent with him. When he came back I had returned his watch and pen to him. He had looked at me as if he did not have much time left. The man who came back to me was a mere shadow of my Michel. I had wanted to nurse him for years to come but he was against it. When we were returning from the mausoleum I wondered why angels had such short lives while demons and vultures seemed to live forever.

From that day onward I had no reason to live except for Maryam: I had to ensure I helped her to achieve her goals in life. From then on my life was a calm oasis. I have since read his diary, written with the fountain pen, hundreds of times: the memories of his years in the camps, particularly that in Siberia. It was totally absorbing and I even translated it into Persian. At the end of his memoirs he had written: 'I died a thousand times and yet managed to go on living because of hope: I wanted once again to see the one whom I loved and to ascertain that she and my daughter were alive. I had both the courage and the incentive to kill myself. I even came across the means on a number of occasions and yet every time I was prevented by my dream. And how very selfish of me; I fear I may have troubled Khanoum and Maryam.'

On the last page of the diary he had written: 'The torment I underwent was compensated for by the years I lived with love. I wish life lasted only a moment: a moment to love and be loved.'

With Maysam's death I, too, was effectively finished. I am not saying anything else about my life. I do not have anything left to say.

CHAPTER 64

When they heard the end of the eleventh tape, Maryam and Narguess were motionless, just as they had been while listening to the others. They rested their chins on their hands or ran their fingers through their hair, swallowing their saliva while listening to them all. None of them dared shed a tear. Narguess was the first to get up and go to the room upstairs to calm down. She regretted not having seen this wonderful woman sooner; from the moment she had left prison, Khanoum had been at hospital or in intensive care, when she had only smiled from behind the glass as if to say, 'I know you, Narguess. I was waiting for you. Welcome aboard.'

The eleven tapes had given Nanaz her material. Maryam already knew a great deal about her mother's life and was well aware of the last years, yet she had never heard the details from her own mouth. She was reminding herself that life was a struggle to exist and carry on. She was ashamed of herself for ever mentioning her four years in prison. For Narguess, however, hearing Khanoum's story at the onset of a new chapter in her life made her sense a message; someone from within was telling her that one should live like Khanoum: one must fight for any worthwhile cause.

Our story could come to an end here; when everyone returned from the cemetery Khanoum's story was effectively over – but not quite. There are many whose death brings the story of their life to a close, but this was not the case with Khanoum. Her story had, over many nights, nurtured a young, delicate girl and prepared her for life. Without Nanaz's story, Khanoum's saga remains open-ended. Maryam seems to have been some sort of intermediary, one of the many intermediaries who witness and then narrate.

However, Maryam had to wait until 1986, the celebration of Nanaz's eighteenth birthday, also the end of her time at school. She accompanied a group of women from the local mosque to the south-west of the country. It was a bloodbath and she witnessed the sacrifice and selflessness of those who, though younger than herself, yet persisted in their determination to go to the front. She had taken photographs and notes relating to the fronts.

She said, 'Khanoum taught me to try to be present at the centre of events, to see people in different situations, to observe them and to ensure that it is not life that passes me by; rather it is I who manoeuvre life.'

During the week that Nanaz spent with the local women she had acted as medic, nurse, photographer and witness to the trenches. She never complained or let fear take over, and she had much to report.

They finally left in autumn, after having paid a midnight visit to the cemetery, to the graves of Khanoum and Maysam. They recited prayers to pay their respects to Khanoum. They went to Monii's grave, Khanoum's mother, whose photograph they had with them, so that they could think of Khanoum, who always remembered her mother and, until the day she died, never forgot about her for a moment. They then left, but, before leaving, Nanaz set up a trust for the house in Shapour Street for Mansoureh's grandchildren and told her mother that she had effectively put the five of them in charge to ensure that no one could let go of it easily.

They were heading for Paris, where Maryam had lived and where they were familiar with the language. Everywhere they went they were reminded of Khanoum: Rue Pasquier in Madeleine, Janine's old place in St Michel, the church in Neuilly and its old hospital where Khanoum had spent two years in the convent, Parc

St Cloud where only one building remained, the house in Avenue Foche, which still existed though without the German soldiers guarding it, Grand Palais where Khanoum had been photographed sitting on a bench in her first year in Paris and ...

Nanaz went to college and Narguess to a language school. Maryam initially tried to find work in an art gallery, as her mother had done, but this was not possible. She leased a small shop near the Louvre where she sold posters, paintings and souvenirs. It was fronted by a framed photograph of Shah Square in Esfahan taken by an Iranian photographer. Two years later, however, they were on their way to the United States so that Nanaz could study political sciences at Harvard. Before 1989 she was in Bush House in London, preparing news reports for the BBC. Her first report on the French intellectuals' hangouts was a huge success. She had followed in the footsteps of Sartre and Malraux, and arranged to meet Khanoum's friends and acquaintances in Montmartre, Monparnasse and La Coupole. Maryam and Narguess remained in Paris, following the details of Nanaz's life. She contacted them from different parts of the world and reluctantly managed to complete her studies at Harvard.

The day after her twentieth birthday Nanaz received an offer from NEWS, a newly established channel which would very quickly go global. The year 2005 saw satellites being positioned in space by two Iranian space engineers. These would make it possible for programmes to be watched across the globe without the need of an aerial. Nanaz was offered a five-year contract worth four million dollars per annum, placing her among the most highly paid producers and reporters in the world. Narguess soon joined the team as secretary and followed Nanaz around the world.

By 1995, Nanaz had reached the pinnacle that Khanoum had wished. They returned to Tehran one autumn day. They were to interview Rafsanjani, then President of Iran, a programme that was to be broadcast globally. Nanaz was wearing Khanoum's scarf.

'Mr President, how do you regard women's role in Iranian society?' she asked, thinking of the documentary on Iranian women she was planning to make.

She had the night before, without the others finding out, quietly slipped into the house in Shapour Street together with Narguess. The modest building was still intact. Nanaz asked Yadollah's son not to touch the house for another year, after which she did not see any reason to stop them demolishing it and having four small flats built instead. The drawings were already done.

Nanaz's interview with the Iranian President, during which he mentioned his government's conditions for negotiations with America, caused a furore in the US. This coincided with her preparations to marry Davoud, the name she began calling her future husband. David Rockwell was a millionaire prodigy who had been her contemporary at Harvard and was later included in President Bill Clinton's tight-knit circle. He had an office in the White House. They decided to delay the wedding until the Lewinsky affair had died down. During this time Nanaz went to Kosovo and prepared a documentary on the fighting in the region. It demonstrated the crimes that Milosevic and the Serbs under his command had committed in Bosnia and Kosovo. At the end of the documentary Nanaz quoted one woman: 'Oppressors are less than they imagine, and perhaps it is this inferiority that drives them to commit big crimes.'

It was she who predicted the fall of Milosevic.

At their wedding, Clinton and his wife Hillary were among the guests, as well as Madeleine Albright, the Foreign Secretary, senators and a number of well-known entrepreneurs. Nanaz was wearing a white gown and took the microphone from Oprah Winfrey, who had named her 'the first lady of the news'.

She thanked everyone and then said, 'I wish to play a tape which is in a language that you are not familiar with and which I shall translate.'

The image of an old woman seated on a cushion, leaning against another while facing the camera, appeared on the white screen.

As Malraux said, life is an invaluable thing and nothing is more valuable than life. Years ago, when I was at the lowest point in my life, someone said to me, "This land was built with hope, despair, love and hatred, and every bit of it is made of these. The only creatures not fearful of the storm are the seagulls; even when they lose direction while flying over the seas unable to find a spot to rest, they either flap their wings until the storm settles down and they manage to find a spot where they can rest, or they die in the storm. Those who fall in the waves are not seagulls; seagulls die in the heights and spend their remaining strength to reach the summit so that they don't see their fall." I was very young when I learned about hatred and spent years of my life with it. In the short time that I experienced love, I felt I could turn every day into a year. When I realised the most powerful monsters are brought down to size upon their encounter with a dainty angel in human form, I understood that "time" makes us, but I made the time for me.

Khanoum's face had filled the entire screen, speaking to people who had locked their eyes into hers: the very people who thought themselves most powerful. Nanaz had videoed Khanoum a year before her death. She kept the video and brought it all the way from Iran to Blairhouse, the guest quarters at the White House.

Nanaz's secrecy made Maryam laugh, and she told herself, 'Can't imagine who could have possibly coached you!'

Maryam had never heard about the video. She got up with a smile and approached her son-in-law. She gave him a peck and presented him with a watch made in the early twentieth century with a date on the reverse. She wrapped the watch round Davoud's wrist; the same watch Monii had placed in a wrapped bundle and handed to Malakeh Jahan at the Russian Embassy in Tehran. Maryam, Nanaz and Narguess knew that this was the same watch that, when returned to Khanoum in the village by the Swiss border, had indicated that Michel had been executed. Maryam also gave Nanaz a necklace with an emerald that had been around for some hundred-and-forty years. It was made in Esfahan and had spent half a century in the quiet of a box in a bank. Nanaz kissed the emerald and placed it on her eye so that she could see Khanoum's picture in it and be as close to her physically as she had once been.

Chapter 65

In November 1989 the Berlin Wall fell. Nanaz was among the jubilant crowd awaiting the demolition of the symbol of the Cold War. She was preparing a report, having interviewed an old woman who described tearfully how her young son was shot at the same spot while he was climbing the wall thirteen years earlier. Everyone sang national songs on both sides of the wall and shouted: 'Down with the Wall.'

Nanaz was back in her hotel room in Grunwald in the early hours of the morning. She was so exhausted that she could not go to sleep. Narguess rang the bell and walked in. They had both been by the Wall well into the night and now Nanaz was writing notes for a documentary she was working on to be called *The Wall*.

She asked Narguess, 'What do you know about walls?'

Narguess explained to her that when she was in prison, she could see the mountains beyond the wall. She would peep through a gap in the wall at break times, and she could see a single tree high up on the mountain.

The prisoners said, 'The tree is there to remind us of the seasons,' and they had all made a pact to climb the tree the day they were released.

'What did Maryam say about the tree?'

Narguess laughed. 'Whenever your mother saw that lonely tree she thought of Khanoum, as though she was standing there.'

'I didn't know that my mother was so romantic.'

'Everyone can occasionally become a romantic. Have you not seen her diary?'

'Yes, I have; hers and Khanoum's, but now I am thinking of my grandfather's, Michel's.'

Ten days after the fall of the Wall, Nanaz and Narguess took their film crew and went to the Reichstag. They had an address for Khanoum's dream house; once they found it, they saw that it looked just the way Khanoum had described it. Narguess found Nanaz standing across the street looking at the house. She knew what she was up to. Nanaz was staring at the windows, letting her imagination take her behind the curtains, at which point she saw a woman with black hair laying a dinner table. Two candles were burning and she was staring at the black telephone, but it was not ringing.

Reclaiming Michel's house was not easy. Their papers were sufficient proof but they knew they had to go to a court that dealt with the estates of those who had lost them in the communist era. Meanwhile, an agent from Deutsche Bank informed them that he was willing to buy the house, and that he would pursue the legal side of things himself. Nanaz asked him what he was planning to do with the house.

'We'll turn it into skyscrapers,' the German replied coolly.

They had no choice, and Maryam was about to sign the paperwork and receive four million dollars, when Nanaz insisted on having the house for one more day so that the crew could video it for the scenario she had in mind. She was standing in a corner, in front of the camera, and spoke as though she was drawing a picture, a picture of Khanoum's life. They looked at every paper and opened every door. In the basement they looked through the bric-a-brac that had piled up over the years but could not find anything specific. Everything had been destroyed over half a century and, as it transpired, the house had been used as a club for senior Party members. They were about to pack up when an old man arrived and noticed they were recording. He said that he had been the warden of the club for many years. Nanaz chatted to him, which was also recorded. At the end of the conversation she asked him whether he had seen anything in that house reminiscent of an Iranian woman.

The old man said, 'Yes, there were many things but everything was discarded.'

But not quite: the old man had kept an old leather case in his home, which he sold to Nanaz an hour later for a hundred dollars. This was a case bearing the sun and lion coat of arms.

'Makes a nice present for Maryam's birthday!'

She then realised that Khanoum had left her mark in different places in different countries, as if she had known Nanaz was going to be looking for them. They did not need to discuss it as the three of them, Nanaz, Narguess and Maryam, knew only too well that the case had belonged to the large fish in Neuilly Hospital; the large fish who didn't know that the nun who frequented his room to check his medication and change his flowers was the very person whose proposed marriage to him was said to have been made in heaven. When Maryam received the case from Nanaz, she kissed it and wondered how Khanoum had come to keep the case. Perhaps, before dying, he had sent it over to Khanoum as a memento of a childhood romance.

The proceeds from the sale of the house in Berlin prompted Maryam to purchase a house for Nanaz in Washington DC. Nanaz, however, was so rapidly gaining fame on the television channels that she hardly needed the money. So they decided to set up an insurance company, something Maryam specialised in and was confident she could make a success of. They leased an office space in the Twin Towers in New York. The managing director's office was decorated sumptuously and Nanaz arrived on the first day carrying a large bouquet of flowers as well as a picture of Khanoum by a Canadian artist. The picture depicted Khanoum in her youth, sitting on a bench in the Grand Palais in Paris with a row of old cars parked behind and a bicycle at her side.

When the picture was hung, Nanaz, Maryam and Narguess spent a few moments looking at it: the Canadian artist had created a masterpiece. The picture depicted Khanoum holding a handkerchief. The original photograph must have been taken in difficult times when Khanoum was at university in Paris, at the time she had first met Michel.

'The photographer seems to have been quite taken by her,' Nanaz exclaimed.

Underneath the picture a framed document introduced Khanoum as the founder of Odessa Insurance Brokers. From then on, wherever Nanaz was, behind her desk in Washington or reporting, she called the office and asked the secretary to put her through to the manager sitting under a large painting of Khanoum on the seventy-ninth floor of the second tower.

Historical Context

Qajar Rulers	Date of Reign
Agha Muhammad Khan	1794–1797
Fath Ali Shah	1797–1834
Muhammad Shah	1834–1848
Nasser al-Din Shah	1848–1896
Mozaffar ed-Din Shah	1896–1907
Mohammed Ali Shah	1907–1909
Ahmad Shah	1909–1925

Of the three prominent historical personages in *The Knot in the Rug* the character and personality of the last Qajar ruler, Ahmad Shah, remains the most remote and opaque. My generation, to say the least, knows very little about him. Ahmad Shah has been greatly misrepresented and maligned throughout the contemporary history of Iran.

Ahmad Shah's upbringing and education in the years away from his parents was supervised by Nasser ul-Molk, a courtier and the first Iranian to get into Oxford University, where he proved to be an outstanding scholar.[24] From 1910 to 1914, Nasser ul-Molk's influence meant that Ahmad Shah became the only Qajar ruler raised with the same standards as any Western monarch. Both his understanding of the limitations of his forebears and the birth of the Persian oil industry could have given rise to a successful and fruitful reign beneficial to the Iranian people.

Ahmad Shah, the teenage king, had inherited a country that was effectively bankrupt and on the verge of disintegration, with a substantial Turkish, German, British and Russian presence throughout the country.

Much of the controversy around Ahmad Shah has to do with the positions he took during his reign from 1914 to 1925, in particular his position on the 1919 Agreement between Britain and Iran and, later, his decision to leave Iran in 1923 in protest over the military coup of his then Prime Minister (initially Defence Secretary) Reza Khan Sardar Sepah (later Reza Shah Pahlavi).

The 1919 Agreement had been meticulously crafted and promoted by Lord Curzon[25] for the British side, and the 'Triumvirate' of Vossough ud-Dowleh, Akbar Mirza Sarem ud-Dowleh and Firouz Mirza Nosrat ud-Dowleh for the Iranian side. Their understanding had been that Ahmad Shah was also in favour of the Agreement, given the assurances and guarantees it included regarding his person and the continuation of the Qajar dynasty. However, the negotiators had failed to take into consideration the changed circumstances in Iran, particularly the existence of a parliament – the parliament – under a newly established constitution (1906), which required the parliament to ratify all such agreements before they could become legally binding. Additionally, the negotiators had failed to secure the consent of Ahmad Shah, who, when presented with the task of approving the *fait accompli*, demurred and asserted his prerogative as constitutional monarch to object to the process and its implications. In the two speeches he gave in England during his visit in 1919, a visit intended to seal the 1919 Agreement, Ahmad Shah chose to remind his hosts of the principles of democratic governance and to reiterate his hope that Britain would treat Iran as an equal within the community of free nations pursuant to the Covenant of the League of Nations signed earlier that year.

In demurring on the Agreement, Ahmad Shah had sealed his fate and, as it later turned out, the fate of the Qajar dynasty as well. In 1923, two years after the military coup by Reza Khan, Ahmad Shah decided to leave the country, ostensibly for an extensive vacation in Europe for health reasons. Official communications from the period tell a different story. These communications show the reason for his refusal to return and his opposition to the increasingly dictatorial powers of his Prime Minister Reza Khan.

In 1925, Ahmad Shah was even offered, by the representatives of the leader of the new Republic of Turkey, Mustafa Kemal Ataturk, the opportunity to return to Iran under Turkish military escort to reclaim his throne and presumably oust Reza Khan. Ahmad Shah's refusal to accept this offer is a matter of historical record but, again, barely known or mentioned in discussions on Ahmad Shah's role. Neither are the reasons for his refusal to enter Iran under the protection of a foreign army to reclaim a throne that was his by right and law. He was not willing to engage in the actions this kind of return would inevitably entail, which would undermine the very legitimacy of the constitutional rule he so cherished.[26]

To add to the portrait we have of Malakeh Jahan from Khanoum, I spent an afternoon in Paris with Soltan Ali Mirza Kadjar,[27] her grandson and Ahmad Shah's nephew, who was seventeen when Malakeh Jahan passed away. Soltan Ali Mirza is the head of the Qajar family today, and very kindly made it possible for me to access the photographs from the family album.

In Malakeh Jahan's letter that was made available to me during my meeting with Soltan Ali Mirza in Paris, she has written to her son, Muhammad Hassan Mirza, who had passed away some two years prior to the date on the letter. The news of her son's death in England had been kept from her to save her yet further torment. In the letter, she complains to her son about his disregard for his mother's feelings by not letting her know of his whereabouts and not informing her of his well-being. This is her last letter. She herself passed away shortly after writing it without ever finding out the truth about her son's death.

Sara Phillips
London
Autumn 2008

ENDNOTES

1   Prominent twentieth-century Iranian female poet.

2   The *kolah*, a Persian national headdress, was introduced by the Qajars. Before then the turban was universal. The *kolah* changed shape over the years; at the beginning of the century it was about a foot and a half in height and sloped up to a peak at the top. It was later usually from six to ten inches in height, rounded at the top and made of astrakhan (Curzon's *Persia*).

3   A centre for the performance of religious ceremonies depicting Persian mythology. This monument was demolished in 1945 and replaced by the new building of the National Bank.

4   As Sufi practitioners, dervishes are enlightened people with wisdom and knowledge in medicine and poetry. Many of the dervishes have taken the vow of poverty. Though some of them are beggars by choice (dervishes are prohibited from begging unless they cannot provide for themselves), others can engage in any profession. There are also various dervish fraternities, almost all of which trace their origins from various Muslim saints and teachers, especially Ali Mohammed, the Prophet Muhammad's son-in-law, and Abu Bakr, his father-in-law. They live in monastic conditions superficially similar to Christian monks. Various orders and suborders have appeared and disappeared over the centuries. The whirling dance, *Sama*, is just one of their practices for trying to reach religious ecstasy. Some deeply religious Sufi masters are looked upon as possessing the divine touch, allowing them to heal the sick and do other miraculous work.

5   Or Malijak (malice/sparrow) in Kurdish. He was brought to the court of Nasser al-Din Shah after his father and his uncle. The first came to be called *malijak* because he was chasing a bird. He was an ugly but witty child who amused the king a great deal. He once accidentally rescued Nasser al-Din Shah from a falling chandelier and the king considered his presence a good omen for his reign. He was rather spoilt as a result of the king's affection,

to the point that when he grew up he took advantage of his position. The women also bribed him so that they could become closer to the king. He accompanied the king on his many trips, and I am told a new book about him, sourced from his memoirs, is now available in Tehran. He never, however, pursued the education available to him, and after Nasser al-Din Shah's death his position at court weakened. He lived off the assets bestowed on him and died a poor man.

6 She was referring to the eighth Shia saint – in troubled times one may call upon him or the other saints for relief.

7 Fruit resembling the mulberry, but pale green and very sweet. It is usually collected by shaking the branches of the tree.

8 North of Iran, the Caspian Sea.

9 In his book *Persia in the Great Game*, Antony Wynn expands on Muhammad Ali Shah's fruitless return to Iran at a time when there was a 'breakdown of order throughout the country' leading to 'demands for restoration of the exiled Muhammad Ali Shah and a return to the old way of doing things'. The Russians, meanwhile, were busy exploiting the situation: 'In July, Muhammad Ali landed in Persia, prompting a stream of frantic telegrams from Sykes to the legation in Tehran.' Sir Percy Sykes was British Consul in Mashad in the north, 'the most sensitive of all British posts, vital for gathering intelligence about Russian military activity'. 'On 25 July, four hundred Turkman horsemen had crossed the mountains occupying Shahrud on behalf of Muhammad Ali Shah. The former Shah was advancing on Tehran via Mazandaran, on the coast, with a large force from Persia and Russia.' He sent telegrams to a number of officials in Mashad to announce his arrival and demand their support. 'The chief of the telegraph office prudently referred these to Sykes, who duly informed a government official, who in turn suggested that instructions should be requested from Tehran. The reply came that the telegrams should not be delivered and that the whole matter should be kept secret.' The former Shah's forces were defeated in Mazandaran and, in September 1911, he fled back across the border.

10 This was an adaptation of a ballerina's tutu. When Nasser al-Din Shah went to France on a state visit, on seeing a ballet performance he took a liking to the outfit and desired that all the women in the harem should be dressed in a version of the tutu with loose trousers underneath.

11 Born in the sixth century AD, Bozorgmehr was the very savvy minister to the court of the Sassanid ruler Ardeshir I. He was initially employed

as tutor to the king's children though was later promoted. A great many stories have been told about Bozorgmehr's wisdom. One recounts the day a question was put to him by a Greek philosopher and an Indian scientist: 'What is the greatest misfortune?' The Greek referred to 'old age' and 'lack of intellect', which he considered equivalent to 'poverty'. The Indian pointed to 'ill health', compounded by 'psychological disorder'. Bozorgmehr, however, referred to 'the coming to the end of one's life and discovering that one had not carried out any benevolent deed'. The Sassanid Empire encompassed all of today's Iran as well as Armenia, Afghanistan, the eastern parts of Turkey and parts of Syria, Pakistan, Caucasia, Central Asia and Arabia. They called their empire, 'Dominion of the Aryans'.

12 *Allah o ma saleh allah Muhammad va aalleh Mohamad*, meaning greetings to Prophet Muhammad and his people. This is recited when the Prophet's name is mentioned, or one survives a critical situation or a task is completed successfully.

13 A small island in the Marmaris – the former king rented a property on the south side of the island. The owner of this mansion was a member of the Ottoman parliament, who was forced into exile in Malta by the British. His beautiful British wife turned the house into a hotel, Hotel Esplanade. On her return to London the house was rented by Ahmad Shah's father.

14 Seven items beginning with the sound 's' in Persian.

15 Coin, symbolizing prosperity.

16 Vinegar, which replaces wine after the introduction of Islam in Iran.

17 Apple.

18 Sumach (Rhus) is an evergreen bush. The fruit is in the form of tiny pouches which are dried and used as seasoning for kebabs. The fact that the plant is evergreen symbolises continuity.

19 Garlic, used to ward off bad omens.

20 A sweet, thick, brown custard-like texture, making a nutritious meal, possibly replacing haoma, a sacred herbal mix with healing properties.

21 Teymour Taash was born into a family of aristocrats and received his formal education in Tsarist Russia, in St Petersburg. He became well versed in English, French, German and Russian. On his return, Iran was in the throes of the constitutional revolution and Teymour Taash entered the second Persian *Majlis* as a parliamentary deputy at the age of only twenty-six. He was heavily involved in the transition of power from the Qajars to the Pahlavis and was a strong supporter of Reza Shah

Pahlavi. He ran the Ministry of Public Affairs and later became governor of several provinces. During this time he was influential in preventing Reza Shah from destroying all the Qajar landmarks, an invaluable contribution to the preservation of the Iranian heritage. The vicious power struggle between him and many of Reza Shah's other close aides eventually cost him his life. In 1933 he was arrested for reportedly setting up secret negotiations with the Anglo-Persian Oil Company. One reason for the dismissal of Teymour Taash had to do with British interference in the politics of Iran. The sixty-year concession for oil, documented in the agreement between William Knox D'Arcy and Mozaffar ed-Din Shah, was due to expire in 1961. The British wanted to extend the concession for another thirty years for five million pounds, changing Iran's royalties from 16 per cent to four shillings/ton, and to acquire the five northern provinces excluded from the original concession for eight million pounds. Iran would have subsequently been getting a total of thirteen million pounds sterling from this deal. Britain had already made the changes mentioned above through the Armitage-Smith Agreement, but they wanted to make it official. Teymour Taash wanted to reserve the right to sell the oil-fields until Iran was free of the concession, so that the rights could be sold to an American company who had offered one hundred million dollars. A court sentenced him to five years of solitary confinement and a total fine of 10,712 pounds/58,592 tomans on charges of embezzlement. His enemies refused to allow him visitors while in prison and he died under torture in solitary confinement on 3 October 1933. The press announced the cause of his death as heart failure. Historians, however, believe he was murdered.

22 Hoveyda was born in Tehran. His father was an experienced diplomat during the latter years of the Qajar dynasty and his mother was a descendant of the imperial family. The senior Hoveyda would serve for much of his adult life. The diplomatic life meant that the Hoveyda family was never based in one residence for any length of time. Studying in various countries gave Hoveyda a unique cosmopolitan background. During the family's stay in Beirut, French literary works by the likes of André Malraux, André Gide, Molière and Baudelaire captivated the young Hoveyda and paved the way for his intellectual growth. He attended a French university in 1938 and during the occupation he was effectively stranded in France. His ability to communicate in several languages, including Persian, French, English, Italian, German and Arabic, helped him climb the political ladder later in life. Hoveyda's return to France in 1939 was short lived as a result of a brewing diplomatic scuffle between the French government and Reza Shah

Pahlavi. Having no choice but to leave France again, Hoveyda enrolled at the Université Libre de Bruxelles the same year and eventually obtained a bachelor's degree in Political Sciences in 1941, under the ever-watchful eye of the occupying German administration. On his return to Iran in 1942, Hoveyda completed his national service. He then applied for employment at the Ministry of Foreign Affairs, where he remained until his execution in 1979 following the Iranian Revolution.

23 Muhammad Mossadeq was born in 1882 in Tehran to a Bakhtiari finance minister and a Qajar princess. When his father died in 1892, he was appointed tax collector of the provinces. He studied political sciences in Paris and received his PhD from the Neuchâtel University in Switzerland. On 28 April 1951 he was elected Prime Minister.

24 Abul Ghassem Khan's extraordinary ability meant that, rather than pursuing an Honours degree, he took up as many subjects as he could, bringing him respect and many influential friends, such as George Curzon. He was later made an honorary KCMG by Queen Victoria during Nasser al-Din Shah's last European tour, when he acted as his interpreter. Gaining huge respect among the British, however, roused the suspicion of his Persian counterparts, who took him for a British agent. (Adapted from the *Journal of the Iran Society*, September 2006.)

25 The then Foreign Secretary, Lord Curzon, negotiated Egyptian independence, resolved an insurrection in the Mandated Territory of Iraq (by sending T. E. Lawrence to report, and adopting his recommendations, which were to grant internal self-government under the rule of King Faisal) and divided the British Mandate of Palestine, creating the Kingdom of Jordan for Faisal's brother.

26 Manoutchehr Eskandari-Qajar, 'Persia's Honor: Remembering Soltan Ahmad Shah', *The Iranian* 24 October 2003; N. S. Fatemi, *Encyclopedia Iranica*, 'Anglo-Persian Agreement of 1919'; Hossein Makki, *Mokhtassari az Zendegani-e Siassi-e Soltan Ahmad Shah*, Amir Kabir, Tehran, 1362 (solar).

27 Some of the princely families prefer to use 'Kadjar' (the French spelling) as opposed to 'Qajar' (English). For further information refer to www. Qajarpages.com.

Author's Note

China, Egypt, India, Greece and Iran, the five standard bearers of civilisation, have never shown as much interest in their own history as civilisations to come. The five nations preferred to picnic on the plains of beautiful fables and welcome the imagination of stylish people rather than make an effort to discover historical truth amid stone tablets and often-neglected historic remains. The Iranian people, perhaps even more so than the others, are keen to blend their history with fables, myths and legends.

Professor Edward Granville Browne, the British orientalist who spent many years living among the Iranians and was a keen supporter of the Constitutional Revolution of 1906, produced a travelogue for British diplomats in which he considered the Iranians a difficult nation to know as the they are not concerned with knowing themselves, or making themselves known to outsiders. For this reason, the history of Persian literature, a country proud of its authors and poets prior to the discovery of oil in 1905, had not been written until Edward Browne committed it to paper at the beginning of the twentieth century.

Until the middle of the last century the most important historic work as far as most Iranians were concerned was Ferdowsi's *Book of Kings*, comparable to Homer's *Iliad* and *Odyssey*. This great, eleventh-century epic was based on a collection of myths. For Iranians, accepting myth in lieu of history has always been easier and more pleasurable than searching for history amid ruins and remains, or entering a never-ending debate on where the truth lies. For years after the Renaissance and the Industrial Revolution in Europe, the Iranians were still content to spend long winter evenings under the *korsi*, a low table covered with blankets with a charcoal brazier underneath, enjoying its pleasant warmth, watching the snowflakes fall from the sky and listening to the great poets, Hafez and Sa'di, and enjoying their grand-mothers' tales of their great past.

After many years of research and study of documents I completed my trilogy of books on the contemporary history of Iran. The three books tell the stories of three women who lived in Europe and spent part of their lives among the Europeans. The first is *Ameeneh*, the story of a woman who was the mother of all the Qajars. In her lifetime Ameeneh met Peter the Great, Catherine the Great, Montesquieu and Voltaire, and was received in the courts of Europe and Russia.

In the third book, *The Broken Urn*, we learn about Alice, the daughter of an English general who served his country in the colonies. She was instrumental in the fate of the last Iranian monarchy, the Pahlavi regime. Alice went to school with the last king of Iran, developing a bond with him and two other Iranian students which led Alice to a long-term interest and involvement in the affairs of Iran, including the 1979 revolution. But what *did* motivate Alice in taking such an active role? Was it love, hatred, or was it, in fact, carrying out her duties as an employee of MI6?

Khanoum (published here as *The Knot in the Rug*) is the second book in the trilogy and spans a period from the fifth Qajar ruler at the turn of the nineteenth century to the events of 11 September 2001. Its heroine, Khanoum, was born at the beginning of the twentieth century and her life is a gripping story encapsulating the history of Iran and Europe across the century and including two World Wars. 'This is a myth that can be believed in' is written on the cover of the first edition of *Khanoum*, now in its fourteenth edition in Persian, although all of my books, including this one, have been banned in Iran since Mahmoud Ahmadinejad has become president. The Iranian people have had no difficulty believing the story, but has there ever been such a woman?

My work is akin to taking a faint old photograph and reviving it with colour: the sky in the photograph is not blue and nor are the trees green, but in these stories they are brought to life. The substance of the story is a picture of reality; this is quite common in the clandestine world of history and Persian stories. Like the fine and intricate Persian rugs found in many Iranian households, when the strong Persian sunlight penetrates through the stained glass of the *Orussi* windows and spreads over the floor every knot in the rug seems to come alive and begin to move; the trees sway with the breeze and the nightingale's song rises from the four corners of the rug.

In his *Book of Kings*, Ferdowsi tells of Rostam, Persia's greatest epic hero, and the equivalent of Samson and Ulysses. Ferdowsi states that Rostam was a local hero from Sistan, and he made him the hero of his story. I spent many years with my hero, Khanoum, and shed many a tear on her grave. She is the most real of all the real creatures on earth and for the readers of this book she is the figure of a beloved grandmother, with whom many Iranians can identify.

M Behnoud
London
Autumn 2008